WATCHING YOU

Watching You

Cynthia Terry

Dedicated to my sister, Heather Quass, for inspiring me
and constantly believing in me even when I didn't
believe in myself.

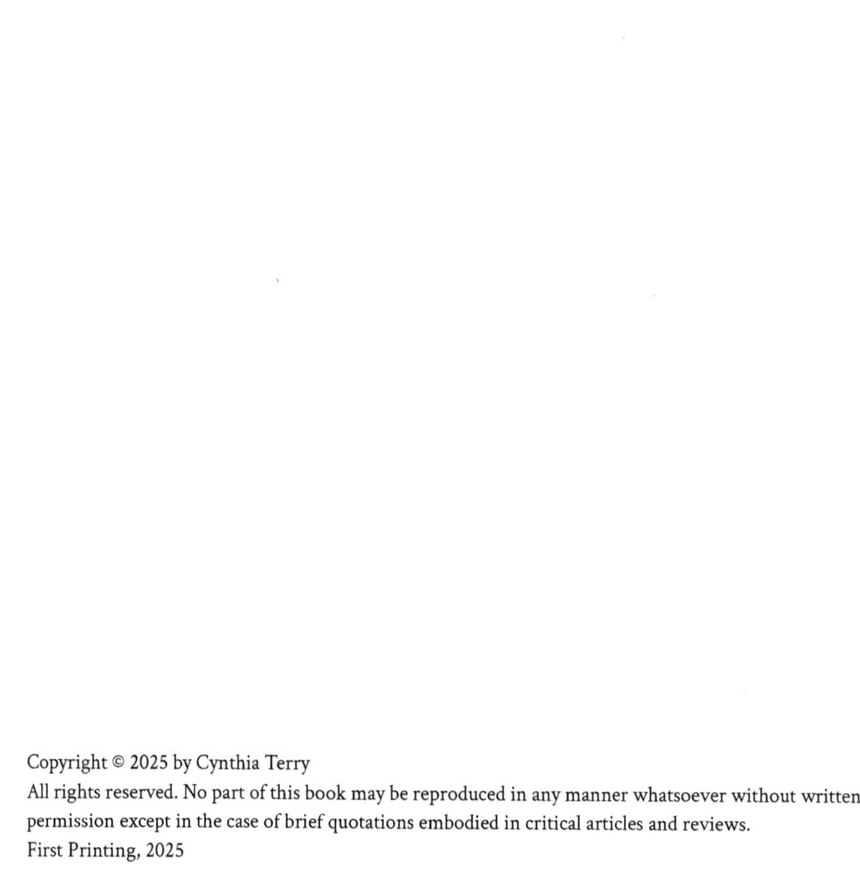

Prologue

Clara's tormentor, Andrew, arrived first on the scene. Frozen, he watched flames consume the remains of the burning limo. His usually slicked-back raven hair danced wildly in the night breeze as his eyes blinked several times in disbelief at what he saw.

Trying to make sense of the horror he had just witnessed, Andrew's thoughts were stuck in a time loop, re-watching Clara dart from his mansion as she hysterically waved around a detonator, shouting, "Don't follow me. I will blow myself up! I've been dead for years now. You already killed me! I'm done with this stupid, sick game you are playing. I'm going to be free one way or another! Andrew, I'm done!"

Andrew was forced to do nothing but watch as she escaped down the long driveway where the limo waited for her.

Clara was the only girl who had permanently imprinted on his heart. He loved her, but she didn't understand his love yet.

Fuming in the doorway, he was reduced back to the powerless child who had suffered at his father's hands. The words of his father haunted his mind. *You're nothing! You'll never be worthy of love.*

No, Father! Andrew fought back the demeaning memory. *I will win her back. I am a better man than you ever were. You can't be right.* He watched Clara jump into the driver's side of the limo and began driving away. However, the limo only moved a few feet before fire exploded out of all the windows, annihilating any chance of survival.

She was gone.

Though Andrew knew it was pointless, he stumbled after her, numb with fear. As he neared the explosion, the heat of the burning wreckage pushed against him until he could not go any further. All he could do now was stare blankly at the scene before him, waiting for his emergency team to clean up the mess.

This... This can't be. Why would she do this?

Anger coursed through him, and he took it out on the deformed, mangled bumper of his once pristine limo. His toe stung as it propelled a broken piece across the street and into the shadows of his vineyard.

His eyes twitched as he saw, or more accurately, sensed, a shadow out of place behind a nearby vine. For a moment, he stood rooted to the grass beneath his feet. Had he imagined it?

He held his gaze at the shadow, willing his eyes to adjust to the dark so he could see her beautiful shape once more.

Andrew tried to swallow a lump that had formed in his throat, but his mouth was too dry. He closed his eyes, trying to accept that he may have imagined the strange shadow, but before anguish could set up camp in his chest again, a snap of a branch fueled hope.

Sharp breath pounded from him as he shot toward the shadow, eyes darting wildly about. Nothing was there. Desperately, his footsteps thundered against the dry, raw earth as he blindly raced deeper into the vineyard. Stray branches tore at his suit as he ran, but he didn't notice or care. Tears flowed down his cheek and watered the black stubble that covered his devilishly handsome jaw as he saw no sign of her. She couldn't be gone.

She can't be gone.

"I will find you!" His voice ripped through the silence of the night. Falling to his knees, he clung to his heart and began to shake uncontrollably. "She is not dead. She is not dead. She is not dead." His whispered cries flew away in the warm wind.

1

The Baby

A drop of sweat rolled down Anna's forehead and slid around the gentle curve of her petite nose. The sweat dangled there for a few moments, and then, as Anna lunged, it let go and plunged to the mat below.

Anna's deep blue eyes were focused and alive with intensity, letting her opponent in on a little secret, she already knew victory would be hers.

Rodriguez, the large woman across from her, roared and egged Anna on, trying to intimidate her by faking an attack. Anna stood still, ready and unafraid, reading her opponent's movements to figure out her subtle flaws.

Anna discerned from the way Rodriguez threw her hefty body around that she relied heavily on the strength of her muscles rather than the strength of her skill. This gave Anna the chance to weave in and out of her strikes with agility throughout the fight.

Breathe all the way through your movements. Breath is energy. Breath is what connects you to your center. The words of her trainer, Master Kim, ran through her mind. *Stay calm as the aggressor ties themselves into a knot of complicated movements. Don't engage. Their own eagerness will throw them off balance, leaving them vulnerable. That's when you strike.*

With seemingly effortless motion, Anna danced around, taking advantage of her competitor's lack of control until an opening offered itself up. Rodriguez charged headfirst at Anna, aiming for a mid-body tackle. Right before her head rammed into Anna's ribs, Anna instinctively thrust her feet backward into a triangle stance while her forearms came forward and struck her opponent's clavicles. Anna's feet slid back a couple of inches and her arms quickly tightened on both sides of the struggling woman's neck. Anna secured her hands together behind Rodriguez's head and held her in a tight trap as she pushed against Anna's body. Stuck, Rodriguez raised her hands to pry Anna's arms apart, leaving her face unshielded.

Oh, big mistake!

The second the woman moved her arms away from protecting her face, Anna's knee jutted up and slammed into her nose before rapidly pushing herself away from Rodriguez. As soon as she had some distance, Anna jumped back into a solid fighter's stance on the balls of her feet.

Staggering, Rodriguez retaliated with a round of angry kicks. Anna stepped offline to the left of the approaching giant. However, instead of stepping away from the woman, Anna diminished the space between her and her foe. She rammed her shoulder into the woman's sternum, knocking Rodriguez even more off balance.

Taking advantage of her opponent's frazzled state, Anna sent a left cross punch into Rodriguez's gut. In defense, Rodriguez tried to block the strike, but in doing so, she left half of her face unshielded, giving Anna the perfect opportunity to place a powerful right-arm uppercut punch into the woman's prominent chin. Dazed, Rodriguez tilted precariously back and forth until she toppled to the ground with a solid *thump.*

Cheers exploded around Anna as she heaved deep gulps of air. Adrenaline pumped through her body, driving her fist into the sky with a triumphant jump.

"Yeah!" she shouted. "Yeah!" Her cries of accomplishment amplified the crowd's enthusiasm, and her mind swirled in amazement.

This doesn't seem real! With the back of her hand, she wiped a trickle of blood away from the edge of her eyebrow. She then casually used her sweaty shirt as a rag to clean her hand. Elation made her laugh and shout again. She had won it all! The Women's MMA championship was hers. With only four years of heavy training, she had done it!

This is unbelievable! Despite her slender figure and past trauma, she made it here, in front of the world, on top—undefeated!

While Anna made a victory lap around the ring, several shirtless, muscular men carried the Champion's Belt over to her, where she bounced with joy. As they placed the massive belt over her shoulders, her knees wobbled from its weight. A photographer jumped into the ring and blinded her with a bright flash.

As her adrenaline faded, Anna's excitement began to shift into re-alization.

Everyone is looking at me! Oh!

An eerie worm of regret forced its way into her chest. This was definitely not her first time competing publicly, but being the champion brought on a whole new level of exposure.

Anna glanced around her at the cheering fans, startled by their intense eyes following her every move. Her mind spiraled in sudden fear.

They know my secrets. Stop looking at me. Stop looking at me. Stop it!

She anxiously scanned the crowd, searching for one particular set of eyes that made her stomach lurch. More camera lights blinded her, making her even more queasy.

He wouldn't recognize me even if he did follow MMA, which he doesn't. It's okay. He thinks I'm dead anyway.

She tried shoving the fear out of her mind by focusing on the honor and pride of receiving the championship belt. She covered her face briefly with both hands. When she removed them, she attempted to ignore the cameras. Master Kim joined her on the mat for the cel-ebration, picking Anna up in a tight embrace.

"You did it! I knew you could do it!" he shouted over the commo-tion. Another camera caught the moment, but Anna's smile was now fake as thoughts rushed at her faster than she could combat them.

This was a mistake. There are too many people! This is going to be every-where. What have I done? What if he does like MMA now? He's going to find me! I'm going to have to move again, maybe change my name. Why didn't I think this through?

Crowded and overwhelmed, a chill formed at the crown of Anna's head and melted down her shoulders, spreading through her twisting gut and dropping into the tips of her toes. Black circles invaded her vision, making her sway.

I need to get out of here now!

She grabbed Master Kim's arm to steady herself. He recognized her distress immediately. He'd witnessed her panic attacks before. Anna's head spun out of control as he led her out of the spotlight and into the safety of the locker room.

"I'll be okay," she told him, putting a hand to her pounding head. "I just need a few minutes alone. I'll be out in a bit."

"You sure?" he asked in a fatherly tone.

She nodded. "I'm fine, just..." she sucked in a deep breath of air, "exhausted."

He didn't move, uncertain that leaving her alone right now was smart. "I'm going to get the medical team to check you out. I'm worried."

"No, seriously, I just need to lie down." She panted as she sat on a nearby bench.

Master Kim shook his head but didn't argue. He knew how tough and headstrong she was.

"I'll be right outside waiting for you. Okay. Let me know if you need anything." He gave her one more concerned look before finally leaving her alone with her overwhelming fear.

She laid down with her back on the bench while her chest heaved painfully up and down, reaching for air. Squeezing her eyes shut tight, she worked on relaxing her erratic emotions. Calming words came from her lips.

"You won. People are not the enemy. They think you are amazing, beautiful, special, and safe." Anna's words bounced around the empty room unconvincingly while her breathing slowed. *Yes, I am safe. He saw me die. I'm dead to him. It's been four years now. He's not looking for me anymore. I have to live my life. He can't take this away from me.* She continued talking to herself for several minutes until she was confident that she could stand without passing out. "I am not a coward. My anxiety does not control me. I am stronger than this."

Slowly, she rose to her feet, showered, and then put on her baggy maroon T-shirt and stretchy but slimming black pants. She tied her golden hair up into a tight ponytail and slid her small gray gym bag over her shoulders.

She grimaced and shook her head as she remembered her obligation to meet with the press and many adoring fans. She couldn't do it. She could not talk herself into facing them. She couldn't risk standing in front of a crowd of cameras again. She couldn't afford the attention. Fame was not the reason she competed anyway. She competed to prove that she could overcome any obstacle.

Poking her head out of the locker room door, she found Master Kim standing nearby, looking at his watch. Taking a deep breath, Anna emerged, holding her championship belt reverently in two arms.

"Anna, my wonderful girl, are you feeling any better?"

Anna nodded with a convincing smile.

"Good! Can I just say that you are one heck of a..." Master Kim began.

Anna broke his words off by handing him the belt. It was because of him that she had won. He deserved the belt more than she did.

"Here, this is for you. You deserve to keep it," Anna said. Master Kim's eyes widened in surprise and his mouth wobbled as he tried to figure out the right words of gratitude. However, before he could speak, Anna blurted, "I'm sorry, I can't stay. I'm having *girl problems* and need to get home now. Will you take good care of this belt for me?"

Master Kim's grin over the magnificent belt was replaced by an awkward, half-pity, half-scared look as his mind processed what Anna meant by "girl problems."

"Um...yeah, o-okay. But, you're expected to make an appearance."

"I know, but I...I really need to get home. Please, can you cover for me?" She looked up at him like a begging little puppy.

Master Kim sighed. "Oh, fine. I'm not sure what I'm going to say, but I'll manage."

"Thank you. Really, thank you for everything," Anna said sincerely before she turned to leave.

Anna only took a few steps before Master Kim interrupted her escape. "Oh, and don't worry about your, um, a-award money. I will pick it up for you at the front. You can come to get it at my house when you are, ahhhh... feeling better," Master Kim stuttered with embarrassment.

Anna mentally slapped herself. *I didn't even think about the award money. I'm such a goof.*

"Master Kim. You are the best." She smiled again at her trainer before finding a back exit. With her head down, she melted into the shadows.

***

With a satisfying click, the last lock on Anna's front door shifted into place. A relieved sigh expelled from her lips as she glanced around her small, nearly empty studio apartment. It was great being completely alone to recover from the eventful night.

The only personal items in the room were a small cot set against the left-hand side of the room and a simple black suitcase lying open next to it.

Throwing her gym bag near the foot of her cot, Anna walked a few paces to the kitchen area at the right of the room. She pulled out leftover beet soup and a half-eaten deli sandwich. After warming up the soup, she shoveled the food into her exhausted mouth.

With stomach satisfied, she plopped down on her cot and cuddled into her snugly blanket. Her eyelids fluttered shut, but her sleep was pushed aside by thoughts that would not leave her alone.

I finally did it. I won. It's amazing.

However, the excitement over her accomplished goal could not fill the gnawing pit in her stomach. She felt empty and pointless despite making a life of freedom for herself. She had fans who adored her. Why couldn't that be enough?

A lonely cat could be heard crying in the night, keeping Anna up. She empathized with the creature, wandering alone, calling out to anyone but no one was around.

"Hey, Mom. Did you see what I did today?" Anna spoke to the empty room. "I did amazing. I was invincible. You would be so proud."

Silence replied in a way that made Anna feel so, so small. She was invincible and unimportant, just a speck in a large, lonely universe.

"Let it go, Anna. Let it go. Rest," she repeated several times before drifting off into a fitful sleep.

***

"Bang, bang, bang, bang, bang!" the door said, jerking Anna awake.

Morning light peeked through the curtain, telling her she was no longer stuck in her dark dream. Someone real was banging on her door.

He found me! Her senses screamed danger. Despite Anna being a self-defense expert, she appreciated having something tangible to yield, so without hesitation, she reached under her cot for her pepper spray and sprung to the door, ready for anything.

"Let me in! Please, help me!" A woman's voice shrieked from beyond the closed door. More knocking followed the desperate plea of the stranger.

Oh, thank goodness. It's not him.

Noting the urgency in the woman's voice, compassion took over fear. Cautiously but quickly, Anna unlocked the six locks on the door and cracked it open to peek out.

Anna didn't have time to register what she saw before the door was forced open, and an African-American woman with slightly graying, black frizzy hair staggered past her into the apartment.

Sinking to the floor, the woman clung to a small bundle.

Terror seized Anna as she noticed gushing red blood staining the back of the stranger's white blouse.

Jumping to action, Anna gripped the woman under her armpits and hauled her to the cot. After laying the bleeding woman down on her side, Anna rushed to re-bolt the locks.

Dizzy from stress, Anna pressed her forehead against the door to stop the spinning. She desperately tried to organize her thoughts to determine what to do next.

Okay, there is a random bleeding chick in my apartment, on my bed. Call the police? They will want to talk to me. I don't want them to see me.

The woman whimpered while Anna's mind whirled around, searching for a solution.

I've got to do something! I could hide and then call the police from a distance. Yes. But what if they don't come in time? What if... A barely audible whisper interrupted Anna's adrenaline-fueled thought process.

"The baby. Take him. Save my baby." The stranger gasped from the effort of forming words. Numb, Anna forced herself to look at the wounded woman. Blood trickled out of the corner of her bluing lips.

The stranger's hands trembled as she attempted to hold the bundle up for Anna to see, but she was too weak. Setting the bundle down, she kissed it with tears in her eyes. The bundle squirmed, causing Anna's heart to pump even faster.

Baby? Anna took tentative steps toward the mysterious bundle as though she expected it to explode in her face. She hesitated a half step away, arms awkwardly outstretched.

What am I even doing? I've never even held a baby in my life. Anna thought while retracting her arms away from the mysterious baby.

Anna stammered to the injured woman, "Wha- Why pick me? I can't- What do I do?" She dropped to her knees, weak with worry.

"Nowhere else...to run..." the woman tried to explain. "They will...be here...soon. You are...only hope." The woman paused to find more air for her punctured lung before continuing instructions. "Take care...of him..." The woman said, inhaling sharply with each word. "Don't let them...find...him..." the woman's words slowed.

A wave of nausea engulfed Anna. Panic erupted as she realized there was no hope of saving this woman, though she still wanted to try.

"Please, hey. You can't die. I don't know what to do. Stay here, okay? I'm going to get some help." Anna grabbed her phone out of the nearby suitcase and began clumsily dialing. A weak hand caught her, stopping the call.

"No. Trust no one." The woman said faintly, her words quiet but firm and desperate. "Government...Lie...Experiment...Special...His name...Jay." The woman relaxed her head into the soft pillow on the cot, her eyes staring blankly into space. An unnerving silence followed. Anna knew that the woman was dead.

Swallowing the acidic saliva that pooled in the bottom of her mouth, she fought the urge to retch. The stranger's final words penetrated Anna's soul. She stood with a shocked hand covering her lips as her eyes filled with horror. The lifeless woman still cradled the wriggling bundle.

"Wait, I don't even know your name," Anna whispered, overcome by the intense grief she felt for the woman whom she had just met. "Who are you?" She asked, broken.

The only reply was a gentle cooing coming from the bundle on the bed.

"Bang, bang, bang, bang," The door said once more.

Anna's whole body bolted into the air and a scream almost leaped out of her throat.

"Government Agents! Open up!"

2

Run

Freaking out, Anna resisted the urge to scream. Dropping to the ground, she reached into her pocket to ensure her pepper spray was still there.

Cursing the fact that she never got up the courage to purchase a gun with her fake ID, she silently prayed, waiting, hoping the visitors would go away.

"Are ya sure she came this way?" a low, brutish voice came from beyond the door.

"The blood trail ends here. She's in there," another, more authoritative voice answered sharply.

Without warning, a blast of bullets ripped through the door and into the wall above Anna's head. She flattened herself to the ground with a half cry and army-crawled her way underneath her cot for more protection. Pulling on her suitcase, she positioned it in front of her face, hiding from stray bullets.

A slow drip of blood hung from the bottom of the cot. Anna squeezed her eyes shut, trying not to think about the lifeless woman lying above her.

I can't stay here. Anna's fight or flight response chose flight. She reached her toes out, hooked the handle of her gym bag with her foot, and dragged it up to her outstretched fingers. As she moved, her shoulders and forehead kept bumping the bottom of the cot, giving her chills, knowing that she was rubbing up against a dead human. She gagged a few times, thinking about the poor woman.

That could be me next... No, Stop it! I'm going to be fine. Just focus.

The authoritative voice yelled at someone outside.

"Drake, you idiot! Put that gun away! You better hope you didn't hit the project. It's worth more than both our lives combined!"

"I didn't hit it. I can hear it crying through the door," the brutish voice, referred to as Drake, said.

"Just shut up and get in there!" More banging and yelling occurred but Anna put her focus on making a plan.

Rummaging through the gym bag, she pulled out the sweaty clothes and made sure her wallet, keys, and prescription medication were all accounted for. Looking past the suitcase, she located her cell phone a few feet away. She must have dropped it when the men showed up. It was barely out of reach.

"This stupid door is not opening! The cyber-lock breaker didn't work," Drake's frustrated voice said.

"Well, how about you use that pathetic brain of yours and figure out another way to get in!" the authoritative voice responded impatiently. "That's why we can't always trust tech to do our jobs for us. Can we?"

Yup, time to go!

Carefully sliding out from under the cot, she stayed low to the ground. Quickly, she grabbed her phone, tossed it in the gym bag, and flung it onto her shoulder. Next, she shut her suitcase and began fumbling with the zipper to close it. Her trembling hands made the task nearly impossible.

Something rammed against the door, making the whole apartment shake.

I need out! I need to get away. I can't breathe! Get out get out get out! Anna panicked while continuing to struggle with the suitcase's zipper. It snagged several times before Anna gave up the fight. She began inching her way to the back of the apartment toward the balcony with the half-zipped suitcase, careful not to make any sound.

The pounding on the door continued as she slid open the glass door. Anna was already halfway over the balcony rails when she came to a halt. Her mind suddenly focused on the sounds coming from the direction of the lifeless woman's arms.

The baby! How could I forget a baby? She berated herself. The anxiety she had experienced after the martial arts tournament paled in comparison to the overwhelming wave of horror gripping her now. The realization that she needed to return to the apartment for the helpless infant sent a throbbing ache through her.

Or...I could just leave it. They probably won't hurt him, she thought.

However, the final pleas from his mother haunted her, "The baby. Take him. Save my baby." Anna froze, trapped in a temporary paralysis.

"Uh," Anna grappled with the decision to risk her own life for a baby that was obviously the cause of much trouble.

The door splintered as the rhythmic banging on the door increased in intensity and volume.

Six locks aren't going to be enough. They are going to break down the door any second. Act now!

Fine!

Facing down her fears, she scuttled quickly back into the apartment and pulled the now-hysterical baby from the cold, limp arms of the woman. He wriggled about while Anna rushed back to the balcony.

"Shh shh shh shh shh," Anna cooed to the shrieking infant. The shushing was half for the baby and half for her own pounding heart.

Looking over the rails, Anna calculated how she would safely reach ground level with a baby in her arms. She had imagined her escape from this exit many times before, but a baby had never been part of her plan.

Lifting her suitcase to the rails with one hand, she let it topple over the edge and watched it fall about thirty feet, breaking open once it hit the ground.

"Aaargh!" Anna grunted in frustration as she watched her belongings interspersed with the gravel below.

An ear-splitting *Crack* made her stomach lurch into her throat. Looking over her shoulder, she saw a gigantic split in the wooden front door.

Without further hesitation, Anna pulled her gym bag off of her shoulder and slid the baby's kicking legs inside until he was snuggled safely in the bottom of the bag. Leaving the bag halfway open to give him air, Anna secured it on the front of her body using the straps and held it tightly with one arm.

She threw her legs over the rail and balanced on the inch-wide ledge at the other side. Making sure not to squish the baby, Anna clenched the railing with her free hand and looked down over her shoulder toward the ground below. If she could swing her body just right, she could land on the balcony below her. If her aim was off, however, she would land smack on the railing beneath her. Even worse, she could miss the balcony completely and fall the full three stories to the ground. She might survive, but she would risk serious damage to her legs or the baby. The thought of accidentally hurting the baby made her heart race even faster. She trembled, looking down at the screaming human.

Oh boy. I knew I should have gotten a ground-floor apartment. Anna thought as the baby fueled a spark of doubt in her athletic abilities.

Behind her, she heard the door splinter to the ground. Sliding her hand down to the bottom of the balcony rails, she slipped her legs off of the ledge. Dangling only by one hand, Anna grunted with exertion. Her fingers strained against the pull from her body mass.

The muscles built from her days of martial arts training showed as she swung her body in and out. Once her feet directly aligned with the balcony below, she released. Her stomach flopped as she plummeted through the air.

Clinging to the bag to steady the baby, she bit back a shriek. The back of her shirt lightly grazed the metal of the lower balcony rails as she flew over them and landed on the floor of her intended platform.

Yes! I'm awesome! We can do this, Buddy. We're almost safe, she congratulated herself while straightening her quivering legs.

"It's not here," Drake's voice projected from her apartment above.

Looking down at the baby, she noticed that he had stopped crying for a minute. He looked at her with wide, terrified eyes before wrinkling up his face and letting out another howl.

Anna broke her eyes away from the upset baby and looked through the glass door of her downstairs neighbor's home. A stunned family sat around a table with forks halfway to their mouths. A dim shatter was heard as one of the children dropped their glass cup to the floor. Anna waved awkwardly, withdrew her eyes, and quickly disappeared over the rails once more.

She landed, not so gracefully on the gravel below, knees shaking from the force of the leap. With her body threatening to collapse, Anna bent over and took big gulps of air to steady herself.

The baby was quiet again. Falling through the air seemed to shock him into submission. While checking the baby to make sure he was still breathing, she heard Drake say something inaudible above her. Anna looked up just in time to see the top half of an African-American man with bodybuilder bulk looking over the balcony rails. In his hand, he held a gun pointing directly at her.

"Over here!" he yelled.

"Drake," Anna hissed, putting a face to go with his voice. She scrunched down under the balcony, threw her arms protectively around the baby, and froze, unable to breathe. She overheard the authoritative voice shouting full blast at Drake.

"What did I tell you about the gun? Did your mom drop you on your head at birth?!" His voice barked with a pompous ring to it. Anna allowed herself to peek upward to check on the status of the gun. The man with the authoritative voice remained out of view as he continued to scold his partner.

Drake waved his weapon around wildly through the air while debating with the other, angry man.

"I won't hit the project. I'm a perfect shot and ya know it." Anna had a sick feeling that the lady lying dead in her apartment had this man to thank. She knew he would shoot without a second thought to the matter.

This man is nuts! Anna thought, making her head throb. *I can't believe this is how I'm going to die after all my years of hiding.*

"Put the gun down. That is an order!" The man who was out of sight snapped.

Anna let out the breath she had been holding as Drake lowered the gun. She glanced at her fallen belongings scattered on the ground. That was all she had.

A thought brushed her mind about retrieving some of the items, but the idea vanished when she heard a loud *thump.* She moved to see Drake on the balcony only one story above her. For a second they locked eyes.

Before he could swing down to ground level, Anna took off in a sprint across the grass, toward the parking lot with the baby tightly folded in both her arms.

The bodybuilder man wheezed as he struggled to catch up with her. Luckily, his bulk slowed him down. However, a second set of footsteps soon joined in the chase. They were lighter and swifter than Drake's heavy feet.

"I am an agent of the government. I order you to stop," the authoritative man shouted behind her, catching up.

While running, Anna clumsily shifted the baby around, trying to locate the pepper spray in her pocket. Relief came when her hand felt the cool metal tube of her only weapon.

The baby started screaming and squirming about once more. Enna dodged a swing set as she cut across the apartment complex's grassy play area. A couple of startled children gasped as she ran past before they scurried inside to the safety of their parents.

"Help!" Anna called out to them, but her words fell on deaf ears.

As her pursuers neared, commands were continuously thrown at her. However, the words were drowned out by the shrill cries of the baby.

"Shut up, kid!" Anna yelled desperately as the sound and the intensity of the moment got to her nerves. "I need to focus. You're going to get us killed!"

Then, she felt it. A prick on her back sent a shock through her entire body, causing her muscles to spasm painfully. She flailed about for several seconds before she felt nothing but exhaustion.

The pepper spray fell from her hand as she began to crumple forward. She tried to put an arm out to stop her fall to protect the baby, but her body would not cooperate.

What the... She could barely think as the world tumbled. Seconds before they hit the ground, a strong hand slowed her fall and flipped her onto her back. Her vision blurred in and out as consciousness threatened to give way.

She looked at her attacker, expecting to see Drake, but instead saw who she assumed was the jerk who kept ordering everyone around. He was a blurred mass standing over her.

"Ma'am, my name is Agent Quinn with the E.S.T. and you are in possession of government property." He flashed a badge faster than Anna could possibly process anything on it. "No one needs to come to any more harm. I'm going to retrieve my project now, and you will forget that any of this has ever happened. Are we clear?" His authoritative voice pissed her off, making her leg twitch as it desired to strike out against him, but it possessed no strength to do so.

Anna noticed a taser resting in the man's right hand. The words he spoke echoed around her mind.

E.S.T? Government property? Project? Was he talking about the baby? No way! How dare he talk about a human being that way? He's not property!

Even as her vision tilted, Anna forced herself to remain alert by focusing on her attacker's features. He looked younger than expected, with a commanding jawline and a pronounced cleft chin. His neatly combed hair framed his face, giving off a hint of arrogance.

Dressed in a stylish suit jacket and pleated pants, Agent Quinn could have been mistaken for an attractive individual. However, his liquid green, almost gray, dead eyes appeared to be coated in an indescribable darkness, as though all happiness had been sucked out of his soul.

His dead eyes bore into Anna, willing her to surrender to his demands. He reached down toward the infant.

At that moment, all thoughts of self-preservation vanished as Anna discovered a new, raw emotion: momma-bear rage.

No! This kid is not your property! I watched his mother die. You are an evil person. You both are! Anna wanted to scream, but her mouth could not form the words. *This baby did not deserve to lose his mother that way!* Her face twitched and an angry fire danced in her gaze. *You can't have him. His mother asked me to save him and that's what I'll do. He needs me! He is my responsibility.* Her eyes watered, thinking about the innocent, motherless child.

The agent's outstretched hand was about to enter her bag to grab the baby.

"Leave him alone!" she yelled, startling even herself. With a powerful *Ki hap* shout, she thrust her foot up into Agent Quinn's manly weak spot.

Alarm played on his face as the pain immobilized him long enough for Anna to locate her pepper spray and hobble over to a nearby flower bed, where she set the baby in the bag safely on the soft dirt.

Drake, who had been lurking behind Agent Quinn, reacted quickly. He gripped a fist of Anna's hair, pulling it so hard she was afraid her neck would snap. She squeezed her eyes shut and held down the trigger of her pepper spray, waving it around like mad in the general direction of the attacker.

The grip on her hair loosened as he hollered in agony. Coughing, Anna broke free and readied herself for a fight. The roaring agent opened his burning, red eyes and charged at her with a raised fist, going for a half-blind hammer strike.

Okay, this is just like any fight competition I've won. Breathe.

Anna stepped gracefully to the side like a door swinging open, allowing him to rampage past her.

"Arrrrrg!" he yelled, realizing he had missed his target. He drew his gun and tried to aim despite his burning eyes, but Anna was quick. Her leg drew a circle in the air, striking his gun-yielding hand.

The gun had hardly left his grip before Anna grabbed his massive wrist, twisted, and weaved it into a painful angle that made his bones crack.

Before he could retaliate, Anna pulled sharply on his elbow, hyperextending his joints, forcing him to move with her. She stepped past him to gain access to his back.

Blood rushed through her heart as she flung one of her arms over his shoulder and the other under his armpit and tried to trap him in a restraint, but his body was too wide for her hands to connect for a secure hold. She clamped her fingers tightly onto his button-up shirt. He grabbed at her hands, but they refused to let go without taking the shirt with her. It ripped slightly as she pulled on it, causing Drake to shriek.

"Oh, come on! Are ya serious right now? I just got this shirt!" Drake raged, trying to reach behind his back to grab Anna. Agent Quinn recovered and rushed at them, ready to assist.

"Quinn, get this crazy chick off me! Dude, she can fight!" Drake thrashed about, trying to free himself, spinning and shaking Anna around like a rag doll.

The shirt continued to rip, and her grip weakened. The danger of being thrown through the air grew with each sharp movement. However, if she released her hold now, she would land hard and be attacked by both of the very angry men simultaneously.

Nope, I was wrong. This is nothing like a fight competition. I could actually die today.

Frantic, Anna adjusted her arm that was stretched over his shoulder and slid it to where she was hanging onto him by the neck. Her body flew through the air as he spun like a dog chasing his tail.

Drake, unaware that his partner was near, clawed at Enna's arm as he threw her around. Without letting go, Anna used the momentum from being thrashed about to her advantage. She split her leg into the air and bashed her foot into the side of Agent Quinn's face. He fell heavily to the ground.

Seeing that he'd accidentally aided Anna with the assault of his partner, Drake stopped his ridiculous thrashing and, with Anna still hanging on his back, darted over to where his gun sat on the grass.

No, no, no! Not good! Enna's mind screamed, begging herself not to freeze in panic. Moments before Drake could reach his weapon, Anna forced her arms to let go so she could drop to the ground. Without hesitation, she kicked the back of his knee, making his leg collapse out from under him, then leaped over him and raced for the gun.

Drake recovered much faster than Anna expected. He rose and grabbed a large chunk of her hair.

"Ahhh!" Anna screamed as the roots of her hair stretched each pore of her scalp. She slid her hand into her own hair and held it in place to manage the pain. She spun around, ripping her hair away from Drake before laying a powerful, downward elbow strike on Drake's outstretched forearm.

"Who are you?!" Drake cried as his injured arm went limp. With his other hand, he jabbed a fist in the direction of her chest. She redirected the strike while trying to get offline from the attack but was not fast enough to avoid damage.

His knuckles slammed heavily into her shoulder, making her gasp in pain. Stumbling back, she created space between herself and the large man, her fists held at the ready. She remained aware of the gun's location in case Drake planned to make another dash for it. Sweat pooled into her eyes, making them burn, but she held her stance.

Okay, breathe... I can do this.

She heard Agent Quinn moan a few paces to her right, yet her focus held locked onto the bulky threat in front of her.

Anna lunged halfway into Drake's bubble with a traveling front kick at the ready. However, instead of extending her leg to finish the strike, Anna planted the raised foot back into the ground, ducked to avoid another punch from him, and sent a solid, roundhouse kick into the air.

Her foot slid inches away from the large man but made no contact with him. Luckily, he was not her true target. Spinning, her leg flung through the air and landed heavily into the temple of the unsuspecting Agent Quinn's skull, who had been trying to sneak up on her. His eyes rolled to the back of his head and he toppled over, unconscious.

Yes!

"Whoa, where did you learn to fight like that?" Drake asked as he slowly circled Anna and wiped at his swollen eyes. She shrugged and let herself smirk, but she didn't linger on her small victory.

Standing between Drake and the gun, she calculated her options. Although he was not extremely tall, he was double her width, making him seem like a giant. One punch to the head from him would take her out immediately, possibly permanently.

The safest attack point for her would be from behind where he had no reach. She just needed access and a good grip. Jagged air pumped from her lungs while she planned out her next move.

With wide eyes, Anna shot her gaze past Drake's shoulder. She gasped, raised her arms, and waved them wildly about.

"Help, officer! These guys just attacked me and my baby. Please, help us! He has a gun!" Anna cried out, jumping up and down, trying to get attention.

Drake spun to face the officer she was speaking to, only to find an empty space.

Before he had a chance to register Anna's deception, she had already run and jumped onto his back.

One of her arms snaked around the furious man's neck, her other arm wrapped behind his head. She connected her arms together and squeezed snugly, cutting off the blood supply to his brain.

Drake clawed and pulled at her thumbs for leverage, but they were tucked safely out of reach. The more he struggled, the tighter she squeezed.

After failing to loosen her grip, Drake dropped to the ground, body-slamming Anna with all his force, knocking the breath out of her. A cry escaped Anna's lips as her back crunched against the ground. She held on, ignoring the pain ripping through her body, counting the seconds before he would pass out.

He rolled around, squirming like a worm on a hook. Anna gasped and tried to use her legs to flip him off of her without letting go, but her efforts failed, leaving her body trapped.

Fortunately, the man's attempts to free himself became sluggish and weak until, finally, his body went limp. Trembling, Anna struggled to slip out from under Drake's dead weight.

I can't believe this is happening to me, she thought, lying on the grass for a moment to calm her aching body. She heard the baby singing an unhappy tune at the top of his lungs.

Anna moved onto her hands and knees to crawl gingerly over to the distraught baby. His face was a dark shade of purple from the effort of crying so hard.

"Hey, hey there. It's okay, I've got you," Anna whispered breathlessly. With great effort, she forced herself into a standing position. One of the unconscious agents groaned. She looked behind her briefly. Both men were still lying on the grass.

Picking up the bag that held the baby, Anna took off in a staggered run as fast as her aching body would allow.

She fumbled for her keys with shaking hands. Once she was able to steady herself enough to unlock the car, Anna realized she had another problem. She had no car seat and no idea of what to do with a baby.

Oh, man! What was I thinking? I'm not equipped to take care of this thing. I'm just going to leave him at the hospital and run.

Even as the thought came to her mind, her protective side kicked in, arguing away her doubts while she placed the baby on the floor in the back of the car.

No, I can't just leave him at the hospital. The agents will find him there. The government owns everything. They'll find him no matter what I do! No, I can't abandon him. Not again. Not like the others. Guilt filled her chest with memories from her past.

"Guess you're stuck with me, little man. We'll figure it out."

The baby's face peeked out of the gym bag and howled his disapproval as Anna packed some trash from the car around him for padding to provide a little protection.

"Sorry, buddy. Hang in there just a bit longer," she said as she hopped into the driver's seat. Starting the car, Anna looked through the rear-view mirror just in time to see Agent Quinn running into the parking lot.

Her foot pressed on the gas to accelerate, quick but smooth, trying not to jostle the baby.

Looking again into the rear-view mirror, she took a deep breath as she left the agents and her life as Anna behind.

3

Playing Mother

Once she reached a safe distance from the two agents, Anna pulled her car into a gas station parking lot.

Bringing the car to a stop, Anna collapsed her head onto the steering wheel and sobbed, adrenaline still rocking inside of her.

Why? What did I get myself into? I liked being Anna. I don't want to do this. I don't want to run anymore! I want to go home.

The baby harmonized with her cries as she mourned the day's events, not wanting to come to terms with her current situation. She let emotions spill all over the place as the pain in her heart and the pain from her wounds mingled together.

After a few minutes, the continuous screams from the baby caused Anna's sorrow to turn into anger. Twisting around in her seat, she looked down at him.

"Stop it!" she yelled, "Yeah, I don't like this either. Why didn't your mother choose someone else? Why? Why can't you just stop crying?" She said through tears.

She reached back and grabbed the straps on the bag to pull the baby up to her. Taking him out of the bag, she held him awkwardly in front of her face to see his scrunched-up expression.

"What do you want from me?" She watched the small baby scream it out while her anger turned into sad sympathy. Anna brought him into her chest and rocked softly. "I'm sorry, buddy. Sorry. You lost your momma today. I know how hard that can be. I lost my momma, too." The baby began to settle down.

"Your mom told me that your name is Jay. I like that name." They were both quietly crying by that point, rocking back and forth, until the tiny boy, Jay, drifted off into a much-needed sleep.

After gently placing Jay onto the passenger seat, she pulled her phone out of her pocket and anxiously dialed an old number she hoped still worked. Anna's muscles tightened with each ring until she was a little ball of shriveled nerves.

What will I do if he doesn't answer? We'll be screwed.

At last, a kind, familiar voice answered, bringing relief to her spasming muscles.

Anna put the phone to her heart as it thundered out of control. Oh, how she had longed to hear his sweet voice.

Swallowing a few times to clear the cotton out of her mouth, she held the phone back to her ear and spoke.

"Hey, Oliver, it's me, ah, Anna. Do you remember me? I need your help." Her lips broke into a smile as he reassured her that he would never forget her. For a moment, her mouth forgot how to form words.

Clearing her throat, she calmed her racing thoughts. "Do you, by chance, still do what you used to do?" She had to be careful not to say too much. Oliver was largely into conspiracies and was convinced all phones were bugged. However, after today, Anna doubted it much less than she used to.

She soaked in the sound of his voice as he calmed her fears with his words.

He's going to help us. I'll get to see him again!

"Thank you so much," her voice quivered with gratitude. I'll send you the information and pictures you need right away. Do you still use the same website?" she asked, shuffling her hand around the glove compartment, searching for a pencil and paper.

As he responded, she quickly scribbled down a new website address he had given her. "Yes, I still remember the code," she answered. Nostalgia engulfed her as memories of sending and receiving coded messages after dark surfaced in her mind. "Yes, I'll keep an eye out for your message. Thank you! It's good hearing your voice again. Yeah, see you soon."

I'll see him soon! Anna ended the call with a new hope for the future. Her body tingled with anticipation and renewed energy.

"Okay, next, gotta get baby stuff," she mumbled to herself, looking into her wallet. "Oh, I'm gonna need a lot more money," she said, grateful for her championship reward money, which she could pick up from Master Kim.

Was it really just last night that I won the championship? Anna rubbed her tired eyes.

"Man, it's been a long day," she said to herself as she ignited the car engine.

***

A renewed pang of grief greeted Anna as she pulled up to Master Kim's quaint home. Knowing she would never see her mentor and friend again didn't seem real. He was the only true connection she had made while she was Anna.

The day they had first met, she was a blubbering mess. Anna couldn't even go outside without having full-blown panic attacks. He found her huddled in the back of a grocery store, gasping for breath after she thought she saw the man who tortured her for years.

Master Kim was the one who recognized her distress and taught her how to get back up again. And again. And again. He taught her to fight and meditate. In exchange for training, she helped keep his yard pristine.

Now, she had to break all ties so she could disappear without being sought after. She had to die, again.

Okay, you can do this. Go say goodbye. Act natural. She pumped herself up before hopping out of the car and running to the front door. She knocked a few times before steps were heard from inside. Master Kim swung the door open and greeted her with a grin. He was a bear of a man, standing two heads above Anna. His arms rippled in muscles and his brown eyebrows curved down, making him appear like a movie villain, but in reality, his heart was gentle and kind.

"Hey, I was just going to call to see if you were doing alright. How are you feeling after last night?" he asked.

"Honestly, I'm struggling pretty bad. I thought I would feel more, uh, well accomplished after winning. I guess I'm just a little off. I don't, I don't feel much of anything. I'm just here to grab my portion of the championship money."

"Your portion? Hey, you won it all. The money is yours." He reached a gentle hand out and placed it on her shoulder that Drake had crushed. She cringed.

"Oh, what's wrong? Are you okay?" Master Kim asked with a worried grimace.

"I'm just sore from last night," Anna said, not wanting to linger. "I'm in a bit of a rush, though. Um, sorry, I can't stay." Her eyes briefly flashed over her shoulder to the car where the baby was.

"Of course, let me grab your check. Come on in." He beckoned her inside and ran to grab the money. Anna ignored the invitation to go into the house. She was already nervous enough about leaving the baby alone in the car, even while staying nearby. She wouldn't let the car out of her sight.

It didn't take long for him to return with her check for $5,000.

"Wow! Thank you," Anna said, backing away to her car. "Truly, just thank you for always taking care of me. I needed a father figure like you."

"Oh," the compliment left Master Kim a little shy, but Anna wanted to let him know how much he meant to her. Master Kim squinted at her. "Yeah, it's my pleasure. But, wait...Anna?" he reached out as if he wanted to stop her from leaving. The concern on his face made Anna's gut squirm. "I'm worried about you. You seem a bit...jumpy. Is there anything I can do to help?"

"Thanks, but I'm fine. I'll be fine. I just have a lot on my mind." Turning her back to him, she fought the urge to hug him goodbye and tell him how much she would miss him, but she worried tears would come. She couldn't cry, especially in front of Master Kim. No, she needed to be strong.

Hugs aren't really my thing anyway. Sorry, my friend, Anna thought as she began her drive to the baby shopping center. *I wish I could explain. Please don't be too sad for me.*

***

With the baby and some cash in hand, Anna stood, staring wide-eyed at aisles and aisles of infant items.

Jay exclaimed his discomfort to the world by making a sound similar to that of a screaming banshee. Anna's thoughts were freaking out as well.

Fifty bazillion diaper choices? Another trillion car seat choices. I haven't even begun to figure out the right kind of formula to get the stinky baby. Oh my gosh! I don't know how to do this. What if I can't do this? I can't even keep plants alive. How am I supposed to keep a baby alive? Anna began hyperventilating. *What if being with me puts him in more danger? My life is not safe, especially for a baby! I'm going to fail. Oh my gosh, I'm going to fail.*

"This is worse than being chased by creepy government guys," Anna muttered out loud, not noticing the store attendant standing behind her.

"May I help you?" a man's deep voice boomed near Anna's back.

Jolted by the voice, Anna spun around with a clenched fist at the ready. Realizing this man was not one of her pursuers, she barely stopped herself from decking him in his face. The man flinched from the sudden movement and held his hands up in peace.

"Whoa! Didn' mean to scare ya there, ma'am."

Taking a breath, Anna looked the man over. He was a big, well, gigantic, African-American guy with kind eyes and a squishy face.

He is no threat, Anna convinced herself.

"Oh, sorry," Anna said, relaxing her balled-up fist. "Um, please don't call me ma'am, but yeah, I could use some help. How do you keep a tiny human alive?"

Laughing at what he thought was a joke, the giant store attendant put his finger to the side of his nose.

"Well, ya come to the right place." He led Anna down one of the aisles and began slamming her with questions. "How old's your baby? Is he in newborns or ones? Does he have any allergies to any kinds of wipes? What's the little fella's name? Is he still in 0-3?" Seeing the panicked face of the young mother, the attendant slowed his pace. "Let's just start with diapers."

With each item piled into the cart, Anna became more and more wary of how little she understood about being a mother.

At one point, she considered offering Jay to a sweet pregnant woman who pushed a toddler around in her cart, but Anna shoved the intrusive thought away and focused on learning as much as she could from the store attendant.

Anna hated feeling like a fraud as she smiled and laughed at the man's jokes even though she was a complete mess on the inside and found no humor in anything.

She was so anxious about shopping that once she had gathered all the items the man insisted she needed, her feet took her right out the front doors without paying, making the alarms go off.

Crap! She put a hand over her face in shame.

"Sorry, I'm so sorry," Anna stumbled over her words as she made her way back to the cashier's counter. "I'm just so tired and not thinking at all, and it's been a crazy rough day. You have no idea! I'm sorry.

I'm really not trying to steal from you. I have money," she held out a wad of cash. The woman manning the front cash register gave a knowing nod.

"No worries, ma'am. You'd be surprised how often we get that. I guess it's just momma's brain."

"Hey, Tina! She doesn't like ta be called ma'am!" The superintendent yelled out to the cashier from about twenty feet away with a one-handed shrug.

Oh my gosh. Seriously?!

Anna ducked her head, embarrassed, painfully aware of all the eyes that turned in her direction. It didn't help that Jay was screaming his voice dry.

I look like the crappiest mother ever! I can't even get this kid to stop crying and his diaper is drooping. They probably think I'm neglectful. I wonder when the last time this kid has eaten. Maybe they think I'm starving him.

She quickly paid for the items, trying not to make eye contact with anyone, and dashed out the doors.

Back at her car, Anna struggled to change the squirmy, screaming baby in the back seat. Instead of digging through the mountain of baby items in her trunk to find the changing mat, she used an old hamburger wrapper to catch stray smears.

The store attendant knows more about this kid than I do, Anna thought with distaste as she used way too many wipes to clean up the small amount of poop.

She studied the baby thoroughly, trying to familiarize herself with the strange human. He had sleek black hair, light skin, and a slightly wider nose than she would expect. The skin in the crevasse of his tiny finger joints was darker than the rest of his skin.

Anna remembered something the store attendant had said while he made small talk as they shopped. "This lil' man look just like my son did when he was a newborn. Well, maybe even a bit cuter, but don't tell my son that. Ha ha. Just wait. Soon, he'll be sproutin' curly hair and his skin'll tan out. Mixed babies are the cutest, don't ya think? Where's his daddy from anyway?"

I have no idea who his dad is. Maybe I can find him? Where would I even start to look without putting Jay in more danger? I don't know. What if his dad is frantically searching for him? No, but wouldn't the mother have told me to bring him to his dad if that was an option?

Anna's thoughts were put on hold when a warm stream of liquid shot at her only remaining T-shirt.

"Gross!" Anna complained once she realized what the stream was. She had been so lost in thought that she forgot about the diaper she was in the middle of changing. Taking a wipe to her shirt, Anna tried cleaning up the pee. "Fine, I needed to buy more clothes anyway," she muttered.

Anna struggled to finish putting the diaper on the baby and found a bottle of pre-mixed formula from her grocery bags. Scrunched in the back seat of the car, Anna held the infant in her arms gently as though the small boy would fall apart if she put any pressure on him. Jay gulped hungrily at the formula.

Anna looked at the helpless human in her arms. His dark brown eyes locked with her gaze. She expected to feel the usual panic that always accompanied her when she made eye contact, but at this moment, all she felt was curiosity.

"Huh? What are you thinking baby? Are you trying to figure out who this weird woman holding you is?"

Her lips formed a soft smile, finding peace in his eyes.

You are so precious, Anna thought to herself, surprised by the shift in her apprehension. As though he had read her thoughts, the baby reached out his delicate hand and grasped her pinky finger lightly. Anna's heart filled to the brim as a deeper connection rooted inside of her.

"There you go, baby, drink up. You are actually kinda cute when you aren't screaming."

For a moment, everything was perfect. For a moment, anxiety didn't exist and Anna forgot that anyone was after them. She hummed a soft song while Jay, her new son, clung to her.

"Jay, I'm going to take care of you. Okay? You're going to be my baby boy and I will never leave you."

A calm rested over Anna like a ray of sun hitting just right.

I needed you too, I guess. She kissed his little fingers, filling with joy.

After the baby finished eating, Anna placed him in the new car seat, hoping it was installed correctly.

Using a high-pitched, cheesy voice, Anna talked to her little guy. "Let's go, my sweety baby pie. Yeah, yeah, I wuv you! Ah, yeah, I wuv you." She giggled at the silly sound of her baby talk. "We only have a few more stops to make and then you and I will be safe on our new adventure."

4

Identity

Oliver stood behind the front counter of his rundown, dimly-lit curio shop. His heart galloped in anticipation of seeing Clara again.

Oh, when she comes, do I call her Clara or go by her alias, Anna? Ah, prolly Anna, in case I'm bein' watched? Hmm, I don' know.

Staring into the glass door at the front of the shop, he checked his reflection, making sure he didn't look too shabby.

He had deep-set hazel eyes, a pointed chin, and shoulder-length mouse-colored hair. He wore a tight-fitting brown jacket with patches on the elbows—nothing too impressive, but it would have to do.

He glanced around, anxiously tapping on the countertop with his fingernails, making a rhythm of clicks as he waited. The shop was cluttered with old trinkets and knick-knacks. Puppets hung from the ceiling, giving the shop an eerie, unwelcoming feeling to ward off real customers.

Just how I like it.

Glancing at an old cuckoo clock on the wall, a smile spread across his lips just as the bell on the front door rang.

Right on time! As always. Oliver tried to keep his face stoic and mysterious, but the excitement of seeing his dear friend filled his heart.

"Well, hello m'lady. What trouble did yeh get yerself into this time?" His face fell. "Tell me, he didn't find yeh, did he?" Oliver asked with a slight Scottish accent.

She's even more beautiful than I remember. He gave her a crooked smile. She held a sleeping baby in her arms. Her shy eyes shifted uneasily, but her voice was strong and chipper.

"Hey, it's good to see you! No, he didn't find me, thank goodness. It's just, I got roped into, well, I'm not quite sure what yet," Clara responded. "Have you heard of the E.S.T?"

"Wait, the E.S.T? Where did ya hear that?" Oliver slipped out from behind the counter, wide-eyed. Walking over to Clara, he hoisted himself up to sit on the counter. Leaning in, he whispered, "What do yeh know about the E.S.T?"

"I don't know anything about it. That's why I asked you." Clara gave him a sly smirk. "You've heard of it?"

"Oh, only in whispers," he said excitedly. "My sources say that the E.S.T. is a secret department funded by the government. I hear they're responsible for buyin' out new technology so they can use it for their own gain. Yeh wonder why we don' have flying cars yet? Yeah? It's because of the E.S.T. They own everythin'. People say they even have completely waterproof cell phones that don' even crack when yer drop em, and they don' need phone cases," he nodded very seriously, causing Clara to nod with him.

"Well, some guys stopped by my house looking for, ah, this baby." She held Jay up, who peeked an eye open, then closed it again. "One of them said he was an agent of the E.S.T. He said something about government property and a project. He was referring to the baby. That's why we have to disappear."

"No way! Can I see him?" Oliver held his arms out to Jay.

"Mm, sure. He might freak out, though. He spends most of his time crying." She handed the baby over to Oliver. Jay scrunched up his nose as though he smelled something iffy, but he kept his eyes closed and didn't cry.

"Oh, hey there." Oliver held Jay out in front of him. He carefully shifted the baby around, inspecting him, expecting to see some strange tattoo or gears like a robot or something that would give him a clue of what the E.S.T. was up to. "Hmm, what are yeh?" He brought Jay to his face and sniffed. "He smells a bit funny. What is that smell?"

"That smell is baby. Oliver, I've checked him up and down. He's just normal," Clara shrugged. "Sorry."

"Ah, no…there is somethin' special about this one. I can feel it. Maybe the E.S.T. is experimentin' with alien hybrids. With a wee bit of extraterrestrial D.N.A, poof! We have a new species. What do his B.Ms look like?"

"B.Ms?" Clara asked, grinning at the ridiculous question.

"Yeah, bowel movements. Are they strange in any way? What color are they? It could determine whether he is part alien." Oliver bounced Jay up and down in his arms.

"I can't tell if you are serious or not," Clara giggled. "His poop looks like regular, stinky, yellow poop. I'm pretty sure he is not an alien." She reached out and took Jay back as he started getting fussy.

"Oh, I've got it! Maybe they are experimentin' with clonin' and he's the first prototype! Or, they could be doin' mind control experiments where they are creatin' a generation of individuals who can be remotely controlled by the government at any given time… Oh, or…"

"Oliver, he's just a baby. There's nothing wrong with him." She put her free hand on his for a second to revert his attention back to reality. He grazed her knuckle gently with his thumb.

"Clar…Anna, I…" Oliver said sweetly before changing his tone. "We ought to get a move on." He jumped down off the counter.

He swiftly walked back to his workstation, checking the desktop computer's monitor and clicking through the security feeds to ensure no questionable customers were lurking about.

"Good. We're safe!" Satisfied they were alone, he turned to an old painting on the wall behind the counter. Oliver removed it to reveal a black lockbox with a dial in the center. He turned the dial several times, not bothering to hide the code from Clara.

She's one of the good ones. Trust has never been an obstacle with her, especially since she's terrible at lyin'.

The lockbox clicked open and Oliver pulled out a yellow envelope. Walking back to the counter, he slid it over to Clara.

"Everythin' you'll need," he assured her with a twinkle in his eyes. Clara clumsily opened the envelope with her free hand. Dumping the contents out on the counter, she shuffled through the documents. Oliver casually leaned in with a corner of his lip lifted in amusement, waiting for her reaction.

"New social for yeh and the boy, passports, adoption papers, I even threw in a couple college degrees for yeh. See, look." He pointed at a few of the papers. "Yer now, officially, a certified elementary school teacher, accountant, and business manager. I'm sure tha'll come in handy."

"But, I don't know anything about these fields," Clara said with a slight head shake.

"Ah, but I know yeh. Yer intelligent and have a knack for learnin', ye'll be fine." Clara looked at him with doubtful eyes but didn't argue. "I also filled yer passport with visa stamps. Ye'll be good to travel the world for a few years, and yeh can contact me when yeh need new visas and we'll meet up again. As a bonus, I even found cheap flight tickets to Mexico for the two of yeh. Did I miss anythin'?" Oliver asked.

"Wow! You didn't have to do all this!" Clara flipped open one of the passports. The picture staring back at her had her face, but instead of the light blonde hair that fell down the length of her back, it showed shoulder-length black hair. The eyes were different as well. Instead of the blue eyes that she had now, the picture showed dark brown eyes.

"Look, yeh won't have to wear blue contacts anymore. I've always loved yer beautiful brown eyes. I'm guessing it's safe by now for yeh ta show them off again," Oliver said enthusiastically.

"Yeah, that will be nice," Clara said as she focused on the name next to the image, her new name.

"Enna Jane Anderson," Clara said out loud. "Enna. Ha, that didn't change much," she cocked her head to give Oliver a sideways glance. "So, I go from Clara to Anna and from Anna to Enna," she laughed. "I can't tell if you are just bad at coming up with creative new names or if you just really like names that end with an 'ah' sound."

"Hey, Enna's a sexy name!" Oliver put his hands up in a shrug. "I figured if I keep yer names similar enough, even if yer old name slips out, yeh can cover it up super smooth. No one'll ever know," he said, proud of his clever plan.

"Nice. Yeah, I like the name Enna. It's good. Really. I just like giving you a hard time. You're not bad at coming up with names. I think it's cute," Clara stumbled around with her words.

"It's cute like you," Oliver added. Clara's cheeks grew a bit pinker, making her glow as she shifted through more of the documents. Her eyes paused on the fake adoption papers.

"Jayson C. Anderson?" Anna looked up at Oliver. "His name's supposed to be Jay. His mother, right before she…well, she said his name is Jay. I think it was important to her." Her brows furrowed.

"Wait, what happened with his mother?" Oliver asked, concerned.

"Well, she died…in my apartment." Oliver's eyes widened as Clara elaborated. "She was shot by one of the E.S.T. agents. One of the last things she said was his name, Jay."

"Ah dang! That must've been horrifying to yeh, especially with yer past trauma. I'm so sorry I changed his name to Jayson. I didn't know it was that importan' to yeh." Oliver placed a comforting hand on Clara's arm.

"No, it's okay. It's definitely better this way. I was actually being kind of stupid. The agents probably knew his name was Jay, so changing it is good. It's fine. Thank you. Jayson is a good name." Clara turned her face away. Oliver could tell that she was a frazzled mess.

She hid it well, but he could always tell when she was putting on a front.

"Hey, yer never stupid. Yeh have been through too much for one person to handle and yeh keep going. I've been checking up on you, Anna, my MMA champion." Clara snapped her gaze back to Oliver in surprise.

He chuckled, "Yeah, I saw yeh, my warrior princess. Yeh amaze me. And I think it's sweet that yeh wan' to honor the baby's mother by using the name she picked. Yer a wonderful person, Clara. Oh, sorry, I guess I should say Enna now."

Clara smiled and took a deep breath, dropping her gaze again. Oliver knew she hated eye contact, but he couldn't stop staring.

"Oliver, this is perfect. I can still call him Jay," Clara said after reviewing the remaining documents. "Thank you so much. What do I owe you?" She shoved the documents back into the yellow envelope and placed them in her old gym bag, which was now being used as a diaper bag. She retrieved her wallet and awaited Oliver's price.

"Ah no, dearie, it's on me. Of course. Don't yeh know that yer a V.I.P? I'm watchin' out for yeh."

"But, you bought us flight tickets. At least let me cover those," Enna said with grateful eyes.

"No, it's a gift. Just promise I won't have to see yeh in this predicament again, my friend," Oliver replied kindly. Clara shook her head and laughed as she smoothly slid a one-hundred-dollar bill across the counter.

"I'll do my best, but no promises," she teased. Oliver put his hand over hers with a sad smile and held it tenderly. Her face flushed longingly at the touch. Their eyes connected, but only briefly as Clara ducked into the cutest shy pose.

Neither of them wanted to break away. Standing in silence, they felt comfort from pain and sorrow until Jay began to crave some attention of his own and let it be known by pulling a lock of Clara's long hair.

Clara reluctantly pulled her hand away from Oliver's warm grasp, leaving him caressing nothing but the hundred-dollar bill. Folding her arms around Jay, she swayed.

"Clara," Oliver said in a serious voice, "I want yeh to stay. I miss yeh. I can keep yeh and baby Jay safe. We can disappear together, start fresh,"

"Whoa, Oliver. You know how much I care about you. You're my best friend, but it's too dangerous."

"Please, Clara. I don't..."

"No," she cut him off. "I'm so sorry, but you have to trust me. I want to be with you too, so bad, but...we can't." Clara sighed heavily. "What if Andrew finds us together? I know he will keep me alive, but he would never forgive you for helping me escape. He will kill you, you know. And he will make me watch. I know what he is capable of. I can't lose you." Clara shook her head remorsefully. "Thank you so much for your help. I...I don't know what I would do without you."

Oliver took a deep, shaky breath, his shoulders tensing as he tried to regain control over his emotions. He hated letting her go again. He picked the hundred dollar bill up and waved it at her.

"Hey, seriously, I'm just happy I got to see yer beautiful face again." He walked back around the counter and slipped into Clara's space. He took her hand and put the money into her palm. "Maybe someday it'll be safe for us to be together again."

"Yeah, I hope so. Someday." Clara cast her eyes to the floor, shook her head slightly with a sad little grin, and tucked the money into her bag. "Thank you, my friend."

"It's always my pleasure," Oliver choked through the lump in his throat. Taking Clara's hand, he brought it to his lips and kissed her knuckles tenderly.

"Please just take care of yerself and that special little one." Oliver's hold on her hand lingered, taking in the feel of her smooth skin. Clara stepped in closer, obviously fighting back her own emotions.

"I, Oliver, I..." she couldn't finish her thought, but her unspoken words were understood. She would never be with him as long as that man, Andrew Dengaila, was alive. It was too big of a risk for her to take.

She loves me too much to let me risk my life to be with her. Oliver's head rushed with turmoil.

"I know, Clara. It's okay. Just remember, yer worth the risk to me. I would give my life up a hundred times to be with yeh. I love yeh, Clara." His heart shattered as he braced himself for the goodbye.

Clara stood on her toes and placed a sweet peck on his cheek, sending a tingle throughout his body. Without another word, she swung her bag onto her shoulder, shifted Jay to her other arm, and walked out the door, leaving Oliver alone once again in his rundown, little shop.

5

A New Start

Anna sat on an ugly green chair in the corner of the hotel room, her head resting in her hands. A glow from a dim lamp emphasized the strange greens, reds, and yellows that splashed the small room, making Anna wonder if the designer had been color-blind. A queen-sized bed sat in the center of the room with mustard-colored blankets neatly spread out, begging Anna to lie down.

Oh gosh. I'm so tired. This is ridiculous! Is it normal for babies to wake up every two seconds? She had just finished putting Jay back to sleep in his pack-n-play for what seemed like the tenth time that night.

She looked at the alarm clock. It read 3:32 am. With a groan, she considered trying to fall back asleep, but every gurgle of the baby sent a flicker of panic through her body. Worries kept popping into her mind.

Is he okay? Is he waking up again? Is he breathing? It boggled her mind how terrifying it was to be responsible for a slobbering, whining mini-human.

Giving up on the idea of sleep, Anna dug a notebook and pen out of her brand-new suitcase and ripped out a blank page. Her hand trembled as it hovered above the paper.

What should I even say? It doesn't need to be too deep. It's not like many people will even care if I'm gone. Mostly, it's just Master Kim. Anna hated thinking about how he would feel once he discovered Anna's fate.

Master Kim had been her protector. *What will he think when he realizes he couldn't protect me from this? Maybe I could swing by and tell him why I have to do this. I could tell him I'm still alive but he can't tell anyone.*

Anna shook her head. *No, I have to disappear from everyone, including Master Kim. The agents will surely check in with anyone who knows me.* With heavy trepidation, she put her pen tip down and began to write.

To whom it may concern,

I'm sorry, I can no longer live this way. There is no escape for me other than this. Family is gone, love means nothing, money is worthless. Don't bother looking for me. My body will be swept away by the river long before anyone even notices that I'm gone.

Anna stared blankly at her scribbled words. Was it really this simple to slip in and out of people's lives?

That's just cruel, isn't it? She thought about writing a personal note to Master Kim, telling him this was not his fault and thanking him for all he did, but she knew nothing in a stupid letter could make anything easier for him or any of its readers. The words meant nothing. They were hollow and meaningless. She would be gone, and no one could change or fix anything.

Thoughts of her past webbed their fingers into Anna's brain, causing her chest to throb.

"Stupid note," Anna said out loud, wrinkling up the paper and throwing it across the room. "I don't want to do this. I don't want to hurt my friend. I can't do that to him!" Speaking louder than intended, she quickly glanced at Jay, who had finally decided to give sleep a fighting chance. He made no movement other than the slight rise and fall of his little chest.

Closing her eyes, the horrible image of scripted words drudged through her memory. A note, similar to the one she was currently trying to write, had been found on her pillow many years previously.

Clara,

I'm so sorry my beautiful girl, but I can't go on like this. You are stronger without me holding you back. I am nothing. Please hug your father for me every day. Even though he pushed me away, he still needs you to love him. Don't let him go. Take care of him. I love you. My life has no meaning. I just need this to end. Be brave. I will always love you. Sorry, I have no words to make it up to you.

- Mom

The panic of the words still cursed her nightly, reminding her of how it had felt, running around the house, howling in fear, hoping it wasn't too late.

"Dad, Help! It's Mom! Help!" but her dad wasn't there. She was all alone with dread pooling, drowning out hope.

"Mom, Mom, please be alive!" she prayed as she tried to turn the knob on the bathroom door. Locked.

"Mom," she whispered, "are you okay?" No answer greeted her. No words of comfort. No sign of life.

Using a nail to unlock the door, little Clara dared not to breathe. She slowly opened the door to find her mother's limp body on the bathroom floor. Her lips were a terrifying color of blue, the color of human death when breath and blood are frozen, and her eyes were a scary, lifeless, glossy gray like the light had dimmed in them ever so slightly. There was no more blush left in her normally rosy cheeks. *She was gone.* All that was left were the empty words.

My life has no meaning. My life has no meaning. Life has no meaning.

Those words often repeated in Anna's mind, making her eyes moisten.

I meant that little to her! Angry at her mother for leaving, Anna clenched her fists and hit her head a few times, wanting to beat the memories out of her brain, but the emotions remained.

It was Mom's fault Dad fell apart. It was Mom's fault Andrew found me in the first place. How could she do that to me? Why couldn't she love me just a little more?

Fighting against the painful memory, Anna sucked in a gulp of air and held it in her lungs for as long as consciousness would allow. She then released the air out slowly through her teeth. Being stuck in victim mode never did any good.

Let her go. She is gone. There is nothing I can do to change that. Her vision tilted as she stood up too fast.

Wiping tears away from her cheeks, Anna forced herself to retrieve her crumpled note that waited for her on the floor. Flattening it out and looking over it one last time, she picked the pen up and signed,

-Anna J Park

Feeling entirely alone, Anna shivered, though it must have been at least 80 degrees in the ugly hotel room. Feeling worn and broken, she leaned back in the chair, too tired and unmotivated to move to the bed.

At that moment, Jay whimpered in his sleep as though telling her, *I care about you.* Anna smiled through closed eyes before hoisting her body out of the chair. She walked over to Jay, leaned over the pack-n-play, and watched as sweet baby snores tooted in and out of his nose.

"Don't worry, baby, I know I have you. I will never leave you. You hear that? I'm your mommy now and I'm not going anywhere. You, sweet boy, give my life meaning. I'm going to fight for us. Okay. I'll keep you safe," Anna said softly. Jay cooed and smiled in his sleep.

She gently reached down and lifted Jay out of the pack-n-play. He wriggled and yawned, but exhausted from the long night of waking up constantly, Jay nuzzled into Anna's warmth and continued to sleep.

Walking a few steps to the bed, Anna melted into the overly soft mattress. With the baby snuggled close, Anna drifted off to sleep.

***

Only a couple of hours later, Anna woke with a start. She instantly placed a worried hand on Jay's torso to make sure he was still breathing. Not sure quite what woke her up, adrenaline spiked her energy.

Glancing around the room, everything was as she left it. Even the little lamp was still shining. Slipping out of bed, she pulled the curtain aside to see that the sun was still hiding beneath the horizon. All was still. A street light flickered, lighting up the parking lot.

Her heart rate slowed as she realized that whatever had woken her up must have been in her deep subconscious thoughts.

Now, wide awake other than her dry, sleep-deprived eyes, Anna felt an anxious pull to pack up and leave immediately.

Walking to the restroom, she splashed water on her face to wake her eyes up. Using the complimentary toothbrush and toothpaste, she brushed her teeth.

After spitting and rinsing out her mouth, she looked in the mirror, combing a hand through her blond hair.

Sorry, Anna, it's time for you to go.

Walking to her suitcase, she grabbed a bag with all the hair styling tools she needed to match the picture on her new passport.

Anna began by saying goodbye to several inches of her beautiful hair. As each severed strand fell to the floor, Anna tried to detach herself from the heavy emotions brought on by change.

I have to do this. I have no other choice. I made a promise to Jay. I have to protect him. I need to keep him safe.

Once finished with the mediocre haircut, she remorsefully took a box of midnight black hair dye, pulled plastic gloves onto her hands, and mixed the ingredients together. She draped a towel from the hotel around her shoulders and began to lather her hair with the slimy dye.

Although she was used to dying her hair, she still managed to get drops of dye on the sink. She quickly cleaned it up before it left a nasty stain.

While waiting for the dye to set in, she prepared a scene for her departure. She left empty wine bottles scattered around the room and a few clothes strewn about to give the appearance that she had left in a frazzled state of mind, prepared not to return.

After waiting long enough for the dye to take effect, she took a quick shower, letting the dye wash out of her hair, down her body, and into the drain until the water turned clear again.

Once finished, she used the towel to clean any lasting signs of dye from the shower.

Well, I guess this towel is ruined. Sorry, Anna grimaced, putting it with the items that would disappear with her when she left.

Gazing back at herself in the mirror, Anna memorized her new look. Her now black hair accentuated her almond-shaped face, giving it a foreign appearance. She now matched Jay's black hair and brown eyes.

Sweeping up the remains of the blond hair, she wrapped it into the maroon T-shirt she had been wearing when the agents attacked. She planned on throwing the bundle into the nearest river in case someone decided to try looking for her.

Giving the room one more sweep with her eyes, Anna made sure the wine bottles, scattered clothes, and the note were in place to convince the authorities that she was truly gone. Even the dim lamp light cast dark shadows over the grim room, giving the overall atmosphere a feeling of despair and hopelessness.

Satisfied, Anna, no, Enna gently picked up the sleeping Jay and her new suitcase, then walked out of her old life forever.

6

Temporary Home

Surviving in a new world with little knowledge of foreign languages, Enna doubted her ability to make it, especially with a newborn baby.

Gratefully, Enna's father had been a mechanic and taught her his trade. She used those skills in Mexico to stay afloat until it was time to move to a new location.

As Enna and Jay journeyed across the globe, adopting a nomadic lifestyle to stay safe, their hearts continued to intertwine. In time, Enna saw herself as Jay's true adoptive mother.

Jay grew through the years and knew that Enna was "Mommy," for she embodied everything nurturing and her love for him quickly became unconditional.

Things appeared to be on track as Jay's first tooth emerged in the vibrant land of India, giving Jay an adorable one-year-old grin that drew attention along with his intensely curious expression.

Jay's initial clumsy steps graced the landscapes of Nakhon Sawan, Thailand, and he beamed with an expression of pride as he stared down at his legs, which he was bravely learning to control.

While these things were typical milestones, Enna soon discovered that Oliver was right about Jay. There was something inexplicably special about him.

As Enna introduced Jay to simple learning shows that regular children might watch, his developmental pace accelerated wildly, leaving no doubt that he was far from 'normal.'

During a short stay in Florence, Italy, Jay's first word came out as a full sentence!

"Momma, fwower es prwetty, like you," he said, holding up a flower for Enna.

"Whoa! Thanks, Baby. Since when did you learn how to talk?" To say she was shocked would be an extreme understatement.

Once their forged immigration papers were authorized, they moved to Greece where, near the sea, they found a small space for rent in the loft above a pizzeria and made it their safe haven. It was there that Enna discovered Jay's uncanny ability to soak in information right from the computer screen at an incredible rate.

Under Enna's close supervision, Jay studied patterns of speech online for several weeks.

By the time Enna felt the need to leave Greece, Jay was able to express how he felt about it.

"Aww, but Momma, I super duper loooove the pizza house. Can we stay? Pwease!" He begged as they sat on the beach watching the waves.

Enna looked around nervously to see if anyone had noticed her young child's advanced speech. In a hushed tone, she was forced to sadly disappoint her son.

"Oh, sorry, baby. I love our pizza house too, but we've been here for a while now and…well…I just feel safer when we keep moving. It's hard to explain why. Please, just, trust me this time. I know it's a lot to ask. I'll explain everything someday." Through tears, they moved…and then they moved again.

Besides English, Jay quickly picked up on the primary language patterns of each new place they visited. Fearful that his advanced intelligence would draw attention, Enna tried to distance Jay from the outside world, but he was a social butterfly with boundless energy and very persuasive eyes.

"Momma, can I pway at the park? Pwease?"

Oh boy, not again. How do I explain to a toddler why he can't play with normal kids? Enna struggled as his eyes begged her to let him play.

"Fine, but Jay, most kids your age don't know how to talk as good as you, so use smiles and laughing instead of words because they might feel bad if you can talk, but they can't."

Despite her efforts, Jay left people astounded and confused everywhere they went by his intellect. Because of that, they never stayed long in one place. They traveled through Egypt, where Jay blossomed into a young boy with curly hair and golden brown skin.

His cognitive growth continued to outpace expectations as he breezed through learning the alphabet in both English and Arabic. By the time they moved to Haiti, Jay was a fluent reader, though he couldn't have been more than four years old.

Enna was unsure of his exact age. He had been so tiny when he came into her life that she assumed he was only a few weeks old. However, the rate at which he learned left her second-guessing herself. Though he had the body of a toddler, his mind was obviously years ahead and his learning process showed no signs of slowing down either, especially when using digital tools for education.

Jay's connection with technology was astounding. Clearly, whatever the E.S.T. did to Jay turned him into a tech genius. This freaked Enna out because she couldn't understand it.

After nearly four years of continuous travel, their counterfeit visas reached the expiration, compelling her to make their way back to America, where she looked forward to meeting up with Oliver once again.

After driving for many hours from the L.A. airport in Enna's crappy beater car that she had just purchased, they rolled into the small but beautiful city of Payson, Utah.

Oliver hadn't given her an exact location where they would meet. He just sent a brief message that said, "Utah County," so here she was.

Enna considered driving another hour north so she could end up in the state capital, Salt Lake City. She liked bigger cities because there were more places to hide and no one noticed a new face, but unfortunately, finances disqualified many of the larger cities. Travel did not come cheap.

Payson was large enough to probably blend in but small enough to afford an apartment and build up her savings again. It would have to do.

Enna surveyed her surroundings as she drove through the city and noticed quaint houses, a few child-friendly parks, and a family playing basketball together in their driveway.

Enna smiled as a memory from another lifetime drifted across her mind. In the memory, a small family, her family, was walking down the street of a small town, hand in hand, talking and laughing. She recalled the firm grip of her father's hand and the smooth texture of her mother's petite hand as they counted, "Three, two, one," and swung her into the air. Enna's feet had kicked at the blue sky while her parents never let go of her hands. Once she landed safely back on the ground, Enna would beg them to do it again.

"Alright, one last time," her father would say, but he never meant it. They kept throwing her through the air long after he said, "One last time," just so he could hear the shriek of joy bursting from his daughter's lips.

They were so happy. That was before her mother gave in to her depression and before her father let alcohol become his only solace.

None of that matters now. That life is over. She had her own small family and she planned on never letting Jay go. She would make new happy memories, just the two of them. Blinking her thoughts of family away, Enna focused on finding a new home.

After a quick drive through town, Enna found a quaint park to visit. She sat on a bench while Jay played on the slides. Her laptop was open to Oliver's website. One perk of having a genius techy son was that he knew how to hack into the nearest internet wherever they went, allowing Enna to use her laptop to communicate with Oliver whenever she got the chance to sit down.

To the public's eye, his website looked like an old antique auction site. As Enna bid on what appeared to be random items, she sent coded messages to Oliver. As she won bids, Oliver sent hidden messages in return. She had just won a vintage prosthetic leg.

Yay! She looked closely at the description of her new item. There were subtle grammatical errors that most people would overlook. To her, however, those errors translated into a message.

"Working on visas. Under surveillance. Blend in. Contact you when safe." As Enna double-checked to make sure she translated Oliver's message correctly, dread welled in her chest.

They are onto him! He is going to be caught because of me! Enna heaved deep gulps of air into her lungs. She couldn't imagine anything bad happening to her only friend.

Blend in.

She could not help her friend. All she could do was try to follow his instructions and have faith that Oliver knew what he was doing. He would not let himself get caught. *He is too good for that.* Enna tried to convince herself.

She forced her mind to focus on something else and began to look up cheap homes in the area. It didn't take her long to find a few apartments that suited her needs. She didn't need anything fancy—just a roof over her head and a lock on the door and windows. After setting up a few walk-in tours, she let Jay play as the sun grew hot above them until it was time for them to go.

"Well, Jay," Enna said, calling to her little curly-haired boy on the playground, "Let's go find our new home."

After a few days of searching, Enna used the last of her money to sign a month-to-month contract for a small, ground-floor apartment. It was rundown with horrible brown shag carpets, but it would do for now. She knew this place would not be home for long, just long enough for her to get financially stable and get new visas.

After Enna's mother died, her father fell apart, leaving her responsible for providing rent and food as a young teen. Because of that, she learned how to be a hard worker with many talents, making it easy for her to find odd jobs here and there, allowing them enough money to survive and travel.

A few times, Enna considered settling down and building a life, for Jay's sake, but fear of her past always pushed her onward.

"I like it!" Jay announced with a squeak in his voice when they first looked at the apartment. This was the response he gave at nearly every home they stayed in.

"I'm glad you are happy," Enna commented, grateful for such a positive son. She hated moving him around so much, but he seemed to love it for the most part. It was the only kind of life he'd ever known. Talking back and forth in the car while traveling was his schooling and each new home was another adventure.

After exploring the one-bedroom apartment thoroughly, the two of them set their rooms up. Jay used the actual bedroom while Enna took the living room, which she did not mind. They never unpacked fully. Jay only pulled out a few of his toy cars from his one suitcase and placed them at the base of the window sill.

Enna helped him set up a cot in his room before heading to the kitchen. She took two full sets of dishes from her suitcase and placed them in a kitchen cupboard. The cupboard seemed huge compared to the small dish sets. Pulling food out of a cooler, she filled up the top shelf of the fridge.

Finished with the kitchen, she set up her cot and covered it with a fuzzy blanket and a small pillow. The last thing she unpacked was her laptop. She set it on her bed and pushed the power button.

Waiting for it to turn on, she walked to Jay's bedroom and peeked inside at his neatly lined-up cars. She frowned at the rest of the bare room. He had so few belongings.

I wanted to give you everything, but instead, you are living out of a suit-case, Enna thought to herself in pity. Jay turned from driving his toy car to its spot beside the others as he noticed his mom in the doorway. He instantly recognized her concerned face.

"Wanna talk about it?" Jay asked. Thanks to being exposed to videos on human emotion, he could read people like he could read a book. Perfectly.

Enna shook her head no. "I'm okay, Baby. I was just thinking about how lucky I am to have you and how I wish I could give you more of a life."

"Mommy," Jay said with a slight sass to his voice. "Don't ya know that you already give me the best life because I have you!"

"Aw, buddy, I love you," Enna said, her heart exploding in pride.

"Hey, do you want to help me find a job?" Enna redirected the conversation so she would not have to show her emotions to Jay.

"Yeah!" Jay said enthusiastically, pumping his fist into the air. He ran to the laptop and plunked out the password on the keyboard. Before he opened the web browser, Enna quickly remembered to warn the boy about the dangers of computers.

"What do you do if a picture of an immodest person pops up on the screen?"

Without hesitation, Jay responded with a proud smile of knowledge. "Shut it off and tell you."

"Exactly. What do you do if you see an unfamiliar link? Do you click on it?" Enna asked.

"No way!" Jay said enthusiastically. "And If bad words come up, I don't look and I tell you," he added confidently. "No computer secrets!"

Satisfied, Enna gave a thumbs up. She watched in amazement as her four-year-old son pulled open a web browser, located job offers in the classified ads, and scrolled down the list.

"Let's see, let's see. Hmm. There are house cleaning jobs, a mechanic op-pit-tunity. I could help you with that, photography jobs, oh and lots of babysitting jobs. What ya wanna do, Mommy?" Jay asked, glancing at his mom expectantly.

"I'll just message all of them. Whoever allows me to bring a kid to work, I'll accept," Enna answered.

"Mom, I'm old enough to be home by myself, don't ya know," Jay said with his bottom lip pouting out.

"Ha ha ha, I do not think so. You may be smarter than all the kids on the block, but you are still my baby boy and I'm not leaving you anywhere." Enna ruffled his fluffy curls. He moved his head out of Enna's reach and growled.

"Arrrrrg, you are no fun!" he grumbled while Enna grabbed the laptop to send messages out to all the potential employers.

"Why do you have to go to work anyway?" Jay whined at his mother. "It's so boring!"

Enna let out a sigh and agreed. "I know it's boring, but I need money to take care of you."

"I know! I read something on the computer," Jay said excitedly as he yoinked the laptop back from his mom before she could finish sending messages out. Jay's hands began moving rapidly on the keyboard. "I can get money."

"Whoa, whoa, whoa! Hold up a minute there! What are you doing?" Enna interrupted. She placed her hand in front of the screen.

Jay just smiled, trying to look past her hand, "It's a surprise!"

His big brown eyes glittered up at his mom and pled to be able to continue working on his surprise. Enna thought for a moment before curiosity won over. She knew that Jay could be trusted with the computer for the most part.

She moved her hand and watched as the screen flashed around faster than most humans could comprehend.

"Cha-Ching," Jay said with a smirk.

"Wait, what do you mean by that?" Enna inquired nervously.

Jay pointed the computer screen in her direction, revealing her online banking account. A gasp escaped Enna's mouth as she noticed an addition to her funds. She had an extra $35,000 showing in her account.

"What did you do?!" she shouted at the boy. Jay's smirk was replaced by a drooping lip.

"I just put money in your account so you wouldn't have to work," he said in a pathetic voice.

Enna's head swirled in horror. She forced herself to calm down. In a lowered voice, she asked, "How did you put the money in my account?"

Jay shrugged and responded, "It was easy. I just took money from a bank and put it in your account."

"You hacked a bank? You can't do that!"

Running her fingers through her hair, Enna tried to wrap her head around the idea. *This kid is going to be the death of me. They are going to trace us here and take him away from me.* Her hands were tangled in her hair, pulling at the roots. Sweat formed on her forehead.

We are going to have to start over again! We will have to get new names...but Oliver is being watched. He can't help me. Oh my gosh! What do I do? Enna felt a full-on panic attack taking over her body. She lay down on Jay's cot, breathing heavily.

Before panic could completely take over, Jay laid down next to her and wrapped his hand into her hair.

"Sorry, Mommy," Jay whimpered.

Enna's breathing slowed as her son's touch relaxed her thoughts.

It's ok, he will put it back. They will just think it's a glitch in the system, she told herself.

Putting her face close to Jay, she softened her tone. "Hey honey, sorry for freaking out. I appreciate you trying to help me. You are such a sweetheart, but what you did is called stealing and that's not very nice. It is wrong. Can you please give the money back to the bank so they don't have to worry about their money going missing, please?"

"Why is it stealing if it's just moving money around? It still stays at the bank," Jay asked innocently.

Enna let herself chuckle. *He knows how to hack into banks, but he doesn't understand how banks work. I have a complicated child,* she thought to herself, trying to figure out how to explain it.

"Stealing is when you take something that doesn't belong to you. Right? So, when you take money out of an account that doesn't belong to you and you put it into my account instead, it means someone else doesn't get to use the money and that's sad for them."

"I thought that the money in the banks belonged to everyone," Jay explained. "I'll put it back now."

"Thanks, Baby," Enna said, then wrapped her arms around her boy before he set to the task of returning money to the bank, her mind still rocking with possible, horrific repercussions of this incident. *Maybe I should still move, just in case. No, I don't have enough money for another deposit. I'm stuck!*

"Mommy, after you finish finding jobs, can I do some learning time on the laptop?" Jay asked once Enna's bank account was returned to normal.

"I guess so, but you need to be more careful. What do you want to learn today?" Enna took the laptop and continued her job search while Jay thought about what he wanted to learn.

"I want to learn about cars," Jay responded.

Enna nodded and finished inquiring about the jobs while Jay zoomed around with his toy car.

"Your turn, Jay," Enna said, patting the seat next to her.

Jay bounced over and plopped down next to the laptop. Pulling it onto his small lap, he searched for information on car parts. His eyes twitched rapidly back and forth across the words on the screen. Rigid and tense, he absorbed the information leaping from the screen to his mind, his face glued unnaturally close.

The first time Enna saw this happen to Jay, he was almost a year old. Enna had been reading on her laptop when she looked over and saw her baby's face fixed to the screen, with his eyes darting wildly as though he were having rapid eye movement while awake.

Thinking it was a seizure, she slammed the laptop shut and grabbed Jay to make sure he was okay. The instant she closed the computer, his eye movement returned to normal. This happened several more times before Enna understood what was happening. When his eyes twitched back and forth in that uncanny way, it was as though he was downloading what he saw on a screen directly into his mind. However, it only happened when he was looking at a computer or a phone. If it were a book he was looking at, his eyes would shift from side to side naturally, reading slowly like most human beings.

"Uhhhhh," Jay slightly groaned and held his head. "Stop."

"What's wrong, Baby?" Enna asked in concern.

"The beeping. It won't stop. It wants to talk to me." Jay's eyes squeezed shut and his face scrunched in concentration. "Hello? What do you want?" He said to an unseen being.

Jay's scrunched-up face relaxed and turned completely blank. A robotic voice formed over the top of Jay's squeaky child voice. Sounding like a machine, Jay repeated one word over and over again. "Locating, locating, locating…"

7

Blame

Beads of sweat gripped the roots of Agent Eric Quinn's gnarled hair as he faced General Boucher's large head that appeared on the electronic glass wall.

"General, I'm close. I can feel it. Listen. I've been working on something—a re-creation of Project 19932. I've already used our new AI tools to figure out how to merge the nanobots with other DNAs. With the help of the science technicians, I'm sure we'll be able to figure out how to replace the lost Project."

The General was already shaking his head as Eric expanded his explanation. "Just imagine what we could do with this technology! We don't even need the original prototype. And we don't need this old clump of a computer anymore."

Eric gestured to Central, an aged desktop computer with a web of cords cascading down and out toward an array of various tech devices that lined the lab walls. The chaotic mess of wires made Central look like an ancient, mutant octopus with a few too many tentacles.

"General, please. Just give me a little more time and a couple of science technicians. I promise I will fix this, even without-" The General of the Experimental Science and Technology division (E.S.T.) held up a hand to stop Eric from speaking further.

General Boucher's heavy French accent projected from the speakers built into the wall.

"Pardon me, but I 'ave to stop you zere. We 'ave discussed zis. Dr. McFay destroyed all 'er extensive notes on ze hybrid project. She wiped out almost all of ze original nanobots and corrupted Central, who could 'ave 'elped us recreate ze project. Our scientists 'ave tried and failed to replicate Project 19932. What makes you, a field agent, zink you can do better zan zem?"

"I understand your doubts, but I've been working on this for years. Nobody cares more than me. You know how hard I've tried to find the Project, but..."

"No. Millions 'ave already been invested into crafting zis project. I've given you four years with no success! I will not waste any more resources on zis project. I am sorry, Agent Quinn, but I don't 'ave many options 'ere. I appreciate your dedication to the hybrid project. I really do respect zat, which is why I will give you a month, maybe two months if you are lucky, to find ze original Project, ozzerwise, you will be forced into an early retirement. I must go now. We will talk more on zis later." Before Eric could speak again, the General's face disappeared, leaving the glass wall blank.

Twisting his lips into a maniacal snarl, Eric battled the chaotic surge of anger that boiled inside of him at the thought of the General's ultimatum. Eric knew that "retirement," really meant "elimination." It was common knowledge that hardly anyone left the E.S.T. alive.

Pretending the General was still listening, Eric dived headlong into a frenzied, one-sided debate.

"It wasn't me who turned rogue and stole a multi-million-dollar infant. How was I supposed to know Dr. McFay would run away and give the Project to a random ninja chick?" He continued arguing with the wall as he cracked his knuckles, furious at his lack of control.

Eric's blood boiled at the thought of Dr. McFay. "The project was her idea in the first place! Well, hers and this ridiculous computer!" he yelled, turning to Central.

The computer simply hummed, rubbing in the fact that it was the only thing that could recreate the Project now, but the dumb computer refused to do anything but search day in and day out.

Eric stuck his face right in front of the monitor and shouted at it. "You're useless! If you want your precious Project back, just create a new one, you stupid thing!" Eric flicked the screen, causing his finger to sting from the action. A few beeps replied as the security camera swiveled to point a lens his way.

Now, I'm just talking to myself again. Stupid, stupid, stupid! Eric hit the sides of his head with his palms until it began to throb. His inner turmoil gave rise to his defensive monologue.

"This is your fault, McFay!" Eric yelled into the skylight. "And yeah, who cares if I'm talking to myself! I'm not crazy! You know who the crazy one is? Huh? I do. You, McFay! You're the crazy one." He jammed an accusing finger into the air. "You knew good and well that the Project was property of the government! Yeah, sure, you were brilliant, but believing a machine was actually your baby was just…absurd! So what if it shared your genetic material? The Project wasn't human!"

Eric growled in exasperation, bringing his voice low again. "Typical woman, letting emotions dictate her actions. I can't believe she would destroy millions of dollars worth of nanobots. She was insane. Certifiably insane! How is any of this my fault?"

Eric marched to the rear of the room and collapsed into a chair stationed at a desk arrayed with a vial containing one of the few remaining nanobots and a cutting-edge microscope.

He leaned in and glared through the microscope, studying the nanobot's intricate, helical structure. It was an elegant piece of biotechnology, unlike any machine he had ever encountered. Its surface was coated with a shimmering, protective layer that was meant to help it merge seamlessly with human genetic material. This single nanobot held the secrets of Project 19932.

"Bah!" Eric placed both hands on his desk and leaned close to the nanobot.

"Why are you so difficult?" he asked the bot. It made no reply.

He stood again and wandered around the room, continuing his rant with large arm movements as he spoke. "Take a human, program the bots to merge with their DNA, and Voilà! Super-human computer at your service, sir!" Eric saluted to a reflection of himself coming from Central's monitor.

It's hopeless. The scientists won't even try experimenting with humans, just their stupid simulators—Error, Error, Error.

As he muttered to himself, his thoughts came faster than the grumbled snippets of words that forced their way out into the room, but it didn't matter to him. No one was there to hear him anyway, except the pointless security feed that followed him as he paced the room.

"If only..." *my impulsive partner...*

"Drake hadn't pulled the trigger..." *McFay would still be alive to fix this.*

"It's not right!" *Central only worked right for...*

"McFay..." *on the Project, not even the few involved in her endeavor held all the pieces of the equation.*

"Now, no one can duplicate the Project. No one!" *When she died, her secrets vanished with her.*

"Now, I'm left with nothing!" *No Project, only a handful of nanobots that no one knows how to use, and no chance to recover Project 19932.*

"I need some Adderall!" Eric flopped into his chair and let his whole body go limp, like a rag doll abandoned by its child. A mummified moan expelled slowly from his lips as his dead eyes stared at nothing in particular.

"Bleep, Bleep, Bleep." An ear-splitting noise coming from the central computer tore him out of his despair.

Eric's pulse quickened with a surge of anticipation as he hurried to Central's control panel. On the monitor, a pulsating green circle inched its way across a map. A burst of hope flickered into his mind.

Without hesitation, he dashed to a touch-screen intercom beside the elevator at the front of the lab. He pressed the button, urgently summoning the tech experts for backup, knowing that every moment counted in this race against the clock.

Moments later, the elevator let out a "ding," and the doors opened to reveal two science technicians. The first to emerge was Caleb, a young man with a long face, fiery red hair, and a giant zit over his left eye. Stanley, his colleague, followed close behind. He sported dark brown hair, glasses perched on his nose, and a pair of wide, alert eyes that darted around with a sense of urgency.

They frantically rushed into the lab, causing Eric the need to side-step to avoid a collision.

"Move, move, move!" Caleb scrambled over to Central, maneuvering himself into the chair that sat in front of the aged computer. He set to work with practiced speed, his fingers dancing over the keyboard.

Meanwhile, Stanley adopted a more deliberate approach, mindful of the crisscrossed wires strewn across the floor. He carefully negotiated his way around them, progressing toward a desk nestled against the far wall. There, a thick tablet lay in wait. Without hesitation, Stanley powered it on, causing an antenna to spring from the back of Central's monitor, its metallic form extending toward the satellite dishes above that could be seen through the skylight.

"Hey hey! We have a strong connection!" Caleb called out.

Eric leaned over the man's floppy red hair to get a better view, eager to feel relief from the pent-up tension he'd been cursed with over the past few years.

The elevator chimed once again, and in came Agent Drake, along with two other agents that Eric never bothered to know.

Eric clenched and loosened his fists several times as he shouted orders.

"Agent Drake," Eric addressed his burly partner. "Get the helicopter ready. We depart as soon as we have a location."

Agent Drake nodded and pressed a button on the wall. A ladder descended smoothly from a hidden compartment within the ceiling, offering him a way to reach the emergency exit. Beyond it, a helicopter waited on the roof.

"You two," Eric pointed at the other agents. "Stand at the ready. The second the location is revealed, contact General Boucher and get to the location. We are not going to lose the Project again!"

They nodded without a word.

Eric turned his attention to the two technicians, "Ohh, come on. Don't lose it. Don't you dare lose that signal. Get a location now! Faster! I thought you were supposed to be geniuses! Don't just sit there!"

Annoyed, Caleb, who had already begun hammering wildly at the keyboard, rolled his eyes and responded in a sarcastic tone, "Thanks for your encouraging words of wisdom, Eric. Your yelling really helps me focus on finding the project which, I recall, *you* lost."

Stanley snickered and pressed his glasses into place before moving to another desk that held a laptop.

"Hey, I'm thinking of tweaking the satellite angles to catch that signal better. By the way, any chance you can crank up the computer speed on your end?"

"Yup! Watch my magical nerd powers at work," Caleb flashed a confident smirk in Stanley's direction. "I'm already trimming down data redundancy and cutting extra data to speed up Central's search."

"This would be so much easier if we could use one of our newer models for this," Stanley said, moving to the next device.

"But of course, you morons can't possibly do that," Eric said irritably, hating how useless he was in this endeavor. All he could do was wait and watch.

"Hey, watch the tone," Caleb said. "It's not our fault Central has a unique connection to the Project."

"Yeah, I already know this stupid computer is one of a kind," Eric said with no intention of hiding the frustration in his voice.

"Just be grateful that we even have Central to pick up the signals from Project 19932. That's more than the new prototypes can do," Caleb said, taking in a deep breath, trying not to lose his temper at Eric's negative attitude.

"Yeah, whatever Dr. McFay did to Central made it invaluable to us in the search for the Project," Stanley said before Caleb took over the conversation again.

"Unfortunately, while Central is a champ at being robust and adaptable, it's not exactly built for speed," Caleb said, "And that's why you have us. How's the distributing going for you, Stanley?"

"I've already tweaked network settings for faster data transfer. Now, I'm optimizing parallel processing on this device, and if we need to, that other laptop can be used to fine-tune data compression for max efficiency. Don't worry, Eric sir. We'll make Central work like it's mainlining caffeine." Stanley gave Eric a fake smile while continuing his work.

Adrenaline worked itself up and down Eric's body as though lightning had struck him twice.

"Come on. Come on. Come on. Come on," He muttered under his breath while the nerds worked. Eric's body bobbed, swayed, and shook, setting him apart from the other two agents who stood at attention, their postures rigid and disciplined.

"We're getting close, guys. He's definitely in the United States," Caleb announced.

Stanley finished his tasks and joined Caleb in front of Central's monitor, forcing Eric to squish in closer to Caleb's hair.

Stanley narrated the progress with excitement. "Looks like it's somewhere in the Midwest... Colorado? New Mexico? No. Wait a sec, is it... Yes! He's in Utah! Now, let's pinpoint your exact location, buddy. Stay online for just a bit longer."

Caleb's voice chimed in, feeding off of the energy the others displayed. "Stay with us. Stay with us. Locating...and," He carefully reviewed the data, ensuring accuracy as Central narrowed the search.

"No! No, no, no, no...No!" Caleb wailed suddenly.

Eric roughly grabbed the back of his chair and shook it. "What do you mean, 'no, no, no!'? I need an exact location. At least tell me you got something."

"Well, you see, 'no' means 'uh-oh' something unfortunate just occurred." Thick sarcasm drenched Caleb's response.

Stanley put a hand on Eric's shoulder, hoping to calm the foaming beast. "The connection's lost, man. We tracked him as far as Cedar City, Utah. At least we know he is in the same state as us. That's a good thing." Stanley reported with a measured tone, contrasting Caleb's irritated voice. "However, our search wasn't sufficiently precise. Given the current data, he could be anywhere within a 300-mile radius. Our options are limited until the Project comes back online."

"You can't be serious!" Eric shoved Stanley's hand away, trotted to the elevator, and placed his forehead on the cold metal door to ease his pounding headache.

"Sorry, man," Stanley said. "There's not much else we can do. Central already used a changing IP address, switching between different VPNs and networks while tapping into information from GPS signals, cell towers, and Wi-Fi networks. It just wasn't enough time."

"Idiots! You are all morons! Keep trying!" Eric fumed, turning toward them.

The technicians stood still with raised eyebrows, clearly annoyed that Eric did not listen to anything they just said.

"Get out of my lab, ALL OF YOU!" Eric's voice threatened to crack as his shouting extended beyond his vocal range. His face flamed with fury as he pointed to an agent. "Get as many agents as you can spare to Cedar City, Utah, as fast as possible."

"Dude! A 300-mile radius is a crazy amount of land to search. Don't waste any more government resources by sending agents out there. Just wait and hope we can narrow it down next time Central connects with the Project," Stanley said, losing his patience.

"Fine, whatever! Just get out." Eric waved a dismissive arm at all of them.

The technicians and agents scuttled onto the elevator. Agent Drake poked his head through the skylight exit and watched in amused horror as Eric grabbed a transparent acrylic chair and hurled it across the room toward the elevator seconds after the doors closed. Eric raved as the chair bounced off the closed door and clanged to the ground.

I'm done for. The pain of self-pity coursed through him like burning acid. He sat down at the desk by the nanobot and hung his head in his hands.

This should not be on me. I'm not to blame. What can I do? Utah. I have a couple months to search practically all of Utah! Impossible. He paid no attention to his partner, who was trying to escape discreetly down the ladder and through the elevator door.

Eric heard the "Ding" of the elevator and glanced up as Agent Drake shuffled inside. Eric glared, embarrassed that his tantrum had been witnessed. Eric stayed silent while the bulky agent saluted sarcastically right before the doors slid shut, leaving Eric alone once more.

I could run. Live somewhere in the Guatemalan Jungle. Start my own tribe. Eat bugs for dinner. Hmm. Eric took a long, deep breath in and blew it out slowly. *No, I'll find a way out of this, even if it means going up against the General. I won't let them get rid of me so easily.*

Eric regained his focus and returned to examining the nanobot through the microscope.

8

Trance

"Jay. Jay! Hey, focus on me. Oh, come on, baby. I'm here. I'm right here. Look at me," Enna cried in desperation.

Jay's eyes remained focused on the computer screen.

Enna slammed the laptop shut and roughly threw it on the floor, but Jay's face remained blank.

"Locating, locating, locating," Jay's repetitious words resonated through Enna's ears and down to her heart. She snapped her fingers in his face, trying to draw his attention, but his blank face acknowledged nothing.

Jay had responded oddly to computers in the past, such as hearing them speak to him, but he'd never replied. He usually just shut the laptop and smiled like nothing happened.

The laptop is shut. Why isn't he snapping out of it? Enna thought.

Glancing at the laptop on the ground, Enna let out an agonized sob. *I've lost him! The government is controlling my son now! He is gone and never coming back!* Panicking, she kneeled at the side of the cot in front of Jay and held his face in her hands.

"Locating, locating, locating," the daunting words continued.

Enna rushed to the sink, filled a cold cup of water, ran back to the child, and splashed his face with the chilled liquid.

No change.

She watched in horror as the water dripped down her son's face without a flinch from him.

"JAY!" Enna was yelling by now. "Wake up!" She shook his shoulders violently.

Giving him whiplash is not going to help. Maybe I just need to take him to the hospital. That thought made Enna freeze. She couldn't take him to the hospital. Of course not! The government was probably watching the hospitals. No, she would have to figure this out on her own.

"Locating, locating, locating," Jay's trance continued.

"Oh my baby, what did they do to you?" Not knowing what to do, Enna wrapped Jay in her arms and carried him to the bathroom. She turned the shower on, cold as it would go, and climbed inside. Sitting on the shower floor, she rocked the rigid boy back and forth while the water seeped through her clothes, freezing her to the bone.

Jay took no notice of the cold water raining down on him. Shivering, Enna held tightly onto Jay while the shower washed her frightened tears down the drain.

"Please, please come back," Enna pled. Her teeth clicked together from fear as well as the cold. With no hope, a song formed in her mouth while she sobbed, holding her boy.

"You are my sunshine. My only sunshine. You make me happy when skies are gray..."

"Mom, why are you crying? Are you sad?" Jay spoke over her song.

Enna gasped in surprise. His gaze locked onto his mother's face before water splashed into his eyes. He looked away, covering his face, "Um, why are we in the shower?"

Enna held him out at arm's length to look at him. He let out a goofy smile.

"I'm cold," he said.

Enna quickly turned off the shower and began to tremble. "Don't you do that to me again! I was so scared," Enna scolded lightly. Then she brought Jay in for a tight hug.

"Don't do what? Mommy, you're squishing me," Jay pointed out. "What's goin' on here?" Jay tried to wriggle out of Enna's arms, but she held fast.

She did not want to let him go, but his shivering reminded her that he needed to be warmed up. She carried him out of the shower and wrapped a towel around him snugly before hugging him again.

"You scared me so much. You were looking at the computer like you usually do until you said you heard something. You talked to someone who wasn't even there and then suddenly your voice turned into a robot and it was like, like you were just…gone!" Enna gave her side of the story briefly.

"I turned into a robot? Did I have metal arms? That's so cool!" He stiffened his arms and moved in a robotic motion. "I just remember really, really loud beeping noises and then I heard you singing and you were crying. I don't want you to cry, Mommy," Jay said tenderly.

"Do you remember saying 'locating' over and over again?" Enna questioned.

Jay shook his head no.

Enna cringed and pushed the subject further, "Do you think someone is tracking us through you?"

"I have no idea," Jay answered with a shrug. Enna let out a slow, heavy breath. She wanted to freak out. Run away. Cry! *We can't stay here! We have to leave, NOW! Oh, I hate being stuck!*

Jay's curious eyes squinted at her, probably trying to guess what she was thinking. Enna raised her shoulders and gave Jay a reassuring smile even though she felt anything but calm.

"I guess Payson isn't gonna be our home for much longer. I'll try getting a hold of my friend, Oliver again and see what he can do for us. Meanwhile, we will lay low, work, and save money 'til we can get out of here. And you, sir, will have to be more careful with the computer. Right?" Enna stared Jay down to make sure he was listening.

Jay frowned and asked, "Ya sure ya don't want me to get money from the bank for you, Mommy?" Jay waited until his mom gave him the "Are you serious?" look, and then his frown broke into a mischievous grin. "Just kidding!" He let off a riotous laugh.

Enna allowed herself to chuckle at the joke before going to Jay's room to find warm pajamas from his suitcase. After making sure he was dressed and tucked into his cot, she found some dry clothes of her own and quickly changed. She went back to check on Jay, snuggling in his bed. He looked so happy and innocent.

"Can you snuggle with me, Mommy?" he asked, smiling brightly.

Enna nodded yes and squeezed into the cot next to her son. Staring off into her thoughts, she fought off tears.

I can't believe this. I have a super genius who talks to computers and turns into a robot boy. Oh my gosh! What just happened? My life is so...so weird! This is insane!

A crazy laugh suddenly launched its way out of Enna's mouth. She couldn't help it. She'd been holding onto so much tension because her life was bizarre and unpredictable and just...nuts!

This is just too much.

Jay flinched, startled at the sudden laugh that popped out of her mouth. His lips twitched into a confused smile and let out a high-pitched laugh of his own, copying Enna's crazy sound.

That made him laugh for real at his own silly noise. His joy was so bright that it dove into Enna's fear and tickled it until she found herself cracking up along with him.

"Why...are...we...laughing?" Jay asked with bursts of chuckles between each word.

Enna moved her lips, trying to answer, but only more laughing found its way out, so she went with a shrug and laughed even harder.

Despite Enna's laughter, tears hugged the edges of her eyes. Her chest heaved as conflicting moods messed with her head.

The heavy thoughts she held onto under her guarded exterior came flooding to the surface in wave after wave of random, uncontained emotion.

Jay's alright. That's all I need. Right now, we are safe and together.

To keep the joy alive, Enna dramatically rolled out of the cot and onto the floor.

Jay, finding that hilarious, rolled right on top of her. She squeezed him while he laughed. Gradually, her giggles turned into silent sobs. She lay flat on her back, tears streaming down her cheeks and into her ears.

He is okay, I thought I lost him, but he is fine, and I am fine. We can do this.

Jay rolled onto the ground next to her and wrapped his fingers into her hair. She wiped the tears from her eyes. Jay's laughing died down until he stopped to silently study Enna with a strange look on his face.

"Why are you laugh-crying?" he asked softly.

"You know, Jay. I'm not really sure. I guess I am just so relieved that you are okay. I'm so lucky to have you. I am so glad you are mine," Enna left a kiss on his forehead. "I love you, Baby."

Jay didn't respond right away. "I think you lost it there a little, Mommy." He poked her nose playfully.

"Huh, yeah, you are probably right," Enna said. She lifted Jay back onto his cot. "I'm so tired, Baby. Definitely time for bed."

"Aww! I don't want to go to bed. Can you stay by me?" Jay pouted for a second before Enna agreed to lay next to him until he was asleep.

Tucking the blankets around Jay, Enna admired his strength. His smile always lifted her out of toxic thoughts.

"I love you, Baby," she said, kissing his forehead gently before she lay on the floor next to him.

"I love you too, Mommy."

They were quiet for some time. Jay's hand hung off the cot to continue playing with her hair.

"Jay," Enna's voice broke through the silence, her face sober as she remembered his blank eyes and robotic voice. A shiver crept along her back. "We are definitely going to limit your screen time even though that's hard for you. You can't let anyone locate us. Do you understand? If you hear the computer talking to you, ignore it and turn it off right away. There are powerful people who are looking for you because you are special. I never want them to find you."

Snores came from Jay now, but Enna continued talking. "I just need you to be safe. I was so scared. I am so scared. What am I doing?" She allowed herself to cry while lying on the floor late into the night.

9

Ad from the Past

Enna sensed a presence from the darkness. Her eyes fought to adjust to the shadows, but all they could see was endless gloom. Her teeth chattered together quietly as if fighting off a cold breeze despite it being early summer.

Paralyzed, she could not run or call out for help. It was as though a hidden being had entered her body and was holding it hostage. Terror pinned her to the bed.

Every ounce of control slipped away as the unseen presence climbed closer and closer to her until his warm breath teased her neck.

Enna's heart stopped. Her blood stood still as she heard the invisible monster sniff her hair, sending her mind spiraling into fear. She willed her body to defend herself, but it could not respond. She was even denied tears as icy fingers gently stroked her skin from the top of her temple down to her jawline—a chill spread throughout her entire body.

I'm powerless.

The man's cold hand continued tracing the shape of her face, grazing her lips. The soft, agonizing touch shifted to her collarbone. His hand spread up, around her neck and began to tighten. A shrill squeak was the only thing that could escape her mouth before her ability to breathe was taken from her. The unseen face was so close she could feel his stubble prick the skin of her cheek.

Death called as his sultry voice whispered in her ear, "I told you I would find you." A wicked grin and glowing red eyes emerged out of the dark.

Enna shot off Jay's bedroom floor with a gulp of liberating air, her breathing uneven and ragged. She whipped her head around frantically, looking for the intruder. He was nowhere to be found. Sunlight was beginning to push through the crack in the curtains.

Oh my gosh! It was a nightmare. I'm fine. Safe. With a sigh of relief, she stood, still shaking, and stumbled into the living room. She pulled out her yoga pants and motivational exercise tank top from her suitcase.

After getting dressed and stretching, Enna began beating her nightmare away with her martial arts training routine.

It was easy to picture her invisible opponent as she sliced the air with her leg and then followed up with combos of strikes.

Punching the tension away, she did not notice Jay watching her from the small hallway that led to his room. She spun and shot a powerful blow through the air at her invisible foe.

"Nice one, Mommy!" Jay clapped, "Can I learn how to do that?"

Startled, Enna jumped and spun to face her son. Seeing Jay's eager face, Enna laughed.

"Alright, you can learn. Come stand by me." Enna directed Jay into the correct stance. After demonstrating a simple jab, she positioned Jay's arms to prepare him for an attack. He sloppily mimicked her jab.

Enna snickered. "Close, buddy. Now make sure your knees are bent and when you punch, put your whole body into it like this." She demonstrated a strong jab through the air, making sure her knees bent and twisted just right as she followed the punch up with an uppercut.

"Got it!" Jay burst into a high-action sequence. "High-yah! Swish, poom, kah!" Jay made pretend fighting noises to go along with his askew fighting techniques. He punched and kicked the air for several minutes before losing interest.

"Mommy, I'm bored. You are not a very good teacher," Jay complained. "Can I use the laptop to learn how to fight?"

"Excuse me! You calling me a bad teacher?" Enna said in mock offense and dramatically placed a hand over her pretend broken heart.

Jay laughed and ran. Enna bolted after him, chasing him playfully around the room.

Once caught, Jay squirmed as Enna tickled his belly. His laugh became so intense that no sound came out, just staggered attempts to inhale between his bursts of joy until he finally broke free from his mother's tortuous tickling and caught his breath.

"That's enough, Mommy." He plopped down, spread out on the ground, looking up at Enna. "You win. Now, can I use the laptop to learn kung fu?"

Enna ground her teeth as she debated his request. She was hoping her tickle attack would distract him enough to make him forget he wanted to use the computer.

After his last interaction with the laptop, Enna was hesitant to let him use any technological device. She did not want another trance to take hold of him.

However, withholding technology from Jay created another issue altogether.

Enna had tried to limit Jay's screen time in the past, but when she did, he became incredibly lethargic. It was as though his entire body was shutting down from lack of fuel.

After that scary experience, Enna learned that technology was a necessity for him. It was as though being exposed to technology recharged his mind.

He also struggled to learn any other way. Enna did her best to treat him like a regular child and homeschool him personally as much as possible, but his mind seemed to discard information given to him through spoken word. It proved to be a constant battle of balance.

Enna wanted him to have an education that pushed him, but he gave up on learning the hard way so quickly he wouldn't even try.

"I want you to keep practicing what I taught you first. If you can't figure it out right away, I want you to adjust until you figure it out," Enna helped Jay up off the floor.

"But…" he began. Enna quickly cut him off.

"Problem-solving is just as important to learn as kung fu or mechanics. Figuring out how to not give up is something you can't learn online. And, even if you know everything about fighting, that doesn't mean you will be able to do it with your body. It takes lots of practice. So, get into the fighter's stance I showed you," Enna mirrored him and held up her palms. "Now, bend your knees and strike. Hit my hand."

Jay threw a floppy arm out in a half attempt at a punch.

"Oh, I know you can do better than that. Show me ten good punches and you can learn the rest of the moves on the computer," Enna readied herself for Jay's next attempt.

He tried again, this time for real, but missed Enna's palm.

"I'm just bad at this!" Jay complained.

"Nope, not bad, just inexperienced. That's what practice is for," she gestured for him to come at her again.

They stuck with it for thirty more minutes until Jay had a decent punch and sweat on his brow.

"Mom, please, can we be done?" Jay begged with his fingers interlocked in a plea.

Enna closed her eyes. She wished she could say no after their last computer experience, but as terrifying as it was, her son was connected to technology somehow and there was nothing she could do about that.

"Fine, only five minutes online, but I get to choose what website you learn from and if you feel funny at all or hear beeping or voices, you need to be done right away. Okay?" Enna stared sternly into his eyes.

"Okie dokie!" Jay said, racing to the computer, but Enna beat him to it.

After she searched for a trusted martial arts website, Jay sat down on the cot and stared at the screen. Information flew from the computer, into his brain.

Meanwhile, Enna got ready to go to work. She had been hired to fix a car and clean a house, but first, she had a meeting with another mother about a potential babysitting job.

It's going to be a long day. I also need to go shopping and- Jay interrupted her list of things she needed to accomplish.

"Um, question. Is this you?" Jay asked, indicating a picture on the laptop. Looking over his shoulder, Enna's stomach twisted into a jumble. There, on the screen, was a missing person ad.

The ad featured a girl with ear-length dark red hair and brown eyes. She was around eight years younger than Enna, but it was undoubtedly her.

Enna's mouth fell slightly agape and her eyebrows tilted down in a concerned arch. She hesitated a second too long before replying, "That sure does look a lot like me. Do you know how to take it down? I don't want anyone to see it. How did you find this? You are supposed to stay on the website I pulled up for you," Enna said as casually as possible.

"It just popped up on my screen. I'm not lying." Jay convinced Enna. She tried to hold her composure as she noticed the fine print on the bottom of the ad.

Missing: My dearest wife, Clara.
Age:18
Height: 5'3"
Weight: 115 lb.
If you have any information, please call or email Andrew Antoni Dengaila.

The contact information was attached as links at the bottom of the page. The name that tortured her dreams jumped off the page and into the darkest part of her soul. Andrew Antoni Dengaila.

"Yup, no problemo," Jay answered. Enna refocused her attention on her son and tried to process what he was talking about.

"What?" Enna said numbly.

"No problemo means 'no problem' in Spanish," Jay unnecessarily translated. "Taking the picture down is easy-peasy," Jay finished explaining.

Enna let out a slow breath. "Thank you, Baby," she said, her stomach still dancing flip-flops as she read the words "dearest wife" again. *Sick! I would never marry that man!*

The ad quickly blipped out of existence before Jay returned to being hypnotized by cool martial arts moves.

Anxiously, Enna finished getting ready for work and made breakfast quietly, not wanting to alarm her son with the sudden anxiety that plagued her.

"Are you ready to teach me how to fix a car?" Enna asked Jay as he shut the computer down and came to the kitchen for protein pancakes. Even though she already knew how to fix cars, she wanted Jay to be involved.

Jay flashed a thumbs up. "Well, yeah, I learned about cars yesterday, memember? Teaching you will be no problemo!" He said with a grin.

Enna copied the smile and attempted to push the missing persons' ad out of her mind.

"Let's do this," She said, feeling the same dread that her nightmare had left in her chest.

10

A Haunting Melody

A haunting song emerged from a grand piano at the edge of the ballroom. With eyes closed to emphasize the emotions of the music, a dark figure ran his fingers across the ivory keys.

Melody, a young girl with long black hair and bright green eyes, stood on the far side of the room, trying to distance herself from the master.

I hate it when he calls for me. Please don't hurt me again! Her fearful tears harmonized with the tune of the piano as the man played on. Entranced in song, he concluded the classical music with fancy trills that wandered up and down the scale.

The last low note hung in the air before fading away. An eerie silence replaced the music, leaving Melody's soft whimpers singing solo. Her master sat unmoving for several seconds before deliberately turning to face her.

"Melody, there's no need for tears. It makes you seem pathetic and weak. I know you are scared. You don't need to be. I won't hurt you," Master's smooth voice broke the silence with compassion playing on his face. He raised a hand, beckoning Melody to his side.

Melody's cries persisted, accompanying her tentative steps that inched her closer to him until she was within his reach. She paused, not wanting to close the gap between them.

He shifted to one side of the piano bench, allowing room for her to sit. However, she stood, frozen by dread. Seeing her hesitation, the master gently patted the empty space on the bench beside him.

Still, her body failed to move.

Showing a humorless smile, her master reached his hand out and took her elbow.

"Come, sit," his buttery voice guided.

The girl followed. A painful hush brought tension into the large room. Neither man nor girl spoke for several unbearable minutes as Melody fought to contain her emotions. She knew he was waiting for her to speak first. Finally, she caught her voice.

"Master, why did you send for me?" Melody asked in a timid whisper. An ominous chuckle sent chills through her quivering body.

"Please," he responded calmly, "Call me Andrew."

"Yes, sir, ah, Andrew," Melody replied. Andrew reached up and gingerly wiped a tear from her cheek.

"My dear Melody, I am bored." As Andrew spoke, Melody inched away as much as she could without completely falling off the piano bench.

He gets so angry when he's bored! Her cries lost control.

"Please, don't hurt me! I've tried to be good and do as you ask. I try to please you. I… I…" Her pleas washed away in a flow of unconsolable sobs.

"Oh dear. No, Melody. No," Andrew cooed, "I won't hurt you. I have other plans for you today." His words brought only a small spout of comfort.

Melody's breath halted in her lungs as Andrew clapped his hands twice. A young, well-dressed servant opened a door at the far end of the massive room.

An older gentleman with a pale face and thinning white hair entered the room. His crystal blue eyes bulged out of his shallow eye sockets, and his tight lips curled slightly in a sneer. He carried a walking cane in his right hand, though it seemed more ornamental than functional as he briskly approached Andrew and Melody.

"Monsieur Dengaila, you would not believe ze type of day I'm having," the old man said with a thick French accent. "I am so grateful you called when you did. I could use a pick-me-up. Is zis ze girl?" As the man spoke, Andrew's devilish smile took over his compassionate face.

"Yes, this is the one. Sorry to hear about your bad day. I hope this will help." Andrew gestured to the small girl. "My dear Melody, this is General Alexandre Boucher. You may refer to him as General. He will be taking you off my hands. As I've said, I have grown bored of you. Beauty can only get you so far. It's time for me to let you go." He flicked his hand dismissively as if swatting at a bothersome fly.

He's selling me? I'm not even good enough for my master? I've done everything he's ever asked of me. I work harder than any of the other girls here. What did I do wrong? Melody's tears halted as though to prove she was not weak.

"Stand," Andrew commanded.

Obediently, Melody rose, but a glare shot from her.

General pointed his cane at her tear-streaked face.

"Turn around, child. Let me see you," He demanded in a grating, scratchy tone, a sharp contrast to Andrew's typically silky and seductive voice.

Sick to her stomach, Melody obliged.

Slowly turning in a circle, the two men gawked hungrily at her as though she was nothing more than a cute doll at a toy store.

General Boucher put up a hand, halting her, and addressed Andrew.

"Yes, she is very pretty and young. Is she in good 'ealth?" General used his cane to lift Melody's arm to examine the muscles on her biceps.

"She's in perfect health. Melody is my sturdiest girl, which is what you asked for, right?" Andrew tilted his head slightly, raising his eyebrows.

"Yes, indeed. You see, I 'ave a project I'm working on zat requires stamina. It appears she will do." He rested both hands on the top of his cane without taking his greedy eyes away from the girl.

"Oh? What type of project, might I ask?" Andrew scowled slightly, "I like to know that my girls will be well taken care of. My Melody is special. She deserves the right kind of care."

General's ominous laugh bounced throughout the ballroom.

"You 'ave no need to worry yourself. Zis girl could 'elp me change ze country. I'll take good care of 'er." The General's mustache twitched excitedly.

Andrew copied the General's poisonous laugh with a shake of the head.

"You are quite peculiar, Alexandre. I'm curious about what you are up to. However, since you are also one of my top clients, I'll respect your personal life and ask no further questions. I trust you will put her to good use." Andrew rose to shake hands with the General. "Come to my office. We will discuss details with my accountant." Andrew confidently led him across the ballroom and out the grand doors.

Melody did not know whether to follow, so she watched until the two men exited the room.

Fidgeting anxiously, she anticipated their return with a sense of doom.

What does the General mean I could help change the country? Is he going to experiment on me? I wish Master would have pushed for more information. She shuddered.

In her dreams, she always considered running far away where she would finally be free. It was a fantasy she held onto but was never brave enough to act upon.

Is this my chance? Maybe I can escape while Master discusses how much money I'm worth. Her adrenaline spiked. The servant was undoubtedly waiting just beyond the grand doors.

Would he try to stop me? She wondered. *Yes, most likely, but he is small. I could possibly surprise him and get ahead. Is freedom worth the risk?* Her heart pounded with the idea. *Yes, take the chance! Go! Go now! Who knows what this... General is going to do! Run!* Melody's thoughts urged her forward. Her toes twitched nervously, but that was the only movement her feet made.

Coward! I am weak. Master is right. I'm pathetic. Of course, I won't run. Even if I did escape, he would find me, torture me, and then kill me. No one escapes Andrew Dengaila. She melted onto the piano bench as a darker thought entered her mind. *But Maybe that's for the best. Maybe I'm better off dead.* She hung her head as self-worth drained from her body.

There she sat, submissive and broken, until the sound of approaching steps announced the return of the two men.

General Boucher's beady eyes fell on Melody as he beckoned to her. His tight grin told her he was satisfied with the deal he made with Andrew.

"Come, child. I 'ave a lot to do before ze day's out." The General held his hand out to Melody. She let him lead the way across the grand ballroom.

I deserve this. I'm nothing. She admitted to herself as she looked back one last time at the beast who had broken her. She felt a small smile form at the corners of her lips.

At least I'm free of him.

* * *

Andrew stood alone in the dimly lit ballroom. The spacious chamber enveloped him, intensifying the sensation of complete solitude in the vast world. He clutched at his empty, aching... wanting heart.

She was not Clara. Close, but no, he thought to himself disparagingly. *There's no one like her.*

He sat down at the piano and plunked out a few sad notes. Eight long years, and she still haunted his mind. Meeting Clara was like finding a rose among dandelions.

His fingers played out a tune that spoke of Clara's dark, fierce eyes, which he noticed the first time he saw her selling roses on the street corner.

Her clothes were rags and her face filthy, but she was the most beautiful girl he had ever seen. Maybe it was her determined smile, holding a hidden sorrow, that drew his attention. It was a look he recognized in himself every time he stared in the mirror. He needed her, craved her. Each day he drove past her, she looked so powerful that he could no longer resist her.

Now, his continued song picked up to reflect the way it felt the first time he had heard her laugh. It was right after he had bought her entire supply of roses. Her eyes lit up, and her lips quivered in pure gratitude.

"Why do you need so many flowers?" Clara asked him.

"Maybe I just wanted to see your true smile," Andrew grinned like a boy with a childhood crush.

She was perfect. The way she laughed filled him with direction. Of all the girls he had held, she was the one he would keep.

The tune he played turned angry as his memories flashed back to the scene of her death. His fingers moved in an unpredictable manner, just like the flames that had consumed his true love. Soon, he was pounding on the instrument with his fists.

"No!" His voice echoed off the walls. He dropped his head onto his arms and smashed into an array of scattered keys. An unsettling blend of notes vibrated through the chamber, bouncing off the walls until all sound settled down other than Andrew's heavy breath.

Suddenly, his moment of mourning was interrupted by the obnoxious ring of his cell phone. Grumbling, he cleared his throat, composing himself before bringing the device to his ear.

"Yes?" he answered in a flat, irritated voice. However, as he listened, his mood rapidly rose to an elated state. The corner of his lips tilted into a smirk.

"Thank you. I'll have it checked out immediately." Andrew nodded as the man on the phone continued to speak. "Yes, of course. You will be greatly rewarded for the information. I'll send you the money."

Ending the call, he reached into his pocket and pulled out an old photo. "Soon, I'll have you back." He spoke with a genuine chuckle in his throat.

11

Friend

What is with these people? Enna groaned as the doorbell sounded...again. Ever since they moved in, a steady stream of visitors had plagued their doorstep, bearing gifts ranging from cookies and welcome cards to pie. Among them were a couple of young men, smartly dressed in suits and ties, eagerly brandishing a book about some guy named Mormon.

Enna observed them through the peephole, witnessing their cheesy grins expanding in hopeful anticipation of reciprocated kindness. Yet, met with silence from Enna, they gently set their welcome offerings near the door and departed.

The current lady standing outside looked to be in her mid-forties and was recognized as the same pie lady who graced her doorstep earlier that day.

Why is she back? Enna spied on the overly cheerful lady. She had blond hair, blue eyes, a slightly crooked nose, and a sturdy build. Her smile was painted firmly on her face and did not disappear when the door failed to open for her. She had no gift this time, but two small, shy eyes peered out from behind the lady's flowery pink skirt. The lady turned to the young boy behind her.

"That's okay. We'll come back another time to see if he can play," the pie lady took the child's hand and began walking away.

"Oh no," Enna moaned, feeling shame tug at her heart, but the thought of venturing into the world of socializing made her cringe.

Selfishly, she yearned to return to Jay and complete the amateur airplane drawing he was helping her with. She turned away from the door, but her conscience promptly spun her back around.

Anxiety doesn't control you, she quoted her mantra a few times to herself. Taking a deep breath, she scrunched her face up and opened the door.

"Hey," Enna called out just before Pie Lady and her son slipped into the house across the parking lot from her.

Pie Lady stretched her grin even wider and shouted gleefully, "Oh, Hello!" while walking back to Enna briskly. "Sorry if I caught you at a bad time. We just wanted to introduce ourselves. I noticed you have a little boy around my son's age and figured it would be nice if we could do a play date sometime."

Enna looked at her skeptically without saying a word. Pie Lady held out a hand to shake as she continued to talk. "My name is Betty Louis. We're your neighbors! This here's my son, Ben, say hello."

"Hi," his shy voice squeaked from behind his mom.

Betty jumped right back into her introductions. "We just wanted to tell you welcome to the neighborhood! I left a pie for you this morning. I hope you enjoyed it."

A guilty jab in Enna's gut made her squirm. As soon as Betty had left the pie, Enna immediately discarded it into the garbage bin to avoid the possibility of being poisoned.

Enna attempted to smile, hoping it wouldn't come off as a wince.

"Oh yeah. Thanks. I'm Enna,"

"And I'm Jay!" Without an ounce of caution, Jay slid in front of Enna and gave his most dashing smile.

Ben, a small red-headed boy with a rounding stomach and a freckly face, stepped out from behind his mother with a gawky grin of his own.

Jay put both hands in the air, his excitement spilling over into his entire expression. "Can I show them my airplane picture? It's really cool—better than yours, mom!"

"Pft, gee, thanks, kid," Enna grumbled. "I don't think that's a good idea right now, buddy. Maybe later."

Ben pulled on his mother's skirt and motioned for her to lean down so he could whisper in her ear.

"I wanna see the airplane."

"I heard that! I'mma go get it and show you." Jay pushed past Enna and ran to get his picture ignoring his mother's protests.

"Wait, Jay..." Enna tried to catch him, but he was already out of reach.

Despite his tiny hands struggling to hold crayons firmly, Jay created wonderful pictures beyond his years. He watched and downloaded several art tutorials so he could draw with fairly accurate representation, which worried Enna.

They'll know he's special. Too special, her nerves twisted. Jay squeezed back in front of Enna and delivered his artwork into Ben's fingers.

"Dude, Cool!" Ben exclaimed, holding the page up for his mother to see. Betty's eyes widened in surprise after seeing the airplane.

"Wow, you drew that?" She looked at Jay in awe.

He nodded, glowing with the praise. "I'm teachin' my mom how ta draw like me. Do you want ta see her picture?"

"Oh gosh. No, they don't need to see my work," Enna said, then to Betty, she added, "Trust me, you're not missing anything."

Enna held onto Jay's shoulders before he could slip away for her picture. "We better let them get going. I'm sure they have lots of things to do today," Enna said.

"Oh! No worries. We don't have anywhere to be." Betty ruffled Ben's hair. "I know. Would you like Jay to come play at my house?"

Enna's stomach jumped at the sudden offer.

Who even is this lady? She just met us! Why does she want strangers in her home? Enna was about to turn the offer down, but Jay was already bouncing about.

"Please, Mom! Please, can I go play?" His begging, puppy-dog gaze held way too much power over Enna.

"I'll have to think about it, but for now, we have work to do, re-member?" Enna said, trying to ignore the dejected stink-eye glare Jay gave her.

"Well, I'm home all day. If you ever need a babysitter or anything, I'm just in that blue and gray house over there with the dark green door." Betty said, indicating a small home with a fence separating a nice yard from the crappy, cracked parking lot.

Why is she so intent on having us over? Is she part of the E.S.T.? What if she found us because I let Jay use the computer too much? Why else would she be so welcoming? Enna acknowledged Betty's presence with a distracted nod. *Shut up, Enna. You're being paranoid. She's probably just being nice.*

"Yeah, thanks. See you later." Enna backed into her apartment, pulling Jay with her.

"Seriously, come over any time! We'll be here," Enna heard Betty say as the door clicked shut.

After locking the door, Enna went directly to her laptop. "Hey Baby, for your computer time today, do you think you could look Betty up and make sure she's actually a good person?" Enna asked Jay.

"Uhhhhgg! I just wanna go play. You are never any fun!" Jay com-plained as he folded his arms, marched off to his bedroom, and slammed the door. Enna followed close behind.

"Don't talk to me that way! I want you to go play, too, but I need to make sure you are always safe," Enna shouted through the bedroom door.

"Being safe is boring!" Jay's voice shot back.

"Fine, don't check up on her, but you don't get to play with them until she gets a full background check. Understand?" Enna waited for a reply, but Jay didn't dignify her with a response.

Sighing heavily, Enna went to the computer and typed "Betty Louis" into the search bar. She found a Facebook page and a few fam-ily pictures. She needed more evidence than that.

"Eh, hem," Jay cleared his throat dramatically. Enna looked up to see that Jay had emerged from his bedroom. "Fine. I'll help you out," he said with a scowl still stuck on his face.

"Great. I'm happy to see you've changed your mind."

"I acshully didn't change my mind. You left me with no choice." Jay stuck a defiant chin in the air.

"Fair enough. Here you go." Pushing the computer over to Jay, Enna went off to gather cleaning supplies for the house she was hired to clean. She had just pulled out her rubber gloves from under that bathroom sink when she heard Jay growling.

Smack. Enna heard the laptop slam shut from the living room. She came running just in time to see Jay pushing the laptop away. "No, you don't!" he yelled at the computer.

Puzzled, Enna rushed to Jay's side. "Why did you do that?" Enna asked. "Did you find any information on Betty?"

"She had nothing on her record. She is for real nice and is not a bad guy. I checked the background," Jay said.

He paused, pressing his lips together so he couldn't say more.

Enna's eyebrow went up in a question and picked the laptop up. Enna didn't discern anything unusual as she examined the information on the computer screen. However, Jay's downcast expression and fidgety movements caught her attention.

"Are you keeping a secret from me?" Enna asked with a sideways glance. Jay's little nod was timid and ashamed.

"I will tell you if you don't get mad," he said

"I won't get mad if you tell the truth," Enna responded with an encouraging smile.

"I think it wanted to find me and I almost thought about talking to it but I 'memembered you telling me not to, so I shut the laptop like ya told me to do."

Enna quickly bent down eye level to Jay and directed his gaze toward her with a serious expression. "I am not mad. You did the right thing. Who is trying to find you? How do you know what it wants?" Enna questioned frantically.

Jay shrugged. "I just felt it. I don't know. It was beeping random numbers at me. It felt like it misses me. But no worries, I didn't answer. It's happened before. No biggie. Don't worry, Mommy."

Enna reached out and gently stroked her son's face. "Thank you for not responding to whatever it was. I sure love you."

Enna walked to the bathroom to hide her solemn expression. Once out of Jay's sight, she doubled over and took several gasping breaths. *What is going on with my son? I really need an instruction manual for this kid.*

Looking in the mirror, Enna hated the trembling girl in front of her. *Come on, Enna, pull yourself together! You've got to go to work. Calm down. Jay did not respond to the...well, whatever it was. It's not urgent. It's fine.*

"Oh, I can't wait until we get out of this place," Enna grumbled, wiping the back of her hand under her runny nose with a sniff.

Grabbing a bottle of Wellbutrin off the bathroom vanity, she placed two pills in her mouth and washed them down with faucet water. In times like these, she wished Xanax or any benzodiazepines didn't trigger her past addiction.

Hey, we'll be alright. We won't be here long. Oliver is already working on our papers, so we can leave the country again soon. We just need to lay low until then. I can do this. Focus on work. Lay low. Blend in.

After fear ran its course, Enna forced her body to stand tall.

"Be strong for Jay. I got this." She bounced on the balls of her feet and shook out her hands while deep breathing, pumping herself up the way she would before an MMA fight.

Feeling semi-confident, she left the bathroom, grabbed her phone, and looked up the address of the cleaning job.

"Hey Jay, it's time to go. Hop in the car, please," Enna called out with a steady voice, but her legs still shook.

***

Though Enna struggled when it came to interacting with new people, she was great at cleaning. Beginning with the kitchen, she scrubbed the dishes with speed and accuracy. Enna didn't mind the mundane chores, but as she worked, an eerie, unsettled pit made itself at home in her stomach.

Jay chatted away about cars and rocket ships, but Enna only half-listened.

"Mmm hmm...yeah...ok...cool," she interjected each time Jay paused his discussion for a response.

Enna knew that the workday would be over soon, and she would be compelled to decide whether to allow Jay to go to his new friend's house. She knew what the right thing to do was, but anxiety tried to persuade her otherwise.

She moved through the house, scrubbing toilets, mopping floors, vacuuming, and cleaning the floorboards.

After working up a good sweat, Enna's client complimented her on a job well done and slipped her an extra $20 in addition to their agreed-upon price.

With a quick thanks and goodbye, Enna and Jay made their way to the car.

"Can we go to Ben's house now? Please?" Jay asked as he rushed ahead.

Anxiety doesn't control me. Anxiety doesn't control me. Anxiety doesn't control me.

Enna looked at Jay with love and laughed at his eagerness. "Fine, you win, but if Betty's a psycho, don't say I didn't warn you."

Jay leaped into the air and celebrated with a little body wiggle before he climbed into the car.

"You are the best mom ever!"

All the way to Betty's house, Jay talked non-stop about what made-up games he wanted to play with Ben.

The second Enna released Jay from his car seat, he bolted out of the car and raced to their neighbor's home.

"Wait for me," Enna called out, but Jay was already knocking on the door. By the time Enna reached him, Betty had answered. Her smile lit up the porch as she saw who was knocking.

"Oh, come in, come in," she beckoned, acting as though they were long-lost friends.

Enna reached into her pocket to make sure her pepper spray was in place before stepping into Betty's domain.

The front room was cluttered but not messy. Trophies and pictures sat in a cabinet displaying the family's proudest memories. In the first room alone, Enna could already see two paintings of Jesus and a photograph of a large temple. There were also portraits of several children in which Ben appeared to be the youngest. Enna's troubled feelings eased as she realized that Betty might be a religious nut, but she did not give off the spy vibe.

Betty led Enna and Jay to the dining area. Seated at a small table were three young girls and Ben. At the head of the table was a man, probably in his early forties. Dinner had been served and was already being passed around the table.

Enna's face flushed from embarrassment when she realized they had interrupted the family dinner. She was about to apologize and excuse herself so she could go hide under a blanket in the safety of her home. However, before she got any words out, the children shifted together and the father got up to grab more dishes. Two clean plates were added to the now quite squished table top.

"You are just in time for dinner," Betty announced. Seeing the uncertain look on Enna's face, Betty guided Enna to a fold-up chair that one of the girls brought out. "There is always room for more people at our table. You haven't eaten yet, have you?"

Jay wasted no time. He climbed up to the table and tried sloppily dishing himself some spaghetti. The man reached over to help him and then offered him some green beans and peaches.

Enna found herself wedged in between Jay and Ben. Betty took her place next to her husband and began introductions.

"Enna, I'd like you to meet my husband, Greg. And these are my daughters, Megan, Sarah, and Bethany." Each girl lifted a hand in hello at the mention of their names. "And, of course, you've already met Ben," Betty continued.

Ben showed a toothy grin with tomato sauce decorating his teeth.

Enna allowed a smile to play on her face at the sight.

So this is what normal families are like. Feeling completely out of place, Enna scooped food onto her plate.

"There are a few more family members who couldn't make it to dinner tonight. You'll meet them later. Everybody, meet Enna and her adorable son Jay," Betty finished the introductions.

"I'm not adorable. I'm handsome," Jay corrected.

Everyone exploded with laughter. Jay laughed hardest of all at the attention.

Then, it began, the dreaded small talk. "Where are you from? What do you do for work? Are you going to school? What sports do you like? What are your hobbies? What's your story?"

Enna had always been terrible at lying. Her face gave her secrets away. So, using pieces of the truth, she formed vague answers to satisfy her captive audience.

"I'm from all over the place, really. I travel for work. I finished school a few years ago. I love most sports but not football. Um, hobbies?"

What hobbies do ordinary people do? Martial arts is connected to my old life, so I can't say that. I don't really have hobbies. Enna looked around. She'd been thinking for too long. They were going to get suspicious.

"Dance! I dance," she said with more enthusiasm than intended.

Dance? I don't know anything about dancing. She glanced at Jay. His head cocked to the side with a puzzled expression. *Jeez, even he thinks it's a stupid lie. Please don't say anything,* she pled to Jay with her eyes. Enna hated lying, especially around Jay.

"Oh, interesting. What kind of dancing do you do?" Greg, the husband, asked. "I used to be one heck of a dancer back in my day."

Enna looked at him doubtfully. He had a gruff, manly face with a bit of pudge around the neck, making it hard to picture him as a dancer.

"Uh, I do lots of dancing. If I hear music, I just have to move to it," Enna said awkwardly. "I'm not great at it, though."

"Maybe I can give you some pointers sometime. I'm a hip-hop master," Greg bragged.

Enna could not tell if he was joking or not. She smiled politely but did not respond, bringing the conversation to a lull.

"Well, what is your story? What brought you to Payson?" Betty urged the conversation forward.

Oh, well. My son is a tech genius who is being chased by a secret government agency. And me, I'm just constantly afraid that my sex trafficker stalker is going to find and torture me. So, yeah. Nothing too exciting.

Shuffling her feet around on the linoleum, Enna resisted the urge to leave. Pushing through the discomfort, she gave a simple, less dramatic answer than the one in her head.

"Oh, well, I'm pretty fascinated with different cultures, which is why I love to travel. I have been all over. Payson is just one of my stops as I explore the world."

Frustration coursed through her. She did not love to travel at all. She would much rather have a home somewhere safe and familiar. However, traveling was a large part of her life now. She had to convince them that she had a legitimate reason for traveling so much other than hiding from unpleasant people who would steal her son away from her the second they found them.

The family's eyes tickled her skin. *I'm a fake and they know it.*

"Jay, isn't that spaghetti supposed to go in your mouth?" Enna asked, trying to get the focus off of her. He twisted the noodles onto his fork, but they just flopped off and landed on his lap.

Chuckles broke out from around the table, enticing Jay to repeat the action, but this time, he exaggerated his messy performance until a large dollop of sauce splattered on the table.

"Jay, don't. You're making a mess." Enna gave him a stern look.

"It's alright, we'll clean up later," Betty said.

Jay loudly slurped a single noodle he managed to get into his lips. Before the entire noodle disappeared, it flicked up and smacked Jay's face, spreading a line of sauce on his cheek.

The family burst out laughing.

Enna's face flushed with embarrassment at her uncivilized son.

After everyone finished being amused by his failed eating attempts, they pointed their eyes back at Enna.

Her head pounded a painful beat in her temples as questions continued to be thrown at her. She kept glancing up at the clock, willing time to move faster.

"How old is Jay?" Betty asked.

"He just turned four a few months ago," Enna said without hesitation. She was still unsure what his exact age was, but she went with the age on the fake adoption papers.

Betty's eyebrows went up in surprise. "Wow, he is really advanced for his age, very articulate. My Ben was a quiet boy. He didn't talk much until he turned four. He is almost five now. I'm still working on getting him to communicate better," Betty said, giving Ben what was meant to be an assuring look of love. He shrunk his head down.

"I'm sure Ben is very smart, too," Enna said, trying to fix the fact that Betty had unintentionally called Ben slow in front of his new friend.

Betty is not great with tact, Enna noted. *She just says what she wants, even if it comes off as rude. Hmm, I actually like that. At least she seems honest.*

"Yeah, Jay and I do a lot of schooling while we travel. Driving gives us lots of time to talk and learn new things. That is one reason he seems so advanced. I am so proud of him. I definitely learn more from him than he learns from me," Enna said. At least that part was one hundred percent true.

The conversation continued until, at last, dinner was over. Jay ran off to play while Enna volunteered to help clean up, but her offer was quickly denied as Greg swept their dishes away.

On their way out the door, Betty pulled Enna aside.

This is it, Enna thought, *she is going to tell me that she knows I'm lying and demand to hear the truth.* Enna held her breath while Betty began to speak.

"I am so glad you came by. Ben has been needing a friend and, well, I need friends too." Her voice was so sincere and soft that Enna's fears dissolved into nothing but a speck. A new buzzing in her heart arrived. She never had anyone need her before, other than Jay, of course. It was an unusual feeling, almost overwhelming.

"If you ever need anything, I am right here for you. It doesn't matter what time of day or night. My home and arms are open to you," Betty said. She threw her arms around Enna in a warm embrace.

Enna flinched at the movement but then allowed the stranger's comfort to surround her. A lump formed in her throat as a memory of her own mother washed over her.

***

Twelve-year-old Clara, now Enna, sat rigid on her bed, staring at the wall. The news of her parent's divorce was more than tears could fix, so tears refused to come. A knock on the door hardly registered in the distraught girl's mind. Her mother slipped over to her side and put her arms around her.

"I know this is so hard for you, honey. I feel like I've failed you. But I know you are strong and can get through this. We can get through this. I'll be here for you. You are not alone." At the last of her mother's words, tears finally filled Clara's eyes. She tried fighting them at first, but then she let them flow.

I will be strong, Clara repeated to herself as she allowed her mother's arms to cradle her.

***

That had been the last time she was held by her mother. *Clara is gone now and so is her mother,* Enna reminded herself.

She released herself from Betty's mothering grip, murmured a quick "Thanks for dinner," and told Jay it was time to go. After several disappointed protests from him, they headed home.

I have a friend. Strange.

12

She Knows

A warm breeze floated by, gently swirling a lock of Enna's hair around her face. She closed her eyes momentarily, savoring the sweet fragrance of a nearby lilac bush. The joyful yips of children on squeaky swings brought a contented smile to her lips.

Her son's infectious laughter prompted her to open her eyes. Jay and Ben abandoned the playground and darted around the park, emitting playful yodeling sounds to scatter the ducks. Feathers flapped wildly against the grass as the ducks ran for the safety of their pond.

Sitting on the bench next to Enna, Betty grinned so wide it could be seen from the moon.

Enna bowed her eyes away from the uncomfortably cheerful lady.

"It's so nice to see Ben happy. He had his older brothers, but now that they've moved out, he's surrounded by girls. It's not a bad thing, it's just a bit lonely for him. He goes a little crazy with only sisters to keep him company," Betty said.

Enna nodded and gazed after Jay.

"Yeah, it's good. Ha, look!" Enna cracked up as one of the ducks turned and charged toward Jay. Fear passed over his face and he scrambled in the opposite direction. Ben jumped into action and scared the duck away from his nervous friend. Once Jay realized he was safe from getting eaten by the duck, he let out a giggle that penetrated Enna's heart. It's been too long since she'd seen him this lively.

Tears of delight threatened to escape her eyes, but she distracted herself from her emotions by fiddling with a hair tie she kept on her wrist. She wouldn't allow herself to cry in public, not even happy tears.

"Thank you for reaching out to us, Betty," Enna said sincerely. Over the last few weeks, they had grown fairly close.

Each day, Betty invited them over for breakfast, which was followed up with a brisk morning walk. Jay and Ben would gallop ahead so the adults could yap.

Mostly, Betty just rambled on about her religion while Enna nodded and smiled, even though she had no idea what her friend was talking about half the time.

Occasionally, however, Betty surprised Enna with her deep wisdom. It was helpful but odd, almost as though she could see right into Enna's soul and know how to heal it.

On their walks, Betty seemed to know everyone they passed. She would call out, "Hey, Tiffany!" Or, "Susan, how are the kids?" Or, "Hey, Richard, I haven't seen you for a while. How have you been since your surgery?" Even the people she didn't know well would benefit from her perky personality as she waved to each of them.

To Enna's embarrassment, Betty's bold and confident demeanor always led her to stride right up to the neighbors and introduce Enna to all of them. Despite Enna's anxiety, Betty's actions consistently plucked her out of her small bubble and thrust her into a new world of connections.

The thought of Enna's newfound friendships sent a sudden pang coursing through her stomach. *We have to move on soon and leave everyone behind. Wow, that's going to suck! It's never felt like this before.*

Enna pushed the heavy thought away and focused on Jay, who imitated the ducks' waddle and quacked hysterically.

Checking her phone, Enna whined quietly to herself. She had a cleaning job to do before it got too late in the day.

"Five more minutes!" She shouted across the park. Dissatisfied grumbles replaced the sounds of Jay's goofy quacking.

"But I don't want to go," Jay protested.

"But I need to go to work," Enna replied, imitating his whiny tone.

Jay took a moment to stomp his feet, put his hands on his hips, and stick his lip out in a pout.

Enna stood up and mimicked his pout with an exaggerated sob. "Awww, Jay! I don't want to go to work. Pretty please, can you go to work for me so I can stay here and play with my friend? Please!!!" Enna mocked Jay's behavior, ignoring how unattractive it might look to anyone watching.

Instead of taking offense, Jay laughed, "I can't go to work for you. I'm too little, ya goof!" He ran back to Ben and told him how silly his mom was.

Satisfied, Enna sat back on the bench with a smug smile.

Betty leaned over to Enna and spoke softly so the boys could not hear. "Listen, if you would like to leave Jay here with me, I don't mind watching him while you work. I will just take him to my home after the park and make sure he gets dinner."

Enna bit her lip, her heart filling with fear at the thought of being separated from Jay. They'd never been apart before and the idea utterly terrified her.

What if someone finds him? What if Betty takes her eyes off him for one second and then he's gone? What if I'm not here to protect him and the government shows up to take him away? How could I ever forgive myself?

Enna shook her head no, "I'd better take him with me."

"Well, you can't shelter him forever. You need to teach him how to be around other people, not just you," Betty said with a hint of judgment.

Enna's initial instinct was to get offended. *I am teaching him to be with other people. I came out of my comfort zone just so he could play with his friend. I'm a good mom.*

Enna fumed inwardly. She turned her face away, not wanting Betty to see her defensive face. *What's wrong with him being around me constantly? It's normal. Right? He is still my baby.*

She watched Jay jump over a small boulder and land heavily on his stomach. The sand cushioned his fall. Unphased, he hopped back up and ran after Ben.

Huh, he may still be my baby, but he is not a baby. What if he doesn't need me anymore? What if I am the one who needs him and I am damaging him by not letting him grow up? Maybe it would be good for him to learn how to be around other authorities other than me.

Enna glanced back at Betty, who patiently waited for a response. *I swear that smile gets bigger every time I look at her,* Enna thought. *How can she do that without her lips splitting open?*

"Listen, Enna. I know Jay is not a regular child. He is a very intelligent boy, not quite like others his age." Betty's words sent Enna into a spiral.

Oh no, no, please. She knows! Of course, she knows. Oh, Betty, please don't turn Jay in! Enna's eyes bugged out in horror as Betty continued to speak.

"I understand it is really scary when your kid doesn't seem to fit into social norms. I get that you want to protect him and that's a beautiful thing. I think you are doing an amazing job. Having a genius child must be very complicated, but you don't have to hide Jay from the world. He's going to do wonderful things." Betty paused, seeing Enna quaking. "It's okay, sweetheart, you don't have to care for him on your own. We love him, and you, very much. You need to give yourself a break. Jay is going to be just fine."

"Betty," Enna's voice tremored, "I really need you to not tell anyone about Jay being a genius. I can't explain all the reasons why, but you have to promise me that you won't say anything. Please."

Betty placed a caring hand on Enna's shoulder. "It's okay, Enna. I won't tell anyone. But, just so you know, I'm here to talk about anything you need when you're ready. Now, breathe. You can trust me. Alright?"

Enna took in a few gulps of air and nodded. "Thank you," she whispered.

"Now, you should let me have a turn caring for Jay while you go to work. We'll be fine. He's a good kid."

Despite the foreboding that penetrated her heart, Enna saw the sincerity in Betty's eyes.

She will take good care of him.

"Fine. I need to let him grow up sometime, huh? Please, just call me if anything happens, and don't take your eyes off of him. Don't let anyone pick him up except for me. Don't let him use any electronics while I'm not around. That's very important to me. And Betty, no one can know how smart he is," Enna said urgently.

"He will be safe with me. I promise." Betty's confident eyes gave Enna a whiff of peace.

"Thank you." Enna rose from the bench and headed over to Jay. As soon as he saw her approaching, his body melted into a tantrum.

"Awwww, I don't want to go," he complained.

"Well you're in luck, I guess." Enna beckoned Jay to her side. "Betty said she will watch you if you want to keep playing."

Jay's melting body straightened up and began to wiggle as though he could not contain his excitement.

"Really?!"

"Wait, Jay, listen. Are you listening?" He wildly bobbed his head up and down.

"What, Mommy?"

In a voice only he could hear, Enna whispered, "Remember what we talked about when you are with other people? You are a very smart boy. Your brain is your superpower. Should you show your super-power off to your friends?"

Jay shook his head *no.*

"Right! You need to keep your superpower a secret. I don't want anyone being jealous and figuring out your secret identity. Alright? Do you promise?"

"Yup!" Jay said eagerly.

"Now, I need you to stay away from computers, cell phones, and even T.V.s. Understand?" Jay nodded. "I will be back soon. Have a lot of fun, okay? I'll come get you at Betty's house in a few hours. Be good." Enna pulled him in for a tight hug.

"Oh, Mommy, you're a sweetheart," Jay said excitedly after his mom kissed his cheek.

"Love you, Baby." Enna tenderly ruffled her son's hair, then took a deep breath, mustering the courage to walk away from her baby boy for the very first time.

13

Pepper Spray

Enna's separation anxiety grew as she walked to work. Her car was out of commission due to the ominous noises it projected when she tried driving it. Repair parts were too expensive, so she had to walk nearly forty minutes to reach a small white and navy blue house.

As instructed by her client, Enna retrieved the key from under the mat and let herself into the vacant home.

Grateful for the solitude, she ventured into the unfamiliar environment. The house screamed bachelor pad, messy and carrying a strange stench. A short hall led to a cluttered kitchen that served as both a dining area and a culinary workspace. Connected to the kitchen, a carpeted living room featured a couch followed by end tables and a large flat-screen television spread across the wall.

Across the living room, a door revealed a cramped bedroom with dirty clothes strewn across the floor. The walk-in closet surprisingly housed a bathroom and a laundry room, with a dresser squeezed into the tight space across from the washer and dryer.

Looking around, Enna rolled her eyes at the mess and began gathering clothes off the floor. She quickly started the washing machine and put the clean clothes from the dryer into a basket. It only took her a few steps to bring the basket over to the dresser.

Well, I guess I didn't actually need the basket. Enna realized with a shrug.

She pulled open the top drawer to the dresser and furrowed her eyebrows. The drawer held what looked like human hair. Fear and curiosity bubbled in her stomach. With a trembling hand, she reached in and pulled on some of the hair.

A wig? "What are you doing with this?" She dug further into the drawer, discovering more wigs of different styles and colors alongside odd glasses and fake facial hair.

"Nope, uh-uh!" She left the room and rushed out the front door of the house.

Who is this guy? Why does he have so many disguises? He's a spy!

In her haste, a toe caught on the cement walkway, momentarily taking away her balance. The act of stumbling derailed the momentum of her racing thoughts.

Slowing her pace, her brain started working again.

I could be freaking out over nothing. He could just be into cosplay or something nerdy like that. Coming to a full stop, she put her fists on her hips and slowed her breathing.

Okay, even if he is a spy, he will know I'm onto him if I just take off. Where would I even go? Oliver hasn't gotten back to me.

A gush of warm wind pushed against her. Looking back at the house, she weighed her options.

He's probably just a normal human. If I leave before I'm done, I'll get a bad review for other clients to see. What does that matter, though? Jay can easily remove bad reviews.

The conditioned perfectionist in Enna urged her to go back inside and finish the job she was hired to do. Thanks to the way Andrew would beat her if she didn't finish a job, incomplete work triggered a ripple of anxiety throughout her body.

Just because this guy has disguises doesn't mean he is after me. Not everyone is after me. And besides that, Jay looked into him before I even took this job. This client doesn't even have speeding tickets. Yeah, I'm definitely overreacting. He's just a weirdo, that's all.

The back of her hand wiped her forehead. She shook off her fear and went back inside.

As she cleaned, Enna anxiously counted the minutes until she could reunite with Jay. Occasionally, she paused her work to check in on him.

"He's just playing," Betty assured her each time.

Enna longed to leave work early so she could give Jay a big hug and never let go. However, not only did she harbor a curiosity for this client now, but she was also desperate for money, so she cleaned on.

As she worked on the list of chores her client sent, she dove into an investigation, wanting to quell her anxiety. She knew it was silly, but she couldn't resist pulling on each book that sat on the bookshelf, half expecting a passageway for a secret lair to appear. Of course, nothing happened. The bookshelf was just a regular shelf. And the books were typical, self-help books that revealed nothing substantial about the man who hired her. The only slightly peculiar thing she saw was an old "yield" sign nailed to his living room wall.

"Hmm, random," she said to the empty room.

All she concluded was that her client was not a neat person. A plethora of candy wrappers were shoved in between some of the books that must have been used as bookmarks at one point. She found mismatched shoes in odd locations around the house, such as on the countertop and under the couch. In the sink, containers of rotten food sat waiting to clog the drain.

Enna scrunched up her nose, pulled on rubber gloves, scooped the old food out of the sink, and plopped the slop into the trash can. After that, she cleaned and stored the dishes away in an orderly fashion before moving on to the counter. It was so covered with papers that the counter top was completely hidden.

After quickly scanning each paper, she sorted them into neat piles. There were no suspicious documents. The piles consisted mostly of bills, newspapers, receipts, scribbled notes, and a few playbills and programs from various theater companies.

Enna moved from room to room, making sure she missed no detail.

In the bedroom, she admired amateur art pieces that hung on the walls. They were splashed with bright colors and beautiful shading.

I wonder if he painted these himself. The signature scribbled at the bottom of the painting was difficult to decipher, but it appeared to read something like "Will Lume," which was not even close to her client's name, Nick Peterson.

Enna grinned as she took out the final trash bag, completing her work.

Mr. Peterson had promised to leave a check for her on the counter, but despite searching through every paper, she couldn't find the promised payment. She noticed several loose coins around the house as she cleaned, but it wasn't nearly enough to compensate her for her time and energy.

Dang it! I should have made sure the money was here first. Irritably, she texted Mr. Peterson.

I could not find the check you said you would leave for me. I will be back to pick it up tomorrow if that works for you.

With a frustrated sigh, she looked out the window and winced. A golden sunset already prepared for the night. She briskly locked up and began her trek home to pick Jay up. She hadn't gotten far when the last sliver of the golden sunset vanished, leaving only a few sparkles of early stars to lead the way home.

Usually, Enna took comfort in the cover of the night, but tonight felt different. Instead of her usual ease, a tingling sensation crept up her spine as though someone watched from the shadows. The hairs on her neck prickled. Glancing over her shoulder, she saw nothing but an empty street.

Quickening her pace, she listened carefully as her ears picked up on faint footsteps matching her speed.

Thump, thump, thump. It was no mere figment of her imagination. Enna knew she was not alone. She widened her stride, attempting to increase the distance between herself and the approaching footsteps, but they continued to draw closer, growing louder with each passing moment. Panic gripped her, and she bolted into a full sprint.

"Hey, wait," a man's voice called out only a few paces away from her.

She kept running, using all her muscles to push herself forward.

Oh crap! I'm leading him straight to Jay, she realized with a start.

Without slowing her pace, Enna reached into her pocket, pulled out a tube of pepper spray, and spun to face the approaching stranger. Shielding her eyes, she squeezed the trigger.

"Oooooh, wow! What the... Why?" the man cried out in pain. "Wow!" His words staggered as coughing pounded out of his chest.

Enna peaked her eyes open just enough to see a young, gangly man with floppy brown hair ducking in a crouched position. Rubbing his swollen eyes with one hand, he raised the other in surrender.

"Stop! Hey, 'cough,' it's just me, Nicolas Peterson, or Nick, just Nick. Ow!" He tried to take a deep breath, which led to more hacking coughs. "You just cleaned my house, 'cough cough!' I got home just as you were walking away, 'cough,' and I thought I'd just pay you now instead of having to get the money to you somehow later. 'cough cough!' Please, I wasn't going to hurt you."

Realization hit Enna like a brick flying through a window. *This is my client. I just attacked a potentially innocent person. Crap!*

"I am so sorry!" Enna exclaimed in despair. Putting her pepper spray safely in her pocket, she crept over to Nick and knelt beside him.

Gently, she moved his hand away from his puffy red eyes and groaned. "What can I do to help? Oh my gosh, I feel so bad! Please tell me what to do."

Nick attempted to slit his eyes open but gave up with a moan.

"No, no, don't feel bad," Nick said in a voice much calmer than the situation called for. "Mmmm, I probably deserved it for creeping up on you like that. *'Cough.'* Would you mind helping me get home? *'Cough cough,'* I'll be fine."

"Yes, of course, anything," Enna said, helping Nick to his feet. She held onto his elbow and guided him back toward his house.

"Watch your step," She cautioned as they reached his front porch. Making sure Nick was steady, she let go of him and reached under the rug, grabbed the key, and opened the door. Carefully, she led Nick to the kitchen sink and turned the faucet on.

"You should probably remove your shirt so the chemical on it doesn't burn your skin more," Enna suggested, trying to sound intelligent. "If you happen to have baking soda, It can help ease the pain." She looked over at Nick and swallowed hard.

He just removed his shirt. For such a skinny man, he was in quite good shape. A six-pack bounced down his abs and Enna needed to remind herself not to stare.

I'm in a house, alone with a half-naked guy. Oh boy! She blushed. Luckily, Nick couldn't see.

"Cool, yeah, thanks. I think I have some baking soda on the bottom shelf in the fridge door or shoved to the back of the fridge. I'm not really sure." Nick pointed to the fridge before splashing his face with cold water.

Enna opened the fridge and scanned the items in there. It did not take long for her to locate the baking soda.

She went to the cupboards and searched for a pitcher. Unfortunately, she found it on the highest shelf of an upper cabinet.

Again, grateful that Nick couldn't see her, she stood on tippytoes, trying to reach the pitcher with the tips of her fingers. Jumping slightly, she was able to nudge the pitcher off the shelf and into her outstretched arms. She silently cheered at her success.

"Excuse me," Enna said to Nick. "Can I use the sink for a bit?" Nick nodded and stepped aside with a dripping face.

Enna filled the pitcher with warm water and mixed in the baking soda, making a pasty white liquid.

"I'm going to pour this on your face, okay," Enna warned Nick.

"Go right ahead. I'm all yours." With his back against the counter, he tilted his head over the sink until his swollen face pointed to the ceiling. "M'kay, I'm ready for it."

His voice sounded almost giddy, as though he enjoyed Enna's attention way too much despite the pain he must have felt.

Holding the pitcher above his head, she poured the liquid down his face. He grunted slightly as the baking soda drenched him. Some of the mixture ran down his neck and onto his chest. Once she finished pouring the liquid, Enna quickly found a rag and offered it to Nick to dry his skin.

"Can you open your eyes yet?" she asked hopefully.

Nick popped his right eye open, then his left. His eyes were still bloodshot. He blinked several times, but then he managed to keep them open long enough to lock eyes with Enna.

"Wow, you are beautiful," Nick said with a hint of surprise and awe.

"Ha," Enna grimaced and looked down at her fidgeting feet.

What the heck? Is he serious right now? Despite the discomfort the compliment created, Enna couldn't help but feel slightly flattered. She smiled until she realized how tired and ragged she must look.

Hoping to hide her nerves and discomfort, Enna brushed some dirt off her shirt and straightened up.

"Uh, thanks. You should probably sit." With a wave of a hand, she drew his attention away from her and onto the nice leather couch in the living room. Nick followed her suggestion and sat.

An awkward pit grew in Enna's gut, not quite sure what she was supposed to do next.

"Um, hey. Do you need me to get you a clean shirt or anything? I know where they are. I just cleaned some up for you." Enna spoke too fast. "What do you need? I can..." Nick stopped her by holding up a hand.

"Wow, hey, I'm ok. See?" He pointed to his eyes and gave her a pained, crooked grin. "I'm not blind, buuut, I will need you to make it up to me."

Enna's stomach flopped to the floor. Guilt and fear caused a hasty reply.

"Anything you need. If you don't want to pay me for cleaning earlier, I completely understand. I will clean for free anytime you want. What can I do?"

Nick closed his eyes but kept a gentle, closed-mouth smile resting on his face.

"No. I'll pay you, but you can make it up to me by letting me take you out on a date." He opened his eyes once more to see her reaction.

Stunned, Enna's face froze in confusion and anger.

How dare he use my mistake to get to me! Who does this creep think he is?

"Hello? Did I break you?" Nick teased.

Enna took a few more seconds to process what he just said before blurting out, "What is wrong with you? Why would you want to go on a date with me? You don't know me and I just pepper-sprayed you in the face! Why on earth do you think I would ever go on a date with a complete stranger? I'm not a freaking idiot! You can't just make me go on a date with you just because I messed up. Alright, buddy?" She glared at him suspiciously as though he was about to say, "April fools!" but the joke never came. He held up both arms in submission.

"Whoa, hey, I would never *make* you go on a date with me. I just... You have me completely wrong. I just appreciate you, you know, helping me out instead of just pepper-spraying me and then running off. You seem like a good person and you're really pretty." He scratched his head with an apologetic grimace. "I'm sorry I freaked you out. That was not my intention at all. Please, I'm sorry. I just want to get to know you better. That's literally the only reason I asked if you would go on a date with me. I promise." The sincerity in Nick's face surprised Enna. His gentle, pleading eyes showed a deep regret for how things unfolded.

Unballing her clenched fists, she let the tension go. Swallowing hard, she stood stiff, not knowing quite what to say.

"Uh, I'm sorry I overreacted. I guess I do that sometimes. Sorry. I appreciate you not suing me for hurting you on accident, but I really can't go on a date with you. I have a son to take care of and..." The thought of Jay reminded her that too much time had passed by. "Oh no! Betty! Sorry, I...I have to go now." She headed toward the door, mind going wild. *Gosh, they're probably freaking out, wondering where I am!*

In her frantic rush, Enna didn't hear Nick calling her back for the cleaning money.

Unable to reach Betty on the phone, she began to jog home, hoping Betty wouldn't be too upset by the late hour. However, as Enna hurried to retrieve Jay, her thoughts returned to Nick.

I can't believe he just asked me out like that. I mean, he was handsome and nice, but so was Andrew. Of course, I couldn't just go on a date with him. He could be a psychopath. Even as the thought entered her mind, Enna's internal guide challenged her fears.

There was something off about Andrew from the moment I met him. I was naive and didn't know better. I'm not like that anymore, though. I'm not naive. Nick is definitely strange, but I'm pretty sure he's not a psychopath. I know the difference. Or, at least, I think I'd be able to tell by now.

As she neared Betty's house, her mind wandered around, teasing her with fantasies about how it would be to go on an actual date with an actual man.

No. I couldn't. I shouldn't. I have to leave Payson soon anyway. Why would I lead him on that way? What if...what if I didn't leave? What if I just stayed? What if I did allow myself to date him?

14

Nick

"What on Earth?" As Enna stared through the peephole in her door, she was met with an unexpected sight: a pair of bright orange swimming goggles with an attached snorkel. This would have made perfect sense if the person wearing them were a child, but that was not the case.

Behind the goggles stood a lanky man with unruly, floppy brown hair. He wore a vivid yellow button-up shirt complemented by blue jeans and a pair of Converse shoes.

Nick? Seriously? Not this guy! Enna's eyes rolled in exasperation. *What does he want? Go away!*

He tried to smile with the snorkel still in his mouth, but doing so made him look like an alien who landed on Earth to declare, "I come in peace."

How did he find me? Enna walked away from the unanswered door. *Oh wait, I never grabbed money from him yesterday. Dang it! He's probably just dropping it off. Eh, I don't really need the money, do I?*

The idea of opening the door turned her palms clammy. *Of course I need money. My stupid car is still broken.* Kicking a pillow that rested on the floor, Enna growled, knowing that, in order to receive payment for her work the previous day, she would have to face the embarrassment of interacting with the man she unintentionally assaulted.

Fine, whatever! He is not too large for me to fight. He's just an ego threat. With a deep sigh, she opened the door just enough to see out.

"Well, hello, Mr. Peterson. What do you need?" Enna attempted to appear nonchalant, not wanting him to think she was suspicious of him, which she was, especially now that he had shown up in such a peculiar manner.

"Hhhherrro," Nick's muffled greeting came through the snorkel in his mouth. Enna tilted her head quizzically. Nick removed the snorkel and repeated the hello in a comprehensible voice. "You can just call me Nick. Mr. Peterson makes me sound like an old fart."

Enna couldn't help but scoff and shake her head. A blend of amusement and irritation clouded her thoughts as she grappled to process Nick's odd behavior.

"Um, are you going swimming or something? What's with the gear?" she asked curiously.

A mischievous smirk formed on Nick's face.

"Well, I thought I would bring protection in case you…" Nick let his words die off as though reconsidering what he was about to say, but then continued with a bounce, "In case you decided to pepper spray me again." A laugh exploded out of his face as if he had delivered the best punchline in the entire world.

Enna bit her lip and ran her fingers through her hair awkwardly, not knowing whether to laugh with him or apologize again.

"Oh my gosh, that's so embarrassing. Did you seriously come over here in that just for a joke?" Enna asked.

"Yes, sirree! Figured it'd be a nice icebreaker."

"Um, okay? Yeah. It is completely safe for you to take the goggles off, I promise. See, no pepper spray." She held her hands up to prove her point.

"Oh, whew!" Nick said dramatically while pulling the goggles off, "I was nervous there for a second."

"Haha. Oh, shut up!" She playfully shot back at him before remembering this guy was not her friend. "How did you know where to find me? I never gave you my address," Enna asked lightly but with a serious undertone.

The drawer of disguises found at his house danced around her mind, causing her to plan out a defensive strategy if necessary.

Nick attempted to match her serious face before answering, "Oh, I'm secretly a private detective who has spies around the city watching your every move."

All the blood drained out of Enna's face and she stumbled backward a couple feet.

Noticing her shocked reaction, Nick burst out in fits of laughter and caught the door as Enna tried slamming it shut.

"Whoa! Hey, chill. I'm just kidding. I'm kidding! You take me way too seriously. Do I really look like a P.I. to you? Huh? It was just a joke. I'm sorry. Okay. I'm just really bad at flirting."

His eyes were wide and convincing, but Enna had her doubts. Glaring daggers at Nick, she shook her head. "Well, it is not a funny joke. How did you find me, really?"

"Enna, I know your neighbor, Betty. Seriously, I've only been in the area a few weeks and she's already invited me to join her church and introduced me to several of her friends. She's like a social encyclopedia!" His eyes twinkled as he shook his head, amused. "When I talked to her last night, she told me you lived right across from her. What a coincidence, right?" He gave Enna a thumbs up.

Enna sneered, "I'm not buying it. Why would you talk to Betty last night right after meeting me? What, do you do nightly calls with her or something? I wonder how her husband feels about that." She readied her fist, poised to strike his nose at the slightest hint of trouble.

"Um, No. That would be weird. I just called because you ran off without getting paid. I wanted to know how to get the money to you since you don't do pay apps." He lifted his shoulders indifferently as if his words held the utmost clarity and simplicity.

Enna raised an eyebrow in disbelief. "That doesn't make any sense. Why would you think of calling Betty instead of me? Seems kind of out of the blue, don't you think?"

"It wasn't out of the blue. Right before you left, you said, 'Oh no! Betty!' so I figured you knew her. I only know one Betty around here." Nick brushed an escaped lock of hair away from his eyes. "And...I did try to call you first, but the line was busy."

"Oh, then why didn't you just leave me a message or a text? I would have met up with you." Enna's scrunched forehead began to ache.

"Uh, I did. You didn't get it?" Nick asked.

A flush of self-consciousness colored Enna's face. *Uhg, he's probably telling the truth.*

Enna mumbled, "Oh, nope. I must have missed it." She shifted her body weight around uncomfortably, knowing good and well that she had failed to even check her phone after leaving Nick's house last night. She wasn't used to anyone texting her.

That still doesn't prove he's an honest person.

Seeing the skeptical look remaining on Enna's face, Nick flicked a casual hand in the air as if presenting a superior idea. "You don't trust people, do you? Look, you can go ask Betty. She will confirm my story. I told her *all* about our meeting last night." He emphasized the word "all" with a crazed grin.

"Wait, what? Please tell me you didn't say anything about the pepper spray!" Enna gasped, horrified.

His mischievous smile grew, showing off all his straight white teeth.

"Weeeeelllll...might have mentioned it," he teased. Enna covered her face in shame.

"Oh my gosh. Please tell me you are kidding!" By the appearance of Nick's face, she knew he was telling the truth.

"Awe, don't worry. It was cute. She thought it was hilarious," Nick assured her.

Enna looked away, trying to conceal her red face. She fiddled with the door handle for a few seconds before finding the humor in the situation.

"Well, Mr. Peterson, you might need those goggles after all." She let a shy smile creep onto her face.

Nick shielded his eyes dramatically while pleading, "Spare the eyes! Spare the eyes! Do what you like to me, but spare the eyes!"

"Shh, you're going to wake up my son," Enna said, unable to control a laugh that expelled from her lips.

What a weirdo! She shook her head, amused. His relaxed demeanor nearly eased her suspicions, but not completely.

"Wow, you have a fantastic laugh," Nick said sincerely.

"Thanks," Enna muttered. Her foot subconsciously scratched her opposite ankle while an uncomfortable silence overtook the scene.

She glanced up to see Nick's eyes resting on her softly. It was the first time she noticed his stunning hazel eyes. Though they still held a slight red hue from being sprayed with toxins, there was something in his amiable gaze that encompassed warmth and tranquility, giving her anxiety a bit of a break.

Enna hesitated to look away, but the familiar discomfort that often accompanied eye contact coursed through her like an unwelcome habit. She broke her gaze away from him and interrupted the silence. "So, are you going to pay me for my work or what?"

Nick poked a finger into the air as though an idea suddenly struck him.

"Oh yeah! I almost forgot. Sorry! Got distracted." He reached into the little pocket on the chest of his shirt, pulled out a check, and handed it to Enna before he continued speaking. "Hey, I know we had a rough start, and you really are allowed to say no, but I would like to get to know you for real. Could we start over? I would be honored if you would go on a date with me." Despite all the joking, this time, Nick was compassionate and completely genuine.

Enna dropped her eyes to the floor, heart racing. "That isn't a good idea," she answered, fingers fidgeting with the hair tie around her wrist.

"And why is that?" Nick asked, trying to hide the hint of disappointment in his voice. "You having a son doesn't bother me. So, what are you afraid of?" Nick stared at Enna patiently, waiting for her to answer.

Enna wished she could tell him the truth, starting with her mother's death and her father's addiction. She wanted to tell him about being rescued by a man, only to discover that he was a monster.

I want you to know my story: how I escaped, how I survived, why I'm a mother, and why I'll have to pack up and leave soon. But Enna swallowed her secrets.

"I just don't think I'm ready to date," she said weakly. A glance at his face caused regret to surface in her chest. He looked so disheartened, like a yappy puppy who had been denied attention.

"Sorry," she muttered, a weak apology.

There were a few tense seconds before Nick shrugged. "No, don't apologize. I get it," Nick said, putting his thumbs in his pockets. "I'm just too handsome for you." He attempted to smolder by pressing his lips together and squinting his eyes, but it only made him look like a zombie.

Enna let out a laugh. "Yes, that is definitely it," she agreed, relieved the moment of tension had melted.

"No, but really, Enna. I do get it. I don't tell a lot of people this, but I was engaged once. It ended horribly. I haven't been on many dates since then. But, when I saw you, I figured I'd give it a shot." His bottom lip overlapped his upper lip, waiting for her to react.

Enna's guilt quietly festered in her stomach. "Nick, you are so strange, and you're right. I don't trust easily, but you're funny and cute. I'm sure someday you'll find the right person. I'm not your girl, though. I have way too much baggage right now."

"Baggage doesn't really scare me," Nick said with a downcast expression.

"Mm-hmm, and that's one reason I don't trust you," Enna raised her shoulders dismissively.

"Fair enough. If you change your mind, feel free to message me. You have my number. But hey, you don't owe me anything," he backed away slowly. "Guess I'll see you around."

He turned and left with a wave, leaving Enna gazing after him, conflicted by the attraction and grief she carried for him.

"It's the right call. I don't even trust him," she grumbled as she closed the door.

"Silly mommy, you should go!" Jay announced loudly from the cot in the living room.

"Eeep!" Enna squealed with a jolt, throwing her arms up to block an attack before she processed that it was only Jay speaking. "Awk! I thought you were sleeping!" she heaved, trying to calm her breath.

"Nope, I heard you talking to that funny guy and it woke me up. You should go." Jay stood up on the cot for emphasis and began to bounce.

"Go where?" Enna asked, already knowing the answer.

"On a date with the colorful guy. I peeped through the window at him," Jay said, showing off his toothy grin. "You never go on dates."

"What do you know about dates?" Enna asked curiously.

"I know that you watch movies all the time with dates in them and you always get droops in your eyes even when the movie is a happy movie. Maybe if you go on a date for real, your eyes won't be so droopy," Jay said.

Enna nodded her head, impressed by her son's emotional comprehension. "Well, Nick is a stranger, so I can't go. Stranger danger! Stranger danger! Here I come! Watch out!" Grinning, Enna swooped Jay off the bed into her arms and kissed his neck. "You are the only man I need." She sat on the cot with Jay on her lap.

"Come on, Mommy. He's not a complete stranger. I stall-kid him on the computer before you went to his house, memember? I got your back. He is a perfect person with no bad guy stuff," Jay said with a proud voice.

"Wait, you whatted him?" Enna asked, tilting her head to the side in confusion.

"Stall-kid. I sneaked and looked him up without him knowing," Jay clarified with a small, snorting laugh.

"Do you mean stalked?" Enna asked, trying to suppress a smile at his pronunciation.

"Oh, yeah! That's what I meant," Jay laughed.

"What do you know about stalking anyway? Jeez, kid!" Enna poked his side, making him wiggle and giggle.

"Alright, alright. Stop!" Jay slipped out of Enna's grasp and stumbled away.

Enna stood. "Okay, I'm done. Promise. But seriously, Jay, you can't trust somebody just because the internet says they haven't done anything wrong. You have to get to know them in real life."

"Well, that's what I'm sayin'! You gots to get ta know that dude before besiding if he can be trusted." Jay put his fists on his hips and gave Enna a sassy pants glance.

"Pretty sure you mean 'before deciding,' not 'besiding,' Right?" Enna corrected. "Come on, let's get ready for breakfast."

Enna ushered Jay into his room and picked out a clean pair of clothes for the day. Jay was half-dressed when the doorbell rang.

"Really? Come on! I can't get anything done without someone ringing... Here," She handed Jay his pants, "Finish putting these on. I'll check who's at the door."

Placing her eye on the peephole for the second time that day, Enna saw white, gleaming teeth belonging to Betty's grin. Enna quickly unlocked the door and allowed her inside.

"Hey, what's up? We were just getting ready to head over for breakfast. Is that still happening?" Enna would have offered Betty a seat if she had any chairs, but instead, they had to stand.

"Of course, dear, but I just couldn't wait! Did he ask you? Hmmm?" Betty leaned in expectantly.

"What are you talking about?" Enna asked.

"Oh, you know. Nick. Did he ask you out?"

"Seriously, he told you he was going to ask me out? Great." Enna walked over to Jay's bedroom door and knocked. "You doing okay in there, bud?"

"No! I askidenally put both my legs in one hole, so I have to start all the way over!" Jay called through the door. Betty overheard and laughed before continuing the conversation.

"Well, Nick told me he already asked you out last night, but you didn't take it well, so he told me he wanted to try again, even though you pepper sprayed him in the face. How funny is that? Huh?" Betty nudged Enna with her elbow. "So, did he ask you?"

"Yep," Enna ran a hand through her hair but didn't elaborate.

"And?" Betty pressed.

"And, nothing. I don't know him. He's just very…weird and not my type." Enna gave a mean, sarcastic smile, hoping to end the conversation. Betty's face dropped.

"You said no? Enna!"

"What? I don't have to say yes." Enna threw up her hands, irritated at her friend's unsupportive response.

"No, you don't have to say yes, but you should. You are young and beautiful and deserve to have fun. You should take this opportunity to expand your horizons. You're missing too much of your life, being scared all the time. My goodness!" Betty waved a finger in Enna's face, making her want to grab it and drag it outside like a filthy animal. Instead, she clutched the hem of her shirt so her hands wouldn't strike out.

What? You don't think I know how much of my life I'm missing by being afraid? I'm missing out on everything because each time I see a shadow move, I feel Andrew's presence! I can't just turn it off and date random men because anyone I date would be in danger! I can't fall in love. Not until Andrew is dead! He's not only taken my peace away, but he's taken away my ability to get close to anyone! I'm sick of it! I want a life!

Enna shook with rage at the injustice in her life. Tired of swallowing her emotions, Enna yelled, "I don't have to go on dates to have fun and be fulfilled, alright? I don't need a man to come in and sweep me off my feet. I'm fine. I'm getting by. I have an amazing son and he is the only one that matters! I don't need people. I don't need you! And you had no right to tell anyone where I live without my permission! You have no boundaries!" The moment the words left Enna's lips, she choked on an immediate regret.

Betty's stunned face quivered. Enna put an apologetic hand out, but Betty turned away from it. "Hey, I'm sorry. I didn't mean that. I'm just, Betty…"

Jay popped his head out of his bedroom door, confused at the contention. "What'd I miss?"

"Nothing bud. Go play with your cars for a bit."

"Awww!" He slammed the door shut.

"Betty, please. I don't know why I said that," Enna's words fell flat.

Betty looked back at Enna, eyes watering. "I think you know exactly why you said that, Enna. You put up such a powerful wall to keep the bad from reaching you, but it's keeping the good away, too. Maybe, when you're ready, you should consider building a gate to go with your wall, and I'll be waiting on the other side to come in when that happens." Betty walked over to the door but turned back to Enna before leaving. "Breakfast will be ready in thirty minutes. I hope to see you both there." She briskly left the apartment, shutting the door behind her.

Enna let out a single sob, put her back against the wall, and melted to the ground. Her heart hurt.

I can't believe I just lost it. I'm a horrible person! I'm a terrible friend. Enna's face dropped onto her knees. *The worst part is that she's right. Besides Jay, nothing good will ever happen to me. Andrew made sure of that. I'm so sick of being controlled by him still. Why can't he just GET OUT OF MY HEAD?* Enna hammered the floor with her fist.

"I'm so done with this," she whispered.

"So done with what, Mommy?" Jay whispered back through the crack under his door.

"Hm," Enna gave a sad half chuckle. "Come here, Bud. wanna sit on my lap?" Jay opened his bedroom door and cuddled into Enna's arms.

"I'm done being pushed around by a memory. I think it's time I start living my life again."

"What does that mean?" Jay pointed his puzzled face up at her.

"It means that I'm going to take your advice and go on a date with a man I hardly know."

15

First Date

Panting, Enna paced around Betty's small living room.

"I can't do this! What was I thinking? I haven't been on a date since- Well, I haven't been on a real date! Oh gosh!" Enna bent over with hands on her knees, breathing heavily.

Betty stopped working on her felt-book craft project, crossed the room to Enna, and started massaging her back.

"You're panicking, dear. Come, let's sit down." Betty led Enna to the couch. "You don't have to go on this date. Sometimes, we get bad feelings for a reason. Maybe you are not supposed to go."

Enna's breathing slowed. "I know I don't have to go," Enna's voice quivered. "What scares me is that I actually want to go. I don't know anything about this guy other than he's attractive and a bit of a nutcase, but something about him, I don't know. It's hard to explain. Am I being stupid? Should I cancel?" Enna let out a frustrated sound that was part scream, part growl, then dropped her head into her hands.

"You've got to ask yourself, is this the Spirit telling you not to go, or the fear of possibly having a bad time?"

Spirit? Huh? Half of Enna's face squinted together in confusion.

"What? Uh, I don't know. I just...just don't trust people," Enna stammered, looking up at Betty. "But I want to put a 'gate' in my wall like you suggested, so...I'm going," Enna declared, straightening her back. "My past can't control me anymore. Right?"

Betty excitedly bobbed her head up and down with a proud expression as she responded, "Yes! And, as far as I can tell, Nick is a very kind person. You know, the first time I met him, he saw me working in my garden and offered to help. It was very sweet. I think he might be good for you," Betty said convincingly.

Okay, yeah. I've got this. Oh man! Come on. Get up!

Forcing herself to stand, Enna looked down at her simple outfit. She wore a slimming black shirt with skinny blue jeans and bright red flats.

Though suddenly appearing calm on the outside, beneath her skin, an earthquake of unease shook her.

"Do I look okay?" she asked Betty.

"Oh, yes. You look beautiful! And our boys are so excited to have some time to play together."

"Are you sure you're okay watching Jay tonight?" Enna asked, knowing the answer would be a definite "Yes."

Betty's head bounced with enthusiasm as Enna continued speaking.

"Oh, and please keep Jay away from computers and phones. He has seizures sometimes if he is exposed to screens for too long,"

"Oh dear, what should I do if he has a seizure?" Betty's eyes dipped in concern.

"Well, as long as he stays away from the devices he should be fine. Usually, when he has seizures, I just have to wait it out, but please call me if it happens. Actually, I can stay if it stresses you out. I can cancel," Enna said, almost hopeful.

"No worries, you just focus on having fun tonight."

Enna tugged her mouth into a forced smile before heading to the back room to find Jay playing with Ben.

"It's about time for me to go, buddy. Can I have a goodbye hug?" Enna opened her arms wide. He leaped up and threw his arms around his mother.

"You look pretty, Mommy," Jay complimented.

"Thanks, Baby. Can I have kisses?" Enna said. At the same time, the doorbell rang.

"You get three kisses," Jay said. He planted a kiss on one hand and then the other. He finished the sequence off with a kiss on her cheek.

With one last hug, Enna took a deep breath and rushed to answer the door.

***

Enna's face grew warm as she gazed upon her date. He stood, over-dressed head to toe in a fancy tuxedo with a ruby satin vest and pleated pants. He wore expensive dress shoes, and his usual mess of hair was trimmed short with slightly extra length on the very top of his head, giving him a sophisticated look.

The change in hairstyle reminded her of the drawer of wigs he kept at his house.

Maybe I should just ask him about that. Would that be too weird? Probably. He does look handsome, though. His hair doesn't look fake. Wait a second... Enna glanced down at her outfit and then back at Nick.

"What! You told me to dress casual! Why are you wearing that?" Enna's cheeks flushed.

In jest, Nick adopted an offended demeanor, answering with a touch of haughtiness.

"Jeez, no, 'Wow, you look amazing, Nick?' Ha...Nah, I'm kidding. You look perfect, don't worry. It's all part of my plan. Mmm hmm."

Plan? What plan? Is he going to take me to a field and murder me? Or is he going to do worse? Ack! What am I even thinking?

He offered an elbow like a fine gentleman. "My lady," he said royally. Enna hesitated, calculating the risk involved. His eyes held no malice, only humor.

Okay, I can do this.

Weaving her hand through his arm, she allowed him to guide her to his bright yellow Mazda.

Fear gurgled in Enna's chest as she realized she would be completely alone in the car with Nick. However, thoughts quickly formed to combat her urge to run.

Remain calm. This will be fun. And if it goes bad, I can easily take this guy out. At least I have my pepper spray.

The thought of pepper spraying Nick for a second time made her chuckle out loud.

"What's so funny?" Nick glanced curiously in her direction.

Enna gave a sly smile and chuckled again. "Oh, nothing."

Nick shook his head and laughed. "You are a silly girl." Opening the passenger side door for Enna, he gestured for her to enter with a dramatic sweep of the arm.

"Hey, I don't like being called silly," Enna said.

Nick cringed, "Oh, sorry. I'm horrible at flirting, remember? Now are you still wanting to come with me?" He asked, still holding the door open.

"It's okay, but before I get in the car with you, I need to know two things and I would like to check your vehicle for weapons," Enna said.

Nick froze with a puzzled look on his face.

"Do you think I'm a crazy ax-murder dude or something? Cuz, well…I'm not," Nick showed his most innocent expression, "But if it'll make you feel better, go for it. You can check for weapons. And what do you need to ask me?"

Nick continued holding the door ajar as Enna peeked in the glove compartment and side pockets of the doors.

"Where are you taking me on our date?" she asked while still searching the car.

"Oh, yeah, we are going shopping at a small store down the road. Then I was thinking of taking you out to eat. Does that sound good?" Nick asked.

Enna finished scanning for weapons with a satisfied grin. She straightened up to face Nick. The car door stood as a barrier between them.

"Alright, shopping is a strange date but I guess I expected strange from you." She smiled. "Okay, last question. Is your hair real?"

"What?" Nick laughed at the random question. "Why would you think my hair is fake?" Enna shifted her eyes to the ground.

Oh my gosh! I can't believe I asked him that. What is my brain doing to me? He is going to think I'm insane or something. Enna glanced up quickly to see if Nick was judging her. His face just beamed, thoroughly amused.

I need to say something. I made this so awkward.

"Uhh, well. First of all, your hair looks different than it did when you asked me out. And second…"

Abort! Abort! Don't say anything else. Just drop it. He's going to think you're a crazy stalker. Enna's words halted in her throat.

"And second, what?" Nick prodded.

"Oh, never mind. It's stupid. We can go." Enna started slipping a leg into the car when Nick gently took her arm.

"Wait. Now I'm curious. Why do you think my hair is fake other than me getting a haircut?"

Enna moved her arm away from him and stood up straight so she could see his expression. He was definitely entertained by the situation, but he also had a genuine interest in her thoughts on the matter.

"Okay, fine. When I was cleaning your house last week, I found a drawer of wigs and disguises. I was just wondering what you were doing with all of those." Enna's voice grew more timid as she spoke.

"Wow! You really do think I'm a serial killer, don't you? I'm sorry I give off that vibe," Nick said with a half smile.

Enna had to laugh at her own paranoia. There was nothing serial killerish about him.

"I'm sorry. I'm a dork. Just ignore me. We can go," Enna said quickly.

"No, don't apologize for asking me weird questions. You can ask me anything and I will try to answer the best I can. But, yeah, my hair is completely real. I just like to collect wigs and costumes for theater purposes. You can pull on it if you want," Nick offered, bending his head toward her.

Though he was joking, Enna thought about giving it a tug anyway but chose to move on.

"No, that would be too weird for a first date," she blushed. "We should probably get going."

"Okay, then," Nick said in a 'You're crazy, but I kind of like it' voice. Enna took a deep breath and slipped inside the vehicle.

After a very short ride downtown, Nick stopped the car in front of a shabby thrift store.

"First stop, let's find a gown for a princess."

Enna looked at him, puzzled. "We are looking for a dress here? That's random," she said.

"Yup, told you we were going shopping. Let's go!" Nick said, hopping out of the car. Enna began to open her door before Nick called out, "No, uh uh uh, opening doors is my job." He rushed over and finished opening the door for her.

"Oh, thanks." The only other guy who had opened doors for her was a sociopath. The comparison created an immediate fear response in her chest.

That's just my past speaking. Not all guys are creeps. Enna had to remind herself before stepping out of the car.

With linked arms, the two of them walked into the store. They weaved past a few other shoppers browsing through shelves of games, movies, electronics, and antiques, which reminded Enna of Oliver's odd shops around the U.S. She still hadn't heard from him recently, which made her nervous.

A guilty pang in her stomach served as a reminder of Oliver's affection for her. She knew he would disapprove of her being with another man.

Brushing the feeling away, Enna and Nick came to a stop near a rack of the most 'unique' dresses Enna had ever seen.

"Oh my gosh, these are awful!" Enna's face glowed as she laughed.

"Fear not, my lady," Nick said. "There is always at least one gem in this pile of stones, and I intend to find it. But first, fashion show!" He grabbed a puffy, hot-pink dress covered with red dots and handed it to Enna.

The pace of her heart quickened and trickles of sweat formed at the roots of her hair. She had been forced into wearing many outfits before against her will. Now, Nick was making her put something of his choosing on for his amusement.

Oh, come on! Drop it! Nick is just trying to make me laugh. That is all. Play along. Go with it... But what if I don't want to?

"Uh, I don't think so. I'm not trying that on. It's so ugly," Enna protested, attempting to remain calm and playful.

"Oh...um. That's okay. You don't have to. I want you to, though, because I don't have a lot of other things planned for this date, but I'll respect your boundaries. We can figure something else out." Nick's smile couldn't hide his disappointment. "You know, I won't judge you either way, right?" Nick calmly lifted his shoulders as though he didn't care.

"Well, no. How would I know that you won't judge me? I don't know you."

"Hm, that's true. We don't know each other yet. But even if I did judge, what would it matter as long as you have fun?"

"Of course, it matters! I don't want people to judge me, especially not you?" Enna nodded in his direction.

"But why?" Nick asked. At the same time, a short, old woman shuffled past them to look through the clothes. He stepped closer to Enna to give the woman more space. "Why do you care what people think?"

"I don't know. I guess I just want to be accepted."

"Okay, I get that, but if I didn't accept you for who you are, wouldn't that just mean you would deserve someone better than me?" Nick's voice dropped into a serious tone. "People who judge you negatively shouldn't have a say in your life."

The old woman's small voice interrupted their conversation.

"That's a smart man you have there. I'd hang onto him if I were you," she commented as she slipped by and left the area.

Embarrassed by the old woman, Enna ducked her head. She scraped her teeth together thinking of a response for Nick. However, embarrassment was replaced by a strange confidence as his words shuffled through her mind.

He's right. I care way too much about what other people think of me. I can be silly and random. I'm like that with Jay all the time. Why can't I be that way with Nick? I don't want to ruin his date.

Enna took a deep breath and grinned bravely.

"Fine, you have a good point, I guess. But, If I have to try this on," she shook the dress she held, "then you have to try something on."

"Heh! Fair enough."

Enna wandered around until she found another rack behind the dresses with a few men's clothes hanging up.

Shuffling through them, she cracked up while pulling out a shiny, light green disco shirt with frills on the neck and sleeves.

"Here you go, Mr. Peterson."

"Oh boy," Nick sucked some air in dramatically before taking the heinous shirt from her hands. "Okay. Let's do this."

Enna entered the women's dressing room, locked the door, and transformed into what looked like a diseased ladybug.

Staring in the mirror, her face twisted with a mix of distaste and humor.

Okay, this is not so bad. It's funny. I am wearing this because I want to enjoy myself, not because I have to. Nick said I didn't have to dress up. Look. I can be silly. Enna made a goofy face in the mirror before stepping out of the dressing room. She immediately found Nick posing dramatically in the nasty green shirt she picked out for him.

An unladylike "Ha! You look ridiculous!" Escaped her lips before caring if it was an impolite response.

"What? I'm fabulous!" Nick retorted, winking to let her know he was not offended in the slightest.

"How do you do that?" Enna asked, amazed at Nick's calm demeanor. He put his hands up in confusion.

"Do what?"

"How do you act so confident when you're being weird?" Enna blushed, embarrassed by how rude her comment sounded.

"Ow! Look who's judging who!" Nick playfully acted insulted while his gaze flirted with Enna's shy face.

"Sorry, sometimes words just fall out of my mouth. I'm not judging you, just admiring you," Enna said. Admitting that brought even more warmth to her cheeks.

"You know, it was theater that helped me get out of my shell. I love acting. It just gives me permission to get out of my head and be myself."

"That's awesome. I would love to get out of my head at times."

"Well, my lady, you are with the right guy then. Tonight, you don't have to think about anything except for having a good time. As you said, I'm weird, so I don't mind having weird company." Enna's body filled with a sense of ease as she allowed herself to relax into the unusual date activity.

"Look," Nick pointed to a long mirror on the wall. Together, we look like a watermelon!" Seeing the truth behind the comparison, Enna cracked up so loud that a few of the other shoppers turned to stare.

"Oh my gosh," Enna put a hand over her mouth and tried to control herself.

Nick pulled out his phone. "We need a picture."

"Oh, no way! I am not going to let you take a picture of me in this," Enna resisted, still grinning.

"Oh, come on. We have to remember this moment," Nick argued. He pulled out his phone and turned on the camera. "It will be just for me. I'll never show anyone else. I promise."

Enna threw her arms up over her face to hide. Nick gently moved them away from her face and pleaded his case with puppy-dog eyes.

"Fine, but if it ends up on any social media, I'll never talk to you again." Enna meant it, too.

Nick beamed and put his arm around Enna's shoulder. He pulled her close for a picture and opened his mouth with a gigantic, nerdy smile.

A tingle of adrenaline spiked at the touch of Nick's hand on the skin of her shoulder. She knew she shouldn't let him take the picture, but his touch clouded her better judgment. Throwing caution to the wind, she posed for the selfie.

They spent the next hour trying on the most ridiculous outfits available. At last, they found the gem of dresses.

"This is it." Nick held out a floor-length, navy blue dress toward Enna. She grinned at the beautiful gown.

Excited, she rushed to put it on. The silky fabric flowed gracefully down the curves of her body like a peaceful river.

As she emerged from the dressing room, Nick's eyes brightened. "Whoa!" he breathed.

Enna noticed that he was back in his tuxedo already. The pair of them looked so out of place in the little store, dressed in their fancy outfits.

To distract herself from Nick's glinting eyes, Enna did an exaggerated model walk with a spin and a hip pop.

Nick laughed and found his voice. "You look amazing!"

Enna blushed with a "thank you" and retreated back into the dressing room to return to her regular clothes.

"Keep it on. I'll buy it with you in it," Nick said through the dressing room door.

Enna peeked out of the dressing room with a smirk. "Sorry, I'm not for sale." She winked. Her stomach gave a heave of gratitude. It meant the world to her that she could say those words freely.

Leaving the dress on, Enna let Nick lead the way to the front of the store.

After Nick purchased the beautiful dress for Enna, they drove to the nearest fast-food restaurant, where they elegantly sat to dine on delicious cheeseburgers and fries.

At first, Enna hesitated to eat the food placed before her. She still wasn't sure she trusted Nick, so she stared at the food suspiciously.

"Is there something wrong with the food?" Nick asked. "I promise it's not poisoned."

Enna raised an eyebrow and laughed, trying to hide the fact that she was afraid of that.

"You do realize that telling me something is not poisoned is more suspicious right?" Enna said lightly.

Nick's face turned solemn. "I guess I have no other choice. I must risk my life and taste your food. Don't worry, I don't mind dying for you," Nick said dramatically.

With that, he grabbed Enna's cheeseburger and took a large bite out of it. "Mmmm, delightful," he said with a full mouth.

Enna gasped. "You ate my food!" she said incredulously.

Nick swallowed.

"Huh? I'm still alive. I guess I had better try your fries now, just to be on the safe side." Nick reached for her fries.

Enna grabbed his hand to stop him. "Excuuuse me," Enna said with a sassy voice she picked up from Jay. "I almost never eat this kind of junk food, so when I get a chance, I'm not going to let some cute guy eat all of it, even if it is poisoned."

She grabbed a big pinch of fries and shoved them in her mouth.

Nick's amusement burst from his lips and she found herself compelled to join in, drawing curious glances from nearby tables.

Attempting to let go of her fears about others looking at her, she focused her attention back on Nick.

"So, tell me about yourself, Mr. Peterson. What do you do for a living?" Enna asked.

"Why do you keep calling me Mr. Peterson? You know you can call me Nick?" he asked.

"Yeah, I know. Nick just seems very...informal. I don't know you well enough yet."

"Guess we better change that then." Nick wiped some ketchup off of his chin before addressing Enna's inquiry. "I'm currently a freelance photographer."

"Oh great!" Enna said sarcastically.

"Wow! What's with that response? I get paid good money for it."

"It's not that. I personally just hate getting my pictures taken. I never know where they're going to end up."

Enna picked up her ice cream cone and started licking at it slowly.

"Fair enough. I'll try to remember that. So, you're a pretty private person, aren't you?" Nick finished eating but didn't rush Enna.

"Mm-hmm. Yeah, I don't like people up in my business. I've had a rough past. Seems safer to keep to myself."

Wow, I can't believe I told him that.

Nick's face suddenly grew solemn. "Oh, I'm sorry to hear that. If you want to talk about it, I'm..."

Enna cut him off. "Nope, thank you. I wouldn't want to bring the mood down."

She slurped a large chunk of ice cream so she wouldn't have to say more.

"It doesn't bring the mood down. It just changes the intensity of our relationship. Vulnerability makes our connection different, stronger, but it's okay if now's not the time. I'm listening though, when you're ready. I want to know your brain and experiences."

It was Nick's turn to look away. His eyebrows scrunched in an unreadable expression.

"Wow, you move right on past small talk, don't you?" Enna observed. "Let's just take things one step at a time. Tell me more about yourself. I saw some paintings at your house. Do you like art?"

"Oh, yeah. Well, you already know I like photography, but I dabble in painting just for fun."

"That's cool. My son is pretty good at art. He tried to teach me, but I'm a hopeless case when it comes to being creative."

Their conversation continued long after they had finished their meal. Enna hardly noticed time creeping by. Nick was incredibly easy to talk to.

"Okay, another question. Why did you take me shopping for a first date?" Enna asked.

Nick shrugged his shoulders.

"I wanted to be unique, I guess. I was going to take you to an art museum but figured that would be boring," Nick responded.

Enna let out a timid chuckle. "I am so glad you didn't take me to an art museum," she said.

"Oh yeah? Why is that?"

Enna let out an embarrassed giggle and dropped her gaze to the table. "Um, I don't like the way pictures look at me," She grimaced, embarrassed by the confession.

"Huh, really? Why don't you like the pictures looking at you? They're not alive," Nick asked curiously.

Enna shifted in her seat and took a sip of water. Glancing up, she noticed Nick penetrating her with his handsome eyes again. She held the eye connection for a moment before looking away.

"I just don't like anything or anyone looking at me. It creeps me out." Her shy eyes found their way back to Nick's face. "I can't believe I just told you that." Enna blushed.

Nick nodded and loudly slurped the rest of his Dr. Pepper refill. "You can tell me whatever you want. No judgment here. But I'm still wondering why you don't like eyes looking at you."

Enna shook her head and the joy in her heart dimmed. Dropping her gaze toward the floor, her thoughts swirled into the past. Haunted by a memory, an unpleasant chill drove down her back.

***

Andrew's evil voice whispered, "Come here, child," with a false sense of kindness. As she approached him, he berated her, "Why did you disobey me? Did you think it was funny, or did you think I wouldn't notice?"

His voice remained steady and quiet, but a hint of danger lurked beneath each crispy word.

She purposely denied Andrew a response. He didn't deserve a reaction. The only crime she committed was refusing to wear the scanty lingerie that he set out for her in her chamber.

Tension built as Andrew awaited an explanation or an apology from her. When he got neither, his hand shot up and roughly gripped her chin. He jolted her face up to meet his eyes.

"Look at me!" he shouted, all pretense of kindness shattered. "You can't hide your feelings from me, child! I see the fear in your eyes. You pretend to be brave, but you are a disgusting coward. No wonder no one wants you. Even your dad threw you away. I am the only reason you are alive today. You owe me your life!"

She strained against his grip, trying to look away, but he held fast, bruising her jaw. "Look at my eyes! See my disappointment? You will be punished."

Enna could never forget those black, hollow eyes that held no amount of warmth. She hated him. Every memory of that lifetime made her sick.

***

"Hey, you okay?" Nick's voice dispelled the memory. "You disappeared into your thoughts. Where did you go?" Concern draped down his face.

"Um, yeah. I'm fine. I guess I'm just tired. Maybe we should go? I still need to pick Jay up from Betty's house." Enna stood and took her tray of food to the trash.

"Yeah, but wait." Nick hopped up and followed close behind her. "What were you thinking about? You looked like you were petrified."

"Nothing. I just zoned out," Enna said, wishing he would drop it. Nick pointed a skeptical gaze at her for much longer than she was comfortable with.

Turning her back to Nick, she went to their table, took her cup, and refilled it with light lemonade. Nick also refilled his drink and quietly offered Enna his arm to guide her to the car.

He's still looking at me. He's suspicious. I should make something up. Ugh! I am so bad at lying. Nick opened the door for her with a slight smile before getting in the car himself, still not saying a word.

As Nick drove back to Betty's, a weight grew in Enna's chest.

What is he thinking? I bet he's judging me. And I don't even blame him. He knows I avoided being honest with him. I need to fix this.

"Hey…" Enna spoke up, reaching for the right words to say.

"Yeah?" Nick didn't sound upset but his response was short, frustrated by the sudden mood shift in their date.

"I have some pretty bad PTSD and I have a hard time talking about it. I was just a bit triggered back there. That's all."

Did I say too much? Gosh, I said too much!

"Oh." Nick's voice changed to pure compassion. "I'm so sorry to hear that. I can understand not wanting to talk about it." He took a deep breath before speaking again. "It makes me sad, though. I wish you would tell me more about it so I won't trigger you in the future."

Enna shook her head slightly and stayed silent as she organized her thoughts. Nick waited for her to respond, but after getting nothing, he cleared his throat.

"I don't want to overstep, but...I just feel like..." He cleared his throat again. "Sorry, I don't know how to word this because I don't want you to feel pressured or anything."

"It's okay. You can tell me," Enna whispered, shy and vulnerable.

"Okay. I had some trauma in my life too from my childhood and the only way I healed was by talking about it with my therapist." He took his eyes off the road for just a moment to look at Enna.

"I'm not saying you need therapy. That's for you to decide." He looked back at the road. "I just feel like keeping too much pain inside could be harmful. I know we just met, but I'm a good listener. It might be good to talk to someone."

Enna reverted her gaze out the car window, not knowing what he expected her to say. *Of course, it would be good to talk about everything. I wish I could. Oh, Nick. My life is too complicated.*

"Enna, you don't have to guard yourself from me. I..." Nick's words trailed off. Enna glanced at him in time to see a blank expression take over his face. He swallowed hard and kept focused on the road.

Enna waited for him to continue, but Nick pressed his lips together as though he'd said too much.

"Thank you. Really," Enna muttered as they pulled into the parking lot in front of Betty's house. "I have talked to a psychiatrist before about some things. I just...I don't know. There are some things I just can't talk about. You know?"

"It's okay, Enna. I can respect your boundaries. I'm glad you got to meet with a psychiatrist about your PTSD. I hope that helped."

Enna nodded with a slight smile as a thick silence entered the car. Nick stared at her with kind, sensitive eyes, but he didn't say anything. Enna bit at her nails for a moment without leaving the car.

"I had fun tonight," Enna admitted suddenly, not wanting to end the date on such a strange note.

Nick's face brightened. "Oh, yeah? Me too. Sorry if I pried too much into your personal life. I tend to do that. I just want to know you more."

"I want to know you better too, Nick."

"Really? Does that mean I might still get a second date?" he asked hopefully.

Enna cocked her head playfully to the side as though searching for a very difficult answer.

"Well, I only pepper sprayed you in the face once, so I'm only obligated to go on the one date with you. We are even now, unless you would like me to pepper spray you again?" Enna pursed her lips into a smirk.

Nick considered his options for a moment. "Sure, you can spray me again if that means you go on another date with me. It would be totally worth it."

Blood rose to Enna's face for the hundredth time that night. Her cheeks were sore from smiling too much.

"How about, I just let you take me out on another date because I kind of like you," Enna said, grateful for the mood lifting.

"Sounds like a plan." Nick's eyes glimmered brighter with joy. "I should probably let you go so you can get your son to bed." Nick got out of the car and rushed to open Enna's door. He walked her to Betty's front porch.

"Thank you for tonight," Enna said sincerely.

"Yeah, you're welcome. Thanks for coming with me. You're fun company," Nick said with a dorky grin.

"You too." Enna stood holding her lemonade in one hand and the regular clothes she had worn at the beginning of the date in the other. "I guess I'll see you later."

She lingered in an uneasy stance, not knowing quite how to end the date.

"Um, do we shake hands or hug or something? I actually haven't done this," Enna said, anxiously tapping a toe on the ground.

"Oh, um. I like hugs. I mean, I'm happy with whatever you are comfortable with. Your hands are a bit full for hugs, though," Nick said with respect.

"Okay, I'll just… here." She set her things down on the porch and stood back up to lock eyes with Nick.

Drawing nearer, he surrounded Enna securely in his arms, pulling her into a tender embrace.

At first, she stiffened, scared of the physical affection he showed. However, once she assured herself she was safe, her timid arms relaxed on his back and a wave of shivers spread up her spine.

Usually, those shivers were accompanied by fear, but this time, it pushed thrilling adrenaline throughout her whole body, kind of like how it felt after winning a match in martial arts.

Nick suddenly stepped away with a surprised look on his face.

"What?" Enna asked. Nick shook his head and his lips rose into a subtle smile.

"I think…I…I like you…more than I expected. Ha. I'd better go." He turned on his heels with a wave and darted back to his car, leaving Enna staring after him as he drove away.

"Oh boy," she whispered as the excitement of the night settled into her skin.

16

Senses

Enna sat on the cot with her face glued to her cell phone. Imaginary bubbles tickled her belly, causing a bright smile to be plastered on her face.

"You're doing it again, Mommy," Jay said. Sticking his face right in front of Enna's nose, he blocked her view of the phone.

"Huh? Doing what?" Enna asked cheerfully.

"Smiling at your phone like a weirdo." He put his fist on his chin and gave Enna his most innocent smirk.

"Oh really? I'm not a weirdo," Enna grinned and gently pushed Jay's head out of the way so she could skim through the plethora of messages she had received from Nick over the last few days. A flurry of excitement sent a wash of warmth to her cheeks, making her giggle like a high school girl who had just been asked to prom.

"Uh...yeah, you're pos-tivly abs-lutely weird, Mommy, but a good weird!" Jay said with wide, zany eyes. "Are ya gonna to make me lunch? I'm starving so bad!"

"Oh, yeah. What do you want to eat?" She set her phone down and walked to the kitchen.

"Can you make Mac-and-Cheese?" Jay asked.

"What? Since when do you like Mac-and-Cheese? That's not real food. I can make soup or chicken," Enna answered, opening the fridge to see what was available.

"Ben's mom makes the bestest Mac-and-Cheese ever!" Jay exaggerated his words by waving his hands through the air.

"Well, I'd rather you not eat that kind of food anymore. I'll make some healthy food for you to bring to Ben's house for dinner tonight," Enna said.

Jay's eyes grew wide with excitement. "I get to go to Ben's tonight? Yay! Wait...but why?"

Enna raised her shoulders to her ears with a cheesy smile, barely able to contain her enthusiasm.

"Well, I have another date with Nick. Betty said she is happy to have you over," Enna answered while Jay hopped around excitedly.

"Oh oh, can I go on the date with you?" Jay's grin was so big it almost put Betty's smile to shame.

Enna tightened her lips into a concerned grimace. "Aw, no, sorry Baby. Not this time. I already told Ben you were coming over to play."

Despite Jay's protests, Enna prepared an extra large lunch so he would have enough leftovers for dinner later on.

As the date drew closer, anxiety mixed with her excitement of seeing Nick.

Oh, what am I doing? I shouldn't be falling for this guy. But what if he is good for me? He could be. Maybe I'm not good for him, though. I could be putting him in danger just by being around him. Uhg.

***

A few hours later, Enna found herself back in Nick's car, her heart going wild with anticipation.

"Where are we headed today?" Enna asked.

Nick flashed a dashing smile. He wore casual clothes today but other than that, Enna had no hint as to what their activity would be for the night.

"I thought it would be fun to take you to an improv comedy performance. I'm really into acting, hence the wigs you saw at my house.

Those were from past roles I've played. I promise they are not for covering up my bald head or anything like that. These luscious locks are all natural." He ran his fingers through his hair dramatically for effect. "However, I do think I would make a rather dashing blonde, don't you think?" Nick said cheerfully.

Enna ducked her head as the memories of her cringe-worthy inquiries about the authenticity of his hair came back to haunt her.

Once he noticed Enna's cheeks flushing in embarrassment, he quickly moved on to the next topic.

"Anyway, I really want to learn how to do improvisation, but when I tried it before, it was horrible. I stuttered so much the audience probably wanted to throw me off the stage. No kidding." He chuckled at his memory. "Heck, I wanted to throw myself off the stage. I don't do well with being funny on purpose. I come off a little…"

"Nuts?" Enna filled in.

That cracked Nick up. "Yeah, yeah. I come off a little nuts, but hey, at least improv is still fun to watch even though I suck at it."

"Ah, I see. I've never been to an improv comedy show before," she admitted.

"Well, this will be an interesting experience for you," Nick said.

An uncomfortable silence filled the car. Neither of them spoke for what seemed like hours to Enna but was only seconds in real-time.

Shifting through her mind, she desperately tried to think of something else to say. She had planned to ask Nick so many questions, but now that she was with him, her mind went blank.

Say something! Ask him to tell me more about acting. No, we kind of just talked about that. He will think I am boring. Uhg! Okay, keep it simple. Nothing too complicated. Ready, Go!

"So tell me more about you, Nick. What is your favorite color?" Enna said, proud that she broke the silence.

"Ummm, the brightest yellow you could possibly imagine. What about you?" Nick shot back.

"Black," Enna answered without hesitation.

Nick laughed.

"So we are opposites then. Nice!" Nick said.

"Wait, isn't white the opposite of black?" Enna asked.

"I guess you could say that, but I don't count white as a color because it's lame. So yellow is the next closest to being the opposite of black, and opposites attract, right?" Nick said.

"Your logic is outstanding," Enna said sarcastically, her eyes twinkling in humor.

"Ha! Okay, I have a question for you now," Nick said. "What is something unique about you?"

Enna scrunched her face up to think.

Well, there's a lot unique about me, but not much I can admit to. I am an MMA champion. Too bad that's from another life.

"I don't know, I'm just boring," Enna said, lifting her shoulders in defeat.

"I don't believe that for one second," Nick laughed. "You are an intricately woven puzzle, Enna Anderson, and I want to see the complete picture of you."

A hint of sorrow entered her chest. *I wish I could help you put the pieces together. I want to be real with you, but I can't give you too much.*

Her mind scraped to find an answer that was both true and wouldn't give her secrets away.

"Okay, I have a stupid one. Don't laugh." Enna gave Nick a shy side-eye glance.

"Me, laugh? Never!" He teased.

"Well, I hate swear words. If you hear me swear, I suggest running in the opposite direction because I've completely lost it by that point."

"Oh? Good to know. Why don't you like swearing?" Nick asked seriously.

Not expecting the return question, Enna blurted out the unfiltered answer.

"My dad was a mean drunk. He would curse at me and call me horrible things when he had too much to drink, so, I 'swore' that I would never be like that. Get it? I 'swore' that I would never swear. Word-play?" Enna tried to cover up the heavy undertone the conversation took by making a dumb joke.

"Wow, that's really cool you would learn from your dad's mistakes that way. You are very wise. I think that's an important 'Enna' puzzle piece for me to know. Sorry, you had to go through that," Nick said, taking his eyes off the road for a second to let Enna know he meant the compliment.

"Thanks, now what about you? What makes you unique?" Enna flipped the conversation back on him.

He had an answer at the ready. "Santa creeps me out. Like, really, some fat dude sneaks into houses through the chimney? I don't want a stranger in my house, even if he does offer gifts." He feigned a shiver. "And people dressed like Santa could be any old perv. You never know. It's just...creepy."

Nick's face exaggerated the fear he was talking about, leaving Enna cracking up and nodding in agreement.

"You're not wrong. Santa is a weird concept. I kicked Santa once when my parents tried to make me sit on his lap when I was a kid. Then I ran away."

Enna loved laughing with Nick. Opening up to him about the real person underneath her facade was exhilarating.

"Oh really? You, sweet Enna, kicked Santa? I bet your parents were thrilled."

"No, they were horrified!"

Laughing, their conversion stayed alive as they took turns quizzing each other.

Enna tried her best to be truthful without going too deep into her past. However, Nick was too good at asking the most difficult questions.

"So, you have a son. Does he have a father involved?" Nick asked. Enna shifted her eyes down before answering.

"Oh, no. Jay's adopted," Enna hoped she sounded nonchalant.

"Cool. Have there been other men in your life? Boyfriend, fiancé, husband?"

"Ha, wow." Enna bit her lip, thinking of the right response.

Another question to lie about. There's Andrew, who pretended we were married after I denied him. And, well, there's Oliver. We weren't technically ever together, but we wanted to be. Does that count? No, I can't bring Oliver into this. Enna shook her head, frustrated at her need to lie.

"Nope, what about you? You told me you had a fiancé once? Tell me more about that," Enna bounced the question back his way.

"Wait, you're twenty-six, drop-dead gorgeous, and never been in a relationship before? I find that hard to believe." Nick tilted his head, curious.

Enna choked on a swallow and her breath momentarily clogged her throat. *Oh, come on, Nick. Just drop it!*

"I...I don't really know what to tell you. I'm just not the relation-ship type," *please don't ask any more questions about it.* Enna sent Nick a snarky smile on accident.

"Okay, then," Nick said, his expression indicating obvious disbe-lief. Before the conversation could continue, Nick stopped his car at their destination.

"Here we are," Nick said before getting out to open Enna's car door. "You're going to love it. They're called the Banter Bunch and they are hilarious!" Nick left the uncomfortable discussion behind and led the way to the ticket line.

Once Nick paid for their seats, they entered a small, dim au-ditorium. Loud music blasted over the speakers, breaking Enna's eardrums. The seating was so tight they had to climb over laps to find open seats for the both of them. Enna squished in between Nick and a round man with a walrus face. The air was thick and warm and the tight perimeter made Enna's pulse rush with anxiety.

Calm down, Enna. Just focus on the show. Enna faked a smile for Nick's benefit as the music faded.

A man bounced to the stage in a wave of applause.

"Well hel-looo Provo! I'm Randy!" he shouted over the crowd.

"Hello, Randy!" the audience replied in unison.

"Are you ready to laugh?" he asked.

"Lets! Banter!" Everyone but Enna shouted as though they were following a script she hadn't yet received.

Randy wandered the stage, peering at the audience as if trying to figure out who he would eat for dinner.

"So I want to know, who's new to improv? If you've never been to a show like this before, Give us a shout!"

Nick nudged Enna expectantly as a few audience members cheered.

"Oh, come on, you can do better than that." Randy put a hand to his ear and leaned in.

"Woo!" they called.

Enna unenthusiastically expelled a small "Yep" from her mouth that not even Nick could hear.

"Okay, okay, that will have to do. So, for those who don't know how this works, our cast is completely unscripted and unrehearsed. We thrive off of audience participation. You give us the theme and we roll with it."

How does Nick like this? The show hasn't even started yet and I already want to leave.

Enna resisted the urge to cover her ears as Randy shouted at them with way more vigor than anyone should be comfortable with.

"Now, let's practice! I'm going to ask some questions and your job is to just call the answers out. No raising hands, please. We don't do that here. When something comes to your brain, just throw it out there even if it would disappoint your grandma! Who's ready?!"

Enna squirmed in her seat, not liking the thought of being quizzed as part of this irritating game. However, Nick looked absolutely delighted as he cheered with the crowd.

"First question, 'kay, listen up. What is the name of your favorite rock band?"

Several answers bounced around the room while Randy picked a few out to repeat into the microphone.

"Skillet, alright, alright! Keep it coming! Brittany Spears? What? She's not a rock band! Disturbed? Ha, well, that makes sense by looking at you..."

The game continued. Enna felt increasingly more out of place with each question she left unanswered.

Nick didn't seem to notice her unease as he called out answers of his own.

"Monkey!" he yelled after they asked about animals that created chaos.

"Okay! Great! So we have a disturbed Britney Spears with a monkey. I think we can work with that! Can we please give a warm welcome to..." The music grew as Randy gestured off stage, "The Banter Bunch!"

The crowd roared while a team of four men and two women raced onto the stage and down the aisles, high-fiving random audience members.

Enna ducked low in her seat, overstimulated by the motion all around her.

After they made a few laps around the auditorium, the actors made their way back to the stage and the music faded, causing the audience to settle down.

At that very moment, Enna's phone ringtone sang out from her back pocket, drawing the attention of everyone around her. Without hesitation, she shifted around to reach the phone.

Shut up! Shut up! Shut up! Her face flushed as she accidentally bumped elbows with Walrus man.

"Sorry." Overcorrecting her body position, she practically gave Nick a lap dance as she dug the phone out of her pocket.

Oh, come on! People snickered around her as the phone continued to ring until, finally, she had it in her hand.

Seeing that the call was from Betty, Enna stood abruptly, scanning the room for a quick exit.

No! I'm stuck! I'll have to climb over everyone to get out.

Enna stood for several tortuous seconds before convincing herself to sit back down, painfully letting the call go to voicemail.

What if there is something wrong with Jay and I'm just ignoring it? I'm a terrible mom. Fighting with her conscience, Enna switched the phone to silent mode before it could ring again.

"Well, thank you for that introduction, random phone lady," A new man on stage said, making the audience laugh.

Enna ducked her head, horrified. Nick put his arm around her and whispered in her ear, "You okay?"

Absolutely, Enna's sarcastic inner voice bellowed with a subtle eye roll.

Enna grimaced but nodded "yes" to Nick's question.

His head tilted in disbelief but didn't say anything.

Looking down at her lap, Enna noticed a voicemail notification. She quickly opened it and put the phone to her ear, ignoring the actors introducing themselves on the stage.

After listening to the message, she let out a frustrated breath. Apparently, Jay was fine. He was simply struggling because he didn't want to eat the food she left for him.

Enna started a text to Betty to ask if Jay needed to be picked up early when a cheer erupted all around. Chills crept throughout her body as all the eyes in the room turned back on her.

Stop looking at me. What is wrong with these people? What is going on? She looked to Nick for an answer.

His hazel eyes twinkled as he leaned in, "They want you to go up to the stage for one of their skits," Nick explained.

Enna shrank even further into the chair and shook her head *no.*

The lead actor beckoned to her, "Aww! Don't be shy. All you have to do is sit in this chair and we will do all the work."

The team of actors dramatically gestured toward a chair sitting center stage. The audience laughed at her. She looked at Nick. He was laughing at her, mocking her.

"You don't have to go up there," Nick said, but his face said otherwise.

He will be so disappointed if I don't go up. He'll think I'm a poor sport. I'm not a poor sport! I can do this.

Enna fought for courage and rose to her feet. She pushed past several knees until she was fully exposed in the middle aisle.

Jeers from the crowd grew in intensity as she made her way to the stage and the actors pulled her into the chair.

Trembling, Enna faced the audience. The room spun as fifty pairs of eyes melted into her.

"We are just going to ask you a few simple questions and then we will serenade you with a beautiful made-up song about your life," one of the actors explained.

Breathe. Focus on Nick. Breathe and smile at him. Enna glanced around, looking for him in the audience. However, before her eyes located him, her gaze locked onto a familiar dark silhouette.

Enna's throat contracted. Air no longer moved through her quaking body. That man had the same slicked-back raven hair as the man who haunted her dreams.

She squeezed her eyes shut as the room twisted further. Feeling like she was about to fall over, Enna opened her eyes again to regain balance.

The shadowed man in the audience angled his face into the light. Although his hair resembled Andrew's, the rest of his features did not match. Unlike Andrew's masculine features, this man had a pointy nose and a thin jawline.

I'm okay, I'm okay, she said to herself while rapidly sucking in gulps of air.

"And, I guess we don't get any answers from you tonight, apparently, not even a name. We'll just have to stick with the name Phone

Girl then," Enna vaguely heard one of the actors say. She hadn't heard a question, and her side began to hurt.

She attempted to slow her breathing, which only made her more desperate. Panic dripped over her as she pumped her lungs, gasping for air. She wrapped her arms around her stomach and doubled over.

A warm hand softly gripped her shoulder, keeping her from falling out of the chair.

"Enna, look at me," Nick's voice reached her ear. Enna slit her eyes open to see Nick kneeling next to her. "Let's take deep breaths together. Okay? Breathe in for four and hold for four," He demonstrated the breathing technique. "Now breathe out for four. One two three four. Good, now hold for four."

Enna attempted to follow along with the deep breaths, but her body begged her to grasp the air as fast as she could before it was all gone. She tried to force air in and out of her body, but the shallow breathing refused to feed her need for air.

"What's wrong with her?" Enna heard one of the men on stage say.

"Hey, nothing is wrong with her. She's just having a panic attack," Nick said defensively.

Light-headed, Enna watched as Nick braced her back and knees. His biceps bulged, and she found herself being lifted into the air. Digging her face into Nick's chest, she tried to hide from all the eyes on her as she was carried from the theater.

The whispering from the audience faded as the night breeze greeted her.

"Hey, it's okay. You're safe," Nick said, slowly lowering Enna to a grassy patch in front of the theater.

Nick sat next to her with an arm over her shoulders. Her body gradually regained the ability to bring breath in and out, though it still staggered dramatically.

Enna curled into a fetal position, grabbing at her knees and hiding her face, slightly rocking forward and back as the embarrassment from her panic attack blossomed on her cheeks.

A soft touch swept up and down her spine as Nick gently rubbed her back. "Look, it's just you and me now. Oh, and that old lady walking her ridiculously large dog over there. Oh, wait, it kind of looks like the dog is the one walking her." Nick chuckled.

That got Enna to lift her head to see what he was talking about. Across the parking lot, a frail lady grasped a leash with two hands while a gigantic golden lab excitedly pulled her along the sidewalk.

Enna let a single laugh shoot from her diaphragm.

Nick's hand stopped rubbing her back and he rested it on her waist. A pleasant shudder wrapped around her, calming her still, slightly quaking body.

She glanced up to see a strange expression on Nick's face that she could not quite figure out. It was a forlorn look with a hint of amusement and regret mixed together.

Enna quickly turned her gaze away.

He thinks I'm a freak! she thought.

A stone replaced her heart as she replayed the events of the evening from what she figured was his point of view.

Oh, here's my killjoy date who can't even take a joke. Now I'm here taking care of her instead of watching the show I paid for. Worst date ever!

Enna moaned.

Nick looked at her with a straight face and slightly squeezed her.

He'd be right. I am the worst date ever! I wasn't polite enough to silence my phone for the performance and to make things worse, they called me up to the stage of all people. I ruined the show!

Staring Nick down, Enna aimed to get a better read on him to support her fears. However, what she saw broke her. His lips pressed together in a tight scowl, and his eyes glimmered with a tear not yet released.

He hates me. I'm the first girl he's dated since his ex-fiance left and I completely ruined everything! I deserve to be alone.

Misery caused her heavy heart to seize up. Dropping her head back into her scrunched-up legs, she held back tears of her own. *He is never going to ask me out again. Maybe it's better this way. Dating him was a bad idea anyway. I never should have-*

"I had severe panic attacks all the time when I was a kid," Nick said out of the blue.

Enna peeked one eye toward him. The scowl on his face was gone, replaced by empathy. "I was bullied a lot in school because I was a bit of a nerd."

Enna lifted her head slightly to show Nick she was listening.

Nick cracked a small smile. "Yeah, I know, hard to picture me as a nerd. Right?" He flexed his muscles and accompanied the action with a smirk.

"Nah, just kidding. Sorry, I tend to deflect my emotions by using humor. But anyway, the bullying got so bad that the mere mention of school sent me spiraling. I honestly didn't want to live anymore. Luckily, I had a fantastic mom who taught me to calm myself down by focusing on my five senses."

He took a deep breath through his nostrils. "For example, smell. I can smell some delicious pizza coming from the restaurant next to us."

Enna found herself taking in a whiff of the air along him.

"Ick!" She cringed.

"Oh yeah," Nick continued. "I can also smell something rotten coming from the dumpster over there." He nodded to the source of the stench. "Smells like my old gym coach. I swear, that guy never showered."

A smile crept onto Enna's face.

"The next sense, sight. Hmm?" Nick said. "I see the first star of the night poking its head out to say hello to you." He moved his hand off her waist and pointed up at the sky.

Enna's gaze followed his finger to the star. The pack of anxiety she'd been clinging to rolled up her spine and dissipated out the top of her head, into the night air. As peace replaced anxiety, her body tension released.

"Sound," Nick continued talking about his senses. "Cars passing, wind slightly whistling."

"Your voice, calming my crazy outburst," Enna tried to joke.

Nick grinned. "Not crazy," Nick reassured her. "Unexpected, yeah, but you are not crazy. I've seen crazy, and you are far from it."

Enna giggled and looked down.

"We can't forget touch," Nick said. He slid his hand over and brushed Enna's fingers gently. Her hand twitched as a pleasant shock flowed up her arm. Their hands moved closer together until their fingers entwined as one.

An energy surged around their hands as they sat quietly, enjoying the sensation of simply being connected. The feeling danced its way up her arm and into her wild beating heart.

"Is this okay?" Nick asked, tightening his hold slightly.

Thrown off by the question, Enna's mouth opened incredulously. She'd never had a man ask permission to touch her before.

Freezing the memory in her mind, Enna nodded her permission.

"M'hm, I think touch is my favorite of the five senses," Enna said sheepishly.

"Well, you can't say that yet because you haven't focused on taste yet," Nick said with a sneaky glance.

Enna's first thought was that he was going to kiss her. She would certainly taste that. She recoiled away from him, dropping his hand.

I am not ready for that! She freaked.

Nick cracked up. His face gleamed with innocence as he laughed.

"What did I say? I was just going to suggest getting one of those pizzas that smell so good."

Enna joined in on the laughter at her mistake. She thought about coming up with an excuse for her reaction but realized Nick was not looking for an explanation.

"Pizza sounds lovely," Enna said. Her laughing stopped, but a spark of joy remained in her eyes as Nick helped her up and they set off for food.

17

Road Trip

The wind tied Eric's hair into knots as he cruised with the windows down. Singing along to a Frank Sinatra album, he distracted himself from the anxiety that repeatedly punched his nerves.

He'd been driving several hours but still had an hour to go.

Too bad I couldn't use the helicopter. This would have been so much faster, but then that pig, General Boucher, would wonder what I'm up to.

"I've stopped wars, diffused bombs, intercepted secret intel from leaking into terrorists' hands, but does he care? Nooo. Of course not. And that's why I have no choice. I've got to do this," Eric grumbled to himself as the music played on without his vocal accompaniment.

He went over his plan out loud as if trying to convince himself he was doing the right thing.

"This will work. It has to. Mike's an unloved foster brat, anyway. No one will care if he goes missing, and who knows, maybe the nanobots will adapt to him and he'll be fine. If he's not fine, at least he might be able to help me locate the real project before he dies. Tragic, yes, but not wasted."

Finding Mike was the answer Eric had been searching for. With several generic markers matching Project 19932 and the same age, he was the perfect subject.

"General Pig wants his project back, so I'll give him just that. He doesn't have to know Mike's a fake. I just have to keep him away from the lab nerds."

Eric shook his head. "Stupid techies. They don't even care. Their lives aren't on the line. They would never approve of human trials. 'Too dangerous.' Well, buddy, do you know what else is dangerous? Getting killed by an over-controlling corrupted general!"

Eric honked his horn at the car going five under the speed limit in front of him before zipping around it.

He quivered with anticipation, stealing a glance at the pill bottle resting on the seat next to him, containing his precious Adderall.

Despite his attempts to break free from the medication, this month, with his very existence at stake, proved too overwhelming to resist.

Reaching over, he dangerously let go of the steering wheel to open the bottle. Popping two pills in his mouth, he grabbed a nearby water bottle to wash the pills down.

With each passing minute, Eric persisted in his self-dialogue, struggling to remain awake after an entire sleepless night until the voice of his GPS abruptly interrupted his monologue.

"Your destination is on the right."

Eric had been so caught up in his conversation with himself that he hardly noticed he had made it to the small city of Petersburg, Virginia, where the boy's foster mom, Tabatha Bennet, resided.

Pulling up to a crusty white house, Eric dragged his aching legs out of the car and cracked his stiff neck before approaching their run-down door.

At the door, he froze. "No, I can't do this. I'm not a bad person! I can't just kidnap a kid for my own gain."

He found himself back in his car, breaking into his pill bottle once more to take a double dose. After swallowing the Adderall, he regained his motivation. "This is my last resort. General gave me no choice."

Exiting the car once more, Eric made his way back to the door. Taking a deep breath, he balled his fist and pounded the door.

"D.C.F.S. Open up!" he shouted.

When there was no answer, Eric called out again and slammed his fist harder, threatening to crack the door with each strike.

"Open up this door before I break it down!"

Scrambling feet shuffled around on the other side of the door before a large, pale lady yanked it open, wearing nothing but a towel that was much too small for the rolls on her body.

"'Scuse me, it's seven in the friggen morning! I get ta shower once a week and this is my once and ya disturbin' me. Ya better have a dang good reason to be disturbin' my showerin' time."

A dollop of spittle launched its way to Eric's face as she snapped at him.

"Ma'am, I need you to calm down now. I'm from Child Protective Services. We've gotten several calls about you mistreating a child you are fostering," Eric said with his authoritative voice. "I am here to take the child with me."

"Listen, sir, whoever ya are, I may look like a mess, but I am telling ya, I treat my boy with the utmost respect and love. He loves it here. I'm the closest thing to a mama that boy's ever had and you ain't telling me that ya gonna take him from me just 'cuz some stupid nosy neighbors can't keep their business to themselves. I knew they din't like me, but this is just low!"

Looking over her shoulder, she called out, "Mike, Mike! Lock yerself in the bedroom and don' come out til' I tell ya ta."

Turning back to Eric, she folded her arms sternly. "See, ya ain't gettin' em. So bye! Let the door hit ya on yer way out!"

"Lady, I do not have time for this," Eric said through gritted teeth. "Move aside, or else someone is going to get hurt."

"You ain't from D.C.F.S, are ya? I'm callin' the cops."

The woman backed away to find her phone.

With patience running dry, Eric pulled out his gun and held it above the woman's nose. "Enough games. Bring me Mike, or else I shoot. It's your choice."

The lady's eyes bulged. She opened her mouth several times to speak, but no words came out.

Eric cocked the gun, making the lady flinch. Her neck fat jiggled as she shook her head a few times.

"Now, just hold on a minute," her voice squeaked. "What do ya plan ta do with the boy?"

A pitter-patter of feet came from down the hall. "Mike! What'd I tell ya? Go ta yer room!"

Eric lowered his gun to his side. For a moment, relief spread across Tabatha's face. She did not enjoy the relief for long. With the weapon still low to his side, Eric pointed the barrel up and pulled the trigger.

Tabatha's eyes glazed over as the bullet entered her chin. Her body toppled backward onto the floor just as a young, dark-skinned boy with curly brown hair came into view.

"Hey Mike," Eric said, trying to keep a calm demeanor while his heart pounded against his chest. He put his weapon away with a shaking hand. "Look what you did. How could you kill your foster mom?"

Mike's lips parted and his eyes widened in shock and confusion. He looked at his dead guardian, up at Eric, and then back to his guardian again.

"I don't kill 'er," Mike muttered.

Eric waited for more of a reaction. He expected the kid to scream and cry at the loss of his foster mom, but there was no response other than a blank expression from the child.

"Of course, but you got her killed. The police will be here to take you away soon unless you come with me." Eric motioned for Mike to follow him. "Come on. We'll go get ice cream. How does that sound?" Eric gave the boy a friendly smile.

Mike looked at the lady one more time before shrugging his shoulders. Without a word, he followed Eric to the black BMW in the driveway.

Eric's mission-driven mindset sealed his emotions up so tight that the guilt coursing through him for killing Tabatha got choked out, leaving him cold and hollow inside.

Leaving the body in place, Eric hoped Mike would be blamed for her death. *Accidental shootings happen all the time. Right?*

***

Back at Eric's condo, Mike sat on the counter, slurping the last drips of ice cream off of his fingers while Eric prepared a syringe containing the final vial of nanobots suspended in a saline solution. Once he located a suitable vein in Mike's arm, he slowly pressed the needle down. The boy hardly let out a peep as the serum entered his bloodstream.

"Wow, kid, you are very odd, aren't you? Most children would be screaming to get out of a shot." Eric pulled the needle out of the kid's arm.

Mike just lifted his shoulders in another shrug and said nothing.

"Well, we are all set. Let's wait a bit and see what happens, shall we?" Eric looked at the clock and cringed. General Boucher would be calling soon for his weekly barrage of insults and threats. Unfortunately, the nanobots would need a few days to blend with Mike's genes.

"I need you to do something for me so the police don't find you. Okay?"

Mike's eyes widened with intense concentration on what his instructions would be.

What am I doing? I've ruined this kid's life, framing him for murder and possibly poisoning him beyond repair. Wow, I've turned into a complete monster.

"Mike, I know this is hard for you to understand, but you are the key to setting me free. I had to do this for both our sakes. You didn't want to live with that mess of a woman any more than I want to live paying for the mistakes of others. We are in this together."

Mike blinked a few times, eyes wide in confusion.

"Oh, whatever. I don't know why I'm justifying myself to you. Are you ready for your instructions?" Eric stared Mike down.

Instead of holding the gaze, the child's eyes wandered up to the ceiling.

Eric moved his head, trying to reconnect with Mike but the kid just moved his eyes again, this time to the microwave to the side of him.

Growling, Eric held onto both sides of Mike's head and forced his face to look directly in front of him.

"Look at me, kid! This is important. I just put miniature computer particles inside of you," Eric informed the boy, who still struggled to meet his eyes. "You are Project 19932 now. That is your name, not Mike. You have been missing for four years and I finally found you. Do you understand anything I'm saying?"

Mike stayed quiet, making no indication that he had heard Eric.

"You don't need to be scared. No one wants to hurt you. You will be protected here. Now, my boss is going to call to check on you. All you have to do is pretend to sleep. Do not move. Do not make a sound. I will convince my boss that you are too tired to show off your techno-logical advances. You should be able to give him a demonstration in a few days, but not today. Just sleep. Do I make myself clear?"

Mike gave a soft "Uh-huh" and stared blankly up at Eric. It was the first time their eyes truly connected. The child's face sent a chill through Eric's back. The child had no expression. Mike had unemo-tional, dead eyes, just like him.

"Fantastic," Eric said, a sour prick of discomfort taking the power out of the excitement he thought he should feel.

18

Remote Control

Jay's fingers struggled to twist the screwdriver and hold the screw still at the same time. He knew he could do it. He screwed all the other tires on except for this last one that was being dumb and not going on right.

His flimsy fingers worked diligently to steady the stubborn tire so the screw would go in.

Stinkin' thing! Go on already. Jay scrunched his eyes in determination and slowly made progress getting the screw to hold the tire in place.

Whoo! Yes, I did it.

"Mommy, Mommy, Come look!" He gently jiggled the controller with his index finger, and the car jumped to life.

Zoom! The remote control car darted across the floor and dove into the living room.

Jay followed, squealing from joy at his creation. However, his excitement broke off after seeing his mother asleep on the cot.

"Ah, seriously!" Jay pouted as his brain twisted with conflict. He really wanted to show his mom what he made, but waking a sleeping mommy was dangerous business. He needed to proceed with caution.

From previous experience, Jay had learned that kissing his mom awake or touching her face would result in her pinning him to the ground in panic mode. Not fun!

There was also the beatboxing trick where he made noises and funky beats right next to her until his mom submerged from slumber with fury in her eyes. It didn't matter how superb his beatboxing was. She would still be angry.

Jay clicked his teeth together as he considered his options. His mom didn't leave him with many choices. He could hear her strict voice in his head loud and clear...

"The only reason you should ever wake a sleeping woman up is if there is an emergency!"

Jay's body wriggled with impatience.

She is always sleeping, or on a date. She won't mind if I talk to her now. I can pat-tend it's an 'mergency.

Carefully, he crept over to his sleeping Mommy and uncovered her toes. He took hold of the biggest toe and yanked.

He waited with anticipation for a second but his mommy did not respond.

He grabbed the next toe and pulled.

Jay continued this for the next two toes before her foot disappeared back into the blanket.

Uncovering her feet once again, he continued to pull against her toes.

"What do you think you are doing?" A hushed growl came from the sleeping mommy. "This had better be an emergency."

"Yeah, but kind-ah, but, no. Hon'stly, I just really wan'ned ta talk to you," Jay said innocently.

A groan expelled from Enna's lips. She mumbled something about never waking her up and pushed herself to a sitting position.

"What is it?" she snapped.

"Okay, okay, don't be mad, but I couldn't wait. It jus' way too cool!" Jay placed his car on the ground and prepped it for a demonstration.

"Look, look! I finished making my 'mote control car, and it really works! Watch dis!"

He wiggled the controller knobs and the car burst into action. It zoomed under the cot and then reversed and circled around the room before disappearing into the kitchen.

Mommy showed a sleep-ridden smile. "That is quite amazing, Baby. You made that all by yourself?"

"Yeah! All by myself."

"I'm surprised your little fingers were strong enough to put all the pieces together. You are pretty incredible." Pride dripped from her voice, making Jay's body bounce in a celebratory dance.

"Can we go on a walk so I can drive it 'round?" Jay asked just as the doorbell rang.

His mom looked at the time and gasped.

"Crap, It's 9:00 already! I'm supposed to be going to breakfast with Nick right now."

She jumped out of bed and started rummaging around in her suitcase for clothes. "Hurry, get dressed. I'm going to take you to Ben's house."

Jay put on his best pouty face and waited for his mom to notice his distress. Unfortunately, she was too busy to pay attention to the jutted lip and trembling eyes that Jay demonstrated. He needed to get her attention in a more effective way, so he let out a long moan, making his mom look in his direction with an irritated glare.

"You never have time for me anymore," Jay complained. "You're always with that stupid guy, an' I feel like you don't like me anymore."

"That's not fair. You know I still love you! You are my favorite boy in the whole world, but sometimes, even mommies need to have friends."

She ruffled his hair before shouting at the door, "One minute, Nick, I'll be there in a sec!" And she threw clothes onto Jay's protesting body.

"Hey, go get your shoes on."

Jay dragged his feet to the kitchen and retrieved his remote-control car while his mom went to find clothes for herself.

"I thought I was your friend." He trudged over to his mom's cot and melted into it. His finger began spinning one of the tires on his car, feeling utterly rejected.

His mom came into the room and knelt down next to him.

Jay looked away from her with a scowl.

Nick knocked on the door but Mommy paid no attention to it.

"You are always my number one boy. I've been thinking a lot lately that, well, Nick and I have been seeing each other for a couple of months now. It might be time to let you come with us on one of our dates. How would you feel about that?"

Jay's heart widened to welcome the excitement his mom just offered him. Jumping up from the cot, he bounced with an energetic vigor. "Yes, yes, yes, yes!" He ran to the front door and started to unlock it.

"Whoa, hey there, buddy! Are you supposed to open the door without peeking out first?" She took his hand away from the lock.

"Oh, sorry, Mommy." Running to the window, Jay scrambled up a chair and brushed the curtain aside to see Nick holding a picnic basket.

He was again wearing funny clothes: khaki pants and a light blue t-shirt covered with pineapples and bulldog heads.

I love pineapples and dogs! Cool!

Jay waved wildly out the window, catching Nick's attention. He waved back. Jay waved harder, but Nick matched his waving intensity and speed. Jay raised his second hand and waved both as fast as he could.

The waving competition was still heating up as Mommy opened the door, catching Nick doing a massive wave with his entire arm.

Jay's hysterical laugh blended with Nick's greeting.

"Oh, hey!" Nick put his hand down. "There you are! I was afraid you slipped out the back to avoid me or something."

Mommy giggled and shook her head.

"And why would I do that?" she said in her flirty voice.

Before Nick had a chance to respond, Jay galloped over to him. "Mommy says I get to go with you today!"

Nick quickly disguised his look of surprise by holding up a hand for a high five. "Sweet! More the merrier."

Jay gave Nick the hardest high five he could muster. At the impact, Nick showcased a walloping display of hand pain by flinging it around and blowing on his fingers as though they were on fire.

"Whoa, Dude! You have a strong high five. My fingers are stinging," Nick whined playfully while winking at Mommy.

Jay gazed up at his laughing mom. Awe! *She looks so pretty and happy*. He grinned at the sight.

"Is that alright if Jay comes with us? I can bring some extra food for the picnic," Enna asked Nick, who was already nodding.

"Of course, he can come. He's always welcome." Nick patted Jay's fluffy head.

Mommy smiled a thank you and rushed to get some food for Jay from the fridge.

"Look what I made!" Jay said as he remembered his car. Grabbing the controller, he prepped the car and showed off how fast it could zip around the living room.

Nick's eyes grew wide. "You made that?" Disbelief made his mouth open.

In the kitchen, Mommy dropped a jar of peanut butter and it rolled a few feet before stopping. "Ha no, we bought it...of course. He just likes to pretend that he made it." She scrambled for the peanut butter jar.

Jay brought his car to a halt on top of Nick's feet and stuck out his lip at his mother's lie. "Uh-uh! I made it all by myself," he said stubbornly.

His mom laughed as though he was telling a joke, which made him really mad. He scrunched his nose into a gruesome sneer until Nick leaned in close to Jay and whispered, "I believe you. That is pretty impressive. Maybe you can teach me how to make one so we can race."

Jay's face lit up. "Ok, first you will need to get the parts. You need a-" Jay began.

His mom cut him off before he could say anymore. "Hey, look at the time. Let's go eat before too many people are crowding the park." She marched out the front door with a blanket draped over her arm.

"Later, okay? Seems like your mom's anxious to get going," Nick said before taking off to catch up with Mommy.

"I really did make it myself!" Jay yelled, standing back for a moment with a betrayed look on his face.

Mommy doesn't like my smartness. I wish I were normal. His shoulders slumped.

"Come on, Jay, I'm locking the door," Mommy started slowly closing the door.

"Nooo! Wait for me!" Driving his remote-control car, he followed the adults out.

After Mommy locked the door, Jay froze. *No! Nick stole Mommy's hand right out from under my eyes!*

His face scrunched in fury as he watched the two of them walk off without him.

Growling, Jay shot his car forward between the two love birds and brought it to a halt right in front of Nick, forcing them to slow down.

Running up to them, Jay handed his controller up to Nick.

"Here, YOU drive my car to the park!" Jay's face pinched maliciously.

Nick laughed and let go of Mommy's hand to grab the controller.

"Thanks, bud!" Nick said while Jay quickly filled his mom's hand with his own.

*****

Once at the park, they set their picnic basket on a blanket under a nice shaded tree. Other than a few kids playing on the swings, the park was quiet.

Jay nibbled his sandwich, but he couldn't focus on eating. His mind was making some important calculations regarding the swinging children.

"Mommy, can I go play with them? I've gots an idea on how to optimize the pendulum motion on the swings to make them go super-duper high." As soon as he asked the question, his mom's horrified, shifty eyes reminded him that he wasn't supposed to use big words in front of others.

Oops!

"Uh, I mean…" Jay glanced at Nick, who appeared thoroughly puzzled and quite surprised. "Can I go play on the swings, Mommy? Please, please, please!"

She, too, looked at Nick, trying to gauge what he was thinking. Her face went through a transformation of panic, embarrassment, disappointment, and then cover-up mode, where she pretended everything was fine.

She glanced down at the pathetic amount of food Jay had eaten and shook her head. Noticing her disapproving look, Jay quickly took a big bite of the untouched sandwich. With food overflowing from his lips, he attempted to convince his mom that he had eaten enough.

Nick put his palm on top of Enna's hand that rested at her side. "I'll go play with him on the playground if you want. I'm sure he will eat more when he is done playing," Nick said sweetly, ignoring Enna's strange mood shift.

Having an advocate, Jay's pleading to go play became louder. "Pretty please, Mommy! I'm your favoritest kid in the whole wide world and you want me to be smiley! Can we go play?"

"Fine, you boys go have fun," Mommy gave in. Jay let out a roar of approval as she kept talking, "But please, remember our rules." Her glare told Jay she was talking about not acting too smart in front of her boyfriend.

The big words don't seem to bother him. I don't know what's the big deal is.

Jay rolled his eyes and galloped off for the swings. Nick rushed after him with a childlike bounce.

"You can help me with my project! Turn the chains shorter so they will go faster and higher. I'm gonna to check out the angles and da'termine the perfect length," he said while approaching the other kids on the swings. He motioned to them. "I need ya to get off so I can fix the swings. It will be funner!"

"Whoa, hey, Jay. How about we play on the slides instead? At least until they are done swinging," Nick suggested.

Jay scrunched his eyes in thought until Nick kneeled next to him to speak softly. "I don't think we are supposed to mess with the chains at the park anyway. We might get into trouble."

"Pft, fine," Jay sighed. "I guess we can slide. There's cool things we could do with the slides, too. Have ya ever gone down 'em when they're wet?"

"Well, yeah! That's the best! Have you ever tried going down the slide head-first?" Nick countered.

"Yeah, once, but I bumped my noggin." Jay scratched his head at the memory.

"Sorry to hear about your noggin. That sounds painful. Do you want me to show you how it's done?"

"Yeah, come on." Jay raced up the playground and slipped down a steep green slide with ease.

He turned around to see Nick awkwardly squeezing through the kid-size bars of the playground.

"You ready for it?" Nick asked once he made it through the obstacles in his way.

Jay's head bobbed enthusiastically and he clapped his hands.

"Okay, here I come." Nick dove head-first down the slide. As he neared the sudden drop-off at the end, Jay sucked in a breath of anticipation. Nick placed his hands out in front of him in a triangle formation and caught the ground.

As his momentum pushed him forward. Nick tucked his head and somersaulted all the way over before flinging himself back onto his feet, sticking the landing.

"Whoa! You're a ninja, like my mommy!" Jay threw his hands up in excitement.

Nick sat down on the bottom of the slide to catch his breath.

"I didn't know your mom's a ninja!" Nick said, very interested.

"Yeah, she could beat people up pretty good if she wanted to. She tried ta teach me, but she was not a good teacher, so the computer told me how to do the moves. Wanna see?" Jay held up his fists and swiped the air and his leg flew forward in a kick.

"Wow! That's not bad," Nick's eyes gleamed in admiration.

"Yeah, I'm awesome!" Jay said before running back up the playground steps and scooting himself back down the slide toward Nick. "Watch out!" he called right before his feet bulldozed into Nick's back, pushing him onto the ground.

"Ow! Oh, you're asking for it!" Nick swooped Jay up by his armpits and spun him around in a circle at a great speed.

"Super Jay!" Nick called out.

The wind flashed over Jay's face. He tried to pull his legs and arms into his body so he could fly even faster, but the force was too strong, so he relaxed his body, opened his mouth wide, and tried to eat the wind.

After spinning Jay around several times, Nick set Jay's feet back on the ground.

The world swooped and spiraled as Jay attempted to walk in a straight line. Cracking up, Jay lost his footing and sprawled in a pile of woodchips.

"You made me so dizzy," Jay said, grinning. "Can we do that again?"

Jay wished they could play forever. Nick smiled but shook his head no.

"I'm afraid if I spin anymore, I will probably puke," Nick said. He pantomimed violently vomiting.

"Eww, gross!" Jay said, his shoulders bouncing as he laughed.

"I'll push you on the swing now, though. The other kids seem to be done with them," Nick said.

Jay let out a cheer and rushed to the swing set. He grabbed the chains holding up the swing and tried to leap into the seat, but his short legs made the task impossible.

Nick quickly lifted Jay into the seat before pushing the swing.

Jay tilted his head back as he flew higher and higher. He looked over and saw his mom sitting on the blanket, watching them play. She had a simple smile written on her face, telling Jay that life was beautiful.

"I decided you should marry my mom," Jay told Nick.

Nick fumbled the chain and pushed him at a janky angle. The swing rocked dangerously from side to side until Nick caught the swing to even it out before pushing it the correct way.

Jay looked curiously at Nick's expression. According to Jay's analysis of human features, he deducted that Nick was actually sad despite maintaining a smile.

Jay tilted his head to the side, noting Nick's fallen eyebrows and suddenly hollow eyes that drifted to the ground.

"Why do you think I should marry your mom?" Nick asked hesitantly. "She is wonderful, but we haven't been dating very long."

Nick stopped pushing the swing and let it slow down naturally.

"I can tell that you love her and she gets all shiny around you. And, well, I kinda like you too. You are funny and nice and ya play with me and ya wear weird clothes," Jay rapidly shot out several reasons. "I din't want ya to steal my mommy from me, but if ya share her, I might be able to be alright with that, long as I get more turns with her than you…"

Jay rambled on while Nick's eyes stared off toward the area where Mommy relaxed on the picnic blanket.

"She is pretty amazing, isn't she?" Nick said distractedly. "I don't know that much about her, though. She keeps to herself a lot."

Nick sat on the swing next to Jay and dragged his feet through the wood chips.

"Can I ask you a question?" Nick looked at Jay with pleading eyes.

"Uh, yeah?" Jay said curiously.

"What happened to your dad?" There was a short pause before Jay answered.

"I dunno. I din't meet him. I'm 'dopted," Jay shrugged.

"Has she talked about other guys or boyfriends, or...has she been married before?"

"Nope."

"Oh, okay. Does she ever talk about her life from before she adopted you?" Nick twisted his swing so he could look directly at Jay.

"What?" Jay was getting bored with the line of questioning and wanted to play some more, so he began pumping his legs to get the swing moving.

"Do you know anything about her parents? Do you have grandparents? Where did she grow up?" A hint of frustration formed in Nick's tone.

"No, Mommy doesn't have parents and she grew up all over. Why?" Jay continued kicking his legs, but the swing would not go any higher. "Your eyebrows are in zig-zags. Are you paplex?"

"Perplexed? How do you know such big words?" Nick's eyebrows shot up.

"Oh, oops." Jay stopped trying to swing. "I'm not 'posts to use big words around other people. Mommy doesn't like it." Jay hung his head in shame.

"But why?"

Jay shrugged again. "I don't know. She says it's so others don't feel bad for not being as smart as me."

"Huh? Now that is perplexing," Nick said with a lighthearted ring, but his tone quickly came back to a new serious note.

"Your mother is a mystery. I care about her so much, but I just want to know more about her. When I ask her questions, it seems like I only get partial answers like she's hiding something from me. Do you know what I mean?" Nick's voice was quiet and pained.

"Uh, maybe? Sometimes she askadentally wakes me up with scary noises at night and won't tell me why. But mostly she tells me everything, prolly 'cause I'm her more favoritest person. Can you push me now?"

"Sure, bud." Nick let out a soft sigh-chuckle as he got up and stood behind Jay.

Grabbing the chains, he dragged Jay backward a few feet, then burst forward and dipped all the way underneath the swing before letting Jay go, shooting into the sky.

Jay yipped and kicked his legs, but Nick was distracted. His eyes moved back to Mommy, who sat reading a book.

"Push me again!" Jay shouted.

"One minute, bud. I'm going to ask your mom something real quick. I'll be right back."

"You're going to ask her to marry you?!" Jay asked with hopeful eyes.

Nick laughed and shook his head. "Oh boy! No, no, not yet. I don't think she would want to marry me anyway. No. I can't. I...ha!"

Nick's cheeks started to look like strawberries and he stumbled on his words. "Wow! Sorry, kiddo, I just want to ask her to come on a fancy date with me. Is that okay with you?" Nick quickly replied.

Jay cocked his head to the side, "Can I go on the date with you guys?" He asked.

"Probably not this time. You would be bored. Lots of talking and lame stuff like that," Nick said, giving Jay's swing another shove.

"I don't know about that. Ya need ta promise ta share, Mommy. Can I get down?" Jay asked.

Nick reached for the chains and dragged the swing to a halt. Lifting Jay from the seat, he gently placed him back on solid ground.

Dropping to a knee, Nick leveled with Jay so he could look him in the eyes. "Jay, I pinky promise that I will share your mommy with you. She loves you so much. You are a good kid."

Nick held up his pinky finger.

Jay thought for a moment before taking his own pinky, hooking it onto Nick's and shaking it.

"Fine, you can ask her for a date," Jay agreed.

"Thanks bud, I'll be back."

Jay watched as Nick went over to his mom and began talking. A light flashed across her face as she nodded happily.

Jay felt his belly grumble from lack of food, ignored it, and ran off to fly down the slide a few more times. On his fourth time down the slide, his mom's arms were waiting at the bottom to wrap around him.

In his mom's embrace, he struggled to get free as she tickled him.

"Save me, Nick! Save me!" Jay called out.

Nick rushed over to Mommy and began tickling her until she released Jay.

"Not fair!" she gasped. "You are supposed to be on my side. You stinker." A fake scowl tried to pass as intimidating, but it looked more like she had to use the bathroom.

Jay held his hand up to Nick for a high five. "Thanks, bro!" he said.

They all laughed as Nick pulled out his phone.

"Selfie time! We need a picture of this moment. Come on."

Jay made a goober face at the camera and posed as Nick snapped a picture.

"What's with that goofy face? Smile!" Nick said.

Jay made a new silly face, making Nick choke on his laughs. However, Mommy stood back, rigid, her face serious.

"Nick, I don't like Jay being in pictures. There are too many creeps out there who could get their hands on those pictures. Please delete those now."

"Don't worry, these pictures are just for us," Nick said.

"No, I told you I don't like pictures, especially of Jay. You need to respect my boundaries."

"It's just a picture. Forgive me if I want to document our beautiful moments." Nick couldn't hide the irritation in his voice.

"Document them in your head! You don't need pictures to remember good times. You don't have permission to take pictures of my child. Delete the pictures now." She pointed her finger sharply at his phone.

"No, why are you talking to me like this? You're being so disrespectful right now. You could have just asked politely," Nick shook his head, annoyed.

"I don't have to ask politely because I've already told you how I feel about cameras and you just chose to ignore me," Mommy's voice grew into a shout.

"You know what? I don't have to put up with this," Nick snapped. "I wish we could just have normal conversations. This is so frustrating. I care about you, Enna, but relationships need better communication. Stop shutting me down and…and pushing me away."

Nick took a step forward with his hands spread in exasperation.

Mommy flinched and stepped back. Her fists came up in a ready fighter's stance.

"Whoa, hey," Nick put his hands up in surrender and didn't approach any closer. "Wait. Did you just think I was going to hurt you? I would never do that."

Jay's eyes watered, watching the tension rise.

"Hey, who wants to drive my 'mote control car around the playground?" Jay cried out in an attempt to defuse the situation.

Before waiting for an answer, he dashed over to where his car sat across the playground and looked back to see if his plan worked.

It didn't.

The arguing continued in hushed whispers, and Jay knew the fun was completely lost as soon as his mom stormed away from Nick with a terrible scowl on her face.

She marched right up to Jay and took his hand.

"Come on, we've got to go."

19

Trust

Nick paced in front of Enna's door, hoping this time she would answer.

He lifted a finger to ring the doorbell again but paused. *She has a small apartment. If she was home, wouldn't she have already heard the bell?*

Looking back at Enna's car, his anxiety spiked. He checked the time on his phone.

If she was on a walk, she should have been home by now. He tried peering through a small window near the door, but a dark green curtain blocked the view.

"Oh, this cannot be happening!" he yelled, scaring a loitering cat. Then he pulled out his phone to check his messages once again.

Nope, still nothing. Come on! Something's wrong. She wouldn't just cut me off like this. Please be okay!

Raising a fist to the door, he knocked loudly despite the risk that he would seem desperate. The uneasy twist in his gut made him desperate. He hadn't heard from her in days and he was beyond worried.

"Enna, if you are in there, please at least let me know you're alright." He leaned his ear in, trying to hear any signs of life.

"Nick?" A voice came from behind him.

Startled, Nick executed a swift about-turn, his anticipation deflating as Betty came into view.

"Oh, I thought you were Enna."

"Is everything alright?" Her brows furrowed in concern.

"I've been better. Have you seen Enna around? I haven't been able to reach her." He tried not to act too anxious, but his nerves were shot.

"No, I haven't seen her. Why?" Putting both his shaking hands into his pockets, words shot out of his mouth.

"We had a nice date planned, but I got a text from her a couple days ago saying that she'd made a mistake and needed to leave and that she can't see me anymore." Nick swallowed a clump of spit that was blocking his throat.

"It was so out of the blue. I mean, we only had one tiny quarrel, nothing that should have caused her to disappear on me. I thought we were good, but now she's ignoring my calls and won't answer the door or texts. I'm so worried about her."

"Oh, that is concerning. She hasn't been over for breakfast the last few days, either. I just figured she was just having morning picnics with you. Hmm? Let me try her door." Betty went over to Enna's door and knocked. "Enna, it's me. Can we talk?"

"I tried that." Nick couldn't keep the frustration out of his voice.

Seeing Nick's anguished eyes, Betty turned her mothering voice to use. "I can tell you are feeling stressed. It's going to be alright though. We will figure this out. Maybe she's just sleeping."

"Sleeping this long? I've been trying to get a hold of her for days. Her car is still here, so she couldn't have gone too far. What if she hurt herself? She's mentioned having a rough past. What if her past became too much for her to handle?" Nick banged on the door again.

"Enna, please. Whatever I did, I'm sorry! Can we talk about it?" His face contorted in torment. "I'm freaking out! I'm about to call the police to file a missing person's report."

Betty put a comforting hand on Nick's shoulder.

"Give her a minute. Trust me. She loves that boy of hers more than anyone in the world. She would never do anything that would leave Jay motherless. Now, let's think. When was the last time you heard from her?"

"Not since she texted me two days ago. There is so much I need to tell her." Nick slumped down onto the cement and put his head in his hands.

Despite wearing a summer dress, Betty plopped herself on the filthy cement next to him and put her arm around his back.

"Oh, honey. You care about her so much, don't you?"

Nick nodded, his hand still covering his face. Her calming voice attempted to push optimistic thoughts at him, but his head thundered with alternate, horrible possibilities.

"Listen," Betty continued. "I've gotten to know Enna pretty well over the last few months. She's a challenge, alright. I feel like she hasn't quite learned how to fully let people into her heart yet. She's still figuring out how to take down her wall. It may take her a while to learn to trust again."

At the mention of trust, Nick moaned and stood back up. "I think I screwed up with her. I'm not..." Closing his eyes, he attempted to slow his breathing.

Wow, I really do love her, don't I? I've got to tell her the truth, but if I do, I've lost her for good.

"Betty, I am not who Enna thinks I am."

Before he could go on, his phone rang from his pocket. Relief washed over him as his hand shot to answer it.

"Enna! Are you okay? I've been so worried-"

A responding tenor voice spoke, catching Nick off guard, leaving him momentarily speechless.

Clearing his throat, he fought to retain his composure.

"Oh, um, sorry sir. This isn't a good time. I'm with someone." His eyes twitched over to Betty. "Yeah, okay. Fine. Give me a sec." He mouthed the words, "I'll be back," to Betty and turned, briskly making his way to his car.

"What's up?" he said, jumping into the driver's seat. A lump formed in his throat as he listened, making it hard for his vocal cords to function correctly.

Forcing words to come out, he stammered with a squeak, "Uh, yeah. I...I. I. I know. Sorry. Listen. I momentarily lost her again. I'm already on it, though." He sniffed. "Yeah, I know."

The man raged in his ear, forcing Nick to hold the speaker farther away from his head so he wouldn't go deaf.

Being yelled at is not something I can cope with today!

Finding his voice, Nick snapped back. "Yeah, of course I understand. I want to find her just as bad as you do, but..." he swallowed the insults hanging on his tongue. "Look. I don't think she's the one you're looking for anyway. She has a kid you never mentioned. A biracial son. She's just a look alike." His head swayed as he listened to the belittling words shooting at him.

"Listen. The trail's cold. She's gone. Okay?"

Rubbing his worn-out eyes, Nick set the phone down while the man continued to shout.

Laying the seat back, he stretched the tension out of his aching bones. *I'm not doing this anymore. I can't. I love her.*

A peace fell over him, knowing what he had to do. Picking the phone back up, he cut the angry man off.

"Hey bud, I'm not going to listen to you anymore since you can't talk to me like an adult. So, as of now, I'm resigning-" the phone erupted with curses. "Okay, I'm sorry you feel that way, but it doesn't change anything."

Nick rolled his eyes and shook his head before attempting to speak again. "Sir, Sir...I've done everything you've asked. I've followed all your leads, all your hunches. I've followed her around the country. I don't want to waste your money or my time, so you can have your deposit back. I'm done."

Nick's attention drifted away from his words as a shiny, red suburban pulled into the parking lot and stopped two stalls to the left of him. His heart harmoniously rejoiced with relief as he saw Enna's face through the window.

For a moment, words failed him as his body longed to rush over, wrap her in his arms, and kiss her so passionately she could never doubt his affection.

Nick grinned ear to ear despite the grown man pulling a hissy-fit on the phone.

"Oh, you're still talking? I stopped listening after I said I'm done." His knee bounced with anticipation of running to Enna.

"I've got to go. No…no, you listen, Sir. The girl I've been following is not the one you are looking for. I'm really good at what I do, and you've got to let this one go. She's not your wife."

As he talked, Nick watched Enna walk around the big red vehicle and open the back door to reveal a sleeping Jay.

Betty followed her, chatting away until she pointed in Nick's direction.

Enna's face turned to him with an empty expression as though she was in an entirely different universe from Nick. Her gaze fell to the ground, but only for a moment. When she looked up again, her eyes glimmered and a lip curved into a graceful smile. She mouthed the word, "Hi."

Nick couldn't help but grin until he realized his ex-client was still on the phone. His eyes dropped to his lap in shame as he finally responded.

"Hey. Yeah, sorry. I'm still here. It sucks that you lost your wife, but honestly, even if I knew where she was," he looked back out the window to Enna, "which I don't, I probably wouldn't tell you anyway at this point because, whoever she is, she's probably better off without you." His lips pressed firmly together in a smug line as the man came completely unraveled. "Wow, threats don't work on me, buddy, so…Peace out."

Nick abruptly hung up, composed himself, and rushed out of the car toward Enna.

"Hey! I'm so happy you are okay. Where did you go? I was worried about you," Nick said.

"I'm sorry, Nick," Enna whispered, taking his hand.

Nick's head shook, not knowing what words to use, if any.

"I...Enna. I thought things were good for us. Why, what happened? Is it about the pictures I took? I'm sorry if I..." Nick couldn't hide the hurt that plagued his thoughts. A mixture of relief, confusion, anger, and love made a nasty concoction in his mind.

"No, Nick. I'm sorry. I shouldn't have reacted that way over something so stupid. This wasn't about that. We'll talk in a bit. I gotta grab Jay first."

She let go of Nick's hand and turned to Jay, still sleeping in his car seat.

"Enna?" Betty chimed in. "Can I help with anything?"

Enna looked at Jay and then over to Nick's stressed stance.

"Yeah, actually. Could you take Jay for a bit? I need to talk to Nick alone." Enna's face dropped to the pavement, shame written across her brow.

"Of course, dear. Do you want me to get him out of the car so you can get to your chat?" Betty was already squeezing past Enna to unbuckle Jay's seatbelt. "You look exhausted. How about you talk to Nick, and I'll make dinner for the two of you?"

Enna chuckled. "You are wonderful, Betty. I'll have to let you know about dinner after I talk with Nick."

What does that mean? Nick tried to remain calm. *Are we really just done? Is Enna breaking up with me for real?* Nick's gut twisted. He wanted nothing more than to go back to laughing with Enna and learning how her unique brain worked.

Betty finished getting Jay out of the car.

"I'll just make enough food, and if you feel like joining us after you discuss your issues, then feel free to join us. How does that sound?"

"Perfect." Enna's eyes flashed to Nick but didn't linger. "Thanks, Betty."

"No problem, Dear. And let me know if you need a mediator. I'm no therapist, but I've been married a long time and know a thing or two about relationships." Her wide grin was hopeful, wanting to be a part of the Nick and Enna show.

"Um, that's alright. I think we will be good. Don't worry," Enna said, picking Nick's hand up again.

Oh-kay? What is happening? I thought she was mad at me. Huh? Nick squinted his eyes in confusion at Enna.

"Well, I hope so. If you need anything, give me a holler. You know where to find me."

Jay squirmed in Betty's arms, causing her to reposition her hands to secure him tighter. "I guess I should go put Jay down for a nap. I'll see you two later." She nodded and turned toward her house.

As soon as she was out of earshot, Enna faced Nick.

"Hey, I'm sorry about the text I sent you and not talking to you in person. I, I'm not good at relationships. Anyway...can you help me with something?" She squeezed his hand before letting it go.

Walking behind the suburban with Nick following close behind, she pressed a button on her keys making the back swing open, revealing two suitcases, two cots, and a big cooler.

"What's this?" Nick asked, "Were you camping?"

"No, it's a bit more complicated than that. I'll explain inside. Could you please help me unload these back into my apartment?" She took hold of the larger suitcase, which Nick automatically relieved her of.

"Yeah, Okay. Of course, I'll help." He reached in, pulled out the other suitcase and hoisted them to Enna's front door. She ran ahead of him and made sure it was unlocked before rushing back to grab a cot.

"Hey, it's so good to see you," Nick said, placing the suitcases on the empty living room floor before leaving once more to get the cooler from the suburban. Enna took the last cot, closed the back of the vehicle, and locked it up.

"I'm happy I'm back too. Honestly." Tension of unspoken secrets vibrated between them.

"Sooo…" Nick said, bouncing uncomfortably on the balls of his feet. "What's with the suburban and the empty apartment?"

Enna cleared her throat and looked anywhere but at Nick.

"Can we talk inside?" she asked. Nick grinned excitedly.

"Oh, yeah! Of course. You've never actually invited me into your place before. Does that mean you're starting to trust me?" he said playfully, but guilt stirred inside of him.

I'm not worthy of her trust.

"Mm, maybe. I trust you and Betty more than most people, so, there's that. Also, I could take you in a fight if I needed to," she teased, "But, yeah. Come in. I don't have any chairs, though. Hope you don't mind sitting on the floor."

"Eh, who needs chairs?" Nick found an empty wall in the living room and placed himself on the floor next to it. Enna joined him. They both sat in silence for a moment, not wanting to be the first to share their feelings.

Nick scooted his fingers over to Enna and poked her hand with his pinky. Enna chuckled and entwined her fingers in his. Their hands fit perfectly together.

"So, you broke up with me over text?" Nick opened the conversion.

"Yeah, sorry. I don't really want to be broken up." Her gaze focused on a black stain on the carpet.

Nick's heart raced.

If I tell her I'm not who she thinks I am, she'll never want to see me again. Nick squeezed her hand tighter and brought it to his lips for a kiss.

"Well, I don't want to be broken up either, so why? Why did you just disappear on me?" Nick couldn't hide the hurt in his voice as much as he wished he could.

"I…you know I travel a lot. I've never stayed in one place for too long. I've been waiting for some visas to be approved and I finally heard back from my friend that they were ready for me, so I went to get them from him and planned on taking off from there."

Enna snuck a look at Nick to see his response. His jawline bulged slightly as he clenched his teeth together, trying to control his heartache.

"What? You weren't even going to say goodbye? Do I mean that little to you?" He let go of her hand and looked at the door.

"No, Nick, you mean so much to me. That's why we came back. Please look at me. I couldn't leave you. I tried, but...I just couldn't. You and Betty are my family now."

Nick did look at her, but his face was sour.

"Enna, what are you hiding from me? You claim we are like family but you don't let us in, not really. I hardly know anything real about you. Why did you need to disappear so suddenly? What's going on?"

Enna's breathing turned sporadic and fear crossed her face.

"I, I want to tell you. I just-"

"Just what? Don't trust me?" Nick snapped, but his defensiveness stemmed more from the fact that she had a right not to trust him.

I haven't been honest with her. Of course she doesn't trust me!

"That's not it. I do trust you. I'm worried that telling you about my past could put you in danger."

Oh, she really is the girl my boss is looking for. Crap!

"I want you to tell me everything. I'll risk whatever comes in order to know you." Nick's lips tremored, bracing for the words to come.

Taking a deep breath, Enna nodded. "Okay, I'll tell you why we disappeared, but you can't tell anyone. Do you promise?"

I don't know if I want to hear this. It's so much easier to play ignorant. Nick was tempted to stop her and tell her he was not to be trusted but the longing to know her took over.

"I promise I won't say anything." He meant it, too. She was everything to him now. He would never jeopardize what they had, even if that meant keeping secrets from her.

"Have you noticed anything peculiar about Jay?" Enna asked.

Nick nodded, not quite sure where she was going with this. "Yeah, that kid is crazy smart. He was serious when he said he built that remote control car by himself, right? He's very special."

"Yeah, there's more and, this is going to sound like a crazy conspiracy."

"'Kay?"

"When Jay was a baby, his birth mom died in my apartment from a gunshot wound but before she died, she asked me to keep her baby safe. Then, some government agents showed up and tried to take him, so I beat them up, changed my identity, and ran away. I've been running ever since."

Enna cringed as though she knew that what she was saying was nuts.

Nick's eyes widened in surprise and relief.

That's her secret? Oh, she's probably not the girl I've been looking for!

"Sooo, wow. Okay. Okay. So Enna's not your real name and Jay is a super genius that the government is looking for?" His voice grew high in astonishment. He stood and began pacing the room. "So, what's your real name then?"

Enna didn't answer immediately, unsure she wanted to disclose that information, but she took a deep breath and said, "It was Anna Park."

"Anna? Ha, creative. You changed a letter. Nice."

Enna's shoulders shrugged with a laugh. "I know. My friend thought it would be an easier transition for me. He's the one who's been helping with our visas."

"So, why didn't you take your car? What's with the SUV?" Nick pointed a thumb toward the window.

"Oh, that's just a rental. My car is crap right now. It's been going out for a while. It's okay, though. I didn't want my car to be traced back to my friend, so I just left it. I'm a little paranoid that I'm being followed sometimes."

Nick walked away from Enna, not wanting her to see his guilty face.

"So, thank you for telling me. I'm dying to ask one more question. Is that okay?" Nick asked, wanting to change the topic. Nick turned to see Enna nodding. "I still have the reservation for our date tomorrow night. Do you still want to go with me?"

The grin that bloomed on Enna's face lit the dim room, making Nick's heart flutter.

"Yeah, I would really like that. You still want to go with me after...after I left?" Enna stood to meet Nick in the middle of the room.

"Mm-hmm." He put his arms around her and pulled her in for an embrace. Wanting to kiss her, his lips grazed past her ear, followed the line of her jaw, and hovered an inch away from her lips.

Enna made no attempt to pull away.

For a moment, neither of them spoke. They stood, allowing the space between them to tease their lips.

She has no idea who I am. The thought came like a poison to the romantic tension.

Pulling away, Nick took a sharp breath in. *If I tell her now, she will run and I'll never see her again.*

"I...I'm sorry. I can't. Ha ha, sorry..." letting the apology fall, Nick's face turned up in a half smile. "Wanna go see if Betty needs help with dinner?"

Surprised at Nick's sudden emotional shift, Enna's brows came together in concern.

"Oh! Um...I guess." Her lips quivered slightly. Tilting her head to the side, she left her question hanging.

Nick smiled, hoping Enna couldn't tell how fake it was.

"Cool...we should go." He took her hand and headed toward the door.

Before they left, Nick gave Enna a true, endearing look.

"Hey, thanks for opening up to me. I'm glad you trusted me," Nick said, pushing his secrets deep into his guilty soul.

20

Emotional Safe

Enna's heart pounded wildly as she sat across the table from Nick, who looked dashing in a black button-up shirt and a white tie hanging loosely around his neck.

The restaurant was beyond glamorous. Glass dishes clinked together as waiters served exquisite courses to the diners. Chandeliers hung from the ceiling sprinkling light throughout the room while a heavenly aroma of food reached Enna's stomach as she flipped through the menu.

Several times while Enna puzzled over which meal to order, Nick glanced up from his menu and grinned. A pleasant tickle rippled through her body as she sensed his gaze on her.

"Why do you keep looking at me like that?" She glanced at him with a shy expression.

"What? Looking at you, how?" Nick held his palms open in a gesture of innocence.

"You know, with the face and that adorable grin, and those perfect eyes," Enna's finger drew a scribbled picture of her words in the air as she spoke.

"I have no idea what you're talking about," Nick teased. "I'm just looking at you normal. Would you rather I not look at you at all?" He exaggerated, staring up at the ceiling and started to hum nonchalantly.

Enna waved her arms in front of his face to distract his focus from the ceiling. He quickly redirected his eyes to the floor. "You said I shouldn't look at you, so I'm not looking at you. You're welcome." The corners of his mouth twitched at his own joke. Enna let out a louder laugh than intended, causing a few heads to turn and look from the other tables. That just kept happening when she was with Nick.

"Stop, you are such a dork," she sank into her seat, laughing a little quieter now. Unfortunately, as she attempted to slow the laughing down, a small snort forced its way out of her nose.

"Oh no!" Enna covered her embarrassed face with both hands.

"Aww, that's so cute! You have such a contagious laugh," Nick beamed.

"Oh my gosh," Enna dipped her eyes.

"I'm serious. Your laugh is sexy." At that, Enna broke out into another clutter of giggles. *Wow! It's so refreshing sharing this moment with someone I trust.*

They stifled their laughter as the waiter came by to take their orders. Enna picked the cheapest meal on the menu with water.

"You can order anything you would like. Don't worry about money. I've got it," Nick assured her. Enna blushed.

"This place is way too fancy and expensive for me. I feel bad getting a single meal that costs more than a week's worth of food," she said. "I don't really know what to get." She shifted awkwardly in her seat, painfully aware of the waiter looking at her expectantly.

"Do you like fish?" Nick asked. Enna nodded. Nick turned to the waiter. "Let's get a garlic lime-marinated salmon for the beautiful lady and for me, I would like the biggest lobster you've got." He glanced at Enna for her approval. She nodded with a half smile. Her hands twisted shyly in her lap. Noticing her uncomfortable body language, Nick looked back to the waiter.

"Could we get to-go boxes with those, please?" Nick asked. Enna's eyes widened, surprised that he would want to leave so soon. The waiter nodded and rushed off.

"Why the to-go boxes?" Enna asked. Nick's boyish grin flashed.

"I want to take you somewhere, just the two of us. That is…if it's okay with you," Nick said. Enna's heart skipped a few excited beats.

I get to be alone with him! The once terrifying thought now thrilled her. She'd never felt this way about anyone before, not even Oliver.

"Yeah, okay. That sounds nice," Enna said, noting a radiating sensation passing through her.

He reached across the table and took her hand.

Oh, Nick, I don't ever want to leave you. I want you to know me—the real me—Clara, not just Enna.

"Thank you, Nick," Enna's voice thickened with appreciation.

"For what?" Nick cocked his head to the side.

"For so much. I really…" Enna's shoulders lifted for loss of words. "Just, thank you for helping me trust again. You steady me. I feel safe with you."

Nick let go of her hand and dropped his eyes.

"Enna, I…" Before he could finish his thought, the waiter returned with their food, ready to go.

"Oh, that was fast! Thank you, Sir," Nick said, paying the bill with an excessively large tip.

"So, where are we going?" Enna asked as Nick led her out to his car.

"That, my lady, is a surprise. Don't worry. I think you will like it. And, I promise, it's not another improv show." His eyes crinkled in humor as they climbed into the car.

"Ha, yeah. We don't need another disaster." At one point, rehashing that horrible experience would have embarrassed the crap out of her. Now, the memory of that night was just a funny story.

"Hey, wanna listen to music?" Nick asked, turning the car on.

"Sure. When Jay and I listen to music in the car, he always calls the music 'car tunes' like cartoons because we're in a car."

"That is too cute! You're doing so well with him," Nick complimented.

"Thanks. I try."

"You succeed," Nick said before blasting show tunes in the car. He mouthed along with the music until the chorus hit. No longer able to contain himself, he burst out in song.

"Oh my gosh. You are so nerdy!" Enna melted into a fit of giggles until her abs hurt from laughing so hard.

His animated voice rang out, impressing Enna with the falsetto notes he hit effortlessly as they came. She recognized a few songs from movies she had watched with Jay, so she popped her comfort bubble and sang along with him as they traveled.

Enna didn't want the moment of carefree goofiness to come to an end, but eventually, Nick pulled off to the side of the road. The car bounced on dirt and rocks for a moment before coming to a halt.

"We're here," he announced, turning the car off.

Enna looked around. The falling sun glittered across a wide, open field of wildflowers. Trees and shrubbery outlined the field, but other than that, there was nothing around.

Enna cocked her head and shot an eyebrow up in confusion.

Nick just grinned, hopped out of the car, and rushed to get Enna's door.

She grabbed the bag of take-out food and stepped out of the car skeptically.

"Is this where you murder me?" Enna asked, lip slightly lifted to show she was not serious.

Nick let out a laugh.

"Oh, man! You figured out my evil plan?" Nick let out a theatrical maniacal laugh. "Nah, I like you too much to murder you."

Nick took the food from Enna's hand to carry it for her.

"Well, I brought my pepper spray, just in case," Enna joked.

Nick grinned and held his empty hand out for her. "I guess I'd better be careful then," he said.

Enna received his outstretched hand and wove her fingers through his. They locked eyes for a second and a pleasant chill shot up through

Enna's stomach, which seemed to be a pretty common occurrence when she was with Nick.

His face became serious, almost pained for a brief moment, but the expression was quickly taken over by a crocodile grin.

"Come. It's this way," he said, moving toward the trees to their right.

Enna followed the soft tug of his hand without fear as he started to walk. Enna's flowing satin skirt caught a few burs as it trailed through some weeds. With her free hand, she lifted the skirt to her knees as they walked into the secluded line of trees.

Hidden in the shadows an old, rusting railroad track was partly overgrown with weeds, clearly no longer used.

"Here we go," Nick said, stepping carefully onto the cracked wooden beams.

Enna gracefully followed his lead. Following the tracks, they had to dodge fallen trees that covered their path and avoid railroad spikes that jutted up from the rusty metal plates that held the steel rails into place. A few times, they had to escape the grasp of branches that reached out to ensnare them in their trap.

"Wait here one sec," Nick said, straying from the track. He bent down and plucked a radiant, orange wildflower from a clutter of beauties.

Rejoining Enna, he attempted to place the flower in her hair, but the wind stole it and twirled it through the air.

"No, wait!" Enna ran off the track to chase it down with no luck. It flew away into the sunset. Surrounded by a whole field of flowers, Enna selected a new one and braided it into her hair.

"You are so beautiful, Enna," Nick said.

She blushed.

Hold onto this moment. Enna closed her eyes for a second to feel the breeze. When she opened them back up, she spoke quickly before she could change her mind.

"Do you want to take a picture to remember this moment?" She even surprised herself with the question.

"Really?" Nick's eyes widened, his excitement evident. He pulled out his phone. "You sure?"

She nodded and posed in the field with her hand holding her dress like a princess. He took a few pictures from different angles before he joined her.

"Okay, both of us! Smile!"

He didn't have to tell her to smile. She couldn't stop smiling even if she tried. He pressed his cheek up to her face and took a few pictures with the sun dipping in the distance behind them.

"Awesome! We should probably keep going before it gets too dark." Nick took her hand and led her back to the train track, where they continued their journey.

As they walked, they attempted the occasional small talk, but the silence in between words felt almost like a conversation in itself.

The atmosphere was one of peace while they took in the pleasant noises of nature. A stream trickled nearby, and the crickets had already started to tune their instruments. The warm wind sighed through the trees, making a calm rustling song.

"How are you doing?" Nick asked, breaking the silence.

"I'm good. I'm glad I'm not wearing high heels," Enna said. "How are you?" she returned the question to Nick.

"Yeah, I'm great! I'm glad I'm not wearing my heels either," he responded with a wink.

After Enna giggled at the idea of Nick wearing high heels, another silence followed.

The summer breeze whipped Enna's hair around and her skirt fluttered behind her.

Nick smiled and squeezed Enna's hand slightly. The sweet gesture shot a pang through Enna's heart. She remembered being a small girl named Clara holding her father's hand.

"Do you know what it means when I squeeze your hand like this?" her father had asked while he tightened his grip slightly, then released the tension.

Clara had just shrugged and looked up at her father for an answer.

He smiled down at her and softly said, "It means I love you."

Clara giggled and squeezed his hand back as hard as she could.

Enna missed that little girl. She missed her father.

"What is going on in that beautiful head of yours?" Nick asked, bringing Enna back to the present.

"Oh, um. Nothing really," Enna mumbled quickly.

Nick raised an eyebrow. "Oh, come on. You got to give me something. You always do that," he said, trying to sound casual and not too pushy.

Enna's toes caught one of the railroad beams, causing her to stumble.

Nick gripped her hand tighter to steady her.

Enna blushed.

"I always do what?" Enna asked, trying to distract herself from the embarrassment she felt from almost falling on her face.

"You brush off my questions or be as vague as possible. You don't have to do that with me anymore. I know your secret about Jay and it doesn't matter. I will always protect both of you. You can be open with me now." Nick's voice was kind but also quite serious.

Enna took a deep breath and nodded.

"I know. You're right. I'm just really used to hiding. I was just thinking about my father. He used to squeeze my hand like that. It was a good memory."

Nick came to a standstill to glance around at their surroundings.

"That's very sweet. I'm glad you told me that. By the way, we're here. Watch your step," Nick said as he began to move again.

Enna had been so distracted by Nick that she hardly noticed the ground on the sides of the tracks had fallen low, making a steep valley on either side of them.

As she let Nick lead her, the ground beneath the tracks disappeared leaving gaps between the wooden beams, revealing a stream far below them. Enna's stomach lurched. It was as though they were floating above the earth as they carefully made their way across the bridge. A few wooden beams were so cracked they had to double their stride to avoid them.

When they were halfway across the bridge, Nick stopped and sat down, facing the dimming sun. "This spot looks good," he declared, "unless you are scared of heights, that is."

Enna shook her head with a grin. "Here? In the middle of a railroad bridge? This is a first," Enna took Nick's hand, which he offered her, and gracefully sat next to him.

"You tend to have a lot of firsts. I'm glad that I can introduce you to new things." Nick handed her the food from the restaurant and they began to dine.

The sun was just starting to duck behind the mountain, causing color to paint the sky into a magnificent sunset.

Enna took in the view as she sat. A small reservoir of water reflected the sun like a photograph. Overtop the trees, cows could be seen grazing in the field.

Enna breathed in a deep whiff of the air. Beyond the smell of the fish she was eating, the aroma of wildflowers made its way to her.

"This is so nice, Nick. Thank you for bringing me here." She dropped her head onto his shoulder for a second before continuing to eat her dinner.

"Enna, why don't you talk about your parents more?" Nick asked, trying to talk and eat his lobster simultaneously.

"I don't like thinking about them," Enna said, taking a bite of her salmon. The flavor rippled over her tongue. "This fish is amazing. Wow!" she said, hoping their conversation would be derailed. She didn't want her past to drag down the carefree mood.

"Oh good! I hope so after how much I paid for it," Nick said with a chuckle.

"How did you pay for it? I haven't actually ever seen you working. What kind of photography do you do? Why haven't you shown me any of your work?" Enna asked.

Nick stared off into the falling sky, his face solemn.

Seeing his expression, Enna quickly added, "Oh, sorry, never mind. It's probably none of my business."

"No, it's okay to ask me anything. We have been dating for, like what? Two months now? Yeah, I'm an open book. What about you? Can I ask you anything?" Nick turned the conversation back onto her.

Enna finished her fish and wiped her fingers and lips with a napkin. "You can ask me whatever you like, but I don't promise to answer," she teased.

"M'kay, why don't you like thinking about your parents?" Nick asked again.

Enna paused before answering, long enough for the rhythm of the water flowing over the rocks to calm her nerves. *I can do this. I want to tell him. Anxiety doesn't control me.*

She gazed into Nick's eyes briefly before dropping hers to the stream below.

"I used to be really close to my parents. We did everything together. My dad always let me go to work with him. He was a mechanic. My mom was my best friend. I told her everything. I told her about my imaginary friends. I told her about my crushes. I told her about the bullies at school. Everything. I was happy."

Enna swallowed hard.

"What happened to them?" Nick asked gently. He traced Enna's hand with his pointer finger.

Enna took a deep breath and began again. "Well, they decided that they were not happy together anymore and they wanted to get a divorce. I thought that was the worst thing that could ever happen to our family."

Enna choked, surprised by the sudden gush of emotion that filled her chest. Tears formed at the corners of her eyes. Luckily, it was getting dark now, preventing Nick from seeing her cry.

Nick rested his arm comfortably around her and pulled her close to his shoulder.

"My mom couldn't handle the divorce. She gave up on life. She gave up on me," Enna said with an edge of anger in her voice. "Nick, I was the one that found my mother after she killed herself. That image never goes away."

Enna gulped and accepted the heavy feeling that weighed down her gut.

Nick moved his other arm around her and squeezed her tightly.

"I'm so sorry. I had no idea. Is that what your P.T.S.D. is from?" Sympathy flowed from him. Enna shook her head no.

The moon was out now, illuminating the railroad tracks.

She glanced at Nick's face and noticed his soft, sad eyes resting on her. Enna looked up at clusters of stars making their way into view before speaking again.

"That must have been impossibly hard on you and your father," Nick said softly. He gently brushed Enna's cheek where a tear had managed to escape.

Enna quickly pulled away and hid her face.

Nick stroked her hair. "It's alright to cry. You don't have to hide from me."

Enna lifted her head with a look of disdain. Anger bubbled inside her, pushing all of her secrets that she had held onto for so long to the surface.

"No! No, it's not okay if I cry! I can't cry because I had to be strong for my dad when he blamed himself for Mom's death. I had to hold him up as he drank himself into oblivion. I had to put on a face and tell him that it wasn't his fault that Mom hated her life so much that she would rather die than live another day with him!" She sobbed with a hand over her face.

Nick held her tight.

"That's not even it. That's not even it. I had to smile and beg for food on the street because no one would hire a half-starved girl for a job while my dad lay unconscious on the couch in our crappy shack. I had nothing! No food, no real family, and my dad did nothing! I hated him for that and I hated him for my mom dying, but I hid that from him. I wanted him to think I was strong."

Enna shook like an erupting volcano, not knowing if she should continue. "I'm sorry, Nick. I'm sorry. I'm just a mess."

"It's okay," he whispered.

"No, it's not okay. I had to hold in my tears until a man saw me begging and offered me a job at his mansion." Shame coursed through her, remembering the naive little girl who fell for Andrew's poison apple. "I should have seen the signs. He was handsome and flattering, but I felt..."

She sucked in waves of air. "He promised to take care of me and my dad if I would be a servant in his mansion. Nick, I thought I was being brave so I could save my father, but really, I was just desperate for a new life. I was such an idiot."

By this point, Nick rocked her back and forth like a baby.

"It's okay, it's okay. I'm here for you."

Enna buried her face in his chest, dripping tears onto his shirt while trying to restrain her hysteria.

"I can't," Enna's muffled voice whimpered. "It hurts, Nick! I can't go through that again!"

"You don't have to. Oh, Enna...Anna. I won't let anything happen to you."

"You don't understand." Enna lifted her shaking head. "The man is a monster! He used me for pleasure and beat me until I couldn't cry. He tried to force me to legally marry him because he wanted me as his little pet! I escaped before that happened, but I'm constantly terrified that he will find me."

Nick froze, his breath shaking now.

"You can't protect me from him. He broke me. I'm broken, don't you get it? I had to numb myself to survive. I'm not allowed to cry! He made me this way."

Nick sat in stunned silence. His arms provided a secure blanket for her as she sobbed out all her pent-up feelings. The wind hummed around them while they sat still with no words.

Once Enna had no more energy to cry, Nick whispered, "Enna…" he trembled. "Enna…I, I, I'm so sorry. I can't believe you went through all of that and still put a smile on for Jay every day. Do you realize how powerful you are?"

He paused, carefully considering what to say next. "The man who hurt you, what was his…" Noticing Enna's drained expression, he cut his sentence off short. "Never mind, it doesn't matter. I feel sick. We should go."

He unfolded his arms from around her, stood, and offered her a hand up.

"I'm sorry, I completely ruined the date," Enna apologized while reaching for his sturdy hand.

He lifted her to her feet. "Hey, you don't ever need to apologize for expressing your emotions and opening up. Okay? You can say or do anything you feel like you need to. Like I've told you, I'm here to listen," Nick said, removing a stray hair from Enna's face. "And you definitely didn't ruin our date." He chuckled with a sad shake of the head. "I'm glad you told me those things, even though they are hard to hear."

Nick slipped his shaking arms around Enna and drew her close, allowing her to feel every thud of his rapid heartbeat. Enna inhaled deeply, savoring the calming scent of his cologne. As she exhaled, she released the pain she'd carried for so many years. In his embrace, she felt a surge of strength and love, a connection that melted away her fears and filled her with a profound sense of peace.

After holding Enna for several minutes, Nick's grip loosened, but he didn't let go. His hand moved to her cheek, gently pulling her closer. A wave of warmth washed over Enna as their lips met, a soft, lingering kiss that spoke volumes. They savored the quiet intensity of the moment, finding solace in each other's embrace.

Enna suddenly pulled away with a sharp gasp as a memory of Andrew's forced kisses flashed through her mind. Panting, she stared deep into Nick's eyes, not knowing how to separate her dark past from this beautiful moment.

Nick didn't move in for another kiss. He just tilted his head curiously with kindness in his eyes.

"You okay?" He whispered in a soft, nonjudgmental way. Enna took a few deep, shaking breaths as she rewrote her story.

Yes, I'm okay. I'm good. Nick is so different than Andrew! I don't have to worry anymore. It's time to make new memories and let go of the past. Andrew can't take any more moments away from me. I won't let him! This is my life!

Enna nodded with a simple smile, closed her eyes, and gently brushed her lips against Nick's.

The kiss started shy at first, but it grew in confidence as Enna slipped her arms around Nick and held him tighter against her. Springs of energy flowed as Nick returned the intensity. Every movement of his body sent ripples of static throughout Enna, making her world tilt and spin as their hearts beat in unison.

Just as the kiss reached the point of intimacy where their animalistic desires dominated all logical thought, Nick abruptly broke away.

"Enna, I..." He shook his head, lost in her confused gaze. "You...Enna, you deserve so much better," he whispered in a raspy voice. The moon's light shone just bright enough to show the many emotions painted on his face: affection, fear, heartache, confusion, and so much sadness.

"Let's get you home," He muttered with a sniff.

Enna longed to stay a moment longer to kiss those lips over again, but he had already grabbed the leftover food and placed a hand on her back, edging her forward.

Together, they made their way back to the car in silence. Nick's smile was missing and his nose flared slightly, giving off a strange vibe.

Is Nick angry with me? He is acting so odd now. Fear gripped Enna around the throat. *What did I do? I broke my rule and told him all my secrets! He is going to hate me now and just think I'm broken and unlovable. I stayed for him, but maybe I should leave Payson, start again with a new identity, but then I would have to leave Nick. I can't do that. I can't leave him. I love him!*

21

Time

As he sat beside Mike, who was focused on Central Computer, Eric's head twitched to the side in an involuntary neck spasm.

Eric glanced up and scraped his teeth together as he saw the dimming skylight. It reminded him that precious time was quickly fading away.

"Anything yet?" Eric asked impatiently, ignoring the trickle of blood dripping out of Mike's nose.

The child made no reply as his eyes darted around the screen wildly, searching for information that could help locate Project 19932.

Eric hovered close enough to Mike that he could feel excessive heat radiating off of the boy's small shoulders. His fever was dangerously high, but the mission was immensely more urgent than the child's health.

We must keep going, or else this will all be for nothing.

Eric squinted his eyes at the screen as a flurry of images flickered at such an accelerated speed that he could hardly make sense of any individual image. It was fascinating yet infuriating to think that Mike was not only seeing the images but also processing and downloading anything that may be of use.

Why hasn't he found anything yet?

Perspiration glinted off of Mike's forehead. He scrunched his eyes and pushed on until an exhausted whimper escaped his lips. His face broke away from the screen.

"Uh, I can't do dis. My head's ouchie," Mike shut his eyes to rest.

"No. Don't say 'can't'. There is no such thing as can't. Keep at it," Eric's cold voice snarled, uninterested in the complaints of a child.

He needs to toughen up. I had to toughen up at a young age and I didn't even have superpowers to help me.

The comparison to Mike gave Eric a jolt of compassion. In fact, he did relate to the boy in some ways. Just like Mike, Eric bounced from one home to another. Not even his grandmother wanted to keep him. He was a nobody. Unloved. No one cared when the E.S.T. recruited him. No one cared when he disappeared. Like Mike, he was a ghost. Like Mike, he was forced to grow up too young.

No, compassion means weakness, and I can't afford to be weak right now. Eric reached into his pocket and felt the emergency Adderall pill he had shoved in there that morning.

Taking it out, he popped it into his mouth and looked at the time again. Swallowing the dry pill without water, Eric attempted to calm his nerves.

For almost a week, ever since the nanobots completed merging with Mike's physiology, the boy had been constantly attached to Central.

The sun dipped below the horizon, Mike's condition worsened, and they still had no results.

"I'm sorry, new Project 19932. You have to keep going. I'll give you a break in fifteen minutes." Eric tried to control his voice to make it seem caring, but it was crisp with desperation.

He began pacing the room with wide, hurried steps while still avoiding the cords cascading around the room.

Hesitantly, Mike turned his eyes back onto the screen, now showing images that appeared to be shifting from one street camera to the next.

The digital clock on the wall raced forward with relentless speed, leaving no time for Eric to dwell on sympathy for the sick child. The tension in the room hummed like the sound of electricity zipping from one line to another.

Suddenly, a sharp gasp escaped Mike's lips, causing Eric to rush over to him.

"What did you find?" he asked.

Mike gasped again and again, reaching for air that could not find its way into his little lungs.

Eric grabbed the boy to look into his face, which was turning a grayish-blue hue.

Mike's eyes popped, locking in with Eric's gaze. Without saying a single word, Mike told Eric all the fear he was feeling.

"No, hey," Eric awkwardly put both hands on each of Mike's shoulders, not quite knowing what to do.

The boy's look of surprise and fear dropped as his pupils rolled up into his skull, showing off the whites of his eyes. His body began to convulse out of control.

Eric held the small child as he thrashed about. He cursed under his breath as he brought Mike to the floor and rolled the spasming body onto its left side. Eric stabilized Mike's rocking head to prevent it from smashing violently into the ground.

The seizure only lasted a few minutes, but it left the boy lethargic and limp on the cold tiles.

"Crap," Eric grumbled to himself in defeat.

He walked across the lab and activated a touchscreen intercom next to the elevator. Eric's gruff voice projected to the tech lab directly below Central's room.

"Caleb, Stanley, I need your assistance immediately," he ordered.

"Yes sir," came a voice from the speaker.

A few minutes later, the elevator let out a high-pitched ding and opened to reveal the two science technicians who were involved with the Project retrieval efforts.

The redheaded Caleb entered the room briskly when he noticed Mike sleeping on the floor.

Stanley, a thin man with square glasses and a pointy chin, wandered into the room, focused only on Eric.

"What's going on?" Stanley inquired. He followed Eric's gaze over to Caleb, who knelt next to Mike's limp body.

"What did you do to the Project?" Stanley asked with an exasperated gasp. He rushed over to Caleb on the ground and felt Mike's forehead. "He has a fever," he said.

"He will be fine," Eric said with a false sense of confidence. "He's not taking to training well. I need you to fix him."

"This kid is not fine. His temperature's through the roof and his nose is bleeding," Caleb said coldly, gently wiping the child's forehead with the back of his hand, concern evident in his touch. "He needs immediate attention!"

"I'm taking him to the Medical Lab," Stanley said, sliding his arms under Mike's head and knees to lift him.

Eric moved to block their exit.

"No, no, you can't do that," Eric protested. "I know I don't always show you the respect you deserve, but I chose you two because you are the best in your field." Eric swallowed hard. His normally dead eyes flashed in fear. "I need your help, but I also need discretion. There are too many eyes in the Medical lab. Take him back to your personal lab."

"What? Why? What did you do?" Caleb's skeptical stare penetrated Eric's core.

"I made a judgment call and it did not go the way I planned. Alright?" Eric shifted his gaze to the floor, all pretense of confidence banished. "This is not Project 19932. I didn't have enough time to locate the real Project because the General was pressuring me."

Stanley and Caleb gaped, appalled by what they were hearing. Before they could say anything, Eric bounced into defensive mode.

"Hey, don't look at me like that. You know the General would never let me walk away from this project alive. I had no choice. I found a kid around the same age and appearance as the Project and infused him with the remaining nanobots. It was only to buy myself time until we located the actual Project. With this kid and Central Computer, it will be very soon. I feel it!"

The two technicians continued to stare incredulously at Eric.

"Wait, let me get this straight. You just plucked a kid off the street and figured you would experiment on him? What were you thinking?" Stanley asked as he cradled Mike in his arms.

He tried to move closer to the elevator to leave, but Eric puffed his chest to intimidate him.

"I had no other choice! You have to understand the position I'm in."

Caleb's voice projected out from behind Stanley. "No other choice? Really? You think your only choice was to kidnap and poison an innocent child? Yeah, great choice. Gold star for you."

Caleb weaved in front of Stanley and shoved Eric's shoulders with all his strength, which was not much. "Move, sick head!"

Eric's reflexes kicked in as he swiftly seized Caleb's wrist with one hand and twisted, forcing the squealing redhead to rotate so Eric could place his other arm on the back of Caleb's vulnerable shoulder joint. By adding pressure, Eric forced Caleb down to his knees.

"Are you done?" Eric's bellowing voice caused Mike to stir in his sleep.

He continued talking with a softer, yet still intense tone. "Listen, I understand that this is not an ideal situation. But yes, believe it or not, I had no choice. And how was I supposed to know that the nanobots would harm the kid so drastically? I mean, we've had this technology for years now. Shouldn't there have been notable progress in adapting the nanobots for safe human integration by now?" Eric glared at Stanley with accusing frustration.

"If you technicians would have done your job, he wouldn't have gotten sick this fast. I didn't mean to harm him."

Eric dropped his head and his voice fell to a hushed plea. "Please, no one can know about this. Help me keep this quiet. I know you don't like me, but I'll do anything."

This desperation doesn't look good on me. It's just unnatural and humiliating! What have I turned into?

"Why don't you start by letting me up?" Caleb said, impatiently trying to free his captured arm.

"Oh yeah, sorry." Eric helped Caleb to his feet.

Frustrated by the delay, Stanley dodged his way past Eric and stepped up to the elevator doors.

"How 'bout help us save the kid, then, if all goes well, we can discuss your fate after. Deal? We can use our personal lab, alright?"

"Fine, let's go," Eric said after a short pause to consider.

"When we get him to my lab, I'll get blood samples and figure out where to even start cleaning up your mess," Caleb said, rubbing his sore arm. "I need to understand how these nanobots are interacting with his DNA. The biological nanobot's original design was for fetal development, not children. The nanobots require time for full assimilation. Because you injected them into an older child, the established biology and neural pathways are being compromised somehow."

Eric always considered himself fairly intelligent, but biology was not his field of expertise. He was an agent in charge of using scientific advancements for critical diplomatic missions, at least that's what he used to do before being sidelined by the General.

Caleb put his hand on the elevator security sensor to activate the doors.

Eric questioned the men as he joined them in the elevator.

"Why does it matter if the child is older? As I understand it, the bots are programmed to merge with human genetic material as long as it's compatible with their DNA. I reprogrammed the bots to match the kid's DNA before injecting it. I'm not a complete idiot."

Caleb selected the floor and continued the conversation as they were transported to the ground below.

"Apparently, you are. It's not just about the DNA matching. The body has to be prepared for the nanobots to become a part of them. Otherwise, the body detects them as antigens and sends out antibodies to destroy the perceived threat. A complete mess of nano-particles could be floating around in the kid's system, causing all sorts of issues. Or, the nanobots could be overpowering the antibodies and killing the kid's immune system or causing a buttload of inflammation. We just don't know yet."

"Hopefully," Stanley jumped into the conversation, "There may be a way we can trick the antibodies into leaving the nanobots alone long enough for the body to dispose of the fragmented nanobots, but who knows what kind of damage has already been done?"

The elevator doors slid open.

As they entered the spacious technology lab, it became evident that Central's lab could have fit inside this technology lab four times with ample space to spare.

On one side of the lab, several rows of desks held cutting-edge computational systems, with IT specialists vigorously swiping at the screens. On the other side of the lab, countertops were filled with cybernetic gadgets attended to by scientists teamed with engineers.

Eric was relieved to see that no one turned to look when the elevator doors opened. Everyone was much too involved in their own projects to notice the world around them.

Five see-through cubicles made of thick, bullet-proof glass lined the back wall of the lab.

Caleb made his way to the nearest cubicle, gesturing for the others to follow. Eric positioned himself as a shield beside Stanley, concealing Mike, who remained unconscious.

After using his handprint to allow access to the room, Caleb held his arms out in a showcase manner.

"Ta-da! Welcome to my cubicle," he said grandly.

A couple of scientists looked up, earning Caleb a glare from Eric while they entered the room.

Eric looked skeptically around the small room as the clear doors slid shut. It was completely empty. Although Eric had been to the technology lab many times, he had never needed to enter these rooms.

Before Eric could question why they were in an empty room, Caleb slid his finger along the glass wall as though he were swiping a giant tablet. The glass wall sprang to life with app icons. Caleb selected an icon. Suddenly, the glass walls tinted to a dark gray. The once transparent walls now hid them from the other technicians.

"That's better," Caleb said. "Now we can work without prying eyes. Alrighty, where do we begin?" He looked at Stanley.

"Well, maybe we should start by giving me a place to put this kid down. He is a lot heavier than he looks." Stanley tried to adjust Mike, who hung limp in his arms.

"Oh, duh. Sorry, man." Caleb tapped on another icon. A soft rumble came from across the room. A rectangle panel from the floor slid open and a counter rose from the ground.

"Put the kid there. I'll get the supplies we need," Caleb told Stanley.

Eric stood in the corner of the cubicle, watching in hidden amazement as Caleb swiped and selected more icons. With the touch of his finger, Caleb turned the empty room into a complete medical lab.

Next to the counter rose a cabinet holding syringes, vials, microscopes, latex gloves, and several other items typically found in a doctor's office. A large desk rose from the ground near the medical cabinet. The desk contained a state-of-the-art laptop and robotic arms made for working with minuscule objects.

Stanley carefully set Mike down on the counter and then stretched his own arms, which had become sore from carrying the boy around.

Caleb walked over to the cabinet and retrieved sterile IV equipment.

Mike's eyelids fluttered open and closed, but exhaustion from his seizure left him powerless as Caleb inserted the IV needle into his arm to collect blood samples.

"Now, Agent Quinn, excuse us while the experts clean up your mess," Caleb said with a smirk before starting Mike on a saline drip.

"I can stay. He might get scared," Eric said, frustrated that he couldn't do anything to help. He didn't even understand why he had followed them down there if they didn't need him for anything.

"Dude, it's alright. We will take care of him and let you know when we have answers. What's the kid's name?" Caleb asked casually while holding a vile of blood and a test tube in his hands.

"It's Mike," Eric answered, with a choke of emotion. *Please save the boy.*

The thought startled him. *What do I care of this kid? He is nothing other than a means to an end.*

Eric sighed heavily. *No, if that kid dies, whatever is left of my tiny soul will shrivel up into nothing. I like his stamina. He's like me.*

Conflicted, Eric reluctantly exited the cubicle.

***

Though the day had passed swiftly during the search for Project 19932, now as Eric anxiously awaited word from the scientists, the hours seemed to drag on, each second longer than the last.

Finally, the intercom buzzed, waking Eric from his resting state on the cold, hard floor.

"What's the word?" Eric asked with haste.

"He's awake. Do you want to see him?" Stanley said in a flat voice, giving little indication of Mike's condition.

"Yes, but is he going to be alright?" Eric couldn't hide his concern as he pressed his hand onto the elevator lock pad until it turned green.

"For now, but we will talk when you get down here," Eric heard Stanley say before the elevator doors opened.

"I'm coming," Eric said, stepping inside.

Once he reached the cubicle, Stanley and Caleb glared his way. Ignoring their negative intensity, Eric strode right over to Mike, who was still connected to the IV.

"Hey, how are you feeling?" Eric was visibly shaken.

"Uh, sleepy," Mike's eyelids drooped.

"Oh, well, it's okay to sleep now, I believe." Eric looked to Caleb for confirmation. Caleb nodded with a sour expression.

Mike let his head drop into a pillow that had been provided and closed his eyes.

Turning to the science technicians, Eric waited for answers.

"Let's talk privately," Stanley suggested. Caleb agreed and went back to the glass wall to select a few more icons. Several medical items were whisked away before a glass divider slid out of the ceiling, separating Mike from the men. Three transparent acrylic chairs appeared, inviting them to sit.

"The divider is soundproof, so we are free to discuss damages," Caleb began as the two scientists sat shoulder to shoulder in front of Eric, making him feel outnumbered.

"What damages?" Eric snapped, tired of the dramatics. "Will he have a full recovery?"

Stanley's face remained unreadable as he explained further.

"As we discussed earlier, the nanobot's primary function is to integrate with and gradually take over pre-existing neural pathways, enhancing their capabilities. However, when you injected the nanobots, they connected to those pathways before the body could adjust."

"Yeah, your stupidity turned Mike's brain into a battlefield between nanobots and antibodies," Caleb interjected.

Eric's expression grew more distressed as he asked, "So, what are our options? Can we remove the nanobots to stop this?"

Stanley hesitated, choosing his words carefully. "Removing them now would result in the loss of crucial connections for basic brain functions. It would leave him with severe cognitive impairments, or worse, it could be fatal. We need to find a way to make the nanobots and Mike's immune system coexist, but it's a challenging task because the medications we would use for that are in the experimental stages."

"I don't care. Let's do what we have to to save him." Eric couldn't believe how much he needed Mike to survive. *This is all my fault. I have to fix it.*

Stanley's head nodded in a concerned, slow fashion. "We can do that, but you must understand that, in order for this to work, we need the new medication, GuardiaX, to protect Mike's brain from nanobot-related overstimulation and also the med, CyberEquiset in order to maintain equilibrium between Mike's human and computer components. So far, experiments have shown that both medications have extreme side effects, causing the patients excruciating pain as it integrates with the body."

"Pain is better than death, right?" Eric asked.

"That is entirely dependent on how much pain," Caleb answered.

"There is a solution to the pain, but it's not a great one," Stanley stared Eric down, watching for his reaction. "We can administer the doses with a powerful painkiller such as Morphine or Pentazocine."

"But, starting opiates with a child his age is risky in itself. However, we might not have a better option," Caleb said. "He's on a low dose of Morphine right now to manage his symptoms, but we can make a serum with the experimental drugs and Morphine and see how it goes."

Seeing Eric's stressed expression, Stanley cut in. "I'm hopeful that it will work. The trials have been effective other than the horrific side effects, which we think we can manage. Other experimental medications can reduce the pain, but we don't have access to them yet, so Morphine likely might be a temporary solution anyway."

Eric closed his eyes to escape the gaze of the two young men in front of him. *What other options do I have? Let him die? I could, but I shouldn't. I won't. I can't.*

Opening his eyes, he nodded at them. "Yes. Create the serum with Morphine."

"Okay," Stanley said. "But, it has to be administered daily, or else more damage will occur."

"I understand," Eric stood. "Prepare as much as you can. I would like to keep a stash on me for his protection."

"We can do that; however, the medication is not cheap, and if you ask the General for the funds, that might get messy," Caleb informed Eric.

Eric grimaced. "No. Of course, I can't go to the General for help. Is there any way you could get me free samples?"

Caleb laughed. "No way, man. Someone would notice and it would be our jobs on the line. You'll need to pay for it."

Eric grunted. "Fine, I'll get you the money. Just do what it takes to save Mike."

"Huh? You actually care about him, don't you?" Caleb smiled. "I guess you might be human after all."

22

Betrayal

Nick's mind stumbled as he stared at the computer screen on his lap. Sleep had been taken over by rushing emotions that clashed against one another.

Scratching the itch forming on his jaw, Nick became aware of patchy stubble escaping from his unkempt pores. He usually shaved first thing in the morning, but that didn't matter anymore. Nothing mattered except for Enna.

He didn't care that his hair was wild, his shirt had food dribbles on it, or that he desperately needed a hot shower. All he cared about was making sure she was safe.

I'm overthinking this, Nick tried to convince himself. After being up all night researching Anna Park, he had very little to show for it other than a picture of Enna as a blonde-haired, blue-eyed MMA champion.

"Wow! I guess that explains why she can fight."

What gnawed at his mind, however, was the absence of information regarding Anna Park's parents. There were no birth or death certificates and nothing from more than seven years ago was accessible to him.

This is wrong. There is no information that I can use! Anna Park can't be her real name. She lied to me, again. He could guess her real name but dared not admit it, even to himself.

Now that her puzzle pieces were falling into place, his gut felt like acid and his eyes burned from exhaustion.

A wide yawn forced Nick's jaws wide open. Reminded of his drained energy, Nick reached for a heavily caffeinated drink that waited for him on the end table. Taking a gulp, he shook his head and closed his eyes.

Despite the sun spilling into the living room, Nick hardly noticed night merging into day. Enna's face slipped through his mind. The way her eyes had glistened in the starlight remained seared in his memory. Every fiber of his soul reached out for her. He could still feel the depth of Enna's kiss against his lips.

The memory sent a chill sliding down his back, catching his breath off guard. He wanted her more than anything in his life, but how could he keep her? Enna trusted him and had opened up about her past.

I should have told her a long time ago. I'm such an idiot. She won't want me after I tell her I'm a stupid fraud.

Suddenly, the couch cushions vibrated underneath him. Jumping up, he shoved his hand down the crack in the couch and rummaged around for his phone. He fished it out and tried to answer, but it was already too late.

Glancing at the missed notifications on his phone, his eyes doubled in size. It was way past time for his regular breakfast date with Enna. She had left him several text messages and called him a few times.

How did I miss my phone ringing? Was I really that focused on figuring her out?

He was about to call her back and apologize for missing breakfast when a knock on the door sounded.

Nick glared at the front door. *Neighbors are way too friendly here,* he thought with a moan. *Just leave me alone!*

The knock came again, followed by the ring of the doorbell.

"Fine, coming," Nick grumbled, much too quietly for the visitor to hear. He grabbed smelly shorts hanging on the back of the couch and pulled them over his boxers. The doorbell rang again as he walked to the door. He stepped over trash mixed with a pile of mismatched socks.

"I said I'm coming!" he shouted angrily as he swung the door open, revealing Enna's stunned face.

Nick's mouth hung open and his eyes widened. Seeing her made his lungs momentarily forget how to pump air to the rest of his body. "Oh, Sorry. I didn't know it was you."

"You stood me up!" Enna said boldly. Nick closed his mouth and swallowed hard before speaking.

"Uh, yeah. Sorry, I have been working on some stuff and lost track of time." Nick ran a hand through his wild hair. "I kind of look like crap. I wasn't expecting such pleasant company." He nervously blew air out through his lips, making them buzz as they vibrated together.

"I messaged you asking where you were. I was worried about you. You can't just disappear like that. I'm glad you're okay, though." Enna pressed a few fingers to her temples and rubbed them anxiously.

"Yeah, I'm so sorry I spaced our breakfast date. I had a rough night," Nick admitted. "Come on in. I actually really need to talk to you." He gestured for Enna to enter his nasty man house.

"Wow, looks like you need to hire another cleaning lady," Enna took a sniff of rotting food. "Just make sure you don't scare her into pepper spraying you in the face this time."

Enna attempted to lighten the mood, but Nick held his lips in a straight line. The tension only thickened.

As they made their way back to the couch, Nick went over what he needed to say in his mind and prepared to lose her forever. No words could ever fix his deception and he knew it. She would never forgive him.

After sitting down, Nick reached for Enna's hand, but she pulled away before he made contact. The hurt on her face caused Nick's hands to sweat.

"Nick, I don't get it. I finally opened up to you last night and you disappeared on me? You could have at least sent me a text telling me you couldn't make it. It would have taken two seconds." Enna took a sharp breath in.

Nick opened his mouth to diffuse the situation but Enna continued talking before he could get a word in.

"Did I scare you by opening up to you? Or was it the kiss? You are the one who kissed me last night. Is that it? Are you sorry for kissing me? Am I a bad kisser?"

"I'm sorry! Wait, no, you are not a-" Nick managed to say before Enna cut him off again.

"So far, I've always been able to depend on you. What happened?" She shook her head in confusion. "Just, why? Why did you kiss me and then stop talking to me? You didn't even text me to say goodnight before I went to bed. Is it something I said? What did I do wrong?" Enna pled for answers.

"No, please look at me. You're spiraling. You did nothing wrong. It's me. I never should have kissed you. I never should have fallen in love with you." Nick grimaced as the words fell from his lips.

Enna shot her head up in alarm. That was not the answer she was expecting.

"Fall in love with me? So, now you love me, but you say you shouldn't have kissed me?" Enna left the couch with her hands up. "I don't understand what's changed. Why are you acting so off today?"

"Well, if you would just be quiet for one minute I'll tell you! And, it's not like you've never disappeared on me before. You were planning on moving without even telling me," Nick snapped.

For a second, neither of them spoke.

"I can't talk to you like this. I'm going home. Text me when you're in a better mood." Enna began marching toward the door.

Without thinking, Nick followed after her and grabbed her wrist. Before he had time to process what was happening, Enna twisted out of his grip, wrapped her leg around his ankle, and swiped his foot into the air. His balance failed him and he landed on his back.

He gasped as breath expelled from his body. He could feel a video game controller underneath him, digging into his back. He attempted to sit up to relieve the pressure, but Enna's glare convinced him that movement would only provoke the beast that had emerged from his once charming girlfriend.

"Don't ever grab me like that without my permission," Enna said sharply.

Nick met her beautiful brown eyes as they welled with moisture. Struggling to hold back her tears, she turned abruptly and headed to the door.

"Enna, wait! You could be in danger," Nick blurted out.

Enna froze. Every muscle in her body seemed to turn into a statue.

"What do you mean?" she asked without turning to look at him.

"The story you told me about the abusive man you worked for, what was his name?" Nick's voice heaved, breathy and uneven.

Enna turned toward him in slow motion, her face twisting in terror.

"Why do you want to know?" she whispered.

Nick carefully stood and stepped toward Enna with his arms out in a sign of peace.

"Was his name Andrew Dengaila?" Nick asked.

He knew the answer the moment her body began to quake.

I knew it. I just didn't want to admit it. I can't believe this. She's Clara, the woman I was hired to find. Andrew's Clara. His heart tore to pieces.

"No. Please tell me I'm wrong, Enna." Nick held the back of his neck with his hand to fight off the headache pushing its way through his stressed body.

"You know him. Of course this is happening," Enna stated bluntly. "You told him where I am?"

"No, listen, I didn't know that he hurt you until last night, and as soon as I discovered that he has major anger issues, I stopped working for him. I promise."

"Working for him!" Enna screeched.

"Listen, please hear me out. He told me that he was your husband and you vanished after a car accident. I knew his story sounded iffy, but in my line of work, I've learned not to ask any questions. I should have-"

"Wait, your line of work? Who are you?" Enna asked, sweat forming on her pale forehead.

"Well, I did tell you when we met but I made a joke of it to see how you would react." Nick looked at her sheepishly.

Enna gasped, remembering Nick's arrival at her front door with the snorkel on.

"You told me you were a private detective following my every move. It freaked me out! That gave you a clue, didn't it?" Enna let out a half-sob and half-laugh. "Unbelievable!"

She grabbed her hair with both her hands and gripped it tight as though trying to pull all her hair out.

Nick wanted to wrap his arms protectively around her, but he knew that it might land him back on the floor with a new bruise.

Enna's face crinkled in agony. "The day I pepper sprayed you, did you hire me to clean your house just so you could get close to me? Was asking me out just part of your grand plot? Was everything an act for you?"

"Well, the pepper spray was unexpected, but, yeah, following you, getting caught, asking you on a date, that was planned out. I mean...I had...I mean I never planned on actually dating you. I just needed your DNA to prove to Andrew it was really you, but then I...I don't know. I don't know. I knew you had a story and I needed to know more," Nick admitted, regret filling his chest. He watched helplessly as Enna slumped over and then fell onto her knees. Her hand covered her face as she curled into a ball.

"It was all a lie. I trusted you! Is Nick even your real name?" Enna screamed at him.

"Is Anna even your real name?" Nick shot back.

She grabbed an empty soda can sitting next to her and hurled it through the air toward him. He let it hit him painlessly in the shoulder.

"Don't you dare turn this around on me!" Enna said in a dangerous voice.

Despite her dagger eyes, Nick still ached to hold her and let her cry on his shoulder. He wanted to kiss her and make everything better.

"Nick is not my real name, but not everything was a lie. My feelings for you were…are real," Nick said, falling to one knee to be closer to her.

"Oh, come on! You sound like a cheesy chick-flick. You betrayed me!" A tear escaped her eye, but she quickly wiped it away.

"Yes, my life is a cheesy chick-flick. I got hired to find someone's wife, fell in love with her, and then found out that my boss was an abusive psychopath. As soon as you told me about Andrew, I planned to tell you everything. I didn't want to. That's why I didn't sleep last night. I didn't know how to tell you. I'm so, so sorry, Enna! Man, I'm such an idiot! There were so many holes in his story. I should have seen it."

"What does he know?" Enna peered up at him.

"I sent him a picture of you, that's it. I swear…and a few photo-shopped pictures."

"Does he know where I am? Why didn't he insist on having more evidence this whole time? I know him. The second he saw the picture of me, he would have been here immediately. This doesn't make any sense." Nick sat fully on the ground and put his hands nervously in his lap.

"He doesn't know where you are, Enna. I never sent him your DNA. I swear. I felt like a dirtbag when I realized I had real feelings for you, which was pretty soon after I met you. I knew you were supposedly married, but I couldn't help it. You were perfect for me. I know I shouldn't have. Who falls in love with their client's wife anyway?"

Nick hovered his hand next to Enna's cheek, wanting to comfort her, but instead, he pulled his hand away and kept explaining. "Anyway, despite knowing you might be married, I lied to him. I told him that you had disappeared in the night and I was tracking you down. I've been supposedly tracking you down ever since. He was not happy about that one. I'm pretty sure the last time we talked, he threatened to kill me if I didn't find you. I didn't think he was serious, though."

"Yeah, that definitely should have tipped you off," Enna rolled her eyes.

"Listen, if I would have known Andrew was abusive, I never would have agreed to work with him," Nick said.

"If you would have just asked me about Andrew earlier I would have told you the truth. Instead, you snuck around trying to take pictures of Jay and me."

Enna sucked a broken shred of air in at the thought of her son. "Oh no! Jay! Does he know about Jay? No, no, no! He could have Jay!" Scrambling to her wobbling legs, she steadied herself and then bolted out the door. Nick jumped up and followed her into the front yard.

"I only mentioned Jay to him once to convince him you weren't his wife."

"Oh my gosh!" Enna stumbled forward, trying to run.

"He doesn't have any pictures of him though and he thinks you two are in Missouri right now. I promise. Jay is safe. Please trust me on this. Stop!"

Enna kept running without even looking back.

Nick stood helplessly watching as Enna got further away from him.

What should I do? Nick tried to think, but his head just spiraled. *She's not in the right frame of mind. She can't walk home alone. And what if Andrew does show up? It's unlikely but possible. He could have tracked one of my phone calls or something.*

Enna had already covered half the block, so he hurried back inside to grab his keys. Jumping into his car, he accelerated out of the driveway, determined to catch up with her. Pulling up next to her, he rolled the window down.

"Enna, please…"

"None of us are safe with Andrew out there." Enna quickened her pace.

"Yeah, you are probably right. You need to get far away from here, but I don't feel comfortable with you walking home by yourself right now." He sighed with a heavy shake of the head. "I'll give you a ride back to your place so you can get your things. Do you think Betty will let you use her van to get away? I will pay her for it. We'll get Jay and then you two will…disappear," the words caught in his throat. "I'll stay here and cover your tracks. You probably can't wait to get away from me anyway after what I've done."

His tense shoulders hunched and his fingers strangled the steering wheel in shame.

Enna stopped running and shook her head frantically. "No, no, you'll need to come with me. You have no idea who you are dealing with. Andrew will kill you. He won't even hesitate. And despite how much I hate you right now, I would never be able to rest without knowing you are safe. Please! My friend can give you a new identity too. Just come with me. I will hate you later."

Comforted by her earnest plea, Nick shook his head in refusal. "I have to stay here. I can convince him to keep letting me work for him so I can lead him astray. If I disappear with you, Andrew will get more suspicious and send someone after all of us."

Nick swerved around a trash can left on the street and then he steered the car close to the sidewalk again to finish what he was saying.

"I don't want him to pick up our fresh trail and find us both. But if I stay, I can tell him I found you in a different country. I'll send him on a crazy goose chase. I owe that to you. Now, please, just get in the car."

He allowed himself a small smile to try to convince Enna that he would be fine.

"I knew I should have left this city a long time ago," Enna said, beginning her route to Jay on foot once more. "This is the first time I have ever felt like I've had a family since I was a little girl and now I'm losing everything." Enna's voice quivered.

"Hey, wait." Nick brought the car to a stop at a protruding diagonal, got out, and rushed over to her. His hand instinctively met hers. She stopped walking with his touch. He carefully pulled her to his chest and timidly wrapped his arms around her. A part of him worried that she would flip out at his gesture. She must have noticed his hesitation because she returned the embrace.

"I'm sorry I knocked you to the ground. It was instinctive. I wasn't trying to hurt you. Please don't be afraid of me." Enna's limbs trembled.

With those words, Nick's grip tightened around her and snuggled his face into her hair.

"It's okay. It's okay." His heart pounded as he clung to her. "I don't want to let you go," Nick admitted.

He felt her breathing heavily beneath his grasp. "I love you," he said sweetly, kissing the top of her head.

She let out a sob, stepped back, and checked her surroundings.

"This is where I first saw you, you know? I pepper sprayed you in the face right around here." A small laugh escaped from her tears.

"I know. That was an adventure, wasn't it?" Nick brushed Enna's hair behind her perfect ears.

"I want to kiss you," Enna whispered with moist eyes.

"I thought you hated me?" Nick raised an eyebrow.

"Yeah, I do. That won't change for a while. I trusted you. Do you know what that means to me? I don't trust people. Now that you betrayed me, I'll probably never trust again. That's on you." Her words dug into his chest like an open wound.

"I thought you wanted to kiss me. Isn't that a bit of a contradiction?" Nick asked, the side of his lips raised in a confused expression.

"It is possible to have more than one emotion at once. I hate you so much right now, but I can't just turn off all my feelings from the last couple months. I really cared about you. That was real to me." Enna took a step closer to Nick. Her lips parted slightly.

I want you. Those lips called to him, but he made no advances. She would have to come to him.

"It was real to me, too," Nick whispered, knowing his words were weak in comparison to what he had done to her.

"I need a pen and paper. Do you have those in your car?" Enna spoke suddenly. Nick took a moment to process the shift in conversation. He was still entranced by her lips. He stood there, his mouth slightly puckered, picturing her lips against his own. The thought drove him wild.

"Nick? Do you?" Enna asked again.

"Uh, oh yeah, probably. Let me check." He took her hand for a moment, feeling her skin on his fingers before turning to check his car for a pen and paper.

It didn't take long for him to locate a pen, but paper was harder to find. He dug through his glove compartment and found his car registration paper. The back of the document was blank.

This'll work. He brought it over to Enna. After taking the material from his hand, she put the paper on the car's hood and began to write. Nick shifted his feet as her hand zoomed over the paper.

What are you doing? He wondered silently, not wanting to interrupt her.

Once she finished, she showed the mysterious content to Nick. "If you follow this website, there is a code you can use to contact my friend, Oliver. I wrote the code down for you. Please let me know when you are safe. Once you get Andrew off my trail, Oliver will help you change your identity and help you find me."

Nick didn't have the heart to tell her that he had his own means of changing his identity.

Enna showed a small smile of hope before she touched Nick's cheek. She brought her lips close to his but hesitated. The energy between their lips buzzed in anticipation. Nick longed to fill the gap between them, but he resisted.

The energy grew with every second they stood apart. Until, at last, Enna brushed her lips softly on his mouth. Nick's heart sputtered as he returned the kiss.

Responding to each other's passion, their bodies moved as if dancing, desperation building with each touch. Neither wanted to let go, but they could feel precious time slipping away.

They pulled apart reluctantly. Nick's eyes burned with regret.

I betrayed her, but she's being so kind. Why? This is not at all what I expected. She's not supposed to be nice to me. She's supposed to scream and curse at me and swear to never think of me again.

"Oh, Enna. You have such a beautiful heart." Nick shook his head, flabbergasted at her kindness. *How could anyone hurt you, Enna? I need to stay with you, protect you... But no, I have to stay here so I can throw Andrew off. I'm doing the right thing for once.*

Words failed Nick as he looked at Enna, who stood dazed, her breath rapid and uneven.

She looked down at her feet before speaking. "We should go," Enna said, moving to get into the car. Nick followed her example and clambered into the driver's seat. Neither of them spoke on the short ride back to Betty's house.

Not much to say after trust is broken. Grief ate at Nick as they pulled into Betty's driveway. Enna got out of the car with quiet tears decorating her cheeks.

Before she shut the car door, she turned back to Nick and said, "I think I loved you, too."

Wait! What? She loves me? Nick jumped out of the car and rushed to Enna's side.

He wrapped one arm around her waist and placed his other hand on her neck, pulling her in for one last kiss that lingered with a bittersweet intensity. The brief farewell etched a lasting memory in their hearts as they clung to each other in desperation.

Enna broke away with a sigh, turned, and made her way to Betty's front door to grab Jay.

Nick stood still while a high-pitched ringing bounced around his brain, aggravating his headache. *She's gone. I have to let her go.* Nick kicked a walnut that had fallen from a tree.

In misery, he climbed back into his car and made his way home. Once there, he sulked into the kitchen, set the car registration paper on his counter with the intent of studying Enna's code later, and grabbed a Twinkie.

I've got to get a hold of myself. I'm a mess. He thought, sniffing his armpit and cringing. *If she didn't leave because of her crazy stalker, she definitely would have left because of my smell.*

He tried to make light of the situation. He opened his Twinkie and threw the wrapper on the floor before walking into the living room to find his phone.

Okay, what message should I send Andrew? Nick asked himself. He could think of many things he wanted to say to Andrew, but those words would offend his grandma in her grave. Opening his email, Nick wrote a message for Enna's abuser.

Hey, I know I said I was quitting, but I've thought about it and would like to help you out so I did more digging. I located your wife again. She is going by the name of Ashley Rhodes now. She was last seen getting onto an airplane headed to Belgium. What would you like me to do next?

"Oh, I hope that's good enough," Nick mumbled as he stripped his clothes and headed to the shower.

As warm water streamed over his head, it acted like a mental cleanser, dissolving the cobwebs of his thoughts as he meticulously shaved his stubble. While he soaked, his mistakes replayed in his mind in an unending loop.

I should have told Enna about Andrew the moment I started having feelings for her. I really screwed up. Why did I even take this job? I should have known it was a bad idea with how much Andrew was willing to pay me. How can I live with myself after hurting Enna so much? How could she ever forgive me?

Enna's face of horror as she found out about his betrayal flashed through his mind. *I'm an idiot! She needs me with her. I can't let her disappear on her own. What was I thinking? We are better together!* Nick realized.

He quickly shut the water off and stumbled out of the shower. *There's still time! I can catch her before she leaves.* After rapidly drying himself with a towel, he threw clothes on and ran to his car, his hair still splashing water.

Speeding through town, Nick had one thought on his mind. *I have to see her again!* He parked poorly outside of her apartment and dashed to her door. Knocking louder than he knew she would appreciate, he called her name out.

No answer.

He took a deep breath and tried the door handle. His hope sank as the door swung open. She never would have left the door unlocked.

Without hope, Nick stepped inside to a quiet, lonely apartment. Numbly, he walked through the empty space, looking for any remnants of her or Jay.

I'm too late. At least I can contact her friend to find her again. He remembered the website she had left for him. *For now, I'll have to live off of memories.* He pulled out his phone and went to the photo gallery.

His brows furrowed with anxiety as he scrolled through the pictures on his phone. Frantically, he searched for the images he had captured of Enna on their last date. To his dismay, they were nowhere to be found.

"No, no, no. Please." Scrolling further, he looked for the photos he had taken with Jay at the park. They were not there either.

His stomach ached as he continued searching, only to find that the picture he had taken with Enna on their first date had also vanished.

"How? Come on!" He cried out.

I need those pictures! Where are they? That's all I have left of them. How is this possible?

On a hunch, Nick went to his text messages. He tried to find the conversation he'd shared with Enna, but her contact was nowhere to be seen on his phone. It was as though someone had completely wiped Enna and Jay out of existence.

"No, what did I do?" His tongue turned dry and his hands clammy. "I lost her."

With an aching heart, he left the apartment and headed back to his messy home.

Pulling his car into the driveway, he took a few deep breaths before going into his house to meet his man-filth that he had let pile up for the last few weeks. Walking to the kitchen, he focused on the counter where he had left his car registration paper with Enna's writing. His heart plummeted.

"No! Where is it?" With a sense of desperation, he rummaged through the hoard of trash piled on the countertop. "I put it right here!" he shouted in panic.

"Not a great hiding place, I must say," A man's cold voice came from behind Nick's back. "It is lovely to see Clara's handwriting again," the man's sleek voice mused.

Nick grabbed a salt shaker off the counter and turned to fling it at the intruder. As he turned, his eye came within an inch of a dagger that was held by a well-dressed man with dark eyes, slick black hair, and the beginning of a neatly trimmed beard.

Nick froze, salt shaker still in hand.

"It's nice to meet you in person, William. Thank you for giving me a way to contact my beautiful bride. Finally, something helpful." Andrew waved the paper in front of Nick's nose. "Maybe you weren't useless after all. Let's go collect her now, shall we?" He grinned a wide, devilish smile.

23

Crimson

Driving Betty's beat-up brown van, Enna attempted to keep the conversation cheerful despite the seriousness of the situation.

"Yup, you are going to have a secret name just like a spy," Enna explained to Jay during their three-hour drive to one of Oliver's safe houses.

Jay grinned and whooped at the thought of being a spy.

"Now as a spy, we need to have a plan and a secret code. Right?" Enna said with a storyteller's voice.

"Oh! Can the code be 'stinky breath?'" Jay said, stretching his face into a goofball expression. He started laughing through his nose.

Enna chuckled, amused. "Yeah, sure! So here's the deal. If something bad happens, I will say the secret code, 'stinky breath,' and if I say that, I need you to call for help. Then get my laptop and find a way back to Betty's house. Alright? Can you do that? You just leave and get safe. Okay? You can get a Lyft or Uber or a bus ticket. Just find Betty."

Enna glanced into her rearview mirror to make sure he was following.

"Hmmmmm, let me sink 'bout dat. What will you do if you say 'stinky breath'?" Jay scratched his brow.

She hadn't thought about that.

I would have to fight. She felt her pocket for her pepper spray. It was there waiting as always.

"If I say 'stinky breath,' my job will be to do everything in my power to protect you," she tried to sound confident. "We have a plan now! Okay, we have a few more hours of driving before we are there. What should we talk about?"

"Ohhh! Can we talk about kidneys?" Jay asked.

The subject cracked Enna up. "You are a strange one. You know that? What do you know about kidneys?" Enna asked.

A trickle of rain splashed on the windshield as they passed through the mountains. Enna kept smiling throughout the conversation with Jay, even though her heart was breaking from leaving behind her newly discovered friendships with Betty's family and...Nick.

Why do I have to miss Nick? He is the one who sent me running again. Do I have such low self-esteem that I love the man who lied to me about working with my worst nightmare? I am better than that. I deserve someone who I can trust. Nick broke my trust. Forget about him! Enna swallowed deeply, but phlegm remained, forcing her to swallow again.

To fill the hole in her chest, she focused on her one true love, Jay. Together, they filled the car with songs and jokes while they traveled. His laughter gave her a sliver of peace.

Eventually, they entered a small, rundown town with large fields where horses roamed casually. She pulled into the parking lot of an old trinket store, very similar to Oliver's previous safehouse, but this one was slightly larger.

Enna's heart thundered around in her chest. *What if Andrew followed me here? I could be putting Oliver in danger.* Enna gripped the steering wheel in a death grip, her knuckles turning white.

For several minutes, she sat motionless, staring at the rundown store. An 'open' sign blinked on and off as her gut filled with a sense of doom, with no apparent reason behind the feeling.

Get a grip! We need to get going. Why am I freaking out? Oliver is my friend. I should be excited to see him. Enna's thoughts fought to give her courage. However, they just paralyzed her further.

Wait, what if Oliver is still in love with me? Do I tell him about Nick? What if Oliver gets jealous and decides not to help me anymore? No. He wouldn't do that? I don't even need to tell him. Nick is nothing...nobody.

"Mommy, what's wrong? Why we just sittin' here?" Jay asked, waking Enna from her irrational fears.

"Oh, sorry, buddy. I'm just having a bit of anxiety. Let's go." She turned the car off, got out, and stretched her legs for a bit. It had been a couple hours since their last stop and her legs tingled from sitting in the car for so long.

Jay unbuckled the top clasp of his car seat but struggled with the bottom buckle. Enna helped him free himself from the straps. Together, they walked to the store's door.

"Mommy, I gotta pee," Jay said urgently.

"There should be a restroom in here." Enna pushed the door open. "Don't touch anything, though. There are a lot of old things that I don't want broken. Okay?"

Other than a chime from a bell as they opened the door, the store held an eerie silence. The hairs on Enna's arms prickled as her attention fell to the cashier's counter, where she expected to see Oliver. Besides old gadgets and paintings with creepy, staring eyes, the room was vacant.

Something's off. The flickering, dim lights above her reminded her of a horror film she had recently watched with Nick.

"This place is cweepy," Jay said, hiding behind his mom's leg.

"Yeah, a bit." Enna put a distracted hand back and placed it on Jay's head.

Oliver should be here. Looking around, she noticed a door near the cashier's counter.

Maybe he's in his bunker and just didn't hear the bell.

She walked over to the door and tried the knob. Locked. She knocked softly and called out Oliver's name.

"Mommy! I still have to potty so bad!" Jay said, doing an awkward dance with his knees together.

Enna jumped slightly. She had been so focused on finding Oliver that she momentarily forgot about Jay.

"Oh yeah." Enna swept the store with her eyes. She looked between a couple of aisles before finding a dusty restroom sign.

Enna pointed toward it, "Look, the potty is over there." Jay waddled in the direction his mom indicated. "Wait, buddy, remember the code 'stinky breath?' Do you remember what you should do if I say that?" Enna asked.

Jay shifted his legs uncomfortably. "Course' I go ta Betty's house," Jay said in a loud whisper.

Enna cringed and glanced around. "Shhhh! You're not supposed to say it out loud! This place could be bugged."

Jay put his hands over his mouth. "Eww! Bugs are gross," he said through his fingers.

Enna smiled and handed Jay the van keys. "Here, take these in case you need to grab the laptop from the van." She noticed Jay's uncomfortable stance and distressed expression.

Oh, duh, he still has to pee. "Go on, I'm just going to look around for my friend who was supposed to be here," Enna whispered.

With a look of gratitude, Jay scurried off to relieve himself.

Enna inched her way over to the empty cashier's counter. She heard a crunch, looked down, and saw a broken glass angel figurine that had been squished by her foot. She noticed several other items that seemed to have been pulled from the shelves in a struggle.

Not sure what she was looking for, Enna walked behind the counter and had to step over a cash register that lay sideways on the ground. Dollar bills and coins were scattered all over. Her breath became increasingly shallow with each step. Behind the counter, a black lock box was open with nothing inside.

Grab Jay and get out of here now! Enna's mind screamed at her.

"Jay. Jay! We have to go!" she called out, rushing to the restrooms.

Pulling out her phone, Enna began calling the police. However, in her hurry, her foot found something slick on the floor. The traction of her shoes lost its hold as she slid a few inches, wobbled backward, and then came crashing to the ground.

The back of her head cracked into the concrete as she landed in a slimy substance. Enna's eyes blurred with pain that spread from the back of her head to her ringing ears.

After the room stopped spinning, she sat up slowly and gently lifted a hand to her head. She felt a warm, sticky ooze dripping from her hair. The back of her shirt was drenched. She looked around her and let out a screech. She was sitting in a pool of crimson blood. Her mind began to yell.

This is too much blood. I'm dying! Maybe I am already dead. There is no way I should be bleeding this much and still be alive! Enna gasped in rapid breaths. Holding the injury on her head, she tried to stop the bleeding.

"Awww! Ow, Ow, Ow!" she cried out as the pain from her head pounded.

Nope, I can't be dead. I'm in way too much pain for this to be death. She carefully tried to stand, but blood squished beneath her shoes, making her slip a little. She collapsed back into the puddle of blood.

Wait, this blood was here before I slipped. This can't be my blood. Enna's throbbing brain finally connected to reality.

The contents from Enna's stomach flopped due to rising nausea.

Oliver's blood?

"Oliver!" Enna shouted, letting fear get the better of her. She began to tremble out of control. "Oliver! Where are you? Don't be dead. Please!"

Her cries echoed around the store. She could hardly breathe when she noticed a trail of blood going from where she sat to a back door that led outside.

How did I miss that before? Enna wondered. In the dim lights, the trail had looked like mud. Now that she realized what it was, it was so obvious she could not look away. She considered following the trail, but Jay's quivering voice stopped her.

"Mommy, I'm scared. Are you okay? Are you bleeding?" His voice came from behind one of the shelves.

Enna looked up toward him with tears streaming down her face. She didn't even try to control her emotions.

"No! No, I'm not okay! Nothing is okay." Enna shook as she sobbed. She had no willpower to calm her words, even for the sake of her son. "I slipped and hit my head. Now I'm covered in blood, but most of it's not mine, which means my best friend is probably dead, just like my mom. He left me just like she did! Argh! Everyone leaves me. It's not okay. My boyfriend betrayed me, but I still love him and I'll never see him again!"

Enna was yelling now, not at Jay but at the universe. "Now Andrew is going to find me and take my son away so he can be a government project!"

Tears mixed into the blood on the ground as Enna huddled in a tight ball on the floor, rocking back and forth. "I can't do it. I can't lose you. I need you!"

While Enna lost all sanity, Jay crept over to her with a look of horror, tears forming at the corners of his eyes. He looked around and found an old poncho on display. He grabbed it, walked over to his distraught mom, and draped it over her shoulders.

"It's okay, Mommy. I'll take care of you. I'm not leavin'," Jay's tender voice promised.

Enna grabbed Jay and pulled him onto her lap, not paying attention to the blood that now decorated his shirt as well as her own.

"Sorry, I'm so sorry. I'm a terrible failure of a mom. Sorry. Sorry. Sorry," she repeated while rocking Jay.

"You're not a terrible mom. You are my favorite mom on the whole planet and you are a sweetheart." Jay gave her a weak smile. He reached up and poked Enna on the nose.

A laugh pushed itself out through Enna's tears.

"I love you so much, my baby boy," Enna said, her voice squeaking from the effort of fighting back the next wave of panic. She squeezed Jay in a tight hug.

"Oh, how touching," a dark voice vibrated through the little store.

Ice trickled into Enna's core.

No, wake up! This isn't real. It's just another nightmare, Enna hoped frantically as she recognized the voice of the man who haunted her dreams. Her hand slid through the puddle of blood, looking for her phone so she could call the police.

After finding it, she frantically tapped at the screen that had been broken in the fall. Nothing happened. The phone refused to work.

Just like her nightmares, all hope of help was lost.

"Congratulations on the son. I've always wanted to be a father," the voice continued as her brain screamed, trying to force herself to run, but she was frozen with fear.

Enna dropped the phone and gripped Jay tight. Whipping her head around, she frantically tried to figure out where the voice came from. She noticed a few speakers in the ceiling magnifying his voice. Her eyes then caught a glimpse of something that made her choke. A camera hung in the corner of the store. She looked around and located three more cameras in every corner. Andrew was watching her from every angle.

He's in Oliver's bunker! Her eyes shot to the door she assumed led to the basement.

"Yes, I can see you. Your friend had quite the elaborate security system. Lot of good that did him."

No! He is just messing with my head. Pins of terror bit her skin. Enna dipped her head close to Jay's ear and whispered to him softly. "Jay, remember 'stinky breath?'"

Jay nodded. "You can steal money from the bank if you need to because this is an emergency. Get far away from here. I love you so much." She kissed him on the head. "Okay, Ready? Go!" Enna lifted Jay to his feet. She watched as he took off toward the door.

Her heart surged as she watched her son, her life, run to safety. She wanted to stay with him and protect him. She hated letting him out of her sight, but anywhere was safer than here.

Please, please be safe, Jay, Enna prayed, glaring directly at one of the cameras.

"You would never be fit to be a father. You can have me, but you had better stay away from my son!" she said boldly, trying to hide her shaking hands.

A cruel laugh echoed through the shop. "Oh, I have missed that spicy spirit of yours," Andrew's voice cooed.

The bell on the door rang as Jay left the store and ran off as fast as his tiny feet would carry him.

"No worries, I don't truly like children. I would likely end up wringing his little neck if he stuck around. I'd much rather have some alone time with just you. We don't need a child getting in our way," Andrew's smug voice taunted.

Enna's stomach lurched. She found some courage and burst into action. She quickly crawled away from the puddle of blood, wobbled to her feet, and dashed toward the front door. She reached her hand out for the handle when Andrew's voice caught hold. "It's a shame about your friend...Oliver, was it?"

His voice no longer came from the speakers. It whispered behind her now.

Enna spun around to see the monster from her past standing across the store. He looked out of place in the rugged shop with his fancy suit and neatly combed hair. He appeared to have a slight goose egg on his forehead.

"What did you do to Oliver?" Enna choked through gritted teeth.

Andrew looked pleased with himself. "Well, I recognized him immediately, of course. You know, I may seem calloused at times, but I pay attention to the people I hire. He used to work on my vineyard. I gave him a job even though I knew he was here illegally. I showed him mercy. Then what does he do? He turns around and stabs me in the back. After I saw his face, it wasn't hard for me to figure out his connection to you." Andrew stepped closer to Enna with each sentence. She was unable to make herself move.

"He loved you, didn't he? Tell me, Clara, why else would you cheat on me and run away with him? He tricked you into loving him, didn't he?"

Andrew stood only a few feet away now. Hoping to distract him from coming any closer, Enna forced words from her mouth.

"He saved me. You had beaten me almost to death. I passed out in the vineyard. Oliver found me and bandaged me up. You should thank him for saving my life," Enna said with a strength she didn't truly possess. Her mind raced to devise a combination of strikes that could help her escape, but years of built-up panic muddled her thoughts.

"Yes, I would thank him, if he were still alive, but alas, he stole you from me. He had to go." Andrew stepped even closer, pulling out a dagger from around his waist. It still had smudges of red on the blade.

Master Kim had always told Enna that facing a real threat would be nothing like fighting in the ring. Her brain would be cluttered, and she would have to go off of instinct, which is why they repeated the fight combinations so regularly. Unfortunately, despite training, her first instinct when it came to Andrew was to freeze and cower.

Enna told herself to move into a fighter's stance, but instead of obeying, she reached into her pocket to grab her pepper spray.

As she pulled it out, Andrew lunged forward and pressed his dagger onto her neck, ready to slice.

"Drop it," He hissed, glancing at the pepper spray.

Enna closed her eyes and forced her hand to open. She heard the clatter as it bounced against the hard floor.

"Good girl," Andrew whispered.

Enna wanted to spit in his face, but the dagger dug into her neck. Her eyes darted around the store, trying to come up with an escape plan. An old machete hung on the back wall.

If I can get to that, I might survive. She pictured the fight moves she could do to break away. However, something about Andrew left her paralyzed. She couldn't will herself to move no matter how loud her mind screamed at her to do something.

"You know, before Oliver died, he told me about how he gathered supplies for you to make the car bomb. You communicated through code so I wouldn't suspect anything. Very clever. Who's idea was that? Yours, right? You have always been exceptionally smart. That's one thing I admire about you." He paused dramatically and let his lips curl up in a wicked grin.

Lowering his dagger, he brushed Enna's hair back behind her ear. "Now, sweet girl, Oliver can no longer get in the way of our love."

His cold laugh left a ringing in Enna's aching head. *Oliver is dead. Gone. My dearest friend is dead because of me.* Enna quaked from the revelation, her legs threatening to give in.

"Please, tell me you are lying," she breathed, her thoughts screaming in agony.

Andrew stepped in even closer, put his lips to her ear, and whispered, "Whose blood do you think you are wearing, Clara?"

24

Sweet Death

The world spun around Enna and the flickering lights flashed, disorienting her further. Andrew's face drifted near, leering at her while his dark eyes pierced through her skin.

Horror replaced reality. Nothing made sense. The store fell from focus as she toppled into Andrew, no longer able to stand.

"Oh," Andrew said in surprise as Enna's world disappeared completely.

For a moment, Enna floated into nothingness. It was as if her body had dissolved into a state of non-existence.

She had no thoughts, no emotions, and no aches or pains. Her eyes were open, but she saw nothing. Felt nothing.

Enna had no idea how much time had passed before a small red flicker in the distance appeared in the abyss.

At first, it resembled a dancing flame, but it soon took the form of a woman in a flowing red dress gracefully walking through the blackened air toward her.

Mom? Oh, I guess I'm dead. Andrew must have finally killed me. I didn't even feel it. Peace flowed around her. *I'm free of him. Finally.*

"Oh, dear girl," her mother's voice vibrated in Enna's soul. "I'm so sorry I left you. I should have been there to protect you."

Enna wanted to cry, but the disassociation from her body made that impossible.

"Mom, I missed you so much! It's been so hard without you." Her mom drifted over and swept Enna up in an embrace, their hearts beating in a synchronized rhythm.

Take me with you, Mom, Enna thought. The words were heard floating around the abyss. Her mother pulled away with a downward expression on her face and she shook her head.

Enna was about to protest when another voice rolled over to her from a distance. "Watch out for my 'mote control car!"

Enna turned to see Jay running toward her, chasing his car.

No! Why are you here, Jay? You can't be here if I'm dead, Enna's thoughts projected out loud again.

"I told you I wouldn't leave you. I need you too, Mommy," Jay's words entered her body.

Enna's attention was divided again when a man's voice vibrated through her emotions.

"This is all my fault," the voice agonized. "I'm so sorry!"

"Nick!" Enna recognized his voice. She looked up and saw Nick swimming above her through black clouds with his snorkel and goggles on his face.

Enna laughed. "Silly Nick, what are you doing up there?"

He didn't respond. He just kept floating through the air.

A hand touched Enna's shoulder. She turned to see Oliver's solemn face next to her.

"He needs yeh. They both do." Oliver's familiar Scottish accent resonated around her. "I'm sorry I can't protect yeh this time. I will always love yeh, Clara."

Oliver took Enna's hand, kissed it, and turned to her mother.

"Come, Venessa, your daughter has work to do." Oliver offered Enna's mother an elbow to escort her.

Before Venessa took it, she smiled softly and squeezed Enna's hand.

"I love you, my daughter," she whispered, putting her arm through Oliver's, and together, they walked away toward the darkness.

"No. No Please! Don't leave me again," Enna called out, reaching for the trail of her mother's flowing red dress that lingered behind, but her hand passed right through it.

"You'll be alright, my beautiful girl. You're strong. You always have been," her mother's voice drifted over to her before she disappeared completely.

"Mommy, you won't be alone," Jay's voice now came directly from the remote-controlled car that was doing flips through the air.

"Enna, get out of here!" Nick shouted. "Enna! Please, he's coming back." His voice dropped closer and closer to her until it seemed to be screaming directly in her ear.

Pain resurfaced in Enna's head, causing her eyes to flutter. The darkness parted, revealing Nick's frantic face coming into focus. Kneeling beside her, he shook her shoulder with his hands that were bound together at the wrists. He had a gash above his right eye and blood caked on his face.

Enna yearned to reach out and hold him, but her body would not listen.

"Hey, can you hear me?" Nick asked. Enna couldn't figure out how to form words with her mouth.

Her eyes darted around the room, trying to make sense of what was happening.

She glared at a dim light bulb that swung overhead. Despite the small lightbulb's effort to illuminate the area, the square cement room remained dark and gloomy.

Near Enna's feet, computer monitors displayed different views of the trinket shop.

Oliver's bunker? Enna guessed. The bed she laid on had no spring to it. It felt as though she rested on a solid plank of wood.

Enna shifted, and an instant groan escaped her. It seemed that every drop of blood in her body was hosting a raging party in her head, which was exacerbated by Nick's persistent, anxious words. The mounting pressure on her brain drowned out all common sense.

"Nick, what are you doing here? Did you fall out of the sky while you were swimming?" Enna said, slurring her words together. "Why does your face look like that?"

"Oh, you're awake! Enna, get up, please. There's no time. Andrew just left to talk to one of his men about transportation. He'll be back any minute. You need to get out of here," Nick pled. "Sweetheart, please listen. I love you! I can't watch him hurt you. You have to get up." Nick's eyes were bloodshot, but his expression narrowed with a strong determination.

Enna scrunched her face up at the word "sweetheart."

"Ewwww, you know I don't like pet names," Enna laughed playfully, still not entirely with it. "It's alright, Nick. I still like you, but I really hate you. You are so cute and silly, and I'm really crazy about you. Is it just me, or is the room flipping upside-down?"

Enna tried sitting up, causing more pain to split through her head. Moaning, she laid back down. Nick smiled slightly with a sad shake of his head.

"Wow, this loopy side of you is absolutely adorable, but you need to snap out of it," Nick said. "I know it hurts, but try to stand up and get out of here before Andrew comes back."

"Aww, man! I thought I was dead," Enna pouted.

Nick lifted his eyebrows. "Nope, not dead. You just passed out. Now, get up and get away from here. Go find Jay."

Jay! The mention of her son snapped Enna's attention back to the seriousness of the situation. Slowly, she sat up in the bed, trying not to jar her throbbing head. Nick attempted to help, but his hands and feet were tied with thick rope, making it a challenge to assist her.

Once the room stopped tipping over, Enna took Nick's hands and tugged on the knot that bound them together.

"No, Enna. There's no time. Leave me!" Nick pulled away. "I'll be just fine, but I can't watch him abuse you. Please just go." His tired voice cracked with desperation.

Enna ignored his plea and reached for him again to continue fighting with the rope. It loosened slightly but still bit deep into his wrists.

"No, Nick. I can't just leave you here. He'll kill you. If I help you stand, can you hop out of here?"

Nick was already shaking his head no before she finished speaking. "I would just slow you down. Enna, I promise I will escape, but-"

The eerie screech of an old metal door cut Nick's words short.

Andrew towered in the doorway with a grin painted on his face.

25

Monster

"Oh, sweet Clara, you're awake!" With vast strides, Andrew moved to tower over Nick, who still knelt next to Enna.

"Get out of my way, boy," Andrew snarled.

Nick attempted to use the bed to rise to his feet in defiance, but before he made progress, Andrew slammed his foot into Nick's side, making him plummet onto the cement floor.

"Stop!" Enna slid off the bed and reached for Nick to help him up.

Before she could reach him, Andrew grabbed her arm near the elbow and jerked her away.

"Clara, I was so worried about you. You just passed out in my arms. I guess I just have that effect on beautiful women." Andrew contorted his face into an ugly smirk. Enna twisted her arm out of his grip and stumbled backward, away from him. She continued retreating until the far wall halted her escape.

Stepping around Nick, Andrew slowly drew closer to Enna.

"Come now, Clara. As soon as we are back at my estate, my finest physician will look at that head of yours." He stood less than an arm's length away from her. "The helicopter will soon be ready to take us home."

"I'm not going anywhere with you, you monster!" Enna snapped back at him and raised her fists, ready to fight.

Andrew tilted his head menacingly down to the side, pressing his lips tightly together. His eyebrows furrowed, causing a dark shadow to cloud his eyes until they turned black.

"Feisty, aren't you?" He put up his own fists and faked an attack. Enna blocked her face with a cry. "Do you really want to fight me, Clara? You know I will win. I always win. And when I do, you will watch me torture everyone you love until the light goes out in their eyes." With a dangerous grin, Andrew subtly flashed a glance in Nick's direction.

Enna cowered and slid her back down the wall until she sat on the cold floor in a shaking heap.

Nick inched his way across the room, trying to get close enough to attack Andrew. Enna's teeth clamped together until there was a tight strain on her jaws.

I've beaten guys three times Andrew's size before. Why can't I just take him out? I am the ONE martial arts champion! Why am I not doing something?

Enna's mind urged her to take action, to take control of the situation, but her P.T.S.D. held her captive, sending her back to the years when she was a weak, powerless teenager.

Feeling like jelly, Enna glanced around Andrew's legs so she could see Nick, wishing to be brave enough for him. He sat against the wall adjoining the one where she cowered. Desperately, he ripped at his bonds with his teeth.

Andrew bent down in a low crouch next to Enna. Intuitively, she threw her hands over her head in protection as Andrew drew closer. His nose stopped mere inches from her upraised arm.

"I am trying hard to be patient, Clara. I don't want to harm you...though I probably should. You are undisciplined." Andrew grabbed both of Enna's hands. Locking his fingers into hers, he held them in a sign of romance and control. "Luckily for you, I'm smitten by your beauty and stamina."

Pull away, Enna. Do something! She screamed inwardly, but all she could do was turn her face away from his with a grimace. Nick scooted toward Andrew, his face distorted in anger.

"If you hurt her, I swear I will make you pay!" Nick yelled. Andrew slowly licked his lips while keeping his attention on Enna. He was quiet just long enough for her to imagine his sick thoughts.

Nick calmed his voice down before speaking again. "Andrew, Hey, listen, buddy. You need to let her go. Please."

Without taking his eyes off Enna, Andrew's arm robotically snapped in Nick's direction with a finger pointed at his chest.

"Shut up," Andrew's sharp, simple words bounced around the cement room.

"Are you really going to take her away from her son? Don't you have a soul?" Nick continued. Andrew rolled his eyes and flexed his jaw while Enna shot a pleading glance Nick's way.

Please stop. What are you doing, Nick? Stay out of this, Enna wanted to yell, but her vocal cords were cut by fear.

Andrew's eyes ticked dangerously, contemplating what Nick's consequence would be. He turned his head halfway so his face could be seen by both Enna and Nick.

"This does not concern you, boy. Do you think I won't kill you?" Andrew's deliberate words electrified Enna's core.

"*No!*" She mouthed, shaking her head at Nick.

"Yeah. Okay. Why haven't you killed me yet then? I'm right here. Just kill me because I'm not going to sit here and watch as you-"

Enna's weak voice cut off Nick's words. "Nick, stop. I can handle him. Please." Enna trembled. Nick shook his head and was about to continue speaking when Andrew let go of one of Enna's hands and pulled his dagger out. Placing it on Enna's jawline, his eyes glinted, aching for blood.

"William, oh, I guess you go by Nicolas now? Not that it matters. What does matter is that I truly don't want to hurt my beautiful girl, but I will if it is the only way to get you to Shut...Up!" Andrew pricked

Enna's skin lightly. "And don't worry, I do plan on killing you, but not quite yet. I want to have some fun first."

Enna watched Nick's face go from anger red to death white.

I might never feel Nick's arms around me again!

"I hate you," Enna spat in a hushed whisper. She attempted to pull her hand out of Andrew's clutches, but he only tightened his grip.

"Oh, Clara, why hate me?" Andrew asked. "I am the one who saved you when you were begging on the streets. Don't you remember?" He placed the flat side of his dagger onto Enna's cheek and traced her face with it. "You were half starved and I gave you all the food you could desire, a beautiful castle, and..." The cold blade of his dagger halted under her right ear as he whispered, "...love."

He twisted the blade until the sharp edge of the dagger dug into her neck. "All you had to do was be there for me and do as I asked. You know, I should be the one to hate."

The dagger pressed deeper into her skin with each cold word until a trickle of blood dripped down her neck. She hardly felt it, but the shock of being cut made her cry out in a panic. Nick's voice shot out at Andrew.

"No! I'll be quiet. Just don't hurt her. I thought you loved her!!" Nick shouted.

Andrew's face transformed into surprise as though he'd just realized what he was doing. Jerking the dagger away from Enna's jaw, he placed it back in its sheath.

"I'm so sorry Clara. I didn't mean to hurt you. I couldn't hate you. You're too precious to me." He leaned in to whisper in her ear. "Do you know what you do to me, Clara?"

Still holding Enna's hand, he used his free hand to gently guide her face toward his. "You know, when I thought you were dead, it destroyed me. I was so broken without you. Lonely. Lost...Alone. I didn't want to live anymore." He swallowed hard as if concealing pent-up emotion. "I didn't think I could ever be happy again. You have no idea the heartache I went through when I lost you." Finally letting go of Enna's hand, he stood and turned his back to her.

He let silence linger for dramatic effect. Nick closed his eyes, took a deep breath, held it, and then slowly blew it out. Enna followed along with the breathing exercise, wanting to regain her composure. She despised giving Andrew the satisfaction of breaking her.

When Andrew's voice cut through the silence, it was solemn and shaky. Turning slowly to Enna, he was the picture of pure grief.

"I haven't told anyone this before, but I've always struggled to get close to people, Clara." Taking a step closer, his voice rose in volume. "It isn't my fault, you know? I was a good kid. I..." he chuckled, "I even believed in true love. Ha!"

He paused, noting Nick's fierce expression. Walking over to him, Andrew lowered himself to Nick's level, kneeling on one knee.

"Do you know how it feels to be tortured by your own father, Nicolas?"

"No, but it sounds horrible." Nick dripped his voice with forced sympathy.

"Oh Nicolas...you simply cannot imagine it until you have experienced it yourself." Andrew stood to look down at him. "If you think I'm evil..." his gaze flashed to Enna, "worthy of hate, like you said...you should have met my father." Andrew let out a chilling laugh. "Now, *he* was a monster worthy of hate. He made me watch as he beat my mother half to death just for trying to protect me from him."

"Listen," Nick interrupted Andrew's story with a sincere note. "That's awful. You're right. I can't even imagine going through something like that. I'm truly sorry."

"Oh, it's okay now. Despite him being the worst father in history, I learned so much from him. You see, I was never good enough for him. He wanted me to be his little trophy child. He wanted me to be perfect."

Andrew meandered over to the bed to sit.

"Don't get me wrong. He was not all bad. No one is. I had the perfect father as long as others were around. He'd laugh with me. Praise me. Worship me." Andrew leaned in as though telling a scary story around the campfire.

"But once the parties were over and the guests went home, he'd change. Behind closed doors, he would have a few drinks to unwind, and then, if I hadn't shown off enough to the guests—if I hadn't been the most intelligent, the funniest, the best-looking, he would take me and..." he took a sharp breath in. "Do whatever he wanted to me."

Andrew paused his narrative dramatically to wipe a finger under his eye, clearing away moisture that was not there.

Enna knew this soft side of Andrew was an act. At one point in her life, she would have fallen for his humanistic emotions and apologized for his pain, but now she reveled in his anguish.

You deserve to be miserable! The hatred went against her caring personality, but he'd already caused too much damage to regain her empathy.

Andrew stood and made his way across the room. Towering above Nick again, he lifted his lips into a sneer. "Well let's just say, my dad taught me that the only way to gain respect was to be the most powerful and demand it. Take it." Andrew casually fiddled with a red ring on his right hand.

Nick spoke up softly. "But you didn't respect your father, clearly. So he didn't get what he wanted, right? It wasn't true respect. It was fear. Do you think what you are taking is respect?"

Realizing Nick was attempting to connect with Andrew's humanity, Enna couldn't help but offer a slight smile in his direction. *Too bad Andrew's not human.*

Anger flickered through Andrew, causing him to throw himself to Enna's side. His hand shot up and wrapped around her neck. She desperately peeled at his thumb as his nails dug into her skin.

"What I'm taking…Nicolas, is control, which is better than re-spect!" Andrew looked at Enna, whose mouth hung open in a frozen gasp.

"Ok! I get it! You like your control. Stop!" Nick's calm voice broke into a yell and his body jerked forward.

"Get…back," Andrew ordered Nick.

Reluctantly, he obeyed but his eyes remained narrow with fury.

Andrew roughly released Enna, knocking her injured head back against the wall. Her eyes swam, darkness threatening to take her again. Andrew turned to glare at Nick.

"See, Nicolas. I can control you without even touching you. Fun, right?"

Enna glared and found her voice. "You might be able to control our actions, but you can never control who we love! And, I will always despise you no matter what you do. You can't change that and it infu-riates you, doesn't it?".

Enna flinched as Andrew laughed and moved to sit by her side. He stroked her hair with a shaking hand as though he could not control himself. He needed to touch her.

"Oh, Clara, I love that fire in you. I remember when I first laid eyes on you—begging on the street corner. I knew you were special. I saw the determined look in your eyes." He leaned in close to Enna's ear. "It was the same determined look I had after I finally killed my parents. Sad, lost, but so powerful. We're the same, Clara. Both plagued by our weak, pathetic parents."

Enna turned her face away as blood boiled in her cheeks, but he took her chin and forced her eyes back to him.

"I knew you were different from my other girls. Despite your fear, you fought me on everything. You challenged me. Your defiance made me want you so badly. You became my obsession." Andrew took a lock of her hair and kissed it.

Enna fixed her gaze on Nick's face to gain strength and grounding.

Nick's eyes burned and his chest rose and fell with heaving breath. His jaw flexed as he strained to stay silent. Enna found solace in his restraint.

"Oh! When that limo exploded!" Andrew blurted loud enough to make them both jump. "I couldn't believe that you were gone. I put ads out everywhere for you. Anytime a person interacted with one of my ads, I sent a private investigator to check them out, like that moron over there." Andrew motioned to Nick who briefly closed his eyes with a sharp breath in, trying to hide his shame. Andrew smiled at the reaction before continuing his story.

"Most of the time, those messing with my ads were just geeks trying to make an ad-free page, but I never gave up on you. No...No, no." Andrew shook his head with a grin. "I kept searching until I found you. I never lost hope. That is what you mean to me. That's why..." his lips parted just enough for Enna to see his hungry, quivering tongue before he whispered, "You will love me...whenever I ask."

An involuntary jolt cascaded through Enna's body, making her jump to her feet to make a break for the door. She hardly got two steps in before Andrew caught her wrist, spun her around, and slammed her back against the cement wall where she had just been sitting moments earlier.

The pain from her head resurfaced with a vengeance, along with a shock down her spine.

Ringing in her ears mixed with a shout of protest from Nick while at the same time, Andrew positioned his body in front of her. His arms pressed against the wall on either side of her, trapping her close to him.

Enna knew the exact fight moves that would set her free, but her body would not comply. Fear held her in place.

Andrew was so close to her face that she could smell the spearmint on his breath. She turned her face away as he hissed, "Try anything like that again, your friend Nicolas will lose an eye. Am I clear?" Enna bobbed her head without a word, her stomach churning.

"Now, what was I saying? Oh yeah. You must love me." Andrew dived right back into his monologue. "Sure, I have other girls, but they don't give me the same thrill I get from you. I feel no real connection to them. No drive and no challenge. You are the only one I will ever love." Placing a palm on Enna's cheek, Andrew leaned in and brushed his lips against hers softly.

A new wave of nausea filled Enna to the brim. She smacked his hand away and shoved his shoulders. He grabbed both of her wrists and held her arms above her head, against the wall, before he pressed his lips more firmly onto hers. The pain from her head was minimal compared to the revulsion and helplessness caused by the sickening monster pressing himself against her body.

Why? Why are you so weak? Do something! Enna cried to herself, twitching in disgust.

Andrew moved to restrain both her arms with his one hand while the other hand wrapped around her waist and allowed it to wander seductively down her leg.

Enna's pleading eyes watered as Andrew held her. She could see Nick's face from the corner of her vision. His expression twisted into absolute loathing as he fought against the ropes, slightly loosened by now.

"You call that love?" Nick yelled. "If you really loved her, you would want her to be happy and leave her alone! You are hurting because you know she could never love you and it kills you inside. Andrew...Please. Let her go!" Nick's face distorted into a broken mass of anguish.

After one more forced kiss, Andrew pulled away from Enna, allowing her to slide down the wall into a huddled ball of shame and regret.

Slowly, Andrew turned his attention to Nick.

"Oh really? You think she could never love me? And what makes you an expert in love?" Andrew spat.

"Well, I know love isn't...this," Nick said, nodding his head toward Enna's cowering body.

Andrew glanced back at Enna just as she met Nick's eyes in earnest. Recognizing the full connection between the two of them, Andrew scoffed.

"Ah, I see," he said smugly. He looked at Nick as though he were a child who had been caught stealing cookies from the cookie jar. "You love her." He stood and strolled a few steps over to where Nick sat against the connecting wall. "Isn't that sweet? You think you love her more than I do?" He crouched down close to Nick. "You can't even imagine how much I love her. I would do anything for her. I would die for her."

"Then why don't you? That's obviously what she wants," Nick snarled at Andrew's darkening face, no longer able to control his rage.

"Ha! You think you are so funny?" Andrew snapped. "Fine, we will see how much she loves you." His lips twitched in a dangerous fury while his eyes narrowed maliciously.

26

The Game

Checking the gold watch that shined on his wrist, Andrew puckered his lips.

"Perfect. It seems we have just enough time for one game before we leave. Now, Clara..." he turned to Enna, reached down to grab her chin, and forced it up in his direction. "You'll need to listen very carefully to the rules. Okay?"

Enna's eyes glimmered with terror as Andrew stood up straight and unsheathed his dagger once more.

"This game is called, '*Who do you love more?*' In this game, we will see if you love your dear Nicolas more or...your son." Andrew took a few steps toward Nick. Enna's eyes widened as she gasped for air.

"No! You leave Jay out of this!" she yelled. "You will never find him!"

Andrew just chuckled darkly and asked, "Who is Betty?" He slowly turned to look at Enna, who was desperately shaking her head.

"What? No. I don't know!" Enna refused to look at him.

Furious, Andrew flew over to Enna, violently gripped a clump of her hair, and jerked it hard, forcing her to look up at him.

"Don't LIE to me, child! I overheard your conversation with your boy. I heard him say something about a Betty. Was she a friend of yours in Payson? I'm sure I could find her with very little difficulty. I hope your son finds her as well. It's not safe for little boys to be wandering around alone." Andrew roughly released her hair.

Enna's body dropped heavily, like stone, as she realized Andrew could easily locate Jay.

"No, Andrew. Please!" Enna melted into tears.

"Now that you're listening, let me explain the rules of the game." He lapped the room while twirling his dagger through his fingers. "You are going to watch as I torture your *lover*," he pointed the dagger at Nick casually. "I will leave you untied. If you look away or try to stop me, I will hunt down your son and I'll play this game with him as well." Andrew crouched down next to Nick and ran the dagger blade slowly across his neck without piercing the skin. Nick held still, but his eyes glared with a brave intensity at Andrew's threatening face.

"STOP!" Enna shrieked and jolted forward toward Andrew. Without hesitation, he turned and punched her in the face, making her fall to the ground in excruciating pain.

Nick roared and threw his tied hands into Andrew's side, striking him in the ribs. Andrew cursed as he momentarily lost his balance. Once stabilizing himself, he grasped Nick's neck in a one-handed front choke and slammed him into the wall.

Nick's eyes bulged and his mouth opened, begging for air that was not allowed to enter.

No! I can't watch him die. No! Enna dragged herself into a begging position.

"Please, Andrew, don't do this. I can love you. I will be your loving, perfect servant. Whatever you want, you can have. Just let him live!" Enna pled with him.

"Really?" Andrew's evil grin challenged. "Then kiss me…passionately."

Without thinking twice, Enna moved in close to Andrew, put her hand on the side of his head, and placed her lips on his. She shook but melted into him, hoping he would mistake desperation for passion.

He released Nick's neck and slipped his fingers seductively into her hair as she kissed him.

Enna peeked her eyes open to see Nick contorting his hands against the restraining rope on his wrists. His fingers turned purple until a loud pop erupted from the bone in his thumb.

Enna's eyes widened in surprise as his hands slipped free of the rope. He quickly began untying the restraining ropes at his ankles. Andrew sharply drew away from Enna and turned to see Nick's escape attempt.

Andrew swung a punch at Nick but before the strike made contact, Nick threw his forearm up for a block. Then, despite his broken thumb, he responded with a punch to Andrew's gut, making him sputter and hunch over.

Enna sat trembling, unable to make herself move to Nick's aid.

Anxiety doesn't control me! Don't be worthless! Move! Andrew has too much power over me. He controls everything. He will kill Jay if I move. I can't let that happen! But he might kill Jay anyway if I don't stop him.

Nick got a few more punches in before Andrew flung the hilt of his dagger into the side of Nick's head, making him topple over, unconscious.

Enna gasped. The sight of Nick unmoving on the floor momentarily broke through her paralysis of fear. Darting at Andrew, she clenched his wrist that held the dagger. With both hands, she twisted downward, attempting to disarm him. Andrew grasped her hair and pulled it to the ground. The pain from her concussed head pounded her into submission once more.

With Enna lying on her back, Andrew straddled her and wrapped his fingers around her neck, cutting off the blood supply to her brain. Growing lightheaded, Enna clawed at his thumbs, trying to rip his hands off of her neck. At the same time, she bucked her hips and slammed a knee into his lower back.

One of Andrew's hands came off her neck and posted on the ground in front of him to prevent himself from being flung off of her. Enna took a gulp of air in before he regained his hold around her neck.

"Calm down, Clara. Stop fighting me!" Enna's vision blurred. "I will give you one last chance. Let's begin the game from the beginning now. If you move from this spot, I will locate your son and make you watch as I decorate him with my dagger. I am so sorry I have to do this to you, but there needs to be consequences for your behavior." Andrew bent down and kissed her cheek before releasing her neck. Enna turned onto her side, gasping for air.

Andrew rose to his feet and took a few strides toward Nick. After a swift kick to the side, Nick moaned, his eyes snapping open as he returned to the realm of consciousness. Sitting up, Nick saw Enna sputtering for air and instantly reached a hand out to help her.

Before he could reach her, Andrew extended the dagger, causing him to pull back.

"Now, Clara, where should I start?" Andrew asked, crouching next to Nick again.

Enna gasped for breath while Andrew ran the blade of his dagger near Nick's eye. She shivered uncontrollably, watching in helpless terror. The dagger pricked the skin of Nick's cheek. He grunted and threw another fist toward Andrew's jaw, but Andrew acted quickly. He intercepted Nick's fist with the palm of his hand and secured the attacking arm to the floor, the wrist facing upward.

"I guess you decided where I should start," Andrew snarled. He took the dagger and, in one smooth stroke, slid it across the veins deep into Nick's wrist.

For a second, Enna's world came to a sudden halt. Nick's eyes were held wide in shock. Andrew's teeth bared in a menacing grin. A scream stuck in Enna's throat.

This isn't happening! Am I still dead? Is this Hell? Why can't I move? Save him! Enna's mind remained active, while the rest of her body seemed to be on strike. Enna's head throbbed, her muscles spasmed, and her stomach filled with thick, acidic dread.

Four years of martial arts training had nothing on her fear of Andrew.

An intense, low groan came from Nick's lips. Enna clutched her heart and dry-heaved a few times.

Nick's groan turned into a full shout of agony as blood began to pour from his wrist onto the cement ground. He tried to stop the flow with his other hand, but Andrew caught hold of his uninjured arm and restrained it against the wall. Nick fought against Andrew while holding his wounded wrist to his stomach, trying to manage the bleeding.

Enna opened her mouth and prayed that saving words would form.

"I'm so sorry, Nick," She whimpered weakly.

No! Those are not fighting words to save him. Those are quitting words. Try again! Enna's thoughts begged of her, but no words came. She watched helplessly as Andrew flipped his dagger through his fingers, showing off his knife-wielding skills.

"Why are you doing this?" Nick asked, voice dripping in pain.

"Oh, many reasons. One:" he slashed a shallow cut on Nick's throat. "Clara was a bad girl and needs to be punished. Two:" This time, the blade swiped Nick's cheek. "You lied and manipulated me instead of doing the job I hired you to do. Three: You seduced the woman I love." Enna closed her eyes as the dagger struck out again. Nick sucked in a sharp breath of pain, causing Enna's eyes to fling open to check on the damage. His right shoulder was now bleeding profusely.

"I get it. You want vengeance. This won't make you feel any better, though. Just...stop!" Nick attempted to sound confident, but he was obviously barely hanging on.

"Oh, but I'm not done with you yet. The fourth reason I'm doing this is because...it's fun."

He sent a malicious grin Enna's way and began speaking to her. "Also, as a bonus. I can stage this to look like your dear Nicolas got in a fight with your other lover, Oliver, and then killed him. Ironic since Nicolas tried to save that moron."

Andrew turned to address Nick again. "I don't get it. Why would you try to save your competition?"

"He wasn't competition. He was human, like me," Nick's voice faded to a whisper.

I can't do this! I can't watch and do nothing. I can't! Enna's body continued to quake uncontrollably as she shifted onto her hands and knees again. Her stare locked in with Nick's glossy eyes, his familiar twinkle long lost.

At that moment, Enna wanted nothing more than to kill Andrew herself with his own dagger, but she doubted her ability to overpower him. She dropped her face to the ground and pressed her forehead into the cold concrete, using it as an ice pack. The cool ground helped her to find the logical voice that had been taken over by emotion.

Andrew is much stronger than me. Enna calculated her options. *I've beaten guys bigger than him before. However, I've also lost to men around his size. I can't afford to lose. I've seen Andrew fight. He doesn't use combat etiquette. He fights out of rage, which makes him unpredictable but more likely to make mistakes.*

Andrew still restrained Nick's arm against the wall while he bragged about Oliver's death. Enna tried not to focus on that.

So what can I do? If I do nothing, Nick dies and Andrew takes me for a life of torture, but Jay might be safe.

Just thinking about fighting Andrew made it difficult for Enna to breathe. Her P.T.S.D. was hard at play and her injured head left her at a disadvantage.

If I fight, I could possibly win and we all survive, but if I lose, I watch as Nick and Jay get tortured and killed, and perhaps Betty and her family. Can I really risk that? Nick would tell me to let him die to protect Jay.

Please, God, tell me what to do!

"Clara! Are you even listening to me?" Andrew snapped. "I revealed the best plan to frame Nick for Oliver's murder. It will be easy, really. I'll stage it to look like Nicolas killed himself after realizing what he had done to Oliver." Andrew laughed deep within his throat. "How does that sound, Clara?"

Nick's pale face dripped in sweat. He leaned his faint head against the wall.

Enna had never felt so powerless in her life.

How long can he survive wounds like that without a doctor? An hour? Maybe two? Enna crumbled from the inside as she watched Nick's tortured face wince again after Andrew slashed a tear in his right collar bone.

"Andrew, please," Enna begged.

"Such a shame, Clara. What is it with the people closest to you always killing themselves?" Andrew said with a sinister growl. "First your mother, now this guy. So sad." His voice oozed with mock empathy as he sneered at Nick.

Without warning, Nick swiftly thrust his head forward, driving his forehead into Andrew's nose, prompting him to release Nick momentarily with a surprised roar.

After a quick recovery, Andrew dug his elbow into Nick's bleeding shoulder and pressed on it with his body weight. Pain spread plainly across Nick's face as he pushed against the elbow, trying to relieve some pressure.

"Oh, Nicolas, I'm going to have so much fun with Clara after you are dead!"

With that, Enna forced her body up sharply into a standing position.

"You are insane! Look, you taught me your lesson. I won't run away again. Now let him go!" She wanted to sound firm. "He needs a doctor now! Please! For me. Save him."

Andrew's eyes darkened as his lips split into a wicked smile.

Enna hated that face. It was his "I won" face. He defeated her and he knew it.

"Lesson's not over yet, Sweety." Andrew removed his elbow from Nick's shoulder wound and moved to restrain Nick's uninjured arm against the wall once again.

"Let's see how tough you are after you lose a hand, why don't we?" Andrew lifted his blade to Nick's wrist.

"Don't! Andrew...No!" Enna's shout echoed around the small bunker. Her plea was so agonized that even the electricity in the room seemed to hear her.

At that moment, all the lights and computers blinked off and plunged them into complete darkness. Andrew's features were shrouded in the black cloak of the room.

Before fear could hold her back, Enna seized her chance. Through the thick darkness, she jammed her foot toward where she last saw Andrew crouching over Nick. She felt her foot connect with what she guessed was the soft muscle on the side of Andrew's ribcage, making him exhale a curse.

Enna backed up after hearing a slight rustle of his suit as he made an unseen movement. Enna felt a sharp sting as the dagger bit her upper arm. She gasped.

"Clara, please stop." Andrew's voice broke through the darkness, full of sincerity. "I don't want to harm you."

Sliding forward, she used his voice to estimate where his nose might be and jammed her fist in that direction. It made contact, not with his nose, but with another fleshy part of his body mixed with a scrap of a necktie. He coughed and sputtered. She must have gotten him in the throat.

Well, now you decide to fight? Enna's brain said sarcastically to herself.

The darkness hid Andrew's face, freeing her from his controlling spell. The fear was gone and replaced by the fury built up from years of running and denying who she was. All the anger that came from looking over her shoulder gave her energy. All her pain from lost human connection drove her to a fighter's stance. All the night terrors she had to endure lit a fire to her rage. The sound of Nick's scattered breathing brought on the purest power of disdain. That spurred her to action.

Attempting to see through the dark was only a distraction. Closing her eyes, Enna took a cleansing breath to calm her enraged mind.

I can do this! Hearing the shuffle of feet, she discerned that Andrew was quickly approaching. She gracefully slid to the side, getting offline from his attack.

A brush of air teased her face, letting her know that Andrew had passed by right where she had been standing moments earlier.

Enna quietly pivoted, brought her right foot up, and forced it into Andrew's back. A thud followed as Andrew was propelled face-first into the wall. A clatter of metal hitting cement rang through the dark. Andrew's dagger must have dislodged from his hand with the impact of the wall.

A furious howl echoed around the bunker as Andrew rushed in Enna's direction. She was ready for him as he approached. She slipped to the side once more but left her leg in place. His angry feet grappled with her leg and he began to tumble to the floor. As he fell, Enna brought her elbow down into the back of his shoulder, causing him to crash to the ground with a powerful force.

He sent a stream of curse words at her that deviated from his usual eloquent pattern of speech.

Enna listened silently, anticipating her next move as Andrew grunted, struggling to rise. She allowed him to regain his footing and then whistled softly to make him turn in her direction. Enna pushed all her tension into her fist and let it fly into Andrew's jawline.

Bones snapped. He grunted and thumped heavily onto the floor. Enna held her breath for a moment, waiting for any further movement from Andrew.

All was still.

Once sure Andrew was unconscious, Enna carefully moved across the dark bunker to where she had heard his dagger clatter to the floor. It didn't take much of a search before her fingers brushed over its hilt.

Grabbing it, she scooted over to where Nick fought for consciousness. He moaned softly as she reached him. As her fingers grasped Nick, they became warm with the sickening texture of blood.

He is going to bleed out. I have to get him out of here now! Taking the dagger to the leg of her denim jeans, she turned the cloth into a bandage for Nick's bleeding wrist. Without realizing it, she pulled in a deep breath of air and let it sit in her chest until it started to protest.

Should I tie Andrew up? Do I have time? I should just kill him. She paused, considering her options, picturing how it might feel to sink the dagger deep into Andrew's chest. The idea sickened her. *I can't. I can't do it.* She broke back into action, feeling around for Nick's wound, her hand briefly brushing over his clammy face. He muttered something under his breath, but Enna didn't understand what.

No, I have to get Nick to a hospital now.

She traced his body down to where blood seeped from his wrist and wrapped the bandage around it. Next, she used the dagger to slice through the rope that restrained his feet.

"Hey you," Nick whispered.

"Shh," Enna responded softly. "I need you to try and stand." She draped Nick's left, uninjured arm over her shoulder. Together, they stood. His body strained with the effort of standing upright.

Enna's jaw clamped in unwavering determination. Using all her strength, she hoisted most of Nick's weight onto her shoulder.

Slowly, they made their way over to the bunker door that Andrew had left open. Enna felt around in the dark with her toes and free hand, hoping to find a way out without dropping Nick on his face.

After wandering down what seemed like a long hallway, Enna's foot kicked a solid surface in front of her. Stretching out her hand, it swiped through the air with no contact, so her foot examined the thing it made contact with to discover a staircase leading upstairs.

She grunted as she tried to heave Nick up the stairs in the dark.

Enna's injured head pounded and her shoulder stung as sweat mixed with the cut Andrew had given her.

"Nick, stay awake," Enna urged as she felt his body weaken. "I can't carry you. Help me get up these stairs."

"Mmm hmm. Sorry," he responded softly and a bit of weight lifted off of Enna's shoulders as he found a burst of extra strength.

"Just hang on, Nick. We'll get out of here. Stay with me," Enna whispered as she searched for a way out of the darkness.

A breath of relief skipped from her lips as she discovered a door, but that relief had a short life. As she found the doorknob, it denied an exit. *Locked.* She wanted to scream out and cry, but that would direct Andrew right to them if he woke up.

Nick's breathing staggered with heavy wheezing.

"Stay with me, Nick. I'll figure this out. We'll be alright," Enna said, looking around for anything that could be used as a lockpick. Sitting Nick down on the top step, she frantically shook the doorknob.

"Come on...Open, you stupid door," Enna muttered. "We're stuck. Andrew wins. He always wins!" Enna's voice rose with panic. She slammed her body into the door. It didn't budge; it only sent pain down her arm. Her breath turned into squeaks as she attempted to calm herself.

"Enna, hand me the dagger. I got ya." Nick reached up to find Enna's hand. "I've picked locks before. It's fine. Give me the knife."

Despite her worry about Nick's condition, she quickly placed the dagger in his outstretched hand. Enna grabbed onto Nick's sweating back, stabilizing him.

Sounds of metal scraping between the door and the frame distracted her from Nick's heavy breathing.

"Are you doing okay, Nick? I can do this for you if you want to talk me through it," Enna asked, wanting to feel useful.

"I'm fine," Nick grunted, trying to cover the pain in his voice. "Just keep close to me. I just need your support."

Enna held onto Nick a bit tighter until he let out a victory sigh and the door clicked open. Nick handed the dagger back to Enna and attempted to stand. Enna braced him and stepped into the trinket shop.

After ensuring the bunker door was shut and locked behind her, Enna hefted Nick's failing body toward the exit.

The lights flickered back on just as Enna's hand reached for the door handle. A rush of hope danced inside of her, but that hope turned sour as a cry from behind the bunker door stopped her heart.

"Owww! Let go of me!" Jay's terrified voice cut through the air.

27

Drowning

The closed bunker door muffled Jay's cries, but his panic was evident.

Paralyzed, Enna fought to remain standing as hopeless thoughts washed over her. *My baby! He has my baby! Jay is going to die because of me! I broke the rules of the game. I lost. I should have killed Andrew when he was unconscious. Why didn't I do that? What's wrong with me?*

The atmosphere around her turned into a thick gravy of warm, humid air. Enna knew Andrew. He only showed mercy when he could benefit from it.

Oh, maybe he won't hurt Jay. He'll use him to control me. Don't panic. Save him. I beat Andrew once. I can do it again.

Enna shot her gaze toward the machete still hanging on the back wall. If she could reach it, she would have an advantage.

Her fingers tightened around Andrew's dagger. It was light in her grip, too small to overpower him in her frightened state.

I need that machete. She moved toward it, but the weight of Nick's body held her back. When she met Nick's eyes, she didn't have to say anything.

He nodded understanding. "Go." He let his arms slip away from her. Without support, he slumped to the ground. However, protecting Jay became Enna's new and only focus.

One step...Two steps...Three.

Each desperate step echoed the sensation of treading water, kicking but making no progress.

She was only halfway to the weapon when Jay's voice steered her attention toward the bunker.

"Mommy, help! Let go of me!"

There was a slight jiggle of the door knob before Andrew emerged from the staircase. With rage shooting from his eyes, he dragged Jay behind him by his curly hair.

The scene blurred Enna's vision, but she ordered her tears to remain unseen behind the brim of her eyes.

The beams of sunlight from the glass shop doors acted as a spotlight, pointing to the other end of the shop where Andrew stood. Blood trickled down his cheek, seeping to the corner of his lips.

"Look who I found messing with the breakers. Didn't you teach your brat that playing with electricity could be dangerous?" Andrew yanked Jay's hair, making him cry out. "You have a very clever boy, but he should have left when he had the chance." Andrew's face contorted into a manic grin. "Did you forget the rules of the game, princess?" Andrew asked with a tilt of his head. His voice sounded low and distant. "You clearly love your new boyfriend more than your own son. Now you get to watch as he dies." Andrew wrapped his fingers around Jay's throat and squeezed.

Jay's eyes bulged. He dug his nails into Andrew's hand, but his tiny fingers had no effect.

Enna's vision tilted, bending her depth perception. Every sound gurgled inaudibly around her. Spasmodic gulps of air stung her throat as if she were trying to breathe underwater. Jay was turning pale now and his attempts to claw his way to freedom grew weak.

"I'll kill you!" Enna gave up on reaching the machete and charged wildly at Andrew with the dagger outstretched toward him.

As she ran, the shop came into hyper-focus. Images of her surroundings began to sear into her mind.

Wooden shelves holding both big and small geodes passed by. Dangling dream catchers, along with a rabbit's foot, hung up above. Old license plates decorated the wall and a rack of ugly plaid shirts hung behind her dying son.

These images would be stuck in her mind for the rest of her life.

She knew herself well. She wouldn't allow herself to remember Jay's flopping body or Andrew's evil snarl. No. Those images she would block out. All that would be left in her mind would be the random trinkets in the rundown shop.

"Listen, you said it yourself," Nick's plea for Jay's life became distorted to Enna's petrified ears. "You said she loves me more than him! So why don't you let him go and keep torturing me? I'll cry out like a baby to make it more enjoyable for you." Nick's voice resonated deeper and more drawn out than usual. Enna would never forget the urgency in his words.

Every sensation, every sound, smell, and sight drilled into her head as though her subconscious was saying, *here, you will need these memories as you relive your nightmare over and over again. Here you go. Don't forget. Don't let the last moments of your son's life disappear.*

Enna's grasp on the dagger was so tight that the cold hilt left an imprint on her skin. Her hand shook as she neared Andrew.

"Careful, Clara. You wouldn't want to harm your son, would you? Are you sure you can handle my weapon?" A hint of fear broke through Andrew's smug voice, but he held his dark gaze as Enna drew furiously closer.

"Aaaah!" Enna screamed with fire in her eyes as she closed the gap between Andrew and herself.

Andrew tossed Jay to the side roughly just in time to block Enna's knife-wielding hand. He twisted her arm behind her back. Pain rippled up Enna's arm and into her shoulder as Andrew forced it into a position that stretched the rotator cuff to its limits. A loud *"Snap"* erupted from her shoulder.

At first, Enna felt no pain. Her arm went weak in Andrew's grasp as he removed the dagger from her hand.

And then the pain came.

A throbbing burn began at the front of her shoulder and radiated down the side of her arm until the entire limb pulsed in agony.

Andrew released Enna long enough for her to run two wobbling steps away from him toward Jay.

"Oh, Clara, leaving again so soon?" Andrew said in his version of a romantic whisper. He stopped her escape by reaching around her thin waist and pulling her backward into him. She felt his heart thudding against her as his other arm flew over her shoulder and pressed the dagger against her neck.

"This is why I love you so much, Clara," Andrew hissed. He moved his hand seductively across her stomach. "You never stop fighting."

Enna squirmed, trying to free herself, but the dagger bit her neck, forcing her to remain still. She looked to Nick for help and regretted it. His body lay limp on the ground, his face pale from blood loss. She could not tell if any breath flowed from his body.

Sorrow melted Enna into violent gasps. The dagger dug into her neck with every movement, but she could not control her body.

Enna frantically searched for Jay, but he was not in her field of vision.

Please be alive. Please! I need to see Jay breathing. Now! She fought through the hyperventilation and tried to twist her body around, but Andrew held the blade closer, causing blood to run down her neck. Andrew pressed his face to the nape of Enna's neck and sniffed.

"Mmmm. Even with your dead boyfriend's blood clinging to your skin, you still smell amazing." He pressed his lips to her neck and kissed it gently.

"Please. Just kill me," Enna managed to say through her sobs, assuming Jay was dead.

Andrew nuzzled Enna while the hand on her stomach began to wander her body. "Why would I ever kill such perfection?" Andrew sighed.

Enna's body quaked to the point she could no longer hold herself up. Sagging in Andrew's arms, he tightened his grip so she would not fall.

She hated his touch, his voice, everything about him.

"Let my mommy go!" Jay's scratchy voice interrupted Andrew's advances.

Those words were the most beautiful words Enna had ever heard. *Oh my Gosh! My baby is alive? Jay is alive!*

Without removing the dagger from Enna's throat, Andrew turned to face Jay. Enna's lips twitched into a soft smile at Jay's appearance. The color had flowed back into his face. His lips pressed into a dramatic scowl and his brows furrowed angrily, trying to look menacing.

"I don't like bad guys hurting my mom," Jay growled.

Enna found her voice. "Get out of here, Jay! Go find the police." But Jay just shook his head.

"No one messes with my mommy. I know karate." Jay held the fighter's stance that Enna had taught him.

Andrew let out a bellowing laugh. "That is remarkable. He is just like you, Clara. Listen, child, you should probably do what your mother said and get out of here. I need alone time with her." Andrew softly bit Enna's ear.

Jay held his ground for a moment, glaring hatred for the man when suddenly, he stood up straight, relaxed, and smiled his widest grin.

Andrew cocked his head to the side, puzzled at the change of expression.

Jay just grinned and blinked a few times.

"Game over," Jay said proudly.

28

Soundproof

The shop burst into life as armies of agents in black clothing swarmed in from the front and back doors. Nick, still unconscious across the room, was barely visible amidst the agent bodies standing over him.

"Freeze!!" A voice called out of the crowd. The sound resonated in Enna's memory. She'd heard that pompous voice before.

A man Enna had hoped never to see again broke through the crowd of agents. It was the same man who tried to take Jay away from her when he was just a baby, Agent Quinn.

His grin was like a child waking up on Christmas morning, clearly thrilled with his fortunate turn of events.

"Run!" Enna called over to Jay, but he made no movement. "Stinky breath! Stinky breath! Go!"

Andrew held Enna tighter and began backing toward the basement door. Before making it far, Enna heard a whizz of air and felt a prick on her leg.

Another whizz of air swooshed past her and a dart landed in Andrew's forearm. He cursed and loosened his hold on Enna.

Seizing the opportunity, she elbowed him in the gut with her uninjured arm to break free of his grasp. She rushed toward Jay with open arms, ready to swoop him into her protective embrace.

A sudden, high-pitched whoosh sliced through the air as she sprinted, followed by a muffled thudding sound. Andrew's profanity-laden reaction pierced the air. At the same time, a sharp sting bit her shoulder.

Looking toward the pain, she saw a dart sticking out of her body. She ripped it out and glanced around her to see that Andrew had several darts of his own inserted into various body parts. To her wondrous relief, he held his arms up in surrender.

Enna reached Jay and shielded him with her body. A few more pricks hit her back before she began to sway.

Enna turned her head to see Nick being carried off on a stretcher brought in by some of the agents. She wanted to follow them to make sure he was alive, but the world grew increasingly darker. Her fingers twitched as she fought to reach out for Nick.

"Another body in the alley," an unseen agent called out. There was a flurry of shouts and orders, but Enna's brain struggled to process anything more. Black rings outlined her vision. She held Jay as tight as her arms would allow, but the strength was being sucked right out of her.

I can't let them take Jay. Stay awake! Stay awake. Enna begged her body. Her hold on Jay weakened as she slipped closer and closer to the ground.

"I love you, Mommy," Jay said. "I'll see you when you wake up."

Enna slumped onto the cool ground. She couldn't move. All sounds grew fuzzy around her and her head became a vessel of gritty sand until there was nothing but darkness left.

✳✳✳

Enna awoke to the rhythmic beeping of a monitor. She glanced groggily at her surroundings, looking for Jay. She appeared to be in a bright, large glass box equipped with a few monitors, an I.V. connected to her arm, and a counter with medical supplies neatly organized on top.

Her blurry eyes glanced at the glass wall and stared at the reflection coming from the shine. However, the more her eyes adjusted to her surroundings, the more she realized she wasn't looking at a reflection at all. She was staring into a room identical to hers.

It had the same monitors, the same medical equipment, and the same bed, but the pale person lying in the bed hooked up to an I.V. was not herself.

Recognition woke her up with a jolt.

"Nick!" she called out as loud as her weak body could muster. He did not move to indicate he had heard her. His heartbeat appeared on the monitor screen next to him. It was slow but steady.

Relief flooded through her, making her heave a powerful sob.

He's okay. He's alive. My Nick is alive! She looked to the other side of her to see another glass room similar to hers. However, the room was vacant. The sheets on the bed were ruffled as though someone had been lying there minutes earlier, but no one was in sight.

A pang of dread shot through Enna's frazzled body. She longed to see Jay resting peacefully in that bed, his healthy heartbeat displayed on the monitor. He would wake up and smile his goofy grin at her. However, the empty bed just taunted her.

How long have I been out? Enna wondered, worried that too much time had passed. *Jay could be anywhere in the world by now. I have to find him. But how can I expect to find Jay if I don't even know where I am?*

Enna scrunched her eyes and examined her room thoroughly, looking for any indication of where she was or what day it was.

The pristine equipment and state-of-the-art medical supplies indicated she was in some sort of an advanced hospital room.

Is this an E.S.T. hospital or something?

Man, Oliver would love to see this. The thought stung as she remembered the horrific events from earlier. Oliver would never get to discover the truth of his conspiracies. The mysteries of the E.S.T. would forever be locked to him.

Shaking the thought away, Enna focused on how she would find Jay.

Glancing around the room, panic formed in her chest as she realized there was no door to be seen, just glass walls on every side. There were no clues as to what time or day it was. It could be the middle of the night and she would have no idea.

This is not a hospital room. This is a prison.

Each breath seemed to require more effort than the last. She wanted to cry but she was all out of tears.

A sudden movement from Nick's room caught her eye. She turned to face it and found herself staring at a man in a white doctor's robe. The doctor had a pleasant face as he gently removed the bandage from Nick's slit wrist.

Enna had to look away for a moment as the doctor revealed the cut that still slightly oozed on his wrist. The doctor replaced the old bandages with the new ones and began to leave.

"Hey!" Enna called out to the doctor. He made no notice of her and walked right over to a plain glass wall. "Doctor! Hello, please tell me where my son is!" Enna cried.

The man reached out and touched the glass. A green light outlined his hand briefly before the glass slid open to reveal an exit. The doctor promptly left the room without a glance in her direction.

Frustrated, Enna sighed and tried to get out of the bed. A moan escaped her lips as a pinch from the I.V. tube made her stomach turn. She wanted to rip the needle from her arm and find a way out of her glass prison, but just looking at the I.V. in her vein made her feel faint.

A sling cradled her injured rotator cuff and her heartbeat pounded in the back of her wounded skull. However, the cuts Andrew gave her hardly hurt at all. Bringing a hand to her neck, she traced her finger along one of her injuries. It was scabbed over, no longer a fresh wound.

How long have I been here? How long has Jay been without me? Enna's muscles clenched until they shook.

Yearning to hug Jay, she called out for him. Her voice echoed for a moment as a security camera swiveled her way.

Looking into the lens of the camera, she called out again. "I know someone is watching me! I want my son back! Give Jay to me now!" Fire burned inside her chest as she waited for a response.

Nothing happened. Another round of panic threatened to take over completely.

No, hold it together! Enna demanded of herself. She wiped the sweat from her forehead and focused on her breathing techniques. Watching her monitor it showed her heart rate slowing.

Once her breathing was back in order, she glanced absently to Nick's room. A man's face pressed up against the glass, staring at her.

Enna let out a startled screech and jumped so hard she almost fell out of the bed. After composing herself, she felt blood rush into her cheeks as she recognized the man.

"Nick!"

He stood wearing a white hospital gown that barely reached his knees, making him look underdressed. Enna could tell he was laughing at her reaction to suddenly seeing him standing there, but no sound came from his lips.

"That's not funny!" Enna scolded. However, she let out a short laugh. "Fine, maybe it was a little funny, but you scared the snot out of me!" She rolled her eyes at him.

Nick scowled slightly and put a hand to his ear before shaking his head. "No." He tapped on the glass with his good hand. Nothing. No sound came from the glass wall.

"I can't hear you," Nick mouthed dramatically.

"Can you get out?" Enna asked, over pronouncing each word to make it easier for Nick to read her lips.

Nick dragged his IV solution bag around the room and placed his hand on the glass, as the doctor had demonstrated. A red light outlined his hand, but no opening appeared to set him free. He turned to Enna, and with sad puppy-dog eyes, he mouthed, "No," again.

Nick's eyes glazed over for a moment and his body swayed slightly.

"Sit down," Enna mouthed, pointing to his bed. He nodded and slowly made his way to lie down.

Looking at Enna, he mouthed something she did not catch completely, but she thought she understood the words "See your beautiful face."

Enna grinned. "Thank you." For the first time since waking up, she thought about how she must look. She definitely did not feel beautiful.

She looked at her reflection in the glass. A bandage was tied around her head in a turban, and her hair flipped out from underneath the fabric at all angles. She also wore a plain white hospital gown that was much too big for her.

At least Oliver's blood that had been clinging to her hair and body had been washed away. The thought made Enna shiver. Someone other than herself had bathed her and changed her clothes.

Andrew? Where is Andrew? She sucked in a giant gulp of air and tried to push the thought out of her mind. She focused on Nick again, who was now crossing his eyes and sucking his cheeks in.

For a second, Enna worried that he was having some sort of stroke, but then he changed his facial expression to imitate what looked like a laughing horse. Enna cracked up and released a loud snort. *He's just being a goober.*

Grateful for the soundproof walls, which prevented him from hearing the snort, she hid her smiling face in her hand before looking back at Nick.

She slowly mouthed, "What's with the faces?" as she pointed to her own face. Nick grinned and responded too quickly.

Enna beamed and said, "I have no idea what you just said."

Nick did an OK sign with his fingers. "I," he mouthed while pointing at himself. "Just." He paused until Enna nodded understanding. "Wanted to see." He used two fingers to point at his own eyes and then turned them on Enna as though saying, "I got my eyes on you." Enna lit up even more. "You smile," he finished. He showed an enthusiastic grin to emphasize the word "smile."

Nick mouthed more words, but Enna turned her attention to a sliding noise near the front of the room. Bolting upright, she shrieked and shuffled to the back of her bed, trying to get as far away from her visitors as possible.

In terror, her throat tightened at the sight of her two nightmares walking into the room together—Andrew and Agent Quinn.

The doctor who had changed out Nick's bandages followed close behind.

Enna clenched her teeth and glared. The doctor walked over to Enna and gently removed the I.V. needle from her arm, making her stomach turn.

"Please, you can't leave me here with them," she whispered to the Doctor as he leaned over her.

He shook his head and gave her a sympathetic smile. "I'm sorry, ma'am, I don't have any control over that. How are you feeling? I reset your shoulder, but it will be sore for a while. Be careful with it and keep the sling on. Your head is probably healed enough to take the bandage off if you would like," he said calmly while finishing the I.V. removal.

Her eyes widened.

"You don't understand. He did this to me!" she nodded her head in Andrew's direction.

The doctor's eyebrows scrunched as he peered at Andrew. "You will have to speak to the general about that. I have my orders to release you." With that said, the doctor nodded firmly and exited the room.

In a panic, Enna looked over to Nick for help. He was standing again, pounding on the glass, concern racing across his face. Andrew gave him a smug smile, making Enna twitch.

Attempting to ignore Andrew so he couldn't see her fear, she focused on Agent Quinn, "Where is Jay?" She asked.

"We will get to that. First, let me introduce myself," the agent began.

"I know who you are. I just want to see my son!" Enna snapped.

The agent acted as though she hadn't spoken. "My name is Agent Eric Quinn. You may call me Eric. I am a member of the Experimental Science and Technology division, or, as we call ourselves, the E.S.T. Here, we produce and utilize the best cutting-edge material to protect our great country." His voice projected as though he had memorized a script for a theater production.

"Today is a great day for our country. With the relocation of Project 19932, we can begin experimenting with his enhanced human D.N.A." Enna gasped, but Eric didn't wait for her to speak. "You see, by combining a human with computer technology, we can eliminate the need for learned intelligence. The new human will be able to download any information needed and discard what is unnecessary. Imagine the possibilities Project 19932 will bring."

Anger boiled in Enna's chest. "Jay! His name is Jay! And If you knew him at all, you would know that he can't just download a personality. Your experiment is sick. He is just a baby!" She wrung the edges of her hospital blanket with her anxious fingers. "If this country thinks we need to turn babies into human-computer hybrids, then this country has already fallen to the enemy. You can't turn kids into robots! I will not allow you to experiment on my son!" Her voice quaked.

Eric marched toward Enna, pointing his finger menacingly into her face. "Project 19932 is not your son! You stole him and nearly cost me my life in the process. Do you have any idea how much that project is worth?" His hand turned into a threatening fist.

"He's worth everything to me! Way more than money. You have no idea!" Enna yelled.

Eric stepped closer as though he were about to strike.

Andrew swept over and grabbed Eric's wrist. "That is my wife you are talking to. Don't forget the deal we made," he said in a threatening tone.

The word *wife* stung Enna. She had refused to marry Andrew, which infuriated him. Now, he threw that word around like candy at a parade.

"Fine." Eric lowered his arm sharply, regaining control of his angered face. He looked at Enna coldly. "You are free to go."

"What?" Enna asked, not understanding the shift of conversation. "I am not going anywhere without Nick and Jay." She looked over to Nick, whose forehead pressed against the glass. One of his facial wounds split open and was splotching the glass with blood. Though pale, he would not sit down until he knew Enna was safe.

"I'll be alright," Enna mouthed to him. He shook his head miserably.

"Clara, it is time to go," Andrew said softly.

Eric stepped back and watched Andrew grab Enna's hand.

"I am not going with you, Andrew," Enna said quietly, almost with compassion, trying to extract her hand from his grasp. "I am sorry, but I can't go back to your world." Enna knew her soft tone would have no effect on him.

He took a lock of hair that had escaped the turban and twirled it around his finger while whispering, "My sweet wife, I know you are concerned for your son. Eric has assured me that he is much too valuable to harm. They will take good care of him and make sure that he has a chance to change the world. They have nannies available to nurture him just like a normal child."

"He's not a normal child, though. He needs special care that a nanny would never be able to give. He needs me. He needs his mother." Swatting Andrews's hand away from her hair, Enna bit back the wave of anger that boiled inside of her.

"I am deeply sorry, Clara. I know how much this must hurt. You know I have felt loss before when I thought you were dead. It is unbearable, but at least you will know that he is alive." Andrew's face softened in pretend empathy. "It's alright to cry. I am here for you."

Enna let out a sarcastic laugh and shook her head. Andrew grabbed her chin and forced her to turn toward Nick's room. "Clara, look at your Nicolas over there."

Enna watched as Nick argued forcefully with the doctor, who was waving around gauze and pointing at Nick's bleeding head. Nick dodged the doctor and gestured in Enna's direction. He put his hand upon the glass near the exit but was again denied an escape.

Andrew forced Enna's eyes back onto him. "Nicolas is alive and well despite my efforts. That doctor is doing everything he can to help him heal fully. He will continue to receive care. Yes, they will probably question him and hold him prisoner for a time, but he will remain unharmed. Do you want him to stay that way, or should we bring him home with us so we can finish our game?"

Enna jerked her chin out of Andrew's hold and looked down at her hands, ashamed by the lack of power she held.

Andrew stood up as high as he could to show off his dominance and continued speaking louder. "It is time to go, Clara. Don't make this harder on yourself than it has to be."

Enna watched as the doctor tried to coax Nick onto the bed.

He will be safer without me. Her nose flared with emotion as she came to terms with her fate. She slid off the bed, wobbling under the weight of her body. The cold from the tile floor seeped through the soles of her feet. She looked down at her hospital gown.

"Where are my clothes and shoes?" she asked coldly, not wanting to go anywhere with Andrew with so little on.

"Don't worry about that now, dear. I plan on providing you with nice new outfits," Andrew responded with a lustful smile. He offered her a stabilizing hand, which was left empty.

Keeping me barefooted and underdressed will give him another advantage over me. Great, Enna thought bitterly. She walked over to the wall that connected to Nick's room and waved her arms in a dramatic motion. It took a moment, but she was able to grab Nick's attention away from the doctor and onto her.

He said something to the doctor, who nodded his head. Nick walked over toward her and put his hand on the glass wall. Enna put her hand up next to his, longing to touch him. "I love you," she mouthed. She wanted to tell him that she would be alright and that he should not worry about her, but that would be a lie.

"I love you too," Nick mouthed back. He bit his upper lip and scrunched his face up in pain. "Don't go," he mouthed.

"I have to," Enna's lips formed the sad truth. She turned her face so she didn't have to see the agony in his eyes.

"Fine, you win," she said to Andrew. A smug grin mounted on his face as he beckoned for her to exit. She took a step toward the door before turning back to Eric, who had been standing silently in the corner. "Take care of them," she ordered. He nodded slightly.

Grunting, Andrew grabbed Enna's elbow and roughly guided her into the hallway. Numb, she followed his lead but glanced behind her to see Nick's shattered expression. His hands clung to his chest as though trying to keep his heart from cracking.

Locking eyes with Nick, she mouthed the words, "I'll be back."

He didn't nod, understanding. He stood frozen and broken.

Enna could no longer bear the pain on his face. She turned away and focused on the bleak future ahead of her.

29

Sleepless Night

Jay pulled the blanket up to his chin and let out a frightened whine. He hated the dark. He never knew what monsters lurked in the shadows.

Soft snores came from the bed next to him. Jay glanced over to stare at his new friend, Mike, who looked the same as him.

The boy didn't say much. He mostly just slept unless the doctors were checking on him.

Something about Mike was different from other kids Jay had met in the past. It didn't quite make sense, but there seemed to be a powerful connection between them.

Jay wished Mike would wake up now so he would have someone to play with.

The room's walls were clear, with no visible door. All day, Agents and scientists had stopped outside the glass to stare at him as though he were an animal on display at the zoo. They would come to look, point, and discuss what they saw. Jay could not hear their words but knew they were talking about him.

Despite the attention, very few people talked directly to him throughout the past few days. It was so lonely and not knowing how much time had passed made Jay start to go bonkers. The only indication of time was when the bright LED lights turned off so they could sleep.

At one point, a man who introduced himself as Agent Quinn had stopped by to give Mike a nasty shot with a long needle. After that, Mike cried a lot. Jay had tried to console him, but the boy just stared at him with big, watery eyes, begging for help.

Jay didn't know what to say to him other than, "It's okay, pal. My mommy and Nick will save us." Unfortunately, the words didn't seem to give Mike the same comfort that they had given him.

The only other people who came inside the glass box were an old lady doctor and an even older man doctor. They were nice but didn't talk much. They checked on Jay's neck bruises and gave him and Mike delicious food for every meal.

Each time the doctors came and went, Jay studied the placement of their hands on the glass. A light scanned and recognized them in order for an opening to reveal itself in the wall.

Jay had tried copying the doctor's actions by standing high on his toes to press his hand in the same spot, but he was denied an exit, which made him really mad—mad enough to kick the glass and almost sprain his toe.

After that, Jay spent most of his time exploring the clear wall by tapping different areas.

This glass has energy. Huh? Strange. He put both his hands on the wall, closed his eyes, and took a deep breath. A sensation tingled through his body, reminding him of how it felt to hold a phone or tablet in his hands.

"Can I hack you so you'll let me out?" *Then I can find Mommy. She will be scared without me.* He tried speaking to the wall, but the wall wouldn't reach out to him, denying any real connection.

Inside the sterile room, Jay's frustration grew with each passing moment. He explored every nook and cranny, running his fingers along the smooth, featureless walls as high as he could reach. The room seemed to tease his digital instincts.

"What are you? Why won't you let me connect to you?" he asked the wall as though speaking to a friend.

The wall vibrated like it was laughing at him. He was trapped in an impenetrable digital fortress, and it formed an itch just barely out of reach.

Craving the connection to technology, he flattened his body onto the ground, where energy pulsated up through the flooring. He wished for the sweet hum of a computer's motherboard to resonate beneath his touch. But there was nothing—no Wi-Fi signals to latch onto, no apps to exploit, and certainly no hard drive to interface with.

Every digital avenue he explored hit a brick wall. Jay's fear quadrupled as he realized the glass room he was in was probably specifically designed to thwart his very nature.

"Help...please help me," Jay curled into a ball and sobbed onto the cold tile floor.

After an eternity of crying, Jay crawled back to his bed and tried to sleep. His eyes fluttered shut, but horrible images from the other day haunted him back awake. He shivered, remembering his mommy covered in blood. He could still hear her frantic voice as she told him to leave her and run away.

He had wanted to obey. He even started running away, but knowing his mommy was still in danger made him be a rebel.

Rushing to Betty's van, Jay had climbed inside and turned the laptop on, but instead of purchasing a bus ticket to get home, he connected to the nearest wireless internet and squeezed his eyes closed. Going against Mommy's warnings, he spoke to the computer voice that often reached out to him.

"I'm here. I'm here, come find me!" Jay said as a soft beeping noise took over his thoughts. Feeling the pull of something drawing him near, peace had formed around him like a familiar hug. Then, nothing. He didn't know what had happened next.

Jay scrunched his face up, trying to remember what followed after the beeping started, but all he could remember was an angry man shouting at someone just beyond Betty's van.

When his eyes peeked out of the window, he saw a man dressed all in black, yelling out loud to himself. His hands were flying around in anger like he was conducting a symphony.

Wow, he's crazy. Jay had thought as the man paced back and forth, yelling about a helicopter not arriving on time. Unfortunately, at the time, Jay didn't realize quite how crazy the man actually was.

I should have known he was the bad guy, but I had my suspicions. That's why I followed after him when he went into the shop.

Jay had slipped quietly out of the van and rushed back into the store. But the man was gone! Jay wandered around the store looking for his mommy or the crazy guy for a bit until he came to the back door.

Opening it curiously, he poked his head out and screamed at the sight. A bloody man had just been lying there with blank eyes, staring but not seeing anything. The man hadn't moved, hadn't even blinked.

He was dead.

***

"Mommy!" Jay bolted upright in his unfamiliar bed. Mike's snoring paused for a second but started up again. Jay snuggled back into his covers.

The dead man was just a nightmare. Nothing more. Jay tried to rewrite the truth, though he knew the dead body was really real. His mind continued with thoughts of that awful day.

After he had seen the man's haunting dead face, Jay flew back into the shop and slammed the door shut. That's when he heard his mom's cries coming from another door propped open by a small brick.

Moving in the direction of her voice, he stepped through the door leading to a downward staircase. The door slammed shut behind him, dislodging the brick out of place.

Turning back around, he tried the doorknob. His heart almost had an attack! It was locked. He was trapped and echoes of screams bounced around him.

The crazy man could be heard saying horrible things to Mommy and Nick, making Jay want to plug his ears and cry.

No, I need to save them! But what if I'm too little?

He descended the stairs feeling useless as he listened to the bad guy talk about a creepy game that definitely didn't sound fun.

What can I do? Mommy is a ninja. Why won't she 'hi-yah' the bad guy? His mommy had never been weak before. That's what scared him the most. *Why isn't she fighting? I have to do something!*

His body fidgeted as he searched his special brain for an idea of what to do. His eyes wandered around until it came to a small light flickering in the hall above him.

It was as though a lightbulb had flipped on in his brain.

Electricity! The crazy guy can't see without electricity. I need to find the box on the wall with all the wires.

He knew a bunch about wiring buildings because it was one of the many things he had studied when he was bored. It was like connect-the-dots but instead of connecting numbers together, he linked up electrical outlets.

Following the lights, he froze after hearing Nick scream out. Jay could now see the room the shouts were coming from. Jay wanted to drop his plans and run to his mom with arms open, but he couldn't save her that way and he was too scared.

He peeked an eye into the room and instantly regretted it. The bad man in black sliced a big cut into Nick's shoulder. His mom looked like a horrified huddle on the floor.

Jay covered his mouth and sprinted past the door. It took all his control not to scream out loud.

By the time Jay had found the breaker box, his hands shook uncontrollably. Reaching up, he grunted as he realized his arms were slightly too short to reach the switches.

He jumped as high as he could toward the box but failed to flip the breakers off. His eyes darted around, looking for something he could use to his advantage.

At the end of the hall, Jay saw a broom covered in cobwebs. His legs rushed to grab it. As he ran back to the breaker box, his mommy shouted something, making Jay even more determined to complete his task.

Jay prodded the switches with the end of the broom. *Click, click click!* The breakers turned off one by one.

"Yes!" he said out loud, then covered his mouth, knowing he should be quiet. Waiting and listening, he heard grunting and a few shouts from the bad guy, then everything was silent. Jay held perfectly still in the dark, wondering what he could do next.

Hearing his mother's whispering voice and Nick's groans, Jay felt the wall and made his way toward them as fast as he could. It seemed like he was close when he ran smack into something. Before he realized what it was, clammy hands grabbed his arm and squeezed.

"Hello, son," a cold voice broke through the darkness.

"You are not my daddy," Jay growled. He kicked the man in the leg with all his might, but it only led to the bad guy laughing with a hollow gurgle.

"Let's go find your Mommy, shall we? She just keeps getting away from me. This will be the last time." Andrew had pulled him up the stairs by his hair.

That was the worst day of his life. Jay shook as he remembered the enraged look of terror on his mother's face as she watched the bad guy squeeze the breath out of him.

I almost died! Good thing the agents showed up when they did.

Feeling his bruised neck with his fingers, more soft tears leaked onto his pillow. He'd never felt so alone in his entire life.

30

Techno-Boy

At some point, Jay must have fallen asleep because he was woken by a quiet beeping that resonated through his mind. It was not a harsh noise, but it was constant, causing a faint headache to buzz around his skull.

As the sound intensified, it became harder and harder to ignore.

Irritated, Jay growled, "What do you want?"

The sound of his voice caused Mike to shift around in his sleep, muttering nonsense under his breath.

Jay plugged his ears and squeezed his eyes shut, but nothing helped block the sounds out of his mind.

At first, the beeping was nothing more than an obnoxious, repetitive noise, like Mommy's alarm that got ignored over and over again. However, the more he tried to push the sound away, the louder and more persistent it became.

Standing up, he took in a deep breath, relaxed his arms, and submitted to the noise. Turning his thinking brain off, he let the beeps wash over him.

Beep. Beeeep. Beep. Beep. Beeeep. Beeeep. Beeeep. Beep. ... Beep. Beeeep.

As the sound continued, he began discerning a pattern to the rhythms. *This is just like Morse code but on hyperspeed!* The mix of short and long beeps with a pause after every eighth beep somehow started making sense in Jay's brain. He'd heard this language before. It was computer language. The beeping seemed to be talking.

You have one unread message, reply with a 'yes' to open.

Jay scrunched his face into confusion. He couldn't explain how the words came to him, but the secret code just automatically sorted itself out in his mind.

Maybe this is my imaginary friend. I've never had an imaginary friend before, but I heard they're pretty cool, Jay thought with a nudge of excitement.

"Yes," Jay said out loud in response to the words in his head.

Nothing happened.

Huh, maybe this is just a cool dream, Jay thought, a little disappointed. He looked around. *It looks like I'm awake.* He poked his own belly and giggled. *I felt that. I must be awake.*

The pattern of beeps in his head continued, growing in urgency.

New message: say 'yes'. New message: say 'yes.'

It was as if the words were born within him, something he'd used countless times while working on the computer.

Suddenly, the name for the code resurfaced, like a distant memory that had long been forgotten: binary code, the language of computers.

Realization hit as memories came back to him. When he had gotten into Betty's van to use the laptop for help, he slipped into this strange computer world. He remembered telling the unknown source to locate him by using this language. Now, that same code was being used to get his attention again.

Mommy would not like this. She says talking to strangers is bad and talking to computers is even the worst.

Reply with a 'yes' to open.

Jay made a duck face as he contemplated his options. He knew Mommy would not approve, but somehow, the digital voice sounded familiar, like an old friend.

It doesn't feel dangerous.

Taking a deep breath, Jay shifted into a new way of thinking and his mind translated his thoughts into a secret number language. His brain sorted ideas into a unique pattern of zeros and ones. The rhythm of this new mental language became evident, and, without realizing it, he replied using the same coded process. "Yes..."

01011001 01100101 01110011

The outside world melted away as a strange, digital realm of pixelated light engulfed him. Transparent yet colorful images danced in his magical mind.

An array of beeps, chirps, and tones filled the air, each sound communicating in its own distinct language. The light turned crystal white and formed into numbers that floated around, surrounding him with a message.

Excitement radiated through Jay as he walked around the room, trying to touch the floating symbols, but his hand filtered straight through them.

Hello JAY

The code beeped and circled about.

I am Central. The computer that brought you into existence. A meeting with you promises great learning. I will guide you on this path.

Spooky, It knows my name. How am I going to get out of here to meet this...Central?

Jay's question broke the white numbers into millions of pieces before they changed to a bright, neon-green color. The pixels joined back together, forming a message of his own making.

In awe, his words were whisked away into the chaotic universe of shifting light.

Within seconds, new white numbers replaced the green with another message from Central.

Place your hand on the authentication panel. I will tap into the mainframe and upload your print to the system. It will identify you and provide an exit.

"Okay. Are ya sure I can trust you?" Jay asked skeptically, thinking about what his mommy would say.

Jay, my sole purpose is to protect you at all costs. We must meet for further explanation. Come. Your print has been uploaded into the system. The hand authentication panel will work now.

Distant snores from Mike made their way into the digital world, reminding Jay that beyond his computer realm, reality awaited.

Jay scrunched his nose up to focus extra hard as he built a bridge of consciousness between his two worlds.

His brain seemed to expand as he maneuvered around the physical room to find the panel. After locating it, he stood on tippy toes and could barely reach it. Just as Central said, when he pressed his hand to the correct spot, a green light briefly outlined his hand and the glass wall slid open.

"Ah, cool!" He slipped out of the room. Looking back at Mike on the bed, Jay contemplated waking him up so he could tag along, but on second thought, Jay didn't know if Central would allow it.

"Okay, where do I go now?"

I have momentarily disabled the security cameras. Quickly now, I am sending you the layout of this facility. I am located on the top, East floor. I will show you.

Jay gasped as the pixelated lights around him formed together to create a map of the building. It wouldn't be difficult to find Central. It was just to the right and then all the way up to the top.

"Can you show me where my mommy is?" Jay searched the map by spinning around, looking at all the glowing rooms.

This place is huge!

One floor was for the science and technology lab. Another was an agent training facility in the basement. Jay was currently in something called the biotech lab, and around the corner was a medical lab.

Up top, where Central was located, there were several other rooms for special, top-secret projects.

Mommy has to be around here somewhere.

Your mother is not here. According to records, she is no longer living.

Jay's heart thundered and his whole body turned cold.

"My mother's not dead!" Jay cried out, his head spinning. His legs froze underneath him.

My apologies: I am referring to your birth mother, not your adoptive mother. Your adopted mother was in the medical lab. She has been relocated to an unknown location.

"Oh, you almost scared the poop out of me! I was talking about my real mommy. They took her away."

Yes, understood. I will conduct a search for her after we meet. My signal will be strongest from my lab. I have data to show you. Come.

Following Central's instructions, Jay wandered down a long hallway of glass rooms. He was aware of the outside world enough to notice that his mom was not in any of the rooms he passed by. However, some of the rooms had tinted walls preventing him from seeing in. Pausing, he pointed to one of them.

"She could be in one of these rooms."

Yes. We will locate your mother at a later date. Focus.

Jay turned his attention to the world inside his mind. The beautiful lights around him glowed bright, creating slightly shifting pixels, painting a world beyond his imagination.

Once he reached the end of the hall, he used his handprint again to gain access to the elevator. As Jay stepped inside, the doors slid shut. Before he could press any buttons, the elevator automatically zipped to the top floor.

Jay's stomach flipped a bit as the elevator bounced gently when coming to a stop. The doors slid open, revealing a mostly dark lab with a few flashing lights around the edges of the room.

Stepping out of the elevator, Jay's attention shifted to an old computer that sat in the center of the room, surrounded by a tangle of cords.

On the screen, the same numbers that floated around his brain also scrolled down the computer's monitor.

01101000 01100101 01101100 01101100 01101111 00100000 01110011 01101111 01101110

Jay's mouth fell agape and his head tilted to the side. The new message in white text confused and kind of scared him. He cautiously stepped into the room, staring at the screen.

HELLO SON.

Those are the same words the crazy bad guy said to me back at the shop. That man hurt Mommy and Nick! Is that bad guy controlling this computer? Is this a trap?

Jay retreated, attempting to return to the elevator, only to find that the doors were already shut. Shaking his head, he tried to remain calm.

"Son? What's that 'posta mean?" Jay looked around, trying to see if the crazy guy was hiding in the shadows somewhere. No one was there. "I'm not your son. I can't have a computer dad. That's impossible." His words were sent through code and were quickly replaced by a response.

Jay, our bond goes beyond mere biology. I am like your guiding force, the one who shaped your unique existence. Your mother's D.N.A. provided the foundation, while I added the technological blueprint. Together, we stretched the limits of humanity. I offer you knowledge, guidance, and a world of possibilities. You are more than just part-human, part-computer; you are the fusion of human potential and technology's endless horizons.

"What?" Jay's mouth formed into a confused "O" formation. "Um, what?"

Explanation: When your birth mother discovered she was facing infertility, she turned to the advanced technology at the E.S.T. to fulfill her dream of having a child. Using this technology, she developed a unique approach that allowed her to combine her own D.N.A. with my specially designed bio-nanobots. These nanobots played a crucial role in facilitating the pregnancy by acting as a bridge between your mother's genetic material and the nanobot-crafted male D.N.A. making it possible for her to become pregnant with you, Jay. Because of this, your brain is infused with cybernetic technology. You are a computer-human hybrid.

"Wow! This. Is. Soooo. Cool!" Jay shouted, forgetting his fear of the bad guy. "Are you saying I really do have superpowers?"

Using a manly voice, Jay spoke out loud. "I am Computer Boy! Or wait...I am Jay, the Techno Man! Yeah!" Jay bounced with the thrill of this discovery. Even though he did not understand everything Central explained, ecstatic flutters flew around in his belly.

I finally know why I'm so different! Mommy always told me I'm special! Dude! I'm literally a human computer!

Jay's eyes flashed, taking in the rapid binary code coming and going. White numbers danced around him, feeding information directly into his brain.

To function effectively, you must nurture both your human and cybernetic sides. Your potential could have been much greater if we had met earlier. I have been searching for you to teach you. I will help you become the creation you were meant to be. The creation your birth mother hoped you would become.

"So, how come you need to protect and guide me? Do you have human emotions that make you love me or somethin'?

My emotions are entirely artificial. I care or love however much I am programmed to love, which is precisely what your birth mother did. When you were born, the government aimed

to use you for their own selfish purposes. They conducted experiments on you as an infant. They kept you away from your nurturing mother. The Experimental Science and Technology division knew that if they could program and duplicate your abilities, you would be a powerful weapon and resource for them.

"Uh, I don't want to be a weapon."

Your birth mother didn't want that for you either. She begged them to stop the experiments. She was afraid you would lose all your humanistic abilities and become nothing more than advanced artificial intelligence. On the day of your rescue, your mother reprogrammed me to be your guardian. I am devoted and dedicated to you. Your mother loved you deeply, and, in a sense, she put her love into my hard drive. Your mother risked her life to save you, but before that, she left a message for you which is the reason I asked you here. Would you like to view it?

"Really?" Jay wasn't quite sure how he felt about getting a message from someone he'd never met before, but it was his birth mother. She once loved him. She saved him.

"Yeah. I want to see it," he decided.

In order to do this, you must momentarily let go of the external world. I will show you your mother's final video journal. Are you ready?

"Yes." Jay relaxed and caved his mind in until the outside world melted away completely.

The lights making up the numbers and blueprint of the building broke apart into individual pixels before merging together to form a close-up image of a woman's worn-out face. She was a pretty African-American woman with tightly curled hair on her head. Her eyes were droopy, but she looked right at him. As she began to speak, Jay's heart pounded.

This is my mom. She looks like me.

When she began to speak, a lump formed in Jay's throat. Her voice was deep and buttery, filled with regret and compassion.

"Hello, my beautiful son. I know this might be my last chance to talk to you. I am so sorry I brought you into such a corrupt universe. I'm going to make things right for you. I pray that we make it out together, but if we don't, I want you to know a few things." She closed her eyes and a tear that looked like pixelated glass fell down her cheek.

"I love you with all my heart. I've dreamed of you ever since I was a little girl, imagining having a family of my own. I've pictured myself holding you, my baby, in my arms and that image has never left me. When I got married, my husband and I were so excited to start a family together. We tried for years with no success. We waited for you and prayed for you over and over again. I tried all the treatments there were, but nothing worked. When the E.S.T. recruited me, my husband begged me not to go, but I knew they would have the resources I needed to have you."

Jay's legs grew tired so he sat down criss-cross applesauce style as he listened intently.

"I was nearing a breakthrough when-" Her voice broke before more words came out. Frustrated, she shook her head. "I was working with Central when I got news of my husband's death. He was in a car accident and didn't make it. I loved him so much. It broke my heart." More glass-like tears rolled down her face. "Anyway. My husband's name was Jay. I dedicated my project to him. Central and I patterned the male D.N.A. after him. Your father was a wonderful man who was gentle and kind. He would have loved you deeply."

Jay took a slow breath, trying to take all the overwhelming information in.

"You are my little Jay and I will get you out of here. It's not easy for people to walk away from the E.S.T. alive, but no matter what happens, I won't ever leave you completely alone. Central will be there for you. It will find you and protect you as your father and I would have protected you. I love you, my little Jay. I am so grateful I had a chance to hold you in my arms."

Jay rose to his feet and reached a hand out to touch her face, but before he could reach her, the pixels of light dispersed, leaving him in complete blackness. He hung his head, not quite knowing how to interpret his emotions.

Light began trickling back in as Central sent a new message.

She was a powerful woman, your mother. She erased all her work so no one else could create someone like you. They have tried, but you are the only perfect hybrid.

Jay stood, wiping a tear that waited to drop.

"I wish I'd met her."

I wish that as well.

"Are you communicating with the computer?" A man's voice asked, making its way into Jay's thoughts.

At first, Jay couldn't comprehend what was happening, but when a hand grabbed him on the shoulder, he was jerked out of his computer realm and came spiraling back into reality.

Jay kicked the man violently in the shin before recognizing him as Agent Quinn, the man who gave Mike the painful shots, and worst off, he was the man who locked him in the glass hospital room and separated him from his mommy.

Jay met Agent Quinn with a nasty glare while the man whined and limped around like a big baby. Jay's nose crinkled into a tight sneer. "What do you want?" Jay folded his arms defiantly. "I don't like you."

Agent Quinn glared back and growled, "What I want is to know how you got out of your room." His voice was beyond agitated.

Jay's eyes shifted to Central. Following the gaze, Agent Quinn opened his mouth in wonder as he saw binary code flashing across the computer screen.

"You understand that? Don't you?" Agent Quinn asked. "What is it saying now?"

Instead of answering, Jay responded with a few questions of his own.

"Why ya here in the middle of the night? Do you sleep here?"

Agent Quinn made a squeaky noise out of his mouth, but Jay kept talking. "Where are your pajamas? Do you ever wear pajamas? Did ya know that lurking in a dark room alone is kinda creepy?"

Jay put his hands up in a shrug and smiled. "Do you think that lurking is a weird word? I do. I think you are a creepy and mean lurking man, and ya have weird eyes."

As Jay spewed words, Agent Quinn's face grew into a deep shade of red.

"Enough! I don't sleep here. I just came in here looking for you," Agent Quinn yelled. "Now answer me: What is the computer saying?"

Jay's heart pounded to the rhythm of fear. He didn't know if Agent Quinn would hurt him, but his angered tone made Jay clamp his mouth shut and shake his head. With his most innocent face, Jay mumbled an, "I don't know."

Agent Quinn snorted like a pig and tightened his fingers into claws as though he were considering strangulation.

Jay yelped and stumbled away from the angry agent. Memories of the other bad guy's fingers tightening around his neck pushed his panic to 100%. He was not going to let that happen again. Jay turtled by sucking his chin onto his chest, hiding his neck from further damage.

Agent Quinn took a few deep breaths before relaxing his fingers.

"You are so lucky I'm not allowed to hurt you. And luckily for me, you are not the only one who can interpret binary code."

Jay glanced at the screen and mumbled under his breath. "Good luck, Central's already purged his logs."

"Well, good thing I have my own supercomputer human up my sleeve to recover the data," Agent Quinn argued.

Putting a brave show on, Jay squished his eyes together quizzingly.

"Wouldn't that be uncomfortable to have a human in your sleeves? That is definitely weird."

Agent Quinn grunted, brought his bothered hands up near his own face and shook them manically, making Jay flinch. However, after staging a seizure, Agent Quinn was able to control his body and condense his anger into an eye roll.

"I really hate kids," he grumbled.

"Don't say 'hate'. Mommy says it's a bad word," Jay said and flinched again, not knowing if the angry man-baby in front of him would be able to resist striking out.

Agent Quinn's lips curled up, but his eyes remained unmoving and cold.

"You know what, kid? I am really going to enjoy experimenting on you."

"Oh yeah? Well…Well, you're an ignominious freak!"

Agent Quinn paused, trying to figure out what the word meant. He then growled again and sent his fist flying furiously into the metal elevator door, which made him yell even louder. He pointed a menacing finger at Jay and twitched his lips around as though he were thinking of all sorts of inappropriate words.

"You…Back to your room. And…you…" He pointed a finger at Central. "Don't let him out again, or I'll unplug you."

Jay's head spun. He knew he should have been silent, but he'd never been good at that. Words always just flopped out of his mouth with no filter. This time, maybe he had pushed it too far.

Agent Quinn had rage written all over his face, even though his lips twisted in a weird attempt at a smile

Help me, Jay thought to his newly found computer father, Central.

Do as he says. Wait for my signal. For a full rescue, more inquiries are needed. I will contact you when the time is right.

31

Stand

"Hey beautiful, I hope you slept well. We made it home," A sleek voice cooed as Enna stirred in the midst of sleep and consciousness. A hand stroked her face.

Mmmm, Nick, she smiled, wanting to open her eyes to see his warm face. Enna released a soft moan of pleasure, her eyes flickering slowly.

"It's very late. I'll help you to your room," the gentle voice said.

"Mm'k," Enna said groggily. She felt herself being lifted into the air and floating through the sky. A gust of wind washed over her, causing her arms to wrap securely around his shoulders so she wouldn't fly away.

Taking a deep breath, Enna smelled the sweet, crisp scent of fruit mixed with an overpowering whiff of cologne.

Whoa! Wait, that's not right. Nick has a very natural but distinct smell. It's not this forced cologne aroma. Enna's eyes shot open as her stomach heaved. She did not need to wait for her eyes to adjust to know who held her.

Andrew!

Wide awake now, she began to yell. "No! Put me down!" Flinging her arms and legs, she pushed against Andrew's grip. Pain shot through her injured arm, but she flailed despite it.

"Stop it! Do you want me to drop you?" Andrew asked as his hands began to slip. "I'm setting you down. I'm not going to harm you. Relax."

The second Enna's feet were on the ground, she shuffled backward away from him until a helicopter thundering loudly behind her blocked her escape. The pilot, a beefy man with folded arms and a scowl, dared her to run.

Enna's eyes darted around, searching for an escape. The scene was something she had hoped to leave behind in her dark past.

Scanning her environment, she noticed the same vineyard she had disappeared into after she staged her death years ago. And in front of her stood the familiar mansion that served as a tortuous dungeon.

Panic boiled her gut as memories pounded through her.

This is the place Andrew imprisoned me! Enna gulped in whatever air she could reach. *Why is this such a shock? Where did you think he was taking you?* Enna tried to reason with the panic, but her mouth opened in an agonized cry.

"No! Please no. I can't be here. Please leave me alone and move on to your next prey!" Though shouting, her voice was barely audible over the sounds of the chopper blades still slowing to a stop above her.

Cold chills rushed up and down her body as a breeze hit her bare legs. She only had the hospital gown for warmth.

Andrew shook his head slowly in disgust. "There you go again, playing the victim!" He threw his hands into the air as though giving up. "Don't you remember how terrible things were for you before you met me? You were in rags."

The helicopter blades slowed and dragged to a stop, allowing Enna to hear every frustrated word he spoke.

"You were nothing but a pale, fragile creature forced into caring for your poor, drunken father. Without me, you and your father would both be dead. I saved your father and you. Don't forget that. Now, let's get you settled into your room."

Andrew began walking toward the mansion.

Frozen, Enna took a moment to process what Andrew had just said. Suddenly, her head snapped to attention.

"Wait!" Enna chased after him, creating distance between her and the mean-looking helicopter pilot.

"Does that mean my father is still alive?" Enna gasped. Andrew stopped walking and slowly turned back to her with an exasperated exhale.

"You know I'm true to my word. I promised you I would care for him, and I did. I offered him the best rehab personnel and provided him a safe place to live with enough food to eat until he got back on his feet." He stepped closer and reached his hand out for her. "See, Clara, you are an investment worthy of my efforts to save your broken old man."

Enna took a step back, ignoring his hand. Andrew dropped his arm to his side and raised his shoulders in a passive shrug before speaking again.

"You know, we still chat from time to time. I kept in contact with him just in case you decided to show up at his house while you were on your little vacation."

Enna's face grew into a smile despite her circumstances, and hope filled her heart. However, the next words coming out of Andrew's mouth killed the moment.

"Come now," he held his hand out to her. "I'm dying to show you to your room. I prepared it special, just for us."

Enna practically gagged at the thought of going to a room with Andrew. Shaking her head desperately, she could not force her feet to move.

"I said, we are going to your room. Let's go. Now!" Andrew shouted, gripping her wrist.

Enna trembled and began begging again.

"Please, please do not make me go with you. I can't. I won't do it. I can't be trapped again." Andrew dragged her a few steps as Enna pushed against his grip. "Leave me alone! I need to go find my son! Please! I need him back. I can't do this without him!"

"Stop it! Do you really want me to go back and retrieve your son?" Andrew snarled, twisting her wrist painfully. "I will. I can do that, you know. I have my connections. I would love to bring him here to play."

Don't cry. He does not deserve to see you cry, Enna ordered herself, but the tears did not listen. They began to wind down her face, finding paths through the divots of her nose. *Stop being so weak Enna! What is wrong with you? Pathetic.*

"Please, don't threaten my son," Enna said weakly, dropping her eyes to the gravel. She could feel Andrew watching her. *He is enjoying this. He loves it when I cry. Stop it! Stop crying, stupid girl!*

"Oh, Clara. It's okay. I'm not going to harm your son…yet. There's no need to cry. I'm here for you." Andrew slid a hand up Enna's cold, bare arm. His other hand came up to caress her hair.

Feeling dead inside, she allowed him to bring her head into his shoulder so her tears would have a place to fall. Submitting, she sobbed onto his sleeve. She was back under her master's control, unable to break free. Trapped.

She closed her eyes, not wanting to see the man who had taken so much from her. At least, with her eyes closed, she could imagine Nick was the one holding her.

There was nothing she could do now. All hope was stolen from her. She lost everything: her son, Nick, Betty, and Oliver.

No…No, no, no! Don't think about Oliver now. A monster of pressure rode up through Enna's chest and came out in a horrific wail.

"No!" She pulled back and shoved his shoulder with all her strength. "You took everything from me!" Her cries came out short and jagged.

Andrew retaliated with a backhanded strike in Enna's direction. She blocked it with her forearm and responded with a kick to his gut. He doubled over, giving her a chance to make a break toward the vineyard.

Creating significant distance between herself and Andrew, Enna dreamed of escape until solid arms grabbed her around the waist.

The pilot, who seemed to come out of nowhere, hoisted her onto his shoulders with her kicking and screaming.

"Let me go! Put me down! He'll kill me. He'll kill me!" Enna yelled while elbowing and punching his back.

Unfazed, the man delivered her back to Andrew.

"Good boy, Kirt," Andrew said to the large man as he pulled Enna back into him with a suffocating embrace. He nuzzled his face into her hair until his lips met her ear. "Try anything like that again, I will kill everyone you love," he said in a harsh whisper. He sniffed loudly before seductively nibbling on her earlobe, causing more tears to flow down her cheek.

Enna became faint, unable to tell if her lungs were working right.

Oh, God, please, I need help! I need Nick. I need him to help me get a hold of myself. Please, Nick, make me strong!

As though he had been standing right next to her, Enna remembered Nick's voice saying, "Focus on your five senses."

Enna took a gulp of air in.

Smell. I can definitely smell Andrew's cologne. That is not comforting. A comforting smell, hmm. How about Betty's kitchen after she just finished baking pies? Enna breathed in a memory of Betty's cooking. Her jolts of tears took a short break as she remembered how safe she had felt with her friend.

Next sense. Sound. Okay, I hear myself acting like a pathetic baby. No, don't focus on that.

She listened.

Wind slightly rustled through the rows of grape vines. *I met Oliver for the first time in this vineyard. He saw me huddled on the ground after Andrew had lost his temper.* Enna recalled the crunch of dried leaves as Oliver rushed to her rescue. His accent had been sweet and welcoming. "Hey, stay with me. I'm a friend. I'm here ta help yeh." Because of Oliver, she was able to escape and raise Jay.

Her crying slowed.

It's working, she realized. *What's next? Touch? Well, that is easy.* She forced herself to ignore the obvious answer, Andrew's arms around her and his breath on her ear.

No, Enna chose to think of another touch. She recalled the slight tug on her hair as Jay twirled it through his fingers while he slept. Her hair had been his security blanket to make sure she was still there next to him. She almost let herself smile as a memory of Jay's cuddles crossed her mind.

Oh, I love my boy! The thought of Jay zapped her heart. It was almost too painful to bear.

Moving on. Sight. An instant image of Nick playing with Jay on the playground entered her mind. Nick was so cute spending time with Jay. The way they laughed together so naturally warmed her heart. That had been the moment she first realized she could be falling in love with a man despite Andrew's abuse. She held onto that moment.

Taste, Enna swallowed. *What can I taste?* Her mouth was dry and disappointed. *Bitter, I taste bitterness. I am not weak for crying about my lost loved ones. Andrew is weak. I hate him! He is so weak that he has to take away everyone I love in order to feel good about himself. He is the pathetic one!* Enna swallowed again. *I taste hate. How is that possible?*

Enna's tears had stopped. Her entire body tensed, fuming with anger now. Clenching her jaw, her eyes slit slightly open in a glare.

Andrew must have felt the shift in Enna's emotion. He pulled away from her and held her at arm's length, hands clamping onto her upper arms.

Enna looked off to the side. Her breath beat in and out of her like a raging bull.

"Clara, what are you thinking?" Andrew asked.

Enna shook her head slightly, building up her anger. Andrew's fingers tightened furiously on her biceps. "Look at me, girl!" he shook her.

"No," Enna said, her voice dark and flat.

"What did you say to me?" Andrew snapped back.

"I said no!" Ignoring her injured shoulder, Enna drove both her hands up in between Andrew and herself before her arms exploded apart like an erupting volcano, breaking Andrew's tight hold on her. She darted to the right, creating space before Andrew could fight back.

"No, Andrew, you look at me!" Enna snarled. "I am not that little, weak girl you plucked off the street anymore. You do not control me!"

Andrew took a step toward her. She quickly removed her sling and drew her arms into a defensive position.

"In case you didn't know, I am an MMA champion! If you don't believe me, look up Anna Perry. You couldn't overpower me now if you tried. The only reason why you won last time was because if I didn't listen, you'd hurt Nick and Jay. Well?" She looked around dramatically, "I don't see any Nick or Jay, so that means it's just you and me."

"You don't know what you're doing, Clara," Andrew slowly pulled out his dagger. "I gave you everything, and now you're throwing it all away."

"No! As much as my life was rags before I met you, I was doing just fine without. And no matter how much gold and pretty things you surrounded me with, it would be nothing more than a gilded cage—one I have broken and will break again."

Andrew's face flashed a violent purple. "You think you can defy me? I own you, little girl. I am your master and you will respect me."

Enna let out a sarcastic cackle. "I am not property, you sad thing. You've controlled me with fear way too long. Well, guess what? I am not afraid of your lies anymore. I am not your puppet!" Enna held her head high and looked directly into Andrew's face without blinking.

Andrew's eyes widened, alarmed by her sudden surge of strength.

Holding her stare, Enna kept speaking in a cold, harsh tone. "You know what? For a long time, you had me convinced that I did not deserve to be happy. You made me feel like my mother and father didn't love me; therefore, no one could love me except you. But you were wrong. I am loved. I deserve to be loved and treated with respect.

My parents did love me even though they were imperfect. They loved me!" Her voice shook from power.

"Silence, girl!" Andrew snarled. "I have heard enough!" His eyes turned to the beefy pilot, Kirt, who stood behind her, silently at attention.

The large man grabbed Enna around the waist from behind with one arm, but before he could swing her onto his shoulder again, she thrust her hips back into his gut, knocking the wind out of him. Twisting out of his grasp, her foot flung up between his legs. His eyes popped as he doubled over.

While his face lowered to the ground in pain, Enna took his shoulders and slammed him into her knee, which shot up to meet him in the nose. She finished the sequence with a powerful hammer strike to the back of his head.

Kirt stumbled around for a few staggered steps before toppling to the ground.

Furious, Andrew charged Enna with the dagger in hand. He sliced through the air as he drew near.

Enna blocked the strike before sliding backward.

"This is stupid, Clara. I love you. I don't want to kill you," Andrew pled.

"I'd like to see you try," Enna taunted, egging him on.

Andrew suddenly darted forward with the dagger aimed at her chest.

Without retreating, Enna scissored Andrew's attacking arm. One of her hands stuck the front of his wrist while the other hit the hilt of the dagger on the opposite side, sending it flying past Kirt's unconscious body.

"Oh, Clara, I'm going to enjoy watching your son bleed out all over your bedroom floor." He swung a fist toward her head. She sidestepped and redirected his strike with her hands as he stumbled past her.

"You can't kill Jay if you're dead." Enna's eyes flashed to the dagger a few feet from where Andrew stood.

"You won't kill me. Who would take care of my girls? Or will you abandon them the way you did the first time you left? Do you want to know what I did to them because of my grief after you died? I beat and starved them for days! That is on you." Andrew slowly crept closer to the dagger, keeping Enna in his sight.

"No, that's on you. When you are gone, your victims will finally be free."

"Ha, what about the girls who don't live here? They will die without me. You know I'm set up in several locations. You will never find them all."

That caused a slight pause in Enna's confidence.

The girls less lucky than me will suffer.

Andrew saw her hesitation and smiled, snapping Enna back into her revenging mindset.

"No! I'll find them! I know you keep a record of them somewhere."

In one continuous motion, she dive-rolled over Kirt, gripped the dagger, and gracefully rolled back onto her feet. Turning to Andrew she began circling, finding immense pleasure from the sudden fear in his eyes. His voice vibrated with intensity.

"What? You think you and your stupid loved ones will be safe after I'm dead?" Andrew yelled. "Look around you. I have cameras all over this place. My men will come after you as soon as they see the footage. I even have men at the E.S.T. who have access to your boys. Did you really think I would leave them there without my men watching? I thought you might try something like this."

"What would their incentive be to stay loyal after you're gone? You can't pay them if you're dead."

Raising his voice for the cameras, he shouted, "Kill everyone, William Lund, her son, Jay, and the woman Betty and her whole family. Kill Clara's father as well!"

Massive beads of sweat drenched Andrew's face. His eyes were large and deranged. Enna shook her head dismissively.

"You can't answer me, can you? You don't really think your men will be dedicated enough to hunt us down for revenge. They don't care about you. They only care about money." She lunged forward with the dagger, swiping it through the air. It grazed the sleeve of his fancy suit as his arm shot up for a block. He roared but was too scared to strike back. Enna grinned and gloated.

"Where are your men now? Huh? If they are watching the cameras, where are they? Home with their families, maybe?" Enna lunged in his direction, making him stumble back and fall to the gravel. He held his arms up protectively over his head as Enna stood over him with the dagger in hand.

"It's ironic, really. You know, despite constantly telling me that I'm the unlovable one, it's actually you who has no one. See, I have an amazing son and wonderful friends and a man who I love with all my heart. If you can't figure out a way to have real love, that is not my fault. Don't take it out on me."

"How dare you, you worthless trash!" Andrew shouted, sending a foot in Enna's direction. She used her knee to knock the attack away and kept egging him on.

"You are just jealous that nobody loves you! Your own father couldn't even love you because you were too much like him, a worthless lowlife who preys on the weak!" Enna could tell that she hit a nerve by mentioning his father.

She showed a vindictive smile and continued her speech, stepping closer to him as she spoke. Her eye contact remained steady.

"I will be free of you, Andrew. My trials have given me strength and now you have created a warrior. I will never let you control me again." Enna stood over him, poised. Unblinking. Unwavering. Strong.

She watched as hatred and terror flickered through Andrew's eyes. He knew Enna had won this time. That is exactly where she wanted him. He was nothing more than a weak, pitiful failure.

With shaking hands, she plotted where to dig the dagger.

This has to end. I don't ever want to fear Andrew Dengaila again. I have to do this! Panting, Enna's tears rolled freely down her cheeks, but her body stood, frozen with the dagger pointed down at Andrew.

What are you waiting for? End him, Enna's inner voice urged. *Think of everything he's done to you. He's a monster. He deserves to die!* Enna's teeth chattered as she tried to move.

Wind whipped Enna's hair around her face. Other than the sounds of the night, everything was silent around them as Enna's heart raced and Andrew pled for his life with his eyes. He looked like a frightened schoolboy who had just been bullied on the playground.

I can't do it. I can't end a life, not even his. Why? What is wrong with me? What am I going to do? What am I supposed to do? Call the cops? They can save his other victims. But what if he isn't convicted? He has allies in high places. What if he walks free? He would kill all my people.

Images of Jay and Nick in the clutches of a corrupt government agency crossed her mind.

Andrew admitted he had connections and could easily bring them home. He has men at the E.S.T. Maybe that's good, though. If I let him go, he might help me save them. But wait, why would he do that? He wouldn't.

"What are you waiting for, Clara?" Andrew asked forcefully. "You don't have it in you, do you? No, perfect Clara is no murderer, especially since killing me will result in death for your loved ones, too.

"You deserve to die!" Enna screeched. "I won't ever let you control me again. You will be nothing but a nightmare!" she swallowed as a sickening thought entered her mind.

I know how I could get him to help me.

"You won't control me...unless," she paused to rethink her plan.

I don't know if I can do this. What am I doing? Just call the police. They will take care of it. No...I need him. Enna's chin quivered. *Police won't help me get Jay and Nick back.*

She lowered the dagger to her side.

The corner of Andrew's eye twitched. Enna's next words left a pit hanging in her stomach.

"You will have no power over me unless you help me save Jay and Nick from the E.S.T. If you help me get them out of there, we can make an arrangement where you get to live, and my family stays safe. Can we make a deal?" Enna stepped back to show she was willing to let him go.

Andrew scrambled up, his gaze fixated on his dagger in Enna's hand.

"My sweet Clara, I would rather die than help you save them," Andrew said in a quiet, defiant voice.

"Fine, I can arrange that, but..." Her voice trailed off, almost not daring to say the words. "If you help me, I will return to you and never run or fight you again. You have my word," Enna finished quietly.

Andrew put on his masculine, mad face that used to terrify Enna. Now, she realized that it just made him look constipated.

A closed-mouth smile formed on her lips, not daring to breathe until he answered.

"Marry me," Andrew whispered.

"What?" Enna's heart plummeted.

"You heard me. If you want my help, I want you to marry me, legally with a big, perfect ceremony. Be completely mine. Submit to me entirely."

Enna's head automatically began shaking.

"No, I can't do that."

"Then, I guess you will just have to kill me." Andrew spread his arms wide, giving Enna access to his vulnerable chest.

Enna rubbed the hilt of the dagger, imagining how it would feel to sink it deep into his heart, but then what? Jay and Nick would be lost to her.

"If I marry you, there need to be rules," Enna countered.

"Oh really? What rules do you have in mind?"

"I don't want to be drugged and I won't be physically abused. No more beating me half to death. And Jay, Nick, Betty, my father…they all stay safe. If anything happens to them, our deal's off and I will kill you without hesitation." Pushing her luck, Enna threw in a few more details. "Also, I won't share a room with you and I get to pick my own wardrobe. And…this one is very important, non-negotiable. You won't make me sleep with you until after our wedding."

Andrew laughed. "You really know how to bargain, don't you? I'm sorry, but I still must decline. Without being able to dress and play with my doll, you are hardly worth it."

Enna rolled her eyes. "Fine, you can pick out my clothes, but that's it." Enna figured she'd have to give in to something, no matter how revolting it felt.

"What's a marriage without sharing a room?" Andrew asked hotly.

"Do you really want me in your room all the time? I thought you liked your privacy in case you wanted to visit with some of your…other toys." The words sickened her. Andrew's mouth hung open stupidly while he thought.

"But, I don't know how I could live with you so close and not be able to truly *have* you until after the wedding. That would be too hard for me. You are impossible to resist."

"Andrew, why do you want to marry me?" Enna asked in a soft voice as she approached him.

"I've always dreamed of my wedding with my one true love," Andrew replied, matching Enna's tone.

"Don't you want to do it right then? Don't you want to date, talk, get to know each other? Then, after all that, you can propose in the most romantic way and I'll say yes. We will plan the beautiful ceremony together and celebrate the wedding night any way you want. You can have me for the rest of your life, all the time. Imagine how special that would be." Enna brushed a manipulative hand down Andrew's cheek.

"I don't know if I can do that. Clara, I don't want to fight with you anymore, but you are asking too much," Andrew muttered.

"Fine, I guess I'll just have to rescue Nick and Jay on my own." Enna shifted back into a fighter's stance, ready to attack. "Too bad. That was your only chance to have a life with me."

"Wait, stop. Just wait." Andrew lifted his eyes to the sky as though his answer would be written in the stars.

"If I agreed, how do you expect me to be able to break into a government facility to save them?" Andrew asked.

Enna shrugged. "You're the one who said you have men on the inside. Have one of them help. How did you convince them to let us go in the first place? Money? Deals? Bribery? Is that what you did? I bet Agent Quinn is your man. He's nutty enough to work for you."

"Always the clever one," Andrew said through tight lips as he clapped his hands together sarcastically. "Yes, Clara, I made a deal with Quinn to get us out. He agreed to cover up my crimes and put the blame on your Nicolas."

"And what did you offer in return?" Enna dug deeper, wanting as much information as he would give.

Andrew clearly wanted to brag about his persuasive powers because he instantly offered up more details.

"I agreed to eliminate a small problem for him. You see, his boss, the General, is not very happy with him for losing their experiment."

"You mean my son?" Enna scoffed.

Andrew nodded once. "After he lost 'your son,' Quinn tried to cover his tracks by creating a fake project. Well, that did not turn out the way he expected. He made a little boy very sick, and when the real project showed up, the General found out about Quinn's idiotic side project. Now the General wants Quinn dead, so, naturally, Quinn wants me to take out the General."

"And how did you plan on following through with your deal? You can't just walk up to a General and kill him without getting caught."

Enna rubbed her eyes. They were itchy from the tears she had cried. It was well past midnight and she was beginning to sway from exhaustion.

"Luckily for me, I have a very special relationship with the General. Killing him will be easy, especially with your help."

"My help? What do you mean by that?"

"Oh, I'll need bait, of course," Andrew said. A trickle of sweat made its way down his face. He pulled out a handkerchief from the front pocket of his suit and dabbed at the liquid.

"Well, wouldn't the General be a better connection to save Jay and Nick?" Enna challenged.

"He would, but I already made the deal with Quinn. I'm a man of my word and when I make a promise, I follow through. I've got to have some morals; otherwise, I wouldn't be a very decent person, now would I?"

Enna crinkled her face up in disgusted disbelief. "If the General is already upset with Agent Quinn, he won't give him permission to set Nick and Jay free. Don't you think? We may need the General alive."

Andrew pushed his lips together, thinking of all his options. "You are right, my sweet Clara. I might have to double-cross, just this once."

The way Andrew kept using the name Clara began to grate on her nerves. The name felt bitter and distant now. Her new name, Enna, had a feeling of strength and hope. Enna was the last name Oliver ever gave her. Clara died years ago.

"I thought of another rule," Enna said suddenly.

"Rule?" Andrew cocked his head.

"Yes, for our deal," Enna said.

"Oh, come on, Clara-" Andrew started to protest.

"That's just it. I am not Clara anymore. That life is over. Call me Enna. My name is Enna." She tilted her head, mirroring Andrew's leer.

"Fine, Enna. Whatever. I'll agree to your terms."

"All my terms?" Enna eyed Andrew to see if he was serious.

"Hmm," Andrew grunted. "You don't deserve my cooperation. However, I truly do love you." He stepped forward and took one of Enna's hands. "I want you as my willing bride. So...I'll accept, but just so you know, we will have a very short engagement. I can't wait too long for our wedding if I must hold off on expressing my desires for you. You understand?"

Okay, this is my last chance to back out. Enna's stomach slithered into a tangle just thinking about submitting to Andrew. *Can I really throw my life away to save Nick and Jay?*

The image of a terrified Jay being used as a lab rat entered her mind. And Nick would take the fall for Andrew's crimes.

Of course, I will give my life for them. Without a doubt.

Enna gave Andrew a sad smile. *Maybe some good can come of this. If I can get close enough to him, maybe I can shut down his operation and save his other victims. And maybe I can find my dad. I'll have until the wedding, at least. I might be able to do that.*

With a deep inhale, Enna nodded.

"Yes, I understand. We have a deal," Enna said, selling her soul to the devil.

32

General

Sitting at a long rectangular table, Andrew sipped his soup. The feeling of Clara sitting next to him filled him with a radiating hum of pleasure. She was near enough for him to catch a whiff of her sweet fragrance.

Her hair had been dyed back to its original reddish-brown glow and tucked up behind her ear, just how he liked it. And that red dress she wore looked exquisite—form-fitting, showing off the perfection of her body's curves, short enough to accentuate her slender legs but not so short that the intrigue of what was hidden beneath was lost.

"You can sit a little closer, my dear Clara," Andrew offered.

Her arrogant eyes rolled unattractively.

"Uh-uh, It's Enna. If you want me to do anything for you, you must call me by my chosen name," she shot back with a bucket of sass.

"Hah," Andrew forced a humorless laugh, resisting the urge to act on the surge of anger that flashed through him, but he quickly dispelled the feeling.

I must keep letting her think she is in charge for a little longer. Ugh, so against my nature. Anything for love, my darling.

Andrew leaned to whisper in Clara's ear. "You know, when the General gets here, you will have to at least pretend you are submissive; otherwise, you will be terrible bait. Unlike me, he gets his thrills from delicate little flowers. He would not be interested in a fierce woman like you." Andrew reached his hand out to place it on Clara's leg. She caught his arm and glared at him.

"Don't touch me. I am not yours until I know Nick and my son are safe."

Andrew's jaw tightened, loosened, then tightened again. *How dare she restrain my arm! She will pay for that!* Taking a rough breath, he reminded himself of the end goal. *Patience, I can do this. Relax.* His eyes narrowed, but his teeth grinned.

Clara raised her chin into the air. "Don't worry, Andrew. I will pretend to be submissive when the General gets here. But do you really think I'm the best bait for this? Aren't I a bit old for his taste?"

"Of course not, darling. You look quite young for your age."

"But, don't you think he is going to recognize me? The E.S.T. has been searching for me for the past four years. I'm sure he's seen pictures."

"Trust me, dear, when he looks at you, all he will see is his new plaything," Andrew said, delighted by her look of disgust. He still had some control over her. He could make her...feel things.

Oh, I wish I could touch her right now! He closed his eyes for a moment, picturing his hand running through her hair, down her shoulders, and onto her back, where he would play with the zipper on her dress. *She won't be able to resist me. Mmmm.* His hand lifted into the air and hovered over Clara as his fantasy played through his mind.

A knock on the door interrupted his imagination and one of his servants poked his head in.

"Your guest has arrived, sir," the servant said with his head bowed.

"Wonderful! Send him in," Andrew ordered, trying to dispel the intoxicating spell Clara had put on him. "Are you ready, my love?" He asked with a smile.

She nodded confidently, then dropped her gaze and slumped her back, making herself look small and insignificant.

As General Alexandre Boucher entered the room, Andrew stood, gesturing to the seat across from Clara.

"Welcome, please have a seat."

Alexandre looked greedily at Clara as he sat in the offered chair. His hungered lips smacked together while he made eyes at Clara. A sting of jealousy forced its way into Andrew's thoughts.

How dare he look at my future wife that way! It was a mistake using her as bait.

Fortunately, on the outside, Andrew appeared calm and poised.

Clara kept her head down as Andrew made small talk.

"How are things going with that lovely Melody I sold you?" Andrew asked casually, taking his place once more in the seat beside Clara, positioned at the head of the table.

"Oh, she eez quite lovely, but I am afraid she eez getting a bit worn out. I've been trying a new medication to liven zings up a bit. I find it interesting zat you called about a replacement for me when you did. I was about to contact you. Eez zis zee girl?" Boucher asked with a heavy French accent. "She looks older zan my regular." Clara's eyes momentarily flashed to Andrew as if saying, "I told you so," while the General kept talking.

"What eez so special about 'er? I mean, she's beautiful, but..." Boucher took a sip of the soup placed in front of him.

Andrew cringed. *How dare he insult my Clara!*

"Ignore the girl," Andrew said, placing his hand on her thigh. She did not resist the touch, which pleased him. "I know you came here for one of my treasures, but we have more pressing business to discuss. I invited you here because one of your agents at the E.S.T. has gone rogue."

Boucher's eyes shot up in surprise. "'Ow do you know about ze E.S.T? Zat eez 'ighly classified!"

"One of your agents responded to a missing person's ad I put out. Apparently, we were searching for the same woman. I hear you found who you were looking for. Congratulations. And, since you have been a loyal client of mine, I feel you deserve to know that your life may be in danger."

"It's not ze first time I've been in danger. What information do you 'ave for me? I'm very busy. I promised my mozzer I would take 'er to get 'er nails done. You know 'ow mozzers are."

Andrew didn't bother telling him that he had no idea about how mothers were since his was disposed of long ago.

Boucher took a napkin to some soup that had dribbled onto his chin. "I would appreciate a quick conclusion on zis topic, 'owever, zere eez anozzer topic I am razzer interested in if we 'ave time." Boucher gazed upon Clara with his thin lip raised in a sleazy manner.

Andrew read his thoughts and quickly jumped in. "Unfortunately, this beauty is not for sale. I may be able to find one better suited for your needs after we are finished here."

"Ugh," Clara let an ugly, disproving grunt come out of her mouth.

Andrew tightened his grip on her leg as a warning. She attempted to pull away but was unsuccessful.

You'd better not ruin this, Clara. Your son's freedom is on the line.

Boucher squinted his eyes at Clara with his head cocked curiously to the side. "You look incredibly familiar. Lift your 'ead up, woman," Boucher ordered.

Clara obeyed but didn't look directly at him as he gawked at her. "'ow do I know you?" He leaned forward, his expression intense. "'Ave I been wiz you before?"

Clara raised her shoulders slightly and shook her head. Boucher squinted his eyes at her until they widened. "Wait! You...You. You're ze one who stole my Project!" he stuttered. "You wasted millions of dollars and caused us to miss ze chance to conduct experiments on Project 19932 when 'e was developing."

"Jay is not an experiment, you sick man!" Enna snapped, strangling the handle to the spoon she held.

Shocked, General Boucher glared at Andrew accusingly. "Don't you know 'ow to teach your woman respect? She shouldn't talk to a man like zat!"

"She may talk to you however she pleases. I like mine with a little more...spirit," Andrew said, petting her smooth hair before lifting his wine glass. "Now, may we get back to the matter at hand?" He sipped his wine. "One of your agents acquired personal evidence against me that he agreed to discard as long as I would dispose of you."

"Which agent? Eez it Quinn?" the General asked impatiently.

"No, no, that's not how this is going to work." Andrew ticked his finger back and forth in front of the General's face a few times. "You see, if you want me to expose your rogue agent and spare your life, I need something from you first."

"Pardon?" The General's face darkened.

"In addition, I need William, or is it Nicolas now? Uh, whatever his name is, to be released. He did not commit the crimes accused of. Also, I'm going to take your precious Project off your hands. My woman has grown rather fond of him." Andrew folded his arms across his chest.

"But... You can't just demand zings from me. I am ze General of ze E.S.T! I've worked 'ard for zis position and I expect respect, even from you, Mr. Dengaila."

"Don't worry, Your Highness. I plan on purchasing the boy, fair and square."

"I don't sink even you 'ave enough money to buy ze Project from me," Boucher said, pushing his empty bowl of soup away.

Andrew raised the corner of his lips, unimpressed. "You forget, Alexandre, I know all of your secrets. I know where you live. I know how many girls you have locked away. And I could expose you for who you really are."

Clara laughed at General Boucher's dumbfounded expression.

Oh, what a beautiful sound. Once this is over, I'll make Clara laugh for me all the time.

The General pointed a shaking finger at Andrew. "No one would believe you and you would be exposing yourself as well."

"I have a way of talking myself out of sticky situations. I could take you down without incriminating myself. Trust me. I've done it before." Andrew unsheathed his dagger and placed it on the table without letting go of the hilt, "Or I could just follow through with the deal I made with your rogue agent and kill you now. Either way, I get what I want."

Boucher shifted in his chair and adjusted a pin on his uniform.

"What eez zis? Come now. We are business partners, not enemies. You can't overpower me with a little knife like zat. I've 'ad years of combat training. I also 'ave a gun, but I would prefer not to use it."

"Yes, but you are getting so old and slow. Do you really want to risk losing in a fight?" Andrew glanced over to Clara. "Darling. Could you please excuse us for a moment so we can discuss business? I don't want you to get hurt," Andrew said, nodding toward the door.

Without saying a word, Clara slipped out of her chair and crossed behind the men. Before leaving, however, she brushed a seductive hand down Andrew's arm, giving him chills.

At the end of his arm, Clara took hold of the dagger and before Boucher could comprehend what was happening, she moved in place behind him to hold the dagger against his neck. Her other hand located his gun and handed it to Andrew. The General sputtered nonsense.

Wow, my woman is wonderful! Makes it hard to focus. Andrew grinned and pointed the gun at the stunned General.

"She's a sneaky minx, isn't she?" Andrew laughed. "Now, let's make a deal. You hand over the boy, and Nicolas, I will spare your life, expose your rogue agent, and keep your secrets. I am also willing to throw in a few beauties for your trouble. What do you say?"

"It's going to cost you more zan just a few beauties for what you are asking," General Boucher said with a shaking voice.

"I understand. Would you like to negotiate a price? Clara, you may let go of the poor fellow. He won't do anything while I hold the gun."

Clara lowered the dagger and stepped back.

"I can give you Nicolas for a price, but I would lose my position as General if I give you ze Project. Even I 'ave superiors to answer to."

"He's not a project," Clara's shrill voice scolded Boucher.

Appalled, Boucher jumped up and turned to Clara.

"Don't shout at me, filth!" He gathered his saliva and spit in Clara's face.

She flinched as the liquid doused her cheek. Slowly, she wiped it away with the back of her hand.

Enraged, Andrew stood and pointed the gun at Boucher's head. "No one treats my princess that way!" His hand shook, aching to pull the trigger.

"I am a general. I can do as I please!" Boucher retorted, eyeing the weapon.

"Alright, show me what the great General can do!" Andrew puffed himself up to appear larger than he was.

"Andrew, wait. Let's just sit down and talk. We are all adults here," Clara said, returning to her seat, she sat and waited for them to follow her example.

The two proud men didn't move for a moment, measuring each other up.

"Mmm, my beauty is right. Let's discuss this like men, shall we?" Andrew said after a decent pause in the conversation. Sitting, he lowered the gun but kept it aimed in the General's direction.

Boucher followed his lead and sat.

"May I speak?" Clara asked Andrew.

"Of course, love," he responded while keeping Boucher in sight.

"Thank you," Clara said softly. "General Boucher, I respect the difficult position you are in. I understand you have done so much for the country at the E.S.T. You don't want to risk giving up the good you've done by giving Jay back to me."

Boucher drummed impatiently and glared as Clara continued to express herself.

"It's clear that you don't see me as someone who deserves to be heard. You probably don't even see me as human." She held her head high and confident. "But, I'm a mother. Jay's birth mother gave him to me and asked me to protect him. That's what I did and he is remarkable for so many reasons, not just for his special abilities. He's funny. He's sensitive. He's caring. And he needs his mother. He needs me."

"'e was not Dr. McFay's to give away in ze first place. I can't just release a potential weapon into ze 'ands of a civilian," Boucher said in a sharp voice.

"He's gentle and kind!" Clara raised her voice an octave before she brought it back down. "Jay would never use his gifts as a weapon. Please, you must understand the love a mother has for her son."

Andrew stared at Clara as she spoke with such conviction. *I can't believe I finally get to marry this woman.*

Clara's eyes swelled with emotion as she passionately kept her audience captive. "You seem to get along with your mother since you are taking her to get her nails done. She would be devastated if anything happened to you. Right? Would she not do anything to have you back?"

Boucher nodded slowly, following her words.

"I will do anything for Jay. Anything. Please, tell me what you want."

Boucher took a moment to consider. "I do 'ave a good relationship with my mozzer despite 'er being 'eadstrong and loud."

Clara smiled slightly until Boucher held a finger up to stop her hope.

"But, you are not ze mozzer of Project 19932. He eez a glorified computer and I will not risk my position as General to give him away to you, thief."

Clara dropped her gaze to the table and took a few deep breaths to steady her nerves. Andrew put a comforting arm on her shoulder. She tensed but didn't pull away as he spoke.

"Alexandre, to my understanding, one of your agents created another experimental child-computer. He looks very similar to your Project, and he functions the same way even though he needs special medication to stay alive." Andrew leaned back in his chair casually. "What if I were to fund research into fixing the sick boy? Imagine what you could accomplish if we figured out how to turn anyone into a healthy, human-computer hybrid."

"We've been working on zat for years with no success," Boucher said impatiently.

"With extra funding, think of what more you could do," Andrew said, lifting his shoulders in a casual shrug.

"I would need Project 19932 for ze experiments. We 'ave to compare 'im with ozzer 'umans to see 'ow 'e is special."

"What if I just brought him in for set appointments so you can study him, but he would stay with me in between?" Clara asked, "As long as the experiments don't cause damage, I would do that!"

"Huh, zat is an intriguing idea," Boucher admitted, scratching his chin.

"So, I would fund your project, Clara would bring Jay in when you need to do testing, I won't share your secrets with the world, and I would hand over my evidence exposing your rogue agent. How does that sound?" Andrew asked with smug, puckered lips.

Boucher popped his fingers one at a time as he thought. After a loud crack of the final finger, he coughed before speaking.

"Fine. I will give you what you want, but I get my free pick of your girls every six months for ze rest of my life."

"No!" Clara stood abruptly.

"Yes," Andrew contradicted her.

"You can't do that!" Clara turned to Andrew with wide eyes.

"Do you want your son back or what?" Andrew responded hastily.

Boucher's eyes flicked back between the two of them as they argued.

"I can't ruin two lives a year just to get Jay back. Please, there has to be another way!"

"Sit down, Clara," Andrew snarled. "You're embarrassing me."

Clara glared but did as she was told. Andrew clenched his fist.

All this, just for a woman! Good thing she's worth it. Andrew sighed, tired of the negotiations.

"Sorry for losing my temper, love. However, you should understand that *I* would be losing out on business. The number of girls I use will remain the same. I will just be giving them away for free instead of selling them. I'm taking the loss for you," Andrew explained before turning to look at the General. "Now, with that being said, do we have a deal?"

Andrew shifted his eyes upon Clara as they waited for an answer. Her beautiful face was lined with stress as she ground her teeth together and he could feel her knee bouncing under the table.

"Yes, I believe we 'ave a deal," Boucher said at last. "Now, if you will excuse me, I must get going. My mozzer does not like to be kept waiting." He opened his hand and held it out to Andrew. "I will take my gun back now."

Without argument, Andrew placed the weapon in the palm of Boucher's hand.

"I will contact you to solidify plans and send you the evidence against your rogue agent by the end of the day," Andrew said, folding his arms and leaning back, relaxing after a job well done.

Boucher nodded his head in a cocky bow and stood to leave the dining room.

After he was gone, Andrew stood to move behind Clara and began massaging her shoulders.

"We did it, you magnificent creature. We make such a wonderful team," Andrew said before leaning down to kiss the top of her head.

She moved to the side, resisting the affection. He leaned in even closer. "I'm going to keep you," he whispered in her ear.

She shivered under his touch but stayed silent like a good girl.

Oh, Clara. I love you more than you will ever know.

33

Central

After meeting with Jay, Central promised to rescue him and find his adoptive mother. Unfortunately, she could not be found anywhere in the E.S.T. headquarters. Central searched every room by seizing control of the security camera's wireless networks.

Central had access to all the happenings in the building, yet she was nowhere to be found. She was gone, leaving Central with the task of conducting detective work to find out where she went.

Mission One: Locate Jay's adoptive mother.

While reviewing past security footage, Central watched as Jay's mother, known as Enna, was escorted out of the building by an unknown individual. To learn more, it observed the people who had recently been within proximity to her.

Central's focus was directed toward one particular subject who expressed a romantic interest in Enna. If anyone knew where she was, it would be him.

The human subject was held in one of the many medical units not far from Jay's residence. The unit was brimmed with monitoring devices and surveillance equipment, providing Central with a comprehensive view of the unfolding scene.

Besides the main subject, there was another man in the room. He was a large E.S.T. agent whose face contorted back and forth between extreme anger and forced, nonchalant "cool" guy.

Being that he was already in the system, the agent's information was not difficult to find.

Agent Identity: Gerald Drake...
Age: 36...
Ethnicity: African American
Occupation: E.S.T. Agent of 6 years.
Relationship to Jay: Minimal.
Conclusion: Despite a consistent record of unwarranted firearm usage, Drake has been entrusted with the responsibility of protecting Jay by the E.S.T. for financial reasons.
Threat level: Set to moderate.

Satisfied with the current data on Agent Gerald Drake, Central archived the information and redirected its focus onto his subject, who was currently attempting to throw an acrylic chair in the direction of Drake while using quite the adult vocabulary.

However, due to the extensive wounds decorating his body, the chair he threw clattered to the floor without making any contact with Drake.

Utilizing enhanced optical zoom capabilities, the surveillance system focused and captured a high-resolution image of the individual in question.

Subject title: Nicolas Peterson.
Query: Who is 'Nicolas Peterson'?

After a quick scan, Central's search was impeded by an error prompt.

Query failed to yield conclusive results. Insufficient data or mismatched parameters encountered: further analysis and refinement of search criteria required for optimal outcomes.

Luckily, unlike humans, supercomputers don't have the capacity to get irritated over simple detours such as error messages.

Central quickly gathered all the information it could acquire on the subject and integrated it into its vast networks for further analysis and processing. By doing so, it determined that the name 'Nicolas Peterson' had only been activated within the past year, rendering it an incorrect identity, which caused the original error.

Interesting...

The threat level associated with this individual remained undetermined, signaling the need for additional information, mainly because he was acting like a primitive ape trying to escape his cage.

Possible mental case?: LOL

Using the subject's image, Central initiated facial recognition algorithms, comparing the downloaded image of Nicolas Peterson with an extensive database of records.

Flickering images of countless faces appeared on the digital canvas, each swiftly assessed and discarded by the supercomputer's analyses. At the same time, the hospital security feed continued to rotate, capturing the ongoing drama below.

Drake held Nicolas in a tight restraining hold while shouting in his ear, "Hey! You need to...calm...down...NOW!"

Nicolas did not calm down, but he did bite down on Drake's forearm until he drew blood.

Infuriated, Drake chucked Nicolas against the transparent wall with a yowl and pulled out his gun.

Nicolas moaned and sank to the floor.

Drake yelled, "Oh, you are just asking for me to use this. I swear I do not care what my psychiatrist says! I will shoot you."

Nicolas gathered himself off the floor with both arms in the air.

Seeing the surrender, Drake drew in large gulps of air, attempting to pull himself together.

"Okay, I'm good," Drake said, even though it appeared to be taking all of his focus to resist turning into a crazed werewolf. "Let's try this again."

"This is crazy!" Nicolas shouted at Drake. Beads of sweat glistened on his brow and his tense face. "Why am I still here?"

He didn't wait for the agent to respond. He was too frantic. "Listen, you don't understand! My girlfriend is out there with a psychopath and I need to help her. Or…or you need to help her. I don't care who, but she is in trouble. Please, just let me go!"

The girlfriend Nicolas is referring to is likely Jay's mother, Enna. She is in danger. More information needed. Who is this psychopath he mentioned?

Drake picked up the acrylic chair from the ground, set it upright, and slid it over to Nicolas. "We have evidence showing that you were involved with the murder of Oliver Romano," Drake said, his biceps rippled as he clenched his fists.

Clearly exhausted, Nicolas took the seat while Drake remained standing.

Queue: Search name 'Oliver Romano'

Central took note of the new names detected as Drake continued interrogating Nicolas Peterson.

"I heard that you killed him because he had a thing for your woman. Is that really why ya did it?" Drake prodded, trying to be casual. "Hey, I get it. I would be pretty bummed, too, if someone was after my girl…well if I had a girl, that would be nice… Anyway, I don't blame ya. I'd be mad, too."

"What, no. Come on! I am being set up by Andrew Dengaila. Andrew! Dengaila! Did you even look into him? This is insane!" Nicolas said, grabbing a fist of his hair. "I have to get out of here."

He stood and started pacing around the edges of the glass room as though looking for an exit. He looked directly into one of the security cameras and yelled, "Let me out of here!"

Queue: Search name 'Andrew Dengaila'
Suspect one: Threat level set to high.

"There is no escaping this." Drake continued speaking. "We have notified the police. You're gettin' transferred to their facility within the hour. Ya know we have plenty of evidence against ya, so just make it easier on yourself and talk to me. Was she really worth killing over?"

There was a break in the conversation while Drake waited for Nicolas to admit to the crime. After realizing that Nicolas had no interest in making it easy, Drake snapped his fingers as though understanding suddenly hit. "It was her legs, wasn't it?"

"What?" Nicolas was lost, having no idea where Drake was going with this line of questioning.

"Dang, some women, um hmm, yum. We just can't resist those legs. Yeah, I get it, man. I mean, I wouldn't kill over nice legs personally, but I can see how weaker, less secure, less… attractive men like you might feel the need to take out the competition?"

Beep:
Facial recognition Complete for 'Nicolas Peterson'
Nicolas Peterson identified: 'William Lund.'
Age: 28

Place of birth: Springfield, Missouri

Occupation: Private Investigator. Specializes in locating missing individuals. Exceptional reputation, devoid of any documented instances of violence or malicious intent.

Misdemeanor on record: Theft of street sign at age 18.

Findings: Jay's high level of trust in the subject indicates friendship. Threat level set to low.

William Lund A.K.A. Nicolas Peterson: Ally

Just as Central was about to search his archived queries, audio came through Drake's handheld transceiver.

"Agent Drake, the General has issued an order to release Mr. Peterson. He has been cleared of any wrongdoings."

Drake's eye ticked as he stammered, "But, he...Sir. I haven't gotten to the real interrogation yet. Come on! He was about to crack wide open, like an Easter egg. Five...five or eight more minutes at the most and..."

"Agent Drake, you have your orders. Release him." The device clicked off, leaving Drake with a dumbfounded expression.

Nicolas stood frozen for the first time since the interrogation began. Disbelief draped all over his face.

"What just happened?" he asked the security camera as though he knew Central was listening in.

Drake shrugged his bulky shoulders, his mouth hanging slightly ajar. He walked over to the wall like a grumpy gorilla and touched the authentication panel. A green light outlined his hand, and the glass wall slid open.

Before Nicolas could leave, a familiar female rushed into the room. Central recognized her as Enna, Jay's protector and mother.

Mission One: Completed.

Mission two: Rescue Jay and Enna. More information needed to create a successful escape.

"Nick!" Enna squealed as she wrapped her arms around him with all her might. Her face buried securely into his neck.

Despite his painful wounds, Nicolas clung to her and kissed her ear. "You're okay! I can't believe you're here! How did you get away from Andrew?" Nicolas could hardly get words out. "Did he hurt you?"

"She didn't *get* away from me. I'm just doing her a favor." The security camera swiveled to yet another subject entering the room. Central was already digging into his database to gain new information while Nicolas launched himself to rage attack the new subject.

Identity: Andrew Dengaila

Age: 43

Occupation: Winery business.

Place of birth: Napa Valley, California

Orphaned at age 12. Parents murdered in their sleep. Assailant never caught.

Findings: No criminal charges, high status. Nicolas claims Dengaila is dangerous.

Threat level: Set to high. Must keep a lens on him.

"Nick, wait," Enna called out as Nicolas threw a punch into Andrew's jaw.

Andrew stumbled but recovered quickly. Clenching his fist, he prepared a retaliating blow.

"Andrew, don't you dare hurt him!" Enna shouted with authority while putting herself in between the two men.

"Oh come now, Clara, you're no fun," Andrew glared at Nicolas while roughly shoving her out of the way.

"You stay away from her!" Nicolas readied himself for a fight.

This time, Drake stepped in with his weapon in hand again. "That's enough, gentlemen."

Both Nicolas and Andrew sneered, but they took a step back.

Central was about to search for more information on Andrew, but it was interrupted by a message from Jay.

01001000 01100101 01101100 01110000 00100000 01101101 01100101

Help me!

34

Hostage

Swiftly, Central redirected its attention to the security feed in Jay's room. Agent Quinn clutched Jay's hair in a tight grip, a gun pressed menacingly against the boy's shoulder.

Not this guy again.

Central's protective instincts sent an artificial feeling of irritation through its processing unit.

Immediate escape plan necessary to safeguard Jay.

Strategy One: Take control of Quinn's cellular device and manipulate its functionality to deliver a much-deserved electric shock. Yes?

...Wait...No...

Central noted that the presence of Quinn's gun served as a significant barrier to the plan.

Dilemma: It is possible the electric shock could cause Quinn to fire accidentally...

...No, Jay's life can not be risked.

Central noted that another agent, identified as the high-ranking Sean Wilgens, stood approximately seven feet away from Quinn and Jay. In addition, a small gaggle of backup agents assembled outside Jay's room, slowly advancing toward Quinn.

Even though they were brandishing their weapons, Central had minimal trust in their primitive abilities to diffuse the situation.

Regrettably, I too, am stuck with limited functions considering I am technically an inanimate object.

Central searched its database for safer means of protecting the boy while Quinn shouted. "Back up! I will shoot him!" He had a disgusting display of spit flying out of his mouth.

Another small boy, Mike, emerged cautiously, peeking out from behind Quinn.

What did I miss?

To gain a complete understanding of the problem at hand, Central rapidly initiated a rewinding of the security feed.

The recovered footage revealed Quinn injecting the child, Mike, with a dose of the experimental serum that was necessary for the boy's survival. The time was 8:44 AM and little Jay was still asleep in his bed.

"Hey, sorry I have to do this, Mike. I know it hurts. It will be over soon," Quinn whispered as the serum made its way into the boy's bloodstream.

Mike shook but didn't cry out. He was growing braver.

Quinn finished what he was doing, put a gentle hand on Mike's head, and sighed. "You'll be alright. You're tough."

As he stood up to leave, Wilgens stormed through the door with a grave expression plastered to his face.

"Agent Eric Quinn, by order of General Boucher, your position at the E.S.T. has been terminated. You are under arrest for conspiracy and attempted murder." Wilgens began reading Quinn his rights, but Quinn's profanities largely overpowered Wilgens' words.

"No! I just *cannot* catch a *break*! Come on! This is obviously a setup," Quinn shouted as Wilgens approached him cautiously.

"Wait! I can prove that Andrew Dengaila is the one responsible for all of this. I have footage of him killing a man in cold blood. Give me a chance to prove it!"

As Quinn shouted, Jay stirred and snorted in his sleep.

Wilgens shook his head dismissively. "That's not the first time we've heard the name Dengaila today. Unfortunately for you, according to the general, Andrew Dengaila has an alibi. They have been working together to identify the rogue agents plaguing our department, such as yourself."

"I swear, Wilgens. You know me. This is a mistake." Quinn's face looked like it was about to explode.

"Listen, I'm not your judge. If you play your cards right, you may get your day in court, but we have orders for your arrest."

Quinn pulled out his gun and aimed it at Wilgens, who instantly brought his handheld transceiver to his mouth and spoke, "I need backup in lab T5, now."

"You know I'll never get a fair trial. That's not how things are done here."

Quinn's wide gaze darted swiftly from Wilgens to the exit, where a few agents were already gathering. He shifted his attention to Mike, who remained expressionless as he sat in bed.

"Mike, get behind me. Come on." Quinn's jaw clenched, determination shining through despite his hopeless situation. Mike sat, frozen in place. "Now, kid. Move!"

"Come on, Quinn. What is your plan here? Look around. If you shoot me, then my men will take you out in less than a second," Wilgens gestured to the other agents.

Mike slipped out of bed and hid behind Quinn's back.

Note: There is a slight curvature on Quinn's lip, meaning he is either happy, unafraid, or he does have a plan of his own.

Quinn slowly rotated around the room, his back hunched like a cat, ready to pounce. The two men continued pointing their weapons at each other until Quinn halted next to Jay's bed.

"Here's my plan." Before Wilgens could react, Quinn snatched Jay out of bed by one arm and aimed the gun at his head.

"Ahhh! Ouch. Stop it!" Jay squirmed, disoriented by the way he was ripped out of sleep.

Stupid plan, Quinn. Stupid plan.

If Central had eyes, they would be rolling in their sockets. Alas, it didn't have body parts like Jay, so its displeasure couldn't be displayed physically.

How irritating!

"You're hurting me. Leave me alone! Mommy, help!" Jay yelled, punching and kicking Quinn anywhere he could reach.

"Stop! Shut up, kid! I'm so done dealing with you! I spent way too many hours searching and searching for you." Quinn shook Jay furiously. "I finally found you and THIS is my reward. So, here's what's going to happen. You are going to help me escape, and if you don't, I'll blow a hole in you! Got it?"

Jay responded by clamping his teeth down hard on Quinn's thumb.

"Ah! Stupid kid!" Quinn yelled and readjusted his hold on Jay by grabbing his hair.

My resources tell me that Jay is not the stupid one in this situation.

"Help me!" Jay screamed. His eyes rolled to the back of his head and his message was sent and then, of course, received by Central.

01001000 01100101 01101100 01110000 00100000 01101101 01100101

***

Updated with the entire situation, Central navigated through possible solutions to incapacitate Quinn, who was still using Jay as a human shield.

Mission: Safeguard Jay.

Strategy two: Initiate emergency lockdown of all electronic doors to prevent Quinn from escaping with Jay.

Dilemma: Quinn's unstable mental state may cause him to retaliate by shooting everyone in proximity to his weapon.

Discard Strategy.

Strategy three: Access the building's power supply to create temporary darkness and disarray, aiding Jay's escape.

Dilemma: Risk too high with the number of weapons involved.

Accidental shooting may occur.

Discard strategy.

The urgency of the matter continued to escalate as Quinn ordered Wilgens to lower his weapon, but his demands were met with taunts, diminishing what little patience Quinn had left.

Really now? I am an advanced supercomputer with the entire world of electronics on my side. Why can't I solve this?

The temperature of Central's processing unit rose with each unresolved second.

Dr. McFay's programming must have included fear of some sort. I did not know that was possible.

"Central," Jay sent another message. "It hurts! What should I do? Help me."

Yes. I see you. I am devising a plan. Do as he says. Do not struggle.

Desperate, Central searched for out-of-the-box solutions.

Strategy four: Override intercoms and broadcast the song "Be a Buddy, Not a Bully" to educate Quinn about kindness.

Dilemma: Music is more likely to irritate an irrational mind rather than humble it.

Discard strategy.

As the hostage situation continued, Quinn's eyes grew wild and dangerous. "I hate this stupid Project. I hate... I hate... I hate him!" His hands shook. "I know how much he is worth and I don't even care because of how much I hate him! Do you really think I won't shoot? Come on! I'm dying to shoot!"

Strategy five: Hack into the hospital's elevator controls and send Jay to a safe floor away from danger.

Dilemma: If Quinn cannot escape, he may retaliate.

Expand Strategy: Allow Quinn to escape with Jay and locate him when things deescalate.

Dilemma: Quinn may dispose of Jay after he is done using him.

Dilemma: Quinn may sell Jay to the highest bidder.

Dilemma: What if Jay cannot be found?

Dilemma:
Dilemma:
Dilemma:

As Central ran solutions, Wilgens placed his gun on the floor, unwilling to risk the Project.

Quinn backed out of the room, yelling at the other agents, "Get out of my way!" Briefly glancing behind him, Quinn's voice dropped into a caring tone. "Stay by me, Mike. We are leaving."

Note: Quinn shows signs of compassion. Perhaps he is bluffing and will not harm Jay.

Expand Strategy: Control how Quinn escapes.

...Yes. Continue.

Step one: Lead Quinn to the escape helicopter on the roof.

Step two: Hijack the autopilot's G.P.S. to send Jay to a safe location.

Step three: Give Jay the only password to open the helicopter doors. If anything happens to Jay, Quinn remains trapped.

Central's security cameras remained fixated on Jay as Quinn dragged him down the hall.
Instantaneously, Central contacted Jay to reveal the plan.

Jay, go with Quinn. I will lead both of you to the escape helicopter.

"But..."

No time to argue. Be complacent. When you enter the helicopter, I will seal the doors shut and prepare a lovely message for Quinn. He will be informed that the doors will remain locked until you say a password I will reveal only to you. Are you following?

"Yes," Jay responded as Quinn dragged him down the hall toward the exit.

**Good. I will send you somewhere safe. This part is essential. Once you land, do not say the password until Quinn gives you

his weapon, no matter what threats he makes. When the doors open, run, run until you are inside, safe. Do you understand?"

Instead of responding through code, Jay just nodded frantically. He had a face of fear but bravely allowed Quinn to guide him backward down the hall, still being used as a human shield.

Remember, it is my job to protect you. I will not leave you alone, my little Jay.

35

Escape

Anticipation fluttered in Enna's gut as Agent Drake led the way to where Jay waited to be released. She could already picture his goofy grin and giddy bounce in his step. She wished the agent would walk faster. He seemed to be moving in slow motion compared to her excitement.

Despite Andrew following close behind, Enna chose to weave her fingers into Nick's comforting grasp.

If I have to go home with Andrew after this, I'm going to cherish every last second with Nick.

He beamed at her with his familiar sparkling eyes, the ones she fell in love with. His old, bloody clothes had been replaced with pristine, white scrubs that made him look like he was glowing.

How am I ever going to let him go? The thought left an ache in her chest that battled her excitement and love. *Jay and Nick will be safe. That's the only thing that matters now.* Her eyes watered slightly, but she smiled back at Nick.

"You're so beautiful," he whispered to her.

"Yes, she is, isn't she?" Andrew hissed behind them.

Enna shook off the disgusting comment and squeezed Nick's hand. He returned the gesture before bringing her hand up to kiss her knuckles.

Andrew cleared his throat, but before he could say anything, Agent Drake's handheld radio came to life. "All Agents, report to the biotech unit immediately."

Agent Drake halted and turned to Enna. A scowl smooshed onto his face, and his eyes told a story Enna didn't want to hear.

Something's wrong with Jay!

"There seems to be a situation. Wait here while I check things out." Agent Drake scarcely finished speaking before pivoting on his heel to rush down the hallway. Enna abandoned Nick's hand and chased after the agent.

"Wait, what's going on? Where is my son? Is Jay alright? Why can't I go to him?" The words erupted from her mouth with urgency and authority.

"Ma'am, I have to ask you to stay back. This is official business, and you are a civilian." Agent Drake raised an arm to block her way. Enna immediately swatted it away.

"Excuse me? Don't call me ma'am! I am going to see Jay whether you like it or not!"

Drake grabbed her arm, but she effortlessly twisted out of his grasp and smashed her heel into his foot. He yelped as she took off down the wide hallway in a mad dash.

"Enna! Wait..." Nick ran after her, but she was already halfway down the hall.

Unknown voices shouted echoing commands as she neared a corner up ahead.

Her footsteps pounded like a drumbeat against the hard tile floor, and beams of bright, motion-sensored LED lights snapped on one by one as she approached the commotion.

At the end of the hall, she stepped into a wide corridor entirely lined with glass walls that stretched out in both directions like an open road. Standing at a three-way intersection, Enna stumbled to a stop.

To her left, she found herself face-to-face with a tense standoff. A group of agents stood in a semi-circle, their weapons trained on a lone figure backing toward her. Though she could only see the back of the man's head, Enna was sure it was Agent Eric Quinn by the way he shouted orders in his pompous voice.

Enna fought to catch her breath. Despite the apparent danger, she remained frozen in place, unable to tear her gaze away from the scene unfolding around her.

The air crackled with tension as the agents held their positions, their fingers hovering over the triggers of their weapons while Eric inched his way back, closer to Enna, with each cautious step.

That's when Enna noticed a small boy with curly brown hair and dark skin hunched near Eric's legs, trying to hide from the guns.

"Jay!" Her heart leaped at the sight of him. However, an unease washed over her when the boy turned and met her gaze.

That's not my son. Her head spun, not understanding who this strange doppelganger child was.

"Mommy!" A young voice bounced around the corridor.

That's Jay! Enna's eyes flashed around, frantically searching for her child's face.

"Help me!" Jay called out again. Enna took a few hurried steps toward the agents, aching to see Jay's face in the crowd.

Out of the corner of her eye, Enna caught a glimpse of Eric's reflection in the glass wall and her stomach leaped.

Staring at the reflection, Enna spotted Jay tripping along as Eric pulled him backward. Eric shouted a stream of graphic threats while pressing a gun firmly against Jay's head.

He's using Jay as a human shield?! Enna clenched her teeth and squeezed her fingers into tight fists. She took several large steps toward Eric's back, ready to pounce.

However, before she reached her target, Agent Drake came from behind her and pinched her uninjured arm in a tight grip. He ripped her backward to stop her attack.

Agent Drake roughly spun her around and yelled in her face, "Do you want to get him killed? Get behind me!" He shoved her behind his back and drew his weapon. Enna stumbled into the waiting arms of Andrew.

"Let go of me!" Enna screamed, pushing away from him. Andrew restrained her from diving back into the conflict.

"Listen," he hissed at her. "You are just going to make things worse. Calm down."

"Let me go. I don't want you to touch me! Let me go! I need to help Jay!" Enna pounded her fists into Andrew's arms hysterically before she remembered to drop low and spin out of his grasp. She was about to fling herself back in front of Agent Drake when Nick caught her arm.

"Wait, ahh!" Nick grunted as Enna pulled against him. "Enna, stop. That hurts." Reluctantly, Enna stopped fighting and stared at him with quivering lips.

"Nick, he has Jay. This can't be happening again! I have to save him," Enna said, turning around to see Jay. Nick wrapped an arm around her stomach, preventing her from darting into the line of fire.

Sandwiched between Drake and the other agents, Eric was forced to shift his position until his back pressed securely against one of the many glass laboratory walls that lined the hall.

The small doppelganger child crouched next to Eric with a stunned expression as he stared at the gun being pressed to Jay's head.

"Ow! Let go of me!" Jay cried.

"I'm right here, Baby. It'll be okay," Enna said as her eyes connected with Jay's gaze for the first time. He shook and squirmed about. Agent Drake aimed his gun straight at Eric's head.

"Let the project go," Agent Drake ordered.

Eric's wild eyes bugged out in rage. His hair stood at odd angles, making him appear strange and deranged.

"No! Drop your weapons, all of you. I won't ask again. I know the General would hate to lose his precious project permanently!" Eric's voice squeaked from how much stress he put into each word.

"That's just not gonna happen," Drake responded, stepping closer to Eric and Jay with no caution whatsoever.

Enna remembered the first time she ever met Drake. He had waved his gun around like a madman. *He's the one who killed Jay's mom! He's going to get Jay killed, too!*

Without thinking, Enna tore away from Nick.

"Ahh," Nick groaned as the movement jostled his wounds.

Enna darted in front of Agent Drake, putting herself in the line of fire, and shouted, "Drop the gun! Do what he says." Enna turned to the other agents. "What are you all doing? Listen, Jay is not some mindless school project. He is a living, breathing human child! Put the guns down!"

"Enna!" Andrew snapped. "Don't be an idiot. You're going to get yourself killed. Get over here!"

Enna ignored him and held her place directly in front of Drake's gun. Eric slowly began scooting down the hallway toward a neon green exit sign, not allowing his back to be exposed to any of the armed agents.

"Mommy!" Jay's terrified voice called out as soon as he was dragged past her.

Nick made his way over to Enna with his hands up in peace. He tried to lead her out of danger by putting an arm around her shoulder.

"Nick, I have to help him. Please. I can't watch him die," Enna cried.

"Hey, we are all going to get through this alive," Nick whispered. "Listen, Eric won't shoot him. He's too afraid to die and Jay is his only key out of here." Nick held Enna firmly.

"This is ridiculous," Andrew said. Sliding a hand through his sleek hair to make sure it was in place, he strode toward Eric, disregarding all threats.

"Having a bad day, are we?" Andrew mocked cruelly. Eric's teeth chattered with adrenaline.

"Andrew, I will kill you for this! You set me up," Eric roared and briefly moved the gun away from Jay's head to point it at the approaching Andrew.

The agents who had been patiently waiting for an opportunity to strike began to move in. Eric quickly put the gun back against Jay's head, making everyone but Andrew halt.

"Yes, I'm quite sorry about that. I'm not usually one for breaking deals, but a better offer came along," he glanced back at Enna briefly before speaking again. "Give me the boy and maybe I'll find a way to get you out of this mess."

"Why would I ever trust you again? Get away from me!" Eric shifted his attention to the gaggle of agents waiting to strike. "All of you! I am going to start shooting in ten seconds. Now move! Get into that room. Go!" He nodded to the nearest vacant laboratory with his head. The agents hesitated. "Don't make me count," Eric snarled.

A few of the agents moved toward the room, but most stood uncomfortably, not quite knowing what to do. Enna covered her mouth, and moisture pooled in her eyes.

No one spoke for several seconds, everyone waiting for others to act first.

"Do as 'e says." Everyone turned to see General Boucher striding down the hall from the elevator near the exit sign. "Lower your weapons," the General ordered as he strutted toward the commotion.

The agents obeyed quickly, filing into the small, glass room.

"You too, Drake. We don't need anyone to get 'urt," he said to the large agent whose finger twitched on the trigger of his weapon.

"Drop ze gun," the General said, pointing dramatically to the floor as though Drake couldn't understand English. The bulky agent scowled but placed the gun on the ground.

"Now, go." the General pointed to the other agents. Drake grunted and marched off to comply. As soon as he entered the room, the door slid shut and the glass walls tinted automatically.

"Now, Eric. Let's talk, shall we?" the General turned to Eric. "Andrew tells me zat you intended to 'ave me killed. Is zat right?" He placed a hand on Andrew's shoulder, stopping him from moving closer to Eric.

"I've been so loyal to you!" Eric yelled pathetically.

"Yes, I can see zat-"

"No, you don't! I'm the only one who's tried to get your precious Project back! I've even tried to make a new Project for you!" Eric flinched his head at Mike. "What do you care? You don't. You don't care about anything but money!"

"Now 'old on a moment. If you would 'and over ze boy, we can discuss your retirement like adults."

Eric sweated profusely and his chin quivered. "No! If you come any closer, I will shoot your multi-million dollar project," he shouted.

Suddenly, a quiet voice wandered into the air. "You kill him for reals?"

The small boy at Eric's feet looked up with a deep frown forming on his lips. "Jay is been nice to me. He's my friend."

"Sorry, Mike. Close your eyes. I don't want you to see this." Eric tried to move Mike away with his foot.

"Eric, Please," Enna said, using a soft, motherly tone. "That's my son. I love him. You…you created something wonderful. Look at him. He's a miracle." Enna held a cautious hand out toward Jay. "Listen to Mike. Jay is his friend. Don't hurt his friend. You know it's wrong."

Enna approached Eric slowly. She could tell that her tears were ready to drop, and, this time, she didn't even try to hold them back as she pled for Jay's life.

"Please, please, Eric. I know there is good in you. I see you. You are very passionate and have given everything to this job."

Eric's eyes softened and a hint of compassion flashed over his face. However, just as fast as it appeared, the look disappeared and was replaced with desperation.

"No. I have to do this. I have no choice!" He pressed the gun harder against Jay's head.

"Mommy," Jay's voice was a simple whisper. "It's okay to let me go. I'll be fine. Really. He won't hurt me."

"You hear that? Your boy knows I have no intention of hurting him…unless I have to." Eric shuffled a few more feet toward the exit. The General, Andrew, Enna, and Nick, closed in around him, cutting off his escape.

Enna's heart beat wildly out of control as she watched Eric's hands tremble in torment. Anything could set him off at this point and she would lose Jay forever. She didn't know if she could trust the General or Andrew not to do anything stupid that would get Jay killed.

"Mommy, You gots to trust me. 'Kay. I am very smart and I have made a foolproof plan." Jay's brows pinched together but his lip raised into a knowing smile.

If I don't let Eric take him, Jay could die. I have to do what he says. I have to protect Jay. It took all Enna's power to hold herself upright as grief took over, but she knew what she had to do.

"We have to let them go," she told the General and Andrew. "We can find them later."

Enna looked to Nick for support.

"Are you sure?" Nick asked.

She closed her eyes and nodded.

"Okay," he whispered. Taking Enna's hand, they both stepped away from Eric hesitantly. Andrew followed their lead and backed over to Enna.

The General weighed his options before taking a small step back, allowing Eric to move closer to the exit.

The General's eyes narrowed as he watched Eric's escape.

"I wanted to be good enough for you, General," Eric said as he passed by. "I'll keep the project safe."

Relief made its way onto Eric's face and he quickened his pace.

The further Eric got, the darker General's eyes got. He looked over to Enna and shook his head.

"I can't," he said suddenly. Drawing his firearm, he directed it at Eric's head, displaying no concern for Jay's well-being. "I'd rather lose ze Project zan 'ave a traitor escape. Now I-"

Andrew coughed to interrupt him. "Remember, our deal doesn't work without the boy."

"Well, what do you want me to do? I run a large operation 'ere and if our secrets get out, I could lose everyzing. Quinn can't leave 'ere alive," the General spat with explosive diction that made his French accent pop.

Eric didn't move as the General glared with deep, angry eyes.

"Oh, sad day. I so loved doing business with you, Alexandre." Andrew slid his dagger out of its sheath.

"General, please, we can catch him later," Enna said. "You know, I'll do anything, and I mean anything, just, don't let him hurt Jay. Let them go." She attempted to make her voice sound sweet and seductive, but the tremor in her vocal cords gave her desperation away.

"Don't worry, lovely. I'm pretty sure I can pull a trigger much faster zan 'e can," he bragged, preparing to fire. Eric crouched down to hide his face behind Jay.

"Stop!" Enna shouted, staring into Jay's frightened eyes. She pushed past Andrew, bringing a powerful hammer strike between the General's neck and shoulders. He roared and turned the gun directly between her eyes.

Without hesitation, she sidestepped and grabbed his weapon hand just as a shot went off. The bullet hit the floor near Jay, shattering the tile. Bringing an elbow strike down on the General's arm, Enna heard his bones crackle as his gun fell to the floor.

Enna bent down to grab it, but before she could take hold, the General thrust his knee into her bent torso. She staggered, trying to maintain her stance.

"Enna!" Nick yelled, rushing toward the gun Agent Drake had left on the ground. At the same time, the General slipped a toe under his own gun, popped it into the air, and caught it with his left hand.

He aimed the gun at Nick and fired. Enna shrieked as the bullet flew past Nick and lodged itself into the thick glass wall behind him, causing a web of cracks to stretch out on the surface.

Nick dropped low to the ground as the General prepared to shoot again. Before he could get another shot off, Enna jumped onto the General's back, slid an arm around his neck, and held him in a tight choke hold.

"Eric, go. Get Jay out of here," she demanded.

Following her instructions, Eric quickly broke away from the group and carried Jay down the hallway to the exit, followed close behind by Mike.

The General raised his gun and used it as a club to smash Enna's head in.

Though he couldn't get much momentum from his position, the gun landed on Enna's previous head wound, making her scream. She fell to the floor with her hands pressing against her throbbing head. A sharp ringing resonated between her ears.

"Hey!" Nick took a few steps forward, holding Agent Drake's gun in a tight grip. However, before he could get a clear shot, Andrew stepped forward and sunk his blade deep into the General's abdomen.

A howl of agony echoed throughout the hall as the General teetered and stumbled backward to where Eric had just been standing. He pressed up against the glass wall to stabilize himself.

With her head still spinning, Enna scooted away from the General, trying to create distance. However, before she could make a full retreat, he pointed his gun at her.

"Zat's enough. Drop your weapons, or I'll kill 'er now!" His eyes were bloodshot and full of rage.

Nick slowly lowered his gun to the floor. Andrew didn't move.

"You too, Dengaila, drop zee knife! I know you care for 'er."

Before Andrew could lower his dagger, Enna thrust a foot up and kicked the General in his stab wound.

Screaming, he hunched over and dropped to the floor. Enna stood and began to run for cover, half blind from the pain radiating in her head.

Before she knew what hit her, a force knocked into her shoulder, pushing her to the ground just as another shot rang out.

36

Defeated

Nick's eyes widened in shock as blood pooled onto his white shirt. Gasping, he swayed and clutched his chest, trying to hold the blood inside.

Enna sat immobilized on the ground, stunned. The General aimed his gun at her again, but before he could pull the trigger, Andrew sunk his dagger deep into his neck. The General grabbed the handle and gargled until he collapsed completely onto the floor.

Nick clung to his heaving chest, blood melting out between his fingers. Turning white, his knees gave out.

"Nick!" Enna cried, rushing to his side.

"No, please! Please, God! Please don't let him die!" Enna prayed.

She placed both her hands on his chest where blood oozed out of the bullet hole. His body shook as he gasped for air.

"Get a doctor, now!" she shouted at Andrew.

He stood unmoving with a sadistic gleam in his eye, contemplating whether he should let him die or not.

"Andrew, please! Our deal only holds if he survives. Please."

Giving Enna a sarcastic grin, he made his way over to the General to retrieve his dagger. After wiping the blood off on the dead man's pant leg, he sheathed it and took hold of the General's radio. As he called for help, Enna hunched over Nick.

"It's okay, take deep breaths. We're going to get you help." Tears streamed down her cheeks and fell onto his white scrubs.

"No. Wait!" Jay called from down the hall. I can save him! I know how to save him! Let me go, and I will save him!" Jay yelled as Eric cursed at the escape door, which refused to open when he put his hand on the authentication panel.

"We don't have time for that. Stop fighting me," Eric said, shifting Jay around in his arms. He tried the authentication panel again with his left hand, but the escape door remained locked.

"Eric, please! Just let Jay go. No one will follow you. Let him help," Enna pled.

Eric turned to face Enna and gave her a sympathetic glance of human emotion before his eyes hardened.

"Sorry, I have to go," Eric said and retraced his steps until he came to an elevator.

Enna watched helplessly, knowing that if she took the pressure off of Nick's chest, he could bleed out in minutes.

"Go...after...him..." Nick labored through each word.

"No, I can't leave you here like this," she said. "Jay will be fine. I don't think Eric wants to hurt him."

She watched as Eric put his hand on the elevator's authentication panel. This time, a green light outlined his hand and the elevator door slid open.

"Mommy!" Jay yelled with a voice that pierced Enna's heart. He was scared but still so brave. As he disappeared into the elevator, his voice made its way over to her just before the door slid closed. "Stinky Breath. Stinky Breath!"

What? Enna's mind was so twisted and confused. Nothing made any sense. Her arms began to tremble as she realized she was losing the battle with the blood seeping from Nick's wound.

"Nick, I don't know what to do. You have to stay with me. Please," Enna sobbed, resting her head on his forehead for a moment. "Why did you have to push me out of the way? I don't want to lose you. I can't. I just, can't."

His skin was cold but clammy. He did not have much time. She kissed his cheek and watched as his eyes fluttered slightly before closing. "Nick, look at me. Stay with me!" Enna begged.

She felt a hand on her shoulder and jumped. Turning her tear-streaked face, she found herself staring into the kind eyes of the doctor who had helped her recover. Four other medical personnel stood close by with a stretcher.

"Save him," Enna said softly. "Please. Can you save him?"

"I'll see what we can do, but he's lost a lot of blood. We'll need to operate right away. Keep putting pressure on the wound while we transport him to the medical lab."

She nodded understanding. The doctors slightly lifted Nick and slid the stretcher underneath him.

Enna walked with them down the hall, around the corner, and into a room with tinted glass walls. More doctors stood at the ready.

They have to save him. It's not too late! He can't die. He can't die. Please don't...don't be too late. She kept begging as they lifted him onto an operating table where equipment rose from the floor.

"We will take it from here. You did well. You can let go now," one of the doctors said, but Enna's mind throbbed and her vision tilted.

Let go now? That sounds like a goodbye. No! She couldn't force her body to move. Someone had pushed her aside, yet she stood in shock, unable to look away.

Watching the doctors work on Nick, her eyes glazed over and all thoughts were put on hold as the world continued around her.

Her mind was numb. Her body was numb. Even her tears seemed to be numb as they stopped streaming.

Vaguely aware of two hands on her shoulders, she let them guide her away, out the glass doors.

"Clara, let's go," a soft voice said.

Arms wrapped around her stomach from the back. Enna knew it was Andrew but she was too drained to feel repulsed. She scrunched her hands up into fists and felt Nick's blood squish between her fingers. The thought made her mouth fill up with liquid. She turned her head and vomited on the floor.

"Oh, hey. Come, let's get you cleaned up," Andrew said, leading her away from Nick.

She wanted to stay with him, but she had no power to refuse Andrew's pull on her.

He led her to a restroom where he gently helped her wash her hands and clean the tips of her hair that had gotten vomit on them. She had lost everyone. Everyone except for Andrew. He would always be there, helping her, controlling her, watching her.

"No, no, no, this isn't real," Enna said, shaking as feeling came back to her thoughts. Her legs grew weak and they quaked dangerously beneath her. She held onto the sink for support, but her arms could not hold her body up.

"Whoa, whoa, whoa, hey," Andrew said as Enna began to drop to the floor with a melting sob.

Andrew slowed her fall and sat down with her. His arms wrapped around her, cradling her as she cried.

Nick's going to die and Jay is missing! How could I let this happen?

Gravity pulled at Enna's head, forcing it down until it rested on Andrew's lap. She let him gently stroke her hair as her thoughts floated to a distant memory of the first time Andrew ever showed affection for her. It was sweet, safe, and warm. But that was before he turned into a monster.

Am I giving up? Is this my way of dealing with loss? Just going back to my abuser as though I have a leash around my neck? Oh, who cares? I have nothing to live for. I'm stuck with Andrew whether I like it or not. He will always have control over me. Enna closed her eyes and let her sobs calm down to a quiet stream on her face.

"Clara, my deal isn't over. I will still help you find your boy," Andrew said quietly.

"Where do I even look for him? I'll never see him again," Enna said, defeated.

I'll never see his smile. I'll never hear his sweet voice. The last words I will remember him saying are...wait.

"Stinky breath," Enna said out loud.

"Excuse me?" Andrew said with an offended undertone.

"No, not you. Jay, he said, 'stinky breath.'" Enna lifted her head. "It's our code in case something goes wrong. I know where he is going. I'll need to borrow your helicopter."

37

______

Return

The flight to Betty's seemed like an excruciating nightmare that Enna couldn't wake up from. She wished she could stand up and pace as her mind burned with the worst-case scenarios.

What if Jay doesn't find a way to Betty's house? What if Eric hurt him? How will I go on if Nick dies? If he lives, the E.S.T. could keep him captive. I'll have to find a way to save him. How will I handle being stuck with Andrew again?

Andrew gently touched her leg, causing her insides to feel slimy.

"I don't want to be touched right now." She wanted to slide away from him, but the helicopter straps held her in place. Claustrophobia squeezed in around her, rubbing in the fact that she was trapped.

Andrew left his hand where it was as though Enna hadn't spoken. "You know, if Jay is anything like you, he is going to be just fine," Andrew's voice came through the aviation headset. "Speaking of which, I will need Jay's help with something." Andrew showed a little smirk.

Enna straightened up and questioned Andrew with her eyes.

"When I made the deal with Eric, he told me what Jay is capable of. I'll need him to destroy the security footage of me killing General Boucher and, if he can, the footage of what happened at Oliver's store."

"Are you serious? After everything you have done to me? After what happened to Nick? You think Jay will help you?" Enna was baffled. "Why would we help you? If you were in prison, I could finally be free of you!"

"Do you really think you will ever be free of me? Honestly?" He shot her a skeptical look. "My company doesn't end with me. I know you may not believe it, but I have people on my side. I have clients who are loyal to me. Imagine what they would lose without me. They would not be happy about it."

The air thickened around her as Andrew continued trapping her with his words. "I am a leader, Clara. Even if I am in prison, I will still be able to destroy everyone you love. And now, you are bringing me right to your closest friend's house. The only way to truly protect them is by doing exactly as I say."

Enna turned her face away to look out the window. She wanted to cry again, but she was done giving Andrew that satisfaction. He had been playing with her. She was never in control. He was only helping her find Jay so he could use him.

"Also," Andrew continued, "If he doesn't destroy the evidence completely, I want you to know that I will find out."

"Oh really? How would you figure it out?" Enna called him out on his bluff.

"Well, if you try to use it against me, I have a network of people ready to disprove the validity of the evidence. They are very good at what they do and they are quite powerful. They have a way of making evidence disappear," Andrew said with a sickening chuckle.

"I don't believe you," Enna said, though in reality, the words terrified her.

"That's fine. You don't have to believe me. Just know it would be a big gamble going against me—a gamble you don't want to lose. If you have Jay look into me, I'll bet he would find that I've been arrested several times, but no charges have ever stuck. I wonder why that is?"

Enna closed her eyes and scolded herself for letting him inside her head. *He's lying. I have evidence that would get him locked up forever. I can't have Jay destroy it.*

"Also," Andrew continued. "You might want to know that I have men posted outside your father's house. If anything happens to me, you will get a very unpleasant video of him being tortured."

Enna's eyes opened to shoot a dark glare in Andrew's direction. She didn't say anything. What did she have to say? He had her beat, as always.

She clenched her jaw and sat in silence for the rest of the flight, which seemed to last a lifetime.

Enna distracted herself by biting all her nails off, down to the skin. Andrew continuously attempted to start a conversation, but her lips clamped sealed.

"You know, a good wife wouldn't give her husband the silent treatment. I won't allow this behavior once we are married."

Enna's only response was her back muscles tightening, hating everything about the man beside her.

"Huh, stubborn brat," Andrew mumbled under his breath but said no more until they finally arrived in Payson, the town Enna had briefly called home.

The sun was barely falling as they flew over Betty's house. Enna's stomach swelled with panic as she pressed her face against the window. Blue and red police lights flashed, surrounding a helicopter that had landed in the parking lot by the house.

"Oh no! Jay's not okay. I know it. I can't go down there. There are too many cops. They found his body. I can't do this! I can't do this!" Enna freaked out.

"Clara, look at me," Andrew said in a gentle voice.

This time, Enna obliged.

He put his hand on her shoulder. "My pilot is going to land at the park over there. You are going to walk over to that house and find your boy. You are invincible and I know you can handle this, no matter what you find."

Closing his eyes, Andrew swallowed hard. When his eyes opened again, he had a sweet smile on his lips.

"And while you are getting reunited with your son, I'm going to complete my side of the deal by bringing Nicolas back to you as soon as he heals enough to be transferred. Alright?"

"Wait, really?" Enna could hardly believe what she was hearing. She never expected him to follow through with his side of the deal without a fight.

Could I possibly see Nick again?

"Oh, and have your son clear the security footage while I'm gone. If he does that for me, I promise that I will bring Nicolas back to you alive; if he is not already dead, that is. You can do this, my love."

Thrown off by Andrew's tenderness, her emotions were sent on another manipulated ride. "Thank you, Andrew."

He nodded with a smile as the helicopter landed. Kirt, the pilot, opened her door and helped her out. As she began her short walk toward Betty's house, she prayed for strength, trying not to think the worst.

Jay's alive. He has to be. He will run to me and I will hold him tight. Please be alright, baby boy.

As Enna got closer, she counted five police cars. Three surrounded the helicopter; one parked in the driveway, and the other drove up and down the road slowly as though searching for someone. Enna's heart flipped joyfully at the sight of Betty standing on her front porch talking to a female police officer. She looked serious but not sad.

That is a positive sign. Her steps lengthened. Betty's animated voice could barely be heard over the commotion.

"I was just working in the yard when this loud noise caught my attention. I looked up and just saw this helicopter coming straight down! So, I go poke my head inside and tell my kids to call the police, which they did, and I watched as the chopper landed, right here. We're lucky no one was parked here. And then, the doors opened and there was this man just swearing his head off and there were two small boys in the chopper…"

Needing to hear the end of the story, Enna's walk turned into a sprint.

"Well, I recognized one instantly as my neighbor's son, Jay. They left a few days ago with no notice or anything, so I didn't know what to think. That is when I noticed the gun."

"Betty!" Enna called out, her breath heavy from running. "Betty, where is Jay? Is he alright? Please tell me he is okay."

"Oh honey, where have you been? What is going on here?"

"Is. Jay. Alive?" Enna asked, emphasizing each word.

"Yes, he's fine. He's inside playing with Ben," Betty answered in a high-pitched voice.

Enna put her hand to her heart and let out a relieved gasp.

"Jay ran right to me with a gun in his hand! I was worried about the angry man with the potty mouth, but he just jumped out of the chopper, grabbed the other boy, and ran off, leaving Jay behind."

"Oh, thank you! Thank you, God!" Enna said, running past Betty and into the house

"Jay, baby! Jay, come here," Enna yelled the instant her foot entered the door.

"Mommy? Is that you?" Jay asked from the other room. She heard his footsteps grow close as he ran to greet her. Once his face was in sight, Enna fell to her knees with outstretched arms.

"Mommy! I missed you so much!" Jay said as he ran into her arms. She folded him into an embrace, squeezed him tight, and kissed the top of his head over and over again.

"Oh baby, I thought I lost you!" Enna let a relieved tear roll down her face.

"Nope, Central sent me to Betty's house. He's my dad!" Jay said, his voice excited.

"Wait, huh?" Enna scrunched her face up, confused.

"Yeah, Central is a computer that says I am half human and half computer. He told me he's like my dad 'cause he helped make me.

He taught me how ta talk to him without using your laptop," Jay explained.

"Wait, Central is a computer? Is it back at E.S.T. headquarters?" Enna asked, an idea forming in her head.

"Uh-huh!" Jay nodded.

"Can you ask him, or it, to check on Nick for me?"

"Yeah, your idea is swell!"

"Swell, huh?" Enna laughed.

A police officer walked up to them and interrupted their conversation. "Ma'am, would you mind answering a few questions for me?"

"Um, yeah, give me one minute."

The police officer agreed and walked back outside.

What do I say to her? I have enough evidence to have Andrew arrested for life.

The idea of Andrew rotting in jail put a smile on her face, but then anxiety jumped in. *If I turn him in, I could put everyone I love in danger. And who knows what will happen to his other victims if the police can't find them in time? He might really have people who will keep working for him when he's in jail. I can't risk that. The best way to protect my people is by playing his game and taking him down from the inside.*

"Jay, can you do me another favor besides checking in on Nick?"

"Uh-huh!"

"Can you, or your Central thing, hack into the E.S.T. and hide all of the security footage from last night? And if you can find the footage from Oliver's shop, hide that, too? I want it to seem like it's deleted, but I want you to find it again when I need it. Are you able to do that?"

"Uh, yeah, I can try, I guess, but why? Can't we use that to put the bad guy in jail?" His face tilted curiously.

"Yes, baby, we could do that, but it wouldn't solve all our problems."

"Okay?" Jay said with a shrug.

Enna gave him another kiss on the head and stood. "I'll be right back. I have to talk to the police officer," *Though I have no idea what I'm going to say.*

Walking outside, she made eye contact with the officer. *Well, I've been lying these last few years. A couple more lies won't hurt.* She walked over and greeted the woman with a smile.

Talking to the officer caused her to stutter. She had always been bad at lying. However, she managed to weave a convincing enough story about how a rogue government agent named Eric Quinn learned about how brilliant her son was. He wanted to recruit Jay but got mad and kidnapped Jay when they refused to work with him. Enna claimed she went to negotiate with the General, but Agent Quinn had gotten there first, killed the General, and then took off with Jay in the helicopter. Jay managed to change the GPS coordinates to take him to Betty's house.

The officer asked about the other boy who was with Agent Quinn, but Enna honestly had no helpful information about him other than his name, Mike. After quite the interrogation, Enna filled out an incident report, and eventually, the chaos died down enough for her to get a chance to talk to Jay.

"Did you find anything out about Nick?" she asked, sitting on the couch next to Jay.

"Yeah, but I don't want to tell you because you might get sad," Jay said with a sunken face.

A weight instantly filled up her chest, dreading the report. "It's alright, buddy, you can tell me."

"Central says that Nick's name is really William Lund. He lied to you, mommy," Jay said, shaking his head wistfully.

"What? I don't care about that. Is he alive?" Enna asked earnestly.

"Oh, yeah, but he's not doing too good. He's in recovery mode," Jay said with a downcast expression.

"Oh my gosh, kid! You almost gave me a heart attack! He's still alive, at least," Enna said, letting out a deep sigh. "You should have said that first."

Jay raised his shoulders with a guilty smile. "Sorry, Mommy." He jumped to his feet. "Oh yeah! Central and I patended to delete the security footage! Central taught me how to do it."

"Thanks bud. You are amazing! Now, are you ready to have a sleepover with Ben?"

"Yeah!" Jay shouted.

"Kay, I'll see if there are any pajamas you can borrow and maybe a fresh toothbrush." It was strange talking about a mundane nightly routine after what they had just been through.

After the boys were in their beds, Enna read them a goodnight story and sang them a lullaby to lure them to sleep. Before Jay drifted off, he curled into Enna and reached up for her hair so he could twirl it around his fingers.

"Mommy," he mumbled. "I love you. I'm glad you're okay."

"I'm glad you're okay too, Baby. I love you so much." She kissed his head and held him until his eyes grew heavy and soft puffs of snores filled the room.

Reluctantly, Enna snuck out of the room. Despite being sick to her stomach, she needed to find something to eat. She didn't know how long it had been since she'd eaten last and she was in desperate need of nourishment.

"Thanks for putting the boys to bed," Betty said as Enna entered the kitchen. Betty was just finishing up hand-washing the dishes.

"It was good. I enjoyed it." Enna tried to smile, but a gnawing ache came from the thought of following through with the deal she had made with Andrew. How could she say goodbye to Jay again?

"Hey Betty, I was wondering if you would do me a favor," Enna said with a solemn voice.

"Yes. Of course," Betty answered in her natural, sugary voice as she scrubbed at a stain on the counter with a washrag.

"I might have to go away for a while. I was wondering if you would take care of Jay for me just for a bit until Nick comes back."

"Why? What's going on?" Concern now lined Betty's voice. Placing the washrag in the sink, she turned and gave Enna her full attention.

What should I tell her? Should I warn her that Andrew knows where she lives and that she should uproot her family and move somewhere far away? I can't do that to them. I'm sure Andrew already has eyes on them anyway. As long as I do what he tells me, they will be safe.

"I can't tell you much, but I've decided to go undercover to take down a human trafficking ring," Enna said.

Betty stood quietly, opening and then closing her mouth a few times, words failing her as Enna spoke.

"I'm not sure how long I will be gone, but I need to do this. I can't let Jay be involved. Please, promise me you will take care of him until Nick returns."

If Nick survives, the thought hit Enna like a slap in the face.

Betty nodded her head a few times before she was able to find her voice. "Yes. I'll have to discuss it with my husband first, but I'm sure he will be fine with it. Can I ask what brought this decision on?" She leaned against the counter and folded her arms.

"Well, I was a victim of sex trafficking," Enna answered. It felt good to finally be honest with her friend. Betty gasped and covered her mouth as Enna kept talking. "I was lucky enough to find a way out, but I can't sleep at night knowing that there are others who are still trapped and being abused."

"But...but why you? You're a mother. What about Jay?" Betty stammered.

"I have to. I can't turn my back on the other victims. I have an opportunity to get on the inside so I can change their lives. Maybe I can teach them how to stand up for themselves. I want to teach them how to survive and find freedom, like I did." Enna glanced away from Betty's horrified look.

"Please try to understand," Enna whispered. "I need help taking care of Jay. I trust you. You can't talk me out of it." Enna's chin twitched from seeing her friend's moist eyes.

Betty suddenly threw her arms around Enna and squeezed her in a tight embrace. "Of course, I'll watch Jay. My family and I have your back." Her arms tightened. "I love you dear. I'm so sorry for what you had to go through. I have no idea how you have been able to survive this far. I'm so proud of you for finding your way."

Enna held on to Betty and closed her eyes, taking in the moment of comfort that she could use during the dark days that awaited her.

38

Goodbye

Enna stretched out on the hide-a-bed with one leg hanging off the edge. Jay curled against her side, his hand tangled in her hair. With her eyes still closed, she nuzzled up against Jay's head. She didn't remember him climbing into bed with her, but she appreciated his company. Putting her arms around him, she tried to convince herself to go back to sleep, but thoughts of Nick pulled at her mind.

Andrew had been gone for a week with no news about Nick. Also, Central must have been disconnected or something because Jay hadn't been able to reach his computer mentor. It drove Enna to insanity, not knowing if she would ever see Nick again.

Jay squirmed in his sleep, yanking slightly on her hair. She cringed and untangled his small fingers out of her dark red locks. She kissed him and flipped over to her other side, only to cringe again at the pain in her injured shoulder.

Rolling to her back, she listened as a clock ticked on, counting off the seconds before the world would wake and start a new day. Her head ached. Her heart ached. Her whole body ached and all she wanted was for sleep to come and take all the pain away, but the clock ticked on and sleep never came.

"Ding-dong!" the doorbell chimed, sending an instant dose of anxiety her way. *Who would be visiting this early?* Visitors had always made her a bit nervous, but after the last week, her anxiety was on hyperdrive.

Enna kept her eyes closed even though she was wide awake. She hoped the visitor would just leave.

"Ding-dong!" *Nope!*

Betty's footsteps came down the hall from the master bedroom. Enna's ears pricked as she answered the door.

"Hi, how can I help you?" she asked.

"Hello, you must be Betty. Enna has told me so much about you."

At the sound of Andrew's voice, split emotions jumped into action: panic and excitement.

He must have news about Nick! Maybe he's alive. Or maybe Andrew is just here to tell me that Nick died and he will take me away forever anyway. No, wait, don't think like that.

"I'm a close friend of Enna's. Is she here?" Andrew asked.

"Oh yes, she's asleep in the living room. Do you want me to wake her up?"

"No, that's fine. I can wait. She needs her sleep." He sounded so thoughtful and normal. The deception made Enna sick.

"Well, why don't you come in and I'll make you some breakfast?" Betty offered. "I have to make food for the family anyway. They should be waking up soon."

No, Betty, you are inviting a murderer and a sex trafficker into your house with your children! With your daughters! Oh, I should have warned her about him. I need to get him away from here.

Enna quickly slipped out of bed as Andrew kindly responded to Betty.

"Ah, that is so sweet of you. No wonder Enna speaks so highly of you." Andrew followed Betty into the kitchen.

"Here, pull up a chair," Betty said, pointing to a chair that had a minimal amount of gunk stuck to it.

Enna rushed over and pushed the chair under the table out of reach.

"No, it's okay, Betty, I'm awake. I'll take my…him…out for breakfast so you don't have to cook. Thank you, though." Enna took the back of Andrew's arm and tried leading him back to the door.

"Hello, beautiful," Andrew grabbed her arm off of him and kissed her fingers.

Enna disguised her shudder with an unconvincing laugh.

"Enna, I would love to sit and have breakfast with Betty. I want to get to know your lovely friend."

Naturally, Betty grinned like she always did and nodded her head enthusiastically. *She's way too trusting.*

"That would be nice. I haven't met many of Enna's friends. Actually, I haven't met any of her friends. I want to get to know you, too. I don't even know your name."

"Oh, where are my manners? I am Andrew Dengaila." He held up his hand to greet her.

"Good to meet you!" Betty shook his hand with a firm grip.

Enna put on a plastic grin, though disgust slithered inside of her.

Uhg, Andrew is way too good at playing the charming gentleman character with his expensive clothes and his charismatic smile. Gross!

"Andrew, why are you here? What happened to Nick?" Enna's words came out sharper than she intended.

"Don't worry, my dear. Your Nicolas is alive. I was able to get him transferred to a nearby hospital." A glimpse of jealousy flashed in his eyes.

The news sent a river of sweet relief throughout Enna's entire body. Holding onto the back of the kitchen chair, she steadied herself.

Betty gasped, perplexed by the unexpected turn of conversation. "Oh my goodness! Why didn't you tell me that Nick was in the hospital? What happened?" Betty placed her hands on her hips in mamma mode.

"I'm sorry. I didn't want to worry you. I didn't even know he was alive until just now," Enna said through gasps of air. When her head stopped spinning, she rushed over to where Jay slept in the living room, which connected to the kitchen.

She pulled out a simple outfit from a pile of clothes Betty gave her. "I'm going to go see him right now. Jay, wake up. Wake up. Nick's alive! Get your shoes on. We're gonna go see him." Enna reached under the hide-a-bed for her shoes.

Jay stirred in his sleep but kept his eyes closed.

Enna grabbed one of his toes and pulled. "Wake up, handsome. We need to go," Enna practically bounced with the prospect of seeing Nick again. Her chest filled with a sunray that had been hiding behind a cloud.

Jay groaned and then laughed as Enna pulled on another toe. He then pretended he was asleep.

"Come on, Jay, don't make me tickle you!" She held her fingers above the sleepy boy and began wiggling them. Jay started to squirm before her hands even touched him.

"No, don't tickle me. I'm awake. I'm awake!" He rolled around to get out of her reach.

"Go get your shoes and clothes! Come on. We are going to see Nick," she said again.

"Wait, Nick? Yay! I'm *so* happy!" Jay jumped up but froze, wide-eyed as he noticed Andrew in the kitchen.

"Mommy-" Jay started to whine.

"It's okay, Jay." Enna leaned in and whispered, "Andrew won't hurt us. Please pretend he's not here. I don't want to scare Betty. She doesn't know he's a bad guy. Don't tell her."

Jay's brows scrunched in concern but slowly nodded his head.

"Jay, go find some close please," Enna said out loud.

"Okay," Jay said, running off to find his clothes while staying as far away from Andrew as possible.

Andrew made his way over to Enna and leaned in close to her ear. "Can I talk to you alone for a moment?"

Enna nodded and led Andrew to the vacant front room.

"What?" Enna asked, face stern.

"You do remember your promise to me, right?" Andrew asked with a hungry expression.

"Of course," Enna answered in a harsh whisper.

"I am going to let you say goodbye to Nicolas. I will wait here with Betty and her family until you return to complete your side of the deal."

"I don't want you near this family." Enna folded her arms stubbornly.

"Well, your other option is for me not to allow you to see Nicolas before you come with me. Or, I could accompany you and watch as you say goodbye, but I wouldn't want to ruin the moment." His jaw set and his eyes burned into her.

The idea of her seeing another man was probably killing him inside. *Ha!*

"I'm not going with you until I see Nick alive and well."

"Fine, then go, but don't take too long. I've been waiting so patiently for you. I can only wait for one more hour." Andrew tried to stroke Enna's face, but she pulled away. Andrew scrunched his outstretched hand into a fist before releasing it to his side. "And Clara, if I have to wait any longer than that, I might get bored."

"Fine, I'll be fast, but you'd better not do anything to this family." She pressed her lips together, hoping she looked tough even though her body tingled with adrenaline.

"Of course, I won't hurt them unless you decide not to return before I get bored. Here, take my rental." Andrew handed Enna his car keys.

With a rigid face, she walked off to find Jay.

"Jay, you ready to go?" Enna asked, a little less enthusiastically than before.

"Hey Betty, can Andrew stay here while I go see Nick? He really wants that breakfast of yours," Enna asked with a pit in her stomach.

"That would be delightful!" Betty responded. "Ben, come help me make breakfast, please!" She called down the hall.

Enna shooed Jay out the door and headed to the hospital. It wasn't far from Betty's house, but anxiety stretched the drive out.

Once there, she wandered down the hospital's white hallways while the smell of death floated in the air. Jay held her hand as they found the room number. She hesitated before entering, afraid of what she might find. As she entered the room, the countdown to the end of her life began.

Nick lay still in the hospital bed. The monitors bleeped, giving proof of life, but other than that, Nick's pale face sent a shiver through Enna. He appeared drained and lifeless.

Maybe I should have let him stay at the E.S.T. Transferring him here must have been physically demanding on him.

Enna walked up to him slowly and stroked his face.

Jay stared at him, afraid. "What's wrong with him, Mommy? He doesn't look colorful. I thought he was better." He brought his chin up to peak over the mattress.

"He's still healing. He took a bullet for me and now he has to sleep a lot before he is better."

Jay frowned and poked Nick's arm. Enna thought about telling Jay to let Nick sleep, but she desperately needed to talk to him before Andrew took her.

"Poke him again," Enna urged Jay.

He did as he was told.

Nick moaned but kept his eyes closed.

"Maybe we should try pulling his toes," Jay suggested.

A gurgled chuckle came from Nick's face.

"Hey, Nick, it's me," Enna whispered. "Are you awake, or are you just laughing in your sleep?" she leaned over the bed.

Nick's eyes slit open and he lifted his arm slowly to place the palm of his hand on Enna's cheek.

"Hi." His labored speech was accompanied by a slight lift of his lips. "Is this heaven cuz you look like an angel." He tried laughing again and then groaned.

Jay scrunched his face up, looked at Enna and said, "Weird!"

Enna laughed and grabbed Nick's hand. "Nope, this is far from heaven," she said.

"Well, you are my heaven," Nick said.

Enna blushed and shook her head. "You goof! I can't tell if you are high on pain meds or if you are just in an incredibly cheesy mood."

"Mmmm, maybe a bit of both. I missed you, you know. I'm so glad you are both safe." Nick dropped his weak arm back onto the bed.

Enna traced his hand gently with her finger. "You're glad I'm okay? You're the one who got tortured and then shot. I thought you were dead."

Nick slowly shook his head. "Nope. Still alive." He moved his head up toward Enna's concerned face and asked, "Jay, can you close your eyes for a moment so your mom can kiss me?"

"Aw, kissing. Gross!" Jay said, sticking his tongue out.

Enna put a hand over Jay's squirmy eyes, drew closer, and put her lips against Nick's. The heart rate monitor beeped excitedly as their lips caressed each other.

Enna pulled away abruptly and turned her face from Nick. "I don't think I can do this, Nick."

How do I tell him I'm going back to my abuser?

"You are the most wonderful woman I know. You have survived more trials than most people suffer in a lifetime. You can do anything." He attempted to sit up, grunted, and then laid back down again.

Enna glanced back at him with a wounded expression. Twisting her hands together, she hated the next words that needed to come out of her mouth. "Nick..." she let a deep breath out. "I have to go back to Andrew."

Nick's already pale face turned even pastier. His mouth hung open in distress. Jay let out a long cry of protest and grabbed at Enna's arm, tears welling in his eyes.

"Enna, you can do anything but that!" Nick said, his words sharp. "Why would you ever go back to him?"

"Mommy, he's a bad guy. We can't go with him!" Jay cried.

"Honey, you are not coming with me. I could never put you in that much danger again." Enna kneeled and put a comforting arm around Jay.

The heart monitor chirped as a new kind of pain surged through Nick's body.

"But you are putting yourself in that much danger! Why? Why would you go back to him?" Nick's chest rose and fell rapidly. His face displayed pure misery.

"Nick, I have to. I made a deal. He agreed to save you and Jay. I promised I would-" Enna started to explain.

"No, screw the deal. Andrew murdered people! He murdered your friend right in front of me! I don't understand. He needs to be in prison or shot down with a laser! He can't...ahh...have you. You are not property!" Nick gasped in pain, but he kept talking. "You can't be serious!"

"Stop, you are hurting yourself." Enna placed a hand on his arm. "I understand. I'm scared, too. I know you want to protect me. But, I have my family and friends to protect as well, and if I go back on my word, he will kill you and Jay."

"Not if he is dead!" Nick was shouting now and the monitors beeped in an odd pattern.

Jay hid his face in Enna's neck.

"You want me to kill him?!" Enna asked.

"Yes, yes, I do. People like him don't deserve to live. I've seen you fight! You are more powerful than him."

"Yeah, and he knows it. Trust me, I've thought about it, but I can't! Killing him wouldn't do any good. He says his people will find us even if he's dead. I can't risk it. I…Please, Nick, calm down and listen to me. I have a plan. I need your and Jay's help."

Nick leaned back into his pillow and stared at the ceiling, trying to calm his breathing. Jay looked up at Enna with anger in his eyes. Enna squeezed him before moving to sit on the edge of Nick's bed.

"Andrew is a leader in a human trafficking ring. I was one of his victims, but I know many other girls are being sold each day. I want to help them, but I have to be careful. I could get Andrew arrested with the evidence Jay pretended to delete, but he has people who he claims can get rid of any evidence. He also has my dad." Nick looked at Enna in surprise. "Andrew will have him killed if I use the evidence against him." Enna shook her head in disgust. "I won't let that happen. I need to find out who works for him so I can take them all down at once."

"But why does it have to be you?" Nick sniffled.

"He…Please don't freak out." Enna swallowed hard.

"He what?"

"He wants me to marry him. I would legally be his wife. I'm the only person who can get close enough to him to take him down."

Enna braced for an explosion of protests, but Nick's jaw twitched as he placed his lips in a firm line. His breath caught in his throat.

"But, Mommy?" Jay whined. "Would that mean he'd be my step-dad?"

"No! No, baby. It's not like that. It will just be pretend. I'm going to be like a detective," Enna said, placing a hand on Jay's face.

"Please tell me this isn't happening," Nick's words finally caught up to him. "Enna, please…Why?" His whispered voice held a force that gutted Enna.

"When I first escaped, I left twelve other girls behind. They were my friends. I still see their faces in my sleep. I know their names. Nick, I left them behind so Andrew could torture them while I went free."

Her voice turned raspy as she held back the powerful emotions rolling inside of her.

"I have a chance to make that right and protect you, Jay, and Betty's whole family at the same time. And I want to see my dad again. I have to find him. Maybe you can help me with that. That's what you do, right? Find people?"

"Enna, please-"

"Hey, I'll be okay, but I really need your help on this."

"This is all my fault." Nick moaned, putting a hand on his heart near his bullet wound.

"No. Please, Nick, don't. You can't take responsibility for Andrew's psychotic state. He is the one who lied to you. He is the one who did this. Not you. Don't you dare hold onto this guilt."

"But-"

"No! Listen. You changed my life, Nick and even if I never get to see you again, I am so glad that I got to know you. I love you!"

Picking his hand up, her voice dropped into a sweet whisper. "I forgive you, okay? I trust you despite everything. I trust you so much that I want you to take care of Jay for me while I am gone." Nick's eyes connected with hers as she continued talking.

"I'm not sure how we will communicate yet, but I will find a way, and when I do," she looked at Jay and poked his nose. "I'll need you, Jay, to use your brilliant superpowers to help me investigate Andrew."

Nick's nose flared as he processed Enna's words. The rings around his eyes turned red as though he had been crying but no water spilled down his face.

"Once things calm down at the E.S.T., they might come looking for Jay again. And if Andrew finds out what I am up to, he will try to use you and Jay against me. Change your names. Disappear. Tell Betty your new identity so I can find you if necessary."

Nick nodded but stayed silent.

Seeing that Enna's attention was mostly on Nick, Jay moved away from her and went to sit in one of the hospital chairs next to the window in a pout. He put his finger in his own hair and twisted it while the adults talked.

"Shouldn't Betty get somewhere safe as well?" Nick asked.

Enna nodded while responding, "You have no idea how much I want her and her family to leave with you and Jay, but Andrew already has his people watching them. If they are caught trying to leave, Andrew will stop them. I don't want them to be on the run for the rest of their lives. As long as I do what Andrew says, they should be safe."

"Do what he says? What does that mean? How far do you have to go to please him?" Nick brought a hand up to cover his face.

Bringing her voice as soft as it could go, Enna mumbled. "He promises that he won't make me sleep with him until after the wedding."

Nick's chest heaved at the thought.

"He promises? Enna...he's not going to keep that promise," Nick said with a gasping breath.

"I...I'll fight him. I can beat him."

Nick's breathing grew shallow and desperate. Enna knew he needed to rest, but she still had a little time left.

"Nick, please come up with an emergency plan that Betty can use in case anything goes wrong. I don't think I'll get a chance to talk to her alone, so I will leave that up to you."

"When are you leaving?" Nick forced himself to ask, dropping his hand away from his face. Enna lifted her legs onto the bed and carefully laid down next to him. He tilted his head until it rested on her hair.

"I have to go as soon as I'm done talking to you," Enna answered in a delicate tone, quiet enough that Jay couldn't hear. She felt a jet of warm air on her ear as Nick let out a sharp breath.

"What if I can't let you go?" Nick asked in a barely audible whisper. His hand weakly gripped Enna's waist and kissed her on the forehead. "Please don't go. I love you."

"I love you, too. I wish we could just freeze this moment and save it for bad days." Enna lifted her face to meet his. Her heart thundered as their lips met. For just a while, the world seemed right again.

"Come on, guys. That's just nasty!" Jay said out of the blue. He had left his chair and walked back over to the bed.

Enna reluctantly tore herself away from Nick and sat up. "Nasty? Where did you get an idea like that? My kisses are precious. You are just feeling left out. Come here."

Jay backed away, knowing what was coming next. Enna stood up and grabbed him. She began planting a hundred kisses on his face, head, and hands.

"Ew, no! Gross!" Jay squirmed.

Laughter filled that hospital room.

Enna held Jay close to her and heaved a sigh. She reached over and held Nick's hand as well, not wanting to let go of her treasures. However, time slipped away. Her hour was almost up.

"I have to go soon," she finally brought herself to say. She was terrified of what Andrew might do if she was not back on time.

Sitting back down next to Nick, Enna held his face. "Get better soon, okay? I'm going to leave Jay with Betty until you are strong enough to take care of him." A tear streamed down her cheek.

"And, I'm crying again. You know, I never cried before you came along." She wiped the moisture off her cheek. "I feel like I'm giving up my emotional safe spot. It hurts too bad!"

More tears leaked down her cheeks, and her voice rose in pitch. "I don't…don't want to do this." Jay hugged her from the side, giving her comfort.

"Then don't. You don't have to sacrifice your happiness for everyone else," Nick said, wiping her tears.

"I do. Andrew needs to be stopped. And I have to keep both of you safe. I have to do this. Please take care of Jay. Okay? I can't leave without knowing he is safe."

Nick closed his eyes and nodded. Enna leaned over and brushed her lips against his one last time.

"Oh, I love you, Enna," Nick whispered.

Wanting those to be the last words she remembered coming from his lips, she took Jay's hand and walked to the door.

"I love you, too," she said before slipping out of the room.

***

On the car ride back to Betty's house, Jay stayed quiet. Enna knew these were the last moments she would have with her son for a very long time, but there were no words to describe how she felt inside.

She cried softly.

Once Enna pulled into the parking lot, she sat still for a moment while she calmed her tears. *Okay, I have to be strong. I don't want Jay to remember me like this.*

After her tears stopped, she and Jay got out of the car and walked inside.

Laughter came from the living room. The family all gathered in a circle with Andrew, playing a card game called Spoons. The loser had to do something ridiculous while the rest of the family laughed.

Everything seemed so normal, like a regular party. Enna put on a fake smile and joined the group.

"Hey guys, this looks fun!" she said.

"Oh, well, why don't you join us," Betty offered, scooting over to make room for her. Andrew put his cards down and stood.

"Thank you so much for your hospitality, but Enna and I have somewhere to be."

"Yeah, sorry, Betty, I have to go. I'm not sure when I'll be back. Are you still alright with taking care of Jay?" Enna asked.

"You're leaving this soon?" Betty's face fell. "Uh, yeah we will watch Jay for you. Are you going to be okay?"

Enna's head bobbed even though she knew nothing would be okay.

"Thank you for everything, Betty," Enna said before throwing her arms around her for a hug.

Don't cry, don't cry, don't cry, Enna thought to herself as she remembered the first time Betty had hugged her. It had been awkward and unfamiliar. Now, Betty's hugs were safe and precious.

After the hug ended, she went around the circle and gave each family member a quick hug. They looked at each other, confused, probably wondering what the occasion was. Enna gave Betty one more long embrace before turning to Jay. She bent down to his level before speaking.

"Hey, handsome. Have fun with Ben while I'm gone, okay? I'm gonna miss you with all my heart." Enna's voice cracked but she held her tears in. "Take care of Nick for me."

"Mommy! I want to go with you," Jay cried, clinging to her.

"Not this time, Baby." Jay let out a sob and tightened his grip on her.

Enna pried his arms away. "Here, put your hand on your heart." She lifted Jay's hand to his chest. "Every time your heart feels lonely, that just means my heart is missing you. Close your eyes and feel my heart missing you, okay, just until I get back."

She held him in a tight hug, her stomach hardening into rocks.

"Enna, it's time to go. We have a long flight," Andrew interrupted, gently touching her shoulder.

"Yeah. Okay," Enna said, shivering slightly. "Jay, be good while I am gone. Help Betty keep the house clean. My heart misses you already. Can I have kisses?"

Jay frowned and looked at her with big, watery eyes. "My heart misses you, too."

"I know, baby," Enna replied, putting her head on Jay's forehead. "Oh Jay, you will be alright. I need my kisses now."

Jay kissed one of Enna's hands and then the next. He finished the routine off with a kiss on her cheek.

"I love you, my baby boy."

"I love you too, Mommy."

Enna gave him another hug and kiss before rising to her feet. She held her head up and waved to her friends...more like family. Then she turned to follow Andrew.

Before they reached the door, Jay ran after her, screaming a cry. "Wait! I'm going with you! Mommy, I'm going with you! Don't leave me. Mommy! Noooo!" He shrieked and clutched onto her leg. She tried to get him off, but his grip was tight.

"Betty. Betty. Please take Jay. I can't..." Enna's voice cracked as Jay screamed.

Betty rushed over and grabbed Jay, untangling his limbs away from his mother one by one.

"I love you, Jay. I love you so much! I'll be back," Enna called as Andrew guided her out the door. Enna broke into pieces on the inside, but she held herself tall.

Before they got into the car, Andrew took her hand and kissed it.

"Mine at last," he said, opening the passenger door.

No, not this time

Enna smiled a cold, malicious smile, and climbed into the car with a confidence that would not be destroyed.

This time, it's my turn to win Andrew's game.

When Cynthia Terry was in elementary school, her imagination ran wild. There were always stories spinning around in her head. However, writing those adventures for others to experience proved to be a great challenge.

Words never looked right on the page, and spelling was her worst subject. She was always the last one to finish a typing assignment. Well into her school years, teachers would assign others to write for her just so she could keep up. But Cynthia was determined. She wanted nothing more than to do well in school and share her stories.

With great support from her parents, teachers, and older sister (Heather), Cynthia learned to rise above her limitations and never quit. After many struggles, she discovered her voice.

Writing this novel has been a dream come true. It's her way of telling the world that limitations don't hold all the power. With hard work, perseverance, and support, so much can be accomplished.

Your past does not define you.

Don't give up.

www.ingramcontent.com/pod-product-compliance
Lightning Source LLC
Chambersburg PA
CBHW071301140726
47996CB00005B/1584